HE WAS TOWERING OVER HER IN TWO GIANT STEPS.

"What did you call me?" His hands wrapped around her hips and he picked her up and stood her on the couch so their eyes were on a more even level.

If he thought she was going to back down, he was crazy. Aunie's chin jutted toward the ceiling. "A lily-livered . . ."

"No, after that." His eyes ran over her from head to foot, taking in everything, missing nothing: her bright eyes, her flushed cheeks, the long, white neck, that T-shirt that had taunted him all afternoon with its cropped neckline that slid all over her shoulders, those skin-tight little grey leggings. "Say it to my face."

"I said it to your face the first time, you big blond baboon. You think you're a stud, but you're only a . . . umm . . ."

James's long fingers had tangled in her hair and his mouth cut off her words. He wanted to force her to eat her words, literally, but then he tasted her mouth under his, felt her bare arms wrap around his neck, felt her body plaster itself up against his, and his brain short-circuited, all coherent thought erased.

BOOK YOUR PLACE ON OUR WEBSITE AND MAKE THE READING CONNECTION!

We've created a customized website just for our very special readers, where you can get the inside scoop on everything that's going on with Zebra, Pinnacle and Kensington books.

When you come online, you'll have the exciting opportunity to:

- View covers of upcoming books
- Read sample chapters
- Learn about our future publishing schedule (listed by publication month *and author*)
- Find out when your favorite authors will be visiting a city near you
- Search for and order backlist books from our online catalog
- Check out author bios and background information
- Send e-mail to your favorite authors
- Meet the Kensington staff online
- Join us in weekly chats with authors, readers and other guests
- Get writing guidelines
- AND MUCH MORE!

**Visit our website at
http://www.zebrabooks.com**

SUSAN ANDERSEN

PRESENT DANGER

ZEBRA BOOKS
KENSINGTON PUBLISHING CORP.
http://www.zebrabooks.com

ZEBRA BOOKS are published by

Kensington Publishing Corp.
850 Third Avenue
New York, NY 10022

All Kensington titles, imprints and distributed lines are available at special quantity discounts for bulk purchases for sales promotion, premiums, fund raising, educational or institutional use.

Special book excerpts or customized printings can also be created to fit specific needs. For details, write or phone the office of the Kensington Special Sales Manager: Kensington Publishing Corp., 850 Third Avenue, New York, NY, 10022. Attn. Special Sales Department. Phone: 1-800-221-2647.

First Printing: February, 1993
Second Printing: December, 2000
10 9 8 7 6 5 4

Printed in the United States of America

For making me laugh and a whole lot more
This one is for two special women in my life
Dedicated with love

To
My mom, Bettie Bell
Whom I'm going to be just like when I grow up

And to
My best friend, Mimi Armitstead
Who knows me inside and out

With a special thanks to Kathy Baker and Ann Marie
Talberg for making this second incarnation possible

—Susie—

CHAPTER 1

The quickest way to Aunie Franklin's heart was not through complimenting her looks. She'd been praised for her appearance since she was five years old and quite honestly didn't understand what the fuss was all about—like most women, she felt she needed a helping hand from the cosmetic industry. Anyway, wasn't the arrangement of one's features pretty much an accident of genes? Not exactly an accomplishment that she could point to with pride, was it? Now, what she would truly find flattering was to hear that she was intelligent, or better yet, competent. At twenty-six she felt that she had already wasted most of her life being nothing more than a decoration—nice enough to look at, she supposed, but ultimately rather useless.

Not, she thought with justifiable irony, that it was likely to be a particular problem today.

She looked up at the facade of the old brick apartment house. It had caught her fancy immediately, with its old-fashioned portico, the warm coloring of its bricks, and the lovely front door that was mostly a large oval of beveled glass. She couldn't believe her luck in spotting this place. The building was not too large; it was close to a community college, and best of all there was a sign, Apartment for Rent, on a peg thrust into the postage-stamp-sized lawn out front. She hadn't even noticed that at first glance. Her eyes had been drawn to the building itself as she'd slowly maneuvered the narrow streets in her rented car. It had an air of shabby gentility that made her feel right at home. She'd lived in places like this one before.

It looked absolutely perfect, which couldn't help making her a bit nervous. Things that appeared too good to be true generally were. She'd discovered that the hard way.

Perfection ceased to be a problem the moment she attempted to find a parking space. In this neighborhood it was obviously an exercise in frustration. She had to drive several blocks, turning several corners in the process, before she finally found a space that was so small it took her three attempts at parallel parking to squeeze into it. Then, of course, she had to find her way back. She'd turned so many corners, she was completely turned around.

But she was not as lacking in intelligence as was popularly believed back home in Atlanta. She had made note of the cross streets and eventually found her way back to the building. She walked up the short path, pressed the intercom button, and peered through the glass into the foyer.

It had a look of having been lovingly restored, all gleaming old wood and new paint. There was an open staircase dead ahead that displayed a polished oak banister. The stairs were covered with an old, thin, tapestry carpet runner that had probably been quite valuable once upon a time.

The speaker next to her ear emitted a static crackle. "May I help you?" asked a disembodied voice.

Aunie leaned into the intercom. "I'm here about the apartment for rent."

"Manager's apartment is 1A on your right." The door buzzed and Aunie pushed it open. Closing it carefully behind her, she shivered in the sudden flow of warm air. She hadn't realized how chilled she was until she stepped out of the moisture-laden wind. After a lifetime in the South, she was going to need a bit of adjusting to this Seattle weather. It wasn't actually raining; yet there was a dampness in the air that cut to the bone.

More heat curled around her when the door to the manager's apartment suddenly opened before she could knock on it. In the doorway stood a tall black woman dressed in layers of colorful cotton, an ankle bracelet gracing one bare foot, and she was wearing a brightly patterned scarf tied turban-style around her head. The woman's welcoming smile faded as she studied Aunie with concern. "Ah, woo-mon," she said in a soft, Jamaican lilt as her warm brown eyes noted the damage to Aunie's face, "What hoppened to you?"

Aunie gave her a polite smile in return, stretching her mouth as far as the still-split lip would allow. "I'm inquirin' about the apartment."

The exotic woman seemed not to take offense that Aunie had not answered her question. She smiled serenely. "Yes, of course; you will like it very much, I think. You come wid me." She stepped back to allow Aunie entrance to her apartment. "I am Lola."

Aunie extended her hand. "Aunie Franklin."

"Pleasured to make your acquaintance, On-nie. Please"—Lola gestured to the overstuffed sofa— "make yourself comfortable while I find the keys."

To herself, Lola thought, *I sign this one up quick, before James catches sight of her.* With her usual decisiveness, she had taken one look at the fragile-looking woman with the battered face and determined she was in need of help and friendship . . . and very likely protection as well.

She also knew that if James were to see her, he would turn her away in a second. He had some ridiculous new notion about not taking care of people anymore. Said he was tired of having everyone's problems dumped in his lap and, from now on, he was looking out for number one . . . period. With that bad-luck family of his, Lola understood his sudden change of attitude. But it was the man's inherent nature to handle trouble, so at the same time it made her impatient. Destiny was destiny, and it was futile to rail against what was meant to be, now wasn't it? Lola knew that, even if James did not.

Grabbing the keys and donning a pair of worn ballet slippers, Lola led Aunie upstairs. The second floor didn't show the same loving care that the ground floor did, but Lola was quick to explain. "Just finished redoin' the first floor and this unit," she said as she opened the apartment door and stood back for Aunie to enter. "The mons, they be starting on the hallway up here come Monday."

"Oh, this is nice," Aunie said a moment later as she wandered about the high-ceilinged apartment. It was light and airy, with stark white walls, and in the small dining area were two tall, narrow, old-fashioned windows that let in the weak afternoon light through

slanted wooden miniblinds. A curved archway sepa-
rated the living room from the dining area, and the
floors in both rooms were polished hardwood. There
had been generous use made of natural woods: framing the windows, in the moldings and foot boards,
and in the built-in bookshelves on either side of . . .

"Oh, a *fireplace*," Aunie breathed reverently. She
didn't actually know how to build a fire, but she was
certain she could learn. She looked over her shoulder
at Lola. "Does it work?"

"Certainly. The mons, they finished redoin' this
place not too long ago. Everything work perfectly."

Aunie's overall impression of the apartment was of
spaciousness even though it wasn't actually all that
large. There was a small, efficient kitchen and an
even smaller bathroom with an old-fashioned claw-
foot tub and pedestal sink. The bedroom was a reasonable size, though, and its floor was covered with thick,
plush, wall-to-wall, pearl grey carpeting. It also con-
tained a huge closet.

"I'll take it." Aunie turned to Lola. "Oh, wait. I
guess I'd better inquire first how much you're
asking."

The rent was only a little steeper than she had
expected to pay but it included heat, so in the long
run she would probably get the best of the bargain.
She had a feeling she was going to go through a great
deal of fuel before she became acclimated to this
damp new climate. With a sense of satisfaction, she
trailed Lola back to her apartment to sign the papers.
First full day in town, and already she'd found a place
to stay and had brochures from the nearby college.

"How do you spell your first name, woo-mon?"
Lola asked her as she filled in the forms. "O-n-n-i-e?"

Aunie corrected her and went on to spell her last

name also. In moments, she was signing a six-month lease and endorsing a number of traveler's checks to cover first and last month's rent and a damage deposit. When everything was in order, Lola offered her a cup of tea.

"Welcome to your new home," she said with cheerful friendliness. "I hope you will be as hoppy here as I have been."

Aunie hoped so, too. Talking with Lola as she finished her tea, she marveled at how uncommonly relaxed and at home she felt. She had never actually known a black person on a personal level before. The few with whom she'd had even the most minimal contact were connected to the service industries, and it was a firmly entrenched belief in her family that people from their rarified echelon of society did not mix with those who served them. She wasn't so sheltered she didn't realize there were many African-Americans in positions of authority far removed from serving others. She had simply never met any and so had never given any thought to how well she'd mix with them in a social situation.

Prejudice apparently wasn't as inbred in her as it was in other members of her family, however; inexplicably, with Lola she felt as though she were talking to an old friend. The woman had a natural dignity and exuded a friendliness that prevented Aunie's old demon shyness from manifesting itself. She felt she could listen to the lilting cadence of her voice forever, could bask in the warmth of the woman's eyes.

The front door banged open, and Lola swore softly under her breath. Gesturing Aunie to remain seated, she rose to her feet and crossed the room in a swirl of colorful skirts.

"Lola!" Aunie watched with interest as a tough-looking, well-built man swept Lola off her feet and swung her around. He had the go-to-hell eyes of someone who'd seen it all and soft, pale blond hair that receded slightly from his high forehead and was pulled straight back into a short ponytail. Aunie had never particularly cared for ponytails on men, but the style seemed to suit this one's face, which was all strong planes and angles. The shape of his skull was delineated faithfully beneath the taut skin of his forehead; he had a bony, prominent nose and a stubborn-looking chin. His cheekbones were flat and angular, his teeth were white, and slashing lines cut from the corners of those rebel eyes clear into his lean cheeks. There were three shallow creases in his right cheek next to his mouth.

"How's my favorite woman?" he asked, grinning at Lola and holding her in a grip that dangled her feet off the ground, even though they were very nearly the same height, perhaps five feet ten or eleven inches tall. Aunie wondered with fascinated speculation if they were married. She'd never met anyone from an interracial marriage, but it wouldn't surprise her, given the ask-me-if-I-care expression in the man's eyes. He looked like the type who would do exactly as he pleased and not give a damn what the rest of the world thought of his behavior.

"James, you fool mon, put me down," Lola said sternly.

"Not until I have your promise you'll dump Otis and run away with me."

"Go on wid you, mon! What is this I'm hearin'?" Lola planted her hands on his broad shoulders and pushed back until she could see his face. He grinned happily. "Will you be forsakin' all your blonde bimbos wid the bra sizes larger than their IQ's to make an honest woo-mon of me, James Ryder?''

"No. But think of the scintillating conversations we could have before I go back to my wandering ways. C'mon, Lola, whataya say? It'll be fun.''

"Take your mitts off my woman, Jimmy,'' a deep voice rumbled. "I'd hate to haveta squash you like a bug.''

"I'd hate to be squashed, Otis.'' Still grinning, James let Lola loose.

Aunie's startled attention was drawn to the black man who had spoken. She'd been so caught up in the blonde's theatrics, she'd failed to even notice the other man; but now that she had noticed him, her eyes widened.

Before he'd smiled, she'd thought the blonde looked tough . . . and it was most likely that he was. Compared to this man, however, he looked like a pussycat.

Otis was tall . . . very tall. To Aunie, who was seated, he appeared to be an ebony giant, all roped muscles, dark gleaming skin, and standing veins. His bald head shone in the overhead light and there was a ridge of scar tissue bisecting his skull from the crown of his head to his temple. A small golden hoop glinted in his ear, and when he suddenly smiled, she was taken aback. He had a surprisingly sweet smile, with the whitest, strongest teeth she had ever seen.

Oh, God, this was too perfect. Aunie nearly hugged herself. If Wesley somehow managed to track her down, coming face-to-face with these two men should at least give him pause. The corners of her lips curled up.

"Who's your dainty little friend, baby?'' The deep rumble made Aunie's head whip up. Otis had crossed the room on silent feet and was standing over her.

Lola joined him, hooking her arm through his and hugging an impressive bicep to the side of her breast. "This is Aunie Franklin. Aunie, this is my husband, Otis Jackson, and our friend James Ryder." She took a deep breath and girded herself. "Aunie's rentin' 2B."

"Oh, shit, baby," Otis whispered. "What did ya go do that for?"

"The hell she is!" James roared and Aunie stared at him in startled confusion. The humorous tease of a moment ago had vanished. In his place stood a furious, scowling man who looked ten times harder than she had thought him to be. She rose to her feet, but she was tiny and still had to crane her neck to look him in the eye as he towered over her. "Sorry, lady," he said flatly, staring down at her with eyes colder than the Pacific Northwest rain. "That apartment's not for rent." Not, at any rate, to another screwed-up little waif looking to make her problems his problems.

Aunie drew herself up. "Ah have a signed contract that says it is," she disagreed in her well-bred, soft-spoken voice. The sudden thickening of her accent was the only outward sign of an escalating inward anger. She didn't know what this man's problem was, but she was not giving up her new apartment.

"Ah, shit, she's a Southerner, too," he muttered in disgust. He turned on his heel and stomped away. "Dammit, Lola, why'd you do it? Look at her face! Some asshole's beat her up, and now you've gone and landed her in my lap." His head whipped around and he impaled Aunie with angry moss green eyes. "Or are you gonna try and tell us *that*"—the wave of his hand encompassed her abused face—"happened to you when you walked into a door?"

"I'm not tryin' to tell you a solitary thing, mistah," Aunie replied with cool disdain. "I don't know you from Adam, suh, and the condition of my face is my business. Not yours."

"You've got that straight, sugar. Remember that when your old man shows up lookin' for blood, because I'm just gonna step aside and wave him by." James turned away. "Lola, *why?*" He raked his fingers through his hair from crown to rubber band. His fist closed around his ponytail and tugged until the roots strained. "Couldn't you see she's trouble? God, I don't fuckin' believe this. I've got a whole truckload of problems to straighten out already, but you just had to saddle me with hers, too, didn't you? I'm never gonna get a minute to myself now, what with handling all the Ryder shit and now Miss Magnolia Blossom's, too."

"Excuse me!" Aunie's infuriated voice sliced through his complaint. "You've got quite an inflated opinion of yourself, haven't you?" Beneath swollen, blackened lids, her brown eyes flashed fire. Breasts rising with indignation beneath her oversized silk-and-cotton-blend sweater, hands clenched into fists at her side, she stalked forward belligerently. Despite her diminutive size, James found himself backing up a step, wondering how she managed to appear to be looking down her nose at him when she had to tilt her head way back merely to meet his eyes.

"Who the devil *are* you, mistah," she demanded, "Superman or somethin'? I purely don't recall him havin' such a filthy mouth." She tossed her head, making her shiny brown hair swing away from her bruised jaw. "That apartment is mine, paid for and signed on the dotted line, and I *am* movin' in on the first. I don't know what you're in such an uproar about, anyway; nobody requested your assistance handlin' my problems." She conveniently chose to forget her momentary excitement over his and Otis's obvious street-aware toughness. It was beside the point, anyway.

"I came here to rent an apartment, period," she informed him with cool disdain, "not to find myself a big brotha to fight my wars for me. But for the record, suh, if Ah did need someone, I think I'd ask Otis here. He looks a whole lot tougher than you, so you can just give your superhero cape a rest. I won't be requirin' it."

She swung away and plucked her coat and purse off the couch. Controlling her outrage with an effort, she managed a weak smile. "Lola, thank you for your warm hospitality," she said. "I look forward to gettin' to know you much better. Otis, it was a real pleasuah to meet you." She turned to James and nodded coolly. "Mistah Rydah."

And then she was gone.

Otis looked at the stunned expression on his enraged friend's face and tried to control his grin, but it refused to be subdued. "Well, I guess you can rest easy, Jimmy. I doubt she's a victim of wife abuse, anyway."

"Why the hell not?" James demanded indignantly. "She's such a midget, it wouldn't take much to subdue her."

"Yeah, well, she may be tiny, Jimmy, but she's got attitude," Otis disagreed. "She backed you into a corner, didn't she?"

"Yeah, *Superman*," Lola murmured with a throaty laugh.

James muttered something truly foul, turned on his heel, and slammed out of the apartment.

Otis put his arm around his wife and dragged her down onto the couch next to him. "You've really stirred up something this time, baby."

Lola shrugged. "She needed a place to stay and she loved the apartment," she replied calmly. "Was I supposed to turn away the steady income because she was sportin' a few bruises?"

"Hell, babe, it is James's apartment house and you know his feelings. You had to know that little gal would be expressly contrary to what he wants."

"That mon doesn't know what he wants."

"And you do, I suppose?"

Lola just gave him her mysterious, three-cornered smile—the one that drove him mad and had led him to pursue her some years back until she had finally agreed to marry him. Laughter rumbled like distant thunder deep in his massive chest. "Yeah, I suppose you do, at that." With a mock growl, he grabbed her up and rolled her over.

After the fact, Aunie was quite amazed at her temerity in standing up to James Ryder. She sat in her rented car ten minutes later, shaking with reaction. Had that really been she, the Aunie Franklin who, up until a year ago, had never made a wave in her life, angrily defying a man with such dangerous eyes? Perhaps she really *was* going to be able to make all the changes in her life she desired to make.

She'd better. It wasn't as if she had any other options.

The first thing she did when she reached her downtown hotel room was call her lawyer in Atlanta. The phone rang several times before she remembered the three-hour time difference. She disconnected and dialed his home number.

The phone there rang several times also and she was just on the point of hanging up when he answered.

"Hello?"

"Jordan? This is Aunie."

"Aunie! Where are you? Are you all right?"

"I'm at the Westin Hotel in Seattle; I'm fine, and guess what? I've already found a place to live."

"That was quick."

"Oh, Jordan, I wish you could see it. It's wonderful." She sat down on the side of the bed and kicked off her shoes. "It's in a beautiful old buildin' just blocks from the college I hope to attend, and it has a fireplace and lots of natural wood and it's filled with such interestin' lines."

"Sounds perfect. Is it a secure building?"

"Yes." She clutched the receiver more tightly and asked with quick alarm, "Wesley is still in jail, isn't he?"

He hesitated then said, "They let him out on his own recognizance."

"NO!"

"Don't worry, Aunie. It was stipulated he could not leave the state before his trial, and he doesn't have the first idea where to find you even if he could leave Georgia. Also, there is some good news."

"Let's heah it. Ah could use a little good news about now." Feeling her grasp on her accent slipping—always an accurate barometer to the amount of stress she was feeling—she took several slow, deep breaths.

"You don't have to return to testify. Because of the threats to your personal safety, the judge has agreed to allow your deposition and the photographs of the damage Wesley did to you to stand in your stead."

"Oh, Jordan, that is good news. The fewer trips I have to make between here and Atlanta, the less chance there is for Wesley to track me." She threaded her fingers through her hair. "Let me give you my new address. Do you have a pencil?"

"Shoot."

She recited it and he read it back to her for verification. "Will you send the things I put in storage?" she requested. "The rest can be sold with the house, or if it's easier to sell it separately, do that. Either way, I don't want it. I'm moving in on the first, so if you could get my stored stuff here by then, I'd sure appreciate it. I realize it doesn't give you a great deal of time . . ."

"Don't worry about it. I'll do the best I can."

"Thank you Jordan. You've been such a comfort through all of this."

"Don't mention it. How do you like Seattle?"

"It's green. And cold." She glanced out the window. "I'm supposed to have a view of the Olympic mountains from my hotel room, but so far I haven't seen anything except clouds where they're supposed to be. They tell me they're quite beautiful, though."

"I'm going to send you the name of a lawyer there," Jordan said. "I'll send him a copy of your file and, Aunie, I want you to go see him. Get a restraining order . . . just in case."

She shivered. "The restrainin' order didn't do me a whole lot of good last time."

"I know, sweetheart. But it should add clout to the case against him, and I want you to have one."

"Oh, Jordan," she said with quiet despair, "is this never going to end?"

"It will, Aunie. Maybe sooner than we think."

"God, I've been prayin' for the day."

"You just enjoy your new life and try not to worry, okay?"

"I'll try."

"Call me again if you need anything or if you just want to talk."

"I will. Thank you again, Jordan."

"You're welcome, dear. Keep in touch."

They rang off and Aunie sat for several despondent moments in the gathering gloom. Finally, she returned the phone to its resting place and rose to pull the drapes and turn on the lights. She bumped up the thermostat and retrieved from her purse the curriculum brochures she had picked up at the college. After briefly consulting a menu, she ordered room service; changed into a warm sweatshirt, leggings, and two pairs of socks; pulled the little writing table and a chair in front of the heat register, and sat down to read.

At her appointment with the college counselor earlier in the day, she had been warned that it was quite late to be registering for the fall quarter. One or two of the classes that interested her had already started this week and another class was full. Aunie had felt a bit discouraged, but the counselor had also offered hope. She had said it wasn't uncommon for classes to be dropped in the first week, so there was still a very good possibility that Aunie could get the ones she desired. Sitting in her hotel room, she finished selecting her alternate choices and filled in the registration form to be returned to the school tomorrow.

Then she didn't know what to do with herself. Her dinner was delivered and she ate it while watching the news on the television. Setting her tray out in the corridor, she wandered around the room, rechecking all its features. She scanned the pay movies listed inside the armoire that housed the television set. Nothing appealed to her. She picked up a paperback, tried to read, then threw it down on the nightstand next to the bed.

Crossing slowly to the window, she pulled back the curtain. It was dark now and her room boasted a panoramic view. Lights formed a cityscape that stretched out before her, and she watched the lighted windows of a ferry in Elliott Bay as it glided slowly toward town. She shivered in the cold emanating off the plate glass and dropped the curtain.

Picking up the evening paper, she read an article about a man who'd been arrested for making obscene phone calls to approximately a hundred women. The article also reported that in an unrelated case, the telephone company and the police were working together to track down a different caller responsible for placing an alarmingly high number of harrassing phone calls to female students at a local college. Aunie tossed the paper aside. She didn't need to hear about other people's troubles; she had enough of her own.

In her wanderings around the hotel room, she had avoided looking into any of the mirrors, but finally, she crossed over to one. Bracing her hands on the small built-in vanity, she slowly lifted her head.

All her life, she had heard how beautiful she was. Sometimes it had been a blessing; sometimes it had been a curse. However she viewed it, one thing was certain. The woman reflected in the mirror would surely never hear such compliments.

There had not been sufficient time for most of the swelling to go down. She had walked out of the

hospital emergency room two days ago, closed her
account at the bank, called a company to crate the
few belongings she would eventually want shipped to
her, packed as many herself as she could carry with
her, and called the airlines for flight information.
She hadn't known exactly where she was going, but
she'd felt the need to cover as much ground as possible while Wesley was still in jail. She only hoped he
wasn't paying private detectives to keep an eye on
her while he was incarcerated. But, surely not. He
hadn't had time to arrange it.

Unless, of course, he hadn't really dismissed the
one he'd already had in his employ, as he'd told her
he had. She wouldn't put anything past him.

Leaving Jordan in charge of her stored belongings
and of putting her house and car up for sale, she
had caught a red-eye to Chicago. At O'Hare, she'd
decided on Seattle as her final destination because
it was far away from home and she didn't know a soul
there. Wesley would have no reason to assume that
she was heading there. She had slipped into a wom-
en's rest room and tried her best to change her
appearance. It hadn't been an easy task with her face
in this condition: the swelling and discoloration made
it conspicuous. Desperate to escape detection if she
were being watched, she had explained her situation
to a large group of businesswomen on their way to a
seminar, and one of them had gone to purchase her
ticket for her. They had then buried her in their
midst, carrying her from the rest room to the gate
of departure.

She didn't recognize that face in the mirror. The
contusions affected its shape, effectively disguising
her much-lauded bone structure. There was a stitched
tear in her left earlobe where Wesley had ripped out

her pierced earring. Both eyes were blackened, but thankfully no longer swollen shut. Her nose had been broken, but the emergency room doctor had assured her that once the swelling went down, it should be good as new. Her lip was split; it, too, would mend. Her skin was eventually going to regain what had once been referred to by a suitor given to flowery compliments as its poreless, alabaster complexion. A gross exaggeration, that, but her complexion was the one physical attribute she took pride in, and anything would be an improvement over its current condition, which was a rainbow of hideous bruises, ranging the spectrum from dense purple to saffron yellow.

But, basically, the doctors had told her, her injuries were superficial. She was lucky, they had said. No other broken bones, no eye damage, no concussion to report, no lost teeth. After the fuss her mama had made in the emergency room, they'd rushed to assure her she would once again regain her former beauty. Those assurances had satisfied Mama, but left Aunie feeling quite ambivalent.

Because, sometimes, her looks had been a blessing.

But, sometimes, they had been a curse.

CHAPTER 2

There was no place quite like the South for one to be a member of the impoverished gentility. Southerners for generations had been raising that condition to an art form and Aunie felt she could write a book on the subject, no research necessary. After all, she had firsthand experience as an only child in a family that was a poor relation to two venerable old Southern names.

Her daddy was L. Martin Franklin III, a dreamer in a family of overachievers. He was a vague, scholarly presence that barely made a ripple in her life. He cared only for his books and his projects, and his lack of business acumen was an accepted idiosyncrasy regarded by his family with the same half-amused, half-irritated tolerance that was accorded Uncle Asa's drinking or Uncle Beau's womanizing.

Her mama was a Pearlin—of the *Savannah* Pearlins? That was the way she always qualified it upon an introduction . . . her voice sweet as sorghum with a gently questioning inflection at the end. The unspoken inference was that a body must surely be lacking in breeding indeed if they had never heard of that august family. Aunie was perhaps five or six years old before she realized that the phrase Pearlin-of-the-Savannah-Pearlins wasn't her mother's exact maiden name.

She was almost as young when she first began to comprehend the expectations her family had of her. It was difficult to remember a time when her looks and an obligation to marry well had not gone hand in hand.

Her mama was an unhappy woman. She hated her lack of wealth, even if the Pearlins and L. Martin's family did see to it that they were never lacking in the amenities. They were nevertheless forced to live in those tacky old apartment houses! She found it impossible to forget that, until her marriage, she had lived in a glorious mansion where she'd been raised to expect that her every wish would be granted.

Then she'd had to go fall in love with a scholar with impeccable antecedents and not one ounce of marketable ambition.

She drummed it into Aunie's mind that she could do better. *It's all very well to marry for love,* she'd often said. *But when the passion fades—and, sugah, it will—you want to make sure something tangible remains. Use the attributes God gave you. Fall in love, if you must. Just see to it that you fall in love with a rich man.* How many times had Aunie heard *that* in her lifetime?

Her daddy never gave her advice at all. . . . He was quite oblivious that she might be in need of it. At the best of times, Aunie was not quite certain he was even more than vaguely aware of her existence.

The rest of her relatives, however, tended to agree with Mama; they talked about her prospects for a good marriage as if it were a foregone conclusion. She grew up in elegant old apartment houses that retained shabby vestiges of their former glory, wearing her cousin Nola's hand-me-down designer clothing. She was waited upon by servants whose wages were paid by her granddaddy. Attendance at private schools was naturally considered de rigueur; the fees were paid by an uncle. Dance classes were financed by another uncle, and she belonged to exclusive country clubs whose dues were subsidized by yet another. Inescapably, at every family gathering, one or another of her male relatives could be counted on to grasp her chin, hold her face up to the light, and murmur, "Yes, suh! This one's a beauty. She'll never have a problem snarin' herself a real catch."

Aunie wasn't quite certain how she was supposed to go about snaring a catch, but she knew it had something to do with her physical attractiveness. As a child she was extremely shy. Everyone at the private schools she attended knew she was a student who needed to be subsidized and with the cruelty of youth, they did not hesitate to taunt her with it. Her own family never credited her with intelligence. All anyone seemed to think she had going for her was her appearance.

And that was before she began to truly blossom.

Life is kinder to the attractive than it is to the unsightly—it's an indisputable fact of life. Acceptance and approval come easier regardless of how undeserved they may be, since they are based, more often than not, on an immediate visceral reaction to outward appearances.

Aunie was not exactly proud of how very much she took advantage of that fact as an adolescent.

Pretty girls are not supposed to feel inadequate, so she hid her shyness as her beauty blossomed, forcing herself to appear vivacious and outgoing. She felt duty-bound to fulfill her family's expectations so she never questioned the rightness of accepting from others the luxuries that her father could not provide. Following her mother's example, she considered them no more than her due.

It never occurred to her to learn to make her own way in life, to use her brains instead of her looks. If someone had told her that the labor entailed in providing her *own* security would ultimately be more rewarding than snaring a good catch to do it for her, she wouldn't have understood. She only knew what had been drummed into her head for so many years. Consequently, it took her longer than most to develop an identity of her own.

She thought her looks *were* her identity. No one had ever lauded her intelligence the way they praised her flawless skin or impeccable bone structure. No one had ever told her she was smart enough to do whatever she wanted to do. It was understood that she possessed one marketable commodity. Her duty was to use her physical attractiveness to marry well. Insecure beneath her bogus surface vivacity, that was what she set out to do.

Upon completing a year of finishing school, she was introduced to a number of eligible, family-approved bachelors: young men with solid family connections and bright prospects. But although she often had fun with them and was even drawn to one or two, there was an elemental spark that was missing. She had been taught that wealth was the primary objective, but in a stubborn corner of her mind she was convinced there had to be more. She wanted love as well.

Then Wesley Cunningham entered her life and swept her off her feet.

Wesley wasn't a boy or a young man; he was thirty-six to her nineteen years. A respected, established gallery owner whose personal collection of rare and beautiful objets d'art was lauded as unequaled in the South, he was an urbane man at ease in the most exalted company. That such a man should exhibit signs of being quite taken with her took Aunie's breath away. His pursuit of her was persistent, sophisticated, and romantic, and it quite turned her head. When he requested her hand in marriage following an eleven-month courtship, she thought she was the luckiest woman alive.

Later, she liked to believe that if she'd had even a glimmer of realization that she was about to become the prized possession of an obsessed man, she would have run as far away as fast as she could. But the truth was, she simply wasn't sure of anything anymore. Maybe the signs had been there all along and she had simply refused to see them. Her ego *had* been inflated by Wesley's attentions and—given her own determination at the time to fulfill every expectation her family had ever had of her—perhaps it was possible she had just turned a blind eye to the flaws in his personality.

She didn't *think* that was the truth of what had happened.

But she had to live with the knowledge that she would never be one hundred percent certain that it was not.

"Afternoon, Otis." There was a soft clatter on the stairs. "I swear, you're one of the hardest workin' men I have ever met. Lola tells me you're a fire fighter, and yet all your free time seems to be spent workin' around here."

James looked up from his crouched position on the floor near the end of the hall. He watched as Aunie reached the top of the stairs. She stopped in the pool of light cast by the hanging trouble light and smiled brilliantly up into Otis's face.

James settled back on his buttocks and crossed his ankles, Indian style. He had been relying on the natural daylight pouring through the hall window to illuminate his work up until a few moments ago when the sun had abruptly gone behind a cloud. On the verge of fetching the other trouble light, he was now glad he'd held off.

It gave him an unexpected opportunity to observe without being observed in return.

He couldn't get over what a looker she was. It had knocked him on his butt every time he'd run across her these past few weeks. Who would have guessed that beneath all those bruises and contusions which she'd been sporting that first day, there would be such creamy, c'mon-and-touch-me skin? The fairness of her complexion was another surprise, a marked contrast to her shiny, dark brown hair, dark brows, and sooty, tangled eyelashes. Her eyes were also a deep brown, large and exotically tilted, the whites almost childlike in their blue-white clarity. That mouth of hers, however, was anything but childlike. The upper lip was narrow and shapely, the bottom lip more lushly full. And just to gild the lily, she not only possessed deep dimples to frame her smile, there was also a tiny mole just to the right of the bow of her upper lip. Talk about a case of overkill, he thought sourly.

Okay, okay, so maybe when he was around her he felt a little bit foolish for the way he'd overreacted the day she'd come to rent the apartment, and maybe it made him regard her with less than rose-colored approval. But he'd be damned if he'd take full blame for it. Her own attitude hadn't helped matters. In fact, instead of graciously ignoring what had happened that day and starting all over—which is what *he* would have done—she seemed to go out of her way to rub it in whenever their paths crossed. Instead of letting bygones be bygones, she was all pretty, dimpled smiles for Otis and Lola, calling them by their first names, while *he* was still *Mistah Rydah*, spoken in that cool, polite manner that never failed to put his back up. Her level, shuttered glances and that damned mister business with his name could really make him feel like a mannerless clod. Which he supposed he sometimes was.

But if she was supposed to be so fucking mannerly, then she sure as hell shouldn't be bending over backwards to make him feel that way.

Ah purely don't recall Superman havin' such a filthy mouth.

James rolled his shoulders uneasily. He'd been hearing those words in his mind repeatedly these past few weeks, and following the casual obscenity of his thoughts, he heard them again now. At first they'd just made him defensive. Not everyone was lucky enough to be born with a silver spoon in his mouth. Some folks had to make do with the cold reality of a day-to-day scramble for survival beneath the uncaring eyes of the Housing Authority.

In the Terrace, the low-income project where James grew up, obscenities were a way of life. He hadn't thought to question his use of them until she'd made him feel like so much dog shit for his spontaneous utterances.

Sounding like the meanest mother in town had saved his ass on more than one occasion in his formative years. James hadn't been naturally drawn to trouble the way his brothers had been. He'd much preferred building things with his hands and drawing his cartoons to knocking heads together. He'd had to fight his way out of his fair share of bad situations, of course, but on the whole he'd preferred to depend on his quick wit and offbeat sense of humor to maneuver him out of a tight spot. Sounding as though he'd as soon rip a man's eyeballs out of his head as look at him sure as hell hadn't hurt, though. Neither had his friendship with Otis.

They'd both been on the verge of adolescence when Otis had moved into an upstairs unit of their Terrace apartment house. Otis had been blossoming into every bigot's nightmare even then: already over six feet tall, showing promise of his future bulk, and losing his hair to a rare dermatological condition. James had hung around the base of the stairs the day he had moved in, sketching rapidly as he'd watched Otis's family pack their meager belongings into their new home. They had marched smartly to the tersely voiced directions of a tall black lady. He'd learned later that when Otis's ma was on a roll, she could put a drill sergeant to shame.

It was, in fact, his quickly drawn cartoon of her in a marine uniform that had more or less introduced the boys. Otis had suddenly paused to stare over James's shoulder, wanting to see what the blond boy was drawing. James had stiffened and held his breath, knowing his cartoon could easily backfire. In their neighborhood, making fun of somebody's mama could get your head laid open by a rusty pipe.

But Otis had roared with laughter and snatched the sketch pad from James's hands. "Hey, Ma," he'd called and carried the pad over to his mother. "This here white boy's already got yer number!"

They'd been friends ever since.

Now, two decades later, he suddenly realized that somewhere along the way Otis had cleaned up the worst of his language, while he never had. Maybe it was time he did. They'd both moved well beyond the need to protect themselves or intimidate others through the use of rough, crude language.

But it was going to be one effin' difficult habit to break.

In any case, he was trying his best not to resent the way the little Southern princess made him feel, because in all fairness, he didn't think she was doing it deliberately—except for that mister business. Hell, he didn't harbor any burning desire to be her good friend. They were two entirely different people and the less he knew her, the less apt he was to get corralled into her troubles. It would be much better all around to keep a healthy distance between them. But he didn't see the need for hostilities either. Living in the same building—hell, on the same floor—they were going to bump into each other. Seemed to him they could at least manage to be polite acquaintances.

"Well, I guess I'd better get going and let you get back to work," Aunie said to Otis. "I've got a ton of homework to do today, myself." She hefted her book bag. As she started to turn away the sun broke through the clouds, illuminating the end of the hallway. She noticed James for the first time, sitting cross-legged on the floor, plaster dust liberally coating his hair, bare shoulders, black tank top, and worn Levis.

Her mouth went dry with a sense of inadequacy she never felt with Otis or Lola. "Hello, Mistah Rydah," she said softly. "I didn't see you back there."

"Hello, yourself, Magnolia Blossom." He gave her a sleepy smile and looked her over with those uncivilized eyes of his. She swallowed dryly.

"Aren't you kind of cold without your shirt?" she blurted. The amusement in his eyes as they roved over her puffy, brightly colored down jacket made her want to squirm, although she couldn't have said precisely why.

"No," he replied politely enough, but Aunie still had the impression he was laughing at her. "Sanding is warm work." His eyes lit on her coat again. "Maybe we should give you a patch of plaster to smooth out. A little physical exertion and you wouldn't have to bundle up like a kid on the first day of snow."

To James's astonishment, her eyes lighted with interest. "Really?" she asked. "I've got homework to start, but I could give you about twenty minutes. Do you mean it?" When he didn't immediately say no—primarily because he was too dumbfounded to speak—she smiled in pleasure. "I'll be right back." She whirled around and raced down the hallway to her apartment like a kid unexpectedly let out of school. The door slammed behind her a moment later.

"I was kidding," James said in amazement to the carpet between his crooked legs.

Otis's teeth gleamed whitely. "You were bein' sarcastic," he corrected his friend. "You thought she was too hoity-toity to take you up on it, so you figured you were safe to embarrass her a little. Maybe you oughtta get to know that little gal a tiny bit better, Jimmy, before you jump to any *more* conclusions about her."

James muttered an obscenity beneath his breath and turned away, feeling unaccountably small-minded. Okay, so maybe he had intended to knock her down a peg or two. She rubbed him the wrong way. Aunie's glowing face when she reappeared a moment later—her jacket replaced by an Emerald City sweatshirt—made him feel even lower yet, and perversely he laid the blame for it at her door.

"What do I do?" she asked him.

"Put a piece of sandpaper around a block of wood and sand the fu . . . uh, the wall," he muttered unhelpfully, and when some of the glow dimmed in her eyes he felt like snapping at her to stop making him feel like such a shit.

"Okay," she murmured and looked around. She picked up a sheet of coarse grit and ran her thumb over it. "This must be the sandpaper."

James's mouth dropped open. She had never seen *sandpaper* before? "Where the hell have you been all your life?" he demanded incredulously.

"In various cities in Georgia, suh, bein' totally useless," Aunie replied with surprising cheer. "But all that's gonna change, Mistah Rydah, just you wait and see. I'm learnin' all sorts of new things every day."

"Here, Aunie," Otis said gently as he wrapped his ham-sized hand around her elbow and steered her down to his section of the wall. He stooped to pick up a block of wood on the way, shooting James a sour look over his massive shoulder. "You can work down here with me. Just wrap the paper around the block like so and stroke the high spots on the plaster like this." He demonstrated for an instant then handed her the block. "Here, you try it."

Aunie applied herself industriously. Several moments later she stepped back to view the results. She shot an uncertain glance down the hall at James, then turned to Otis. "It's not as flat and smooth as the patch you did," she said in a low voice.

"You don't have my upper body strength, girl," Otis said with a smile. "It's just gonna take you a little bit longer, is all."

"Okay, good." She flashed him a smile that expressed gratitude for his forbearance in not making her feel as inept as she knew she most likely was and then applied herself once again with renewed vigor. She didn't stop until Otis tapped her on the arm.

"You've been out here for nearly an hour," he said and removed the block from her hands. "You'd better get started on that stack of homework you were tellin' me about. I wouldn't want to be responsible for preventin' you from getting a good grade."

"Oh. I suppose you're right." Aunie flexed her fingers and knocked plaster dust from her arms and legs. She shook her head like a wet puppy and dust flew. Raking her fingers through her hair to hold it off her forehead, she peered up at Otis. "This has been fun. Thanks for broadening my horizons, Otis."

"My pleasure."

She laughed. "You're a nice man." Then, peering down the hall, she nodded to James, who had stopped sanding to watch her. "Mistah Rydah, you were certainly right. Sandin' keeps you nice and warm." She left them to their work.

Aunie laughed at her dusty image in the bathroom mirror a few moments later. Wouldn't Mama die if she could see her now? She took a quick shower and dressed in jeans, a cotton turtleneck, warm socks, and a warmer sweater. Pouring herself a glass of juice, she lined up her books and papers on the dining room table and sat down to study. It took her some time, though, before she could give it the concentration it deserved.

Smoothing that plaster had been fun; it had made her feel a little less ineffectual than usual. It would be awhile, however, before she'd forget the look on James Ryder's face when she had stupidly identified the sandpaper. He'd looked at her as though wondering how she'd ever managed to navigate the face of the earth as long as she had, when it should be quite obvious to anyone with eyes in their head that she didn't possess the most basic knowledge.

Gawd, that man made her uncomfortable, and instinctively she maintained a formal distance between them. It wasn't because of James's reaction on the day she had rented the apartment that she refused to call him by his first name; well, not entirely at least. Mainly it was because he looked at her as though she were inherently deficient when she was trying very hard to become a competent, independent adult. She'd admit she was starting later in life than most people did, but better late than never. She *was* making the attempt and she didn't need him to undermine what was already a limited confidence in her ability to become useful and productive. She was also intimidated by all that he had accomplished when she had never accomplished a damned thing on her own.

Not only did he own this apartment house, which she never would have guessed that first day, he was also J. T. Ryder. *The* J. T. Ryder, the inventor of "A Skewed View," the hottest cartoon to grace the Sunday papers in years. And his cartoons weren't just in the newspapers, either; there were Skewed View calendars and two collections of cartoons in paperback. Why, just the other week, at the bookstore at school, she had purchased a coffee mug with one of his cartoons on the side. She kept her pencils and pens in it. It was when she was showing her purchase to Lola, actually, laughing once again at the offbeat humor displayed on its side, that she had discovered it was James's work. She was floored. *He* was its creator? She had been almost positive that he was a drug dealer.

His apartment was down the hall from hers, and she couldn't help seeing the steady procession of men who had come and gone at odd hours ever since the first day she'd moved in. Well, there hadn't actually been that many of them, but they never seemed to stay for more than five minutes at a time and a couple of them had been so motley in appearance. Was she ever glad she hadn't mentioned her suspicions to Lola; God above, she'd feel even more worthless than she already did.

Both James and Otis had made something of their lives, and neither of them had had a tenth of her advantages. Lola had told her something of the neighborhood where they'd grown up, and Aunie cringed when she thought of everything she had ever been given. She had never had to earn a thing for herself; yet she'd still made a mess of her life in spite of her privileged beginning.

What most shamed her was knowing that at the beginning of her marriage, she had been totally satisfied with her situation. Well, *almost* totally. Her love and sex life had been a frustrating disappointment right from the start, but materially, she couldn't have been happier if she'd won a multimillion-dollar lottery.

Aunie stared blindly at the text in her book, rapidly tapping her pencil eraser against the tabletop. In her mind's eye, she saw the well-developed muscles in James Ryder's shoulders and arms, the ridges of muscle beneath the black material that had been sweat-soaked to his stomach. She had never in her life been so close to two such masculine men as he and Otis.

Wesley had been baby-soft compared to them. He had looked fit and urbane in his flawlessly tailored suits, but out of them . . . well, he hadn't been Michelangelo's *David*. Not that it would have made a lick of difference if only he had been lusty and passionate with her, but unfortunately, he'd been anything but. The romantic streak that had swept her off her feet had disappeared almost as soon as he'd said, "I do."

It had been terribly confusing . . . not to mention a debilitating blow to her sense of desirability. She had assumed at first that he was trying to be considerate in the face of her lack of sexual experience; she had been a virgin, after all, and years younger than her new husband. Only gradually had it dawned on her that he quite simply was not often interested in that particular aspect of their marriage. She'd always had the uneasy feeling he'd much prefer to admire her from a distance like one of his rare objets d'art than to engage her in anything as sweaty and vital as sex.

She, on the other hand, had been looking forward quite eagerly to some sweaty, vital sex with her new husband. She had always had an intense secret interest in the subject, even if she hadn't had an abundance of hands-on experience. Ultimately, however, she'd had to concede that their love life was most likely not going to improve, a concession that had left her feeling restless and frustrated in a way she hadn't quite known how to alleviate. She knew it

wasn't to her credit that she'd managed to console
herself fairly well for a while with her newfound
wealth.

Finding herself undesired as a woman and having
no useful purpose, however, had begun to pall after
the second year of marriage. There were too many
empty hours in the day and she could only fill a
fraction of them with shopping, lunches, workouts
with her personal trainer, and tennis on Tuesdays
and Thursdays. Her husband paraded her at business
deals and took her out several evenings a week to
popular restaurants and watering holes where they
could see and be seen by those he considered
important, but she wanted to be more than a decoration
on display. She wanted to seek gainful employment,
but Wesley wouldn't hear of her going to work.

Part time? she had pleaded.

NO.

She had waited a couple of months and then had
suggested volunteer work, thinking he could not possibly object to that. Many of the women in their social
circle gave their time to worthy charitable organizations.

She was wrong in her assumption, as Wesley was
swift to point out to her in no uncertain terms. He
wanted her on call at a moment's notice to grace his
gallery openings, his business lunches, dinners, and
social functions. He expected her to be impeccably
turned out at all times in the clothes that he'd
selected. He did *not* intend to compete with anyone
else for her time.

For another two years, she tried to accommodate
him. She tried equally hard not to resent being made
to feel more like a valuable collector's item than a
desirable woman. She wanted someone who would
throw her down on a bed and make mad, impulsive,

passionate love to her. She wanted someone who would muss her up without a moment's thought. She hated feeling as if she weren't bright enough to climb down off her state-of-the-art lighted pedestal and actually do something useful.

When she told him she wanted a baby and **he** refused even to consider the notion, it was the beginning of the end.

She'd thought about it long and hard before she ever proposed the idea to Wesley. She would love to have a child. She had a wealth of love stored up inside of her just waiting for someone on whom she could lavish it. Wesley had denied her himself for that purpose, but children thrived on love. God knew she had an abundance of time and energy to spare. And all men wanted an heir, didn't they? Surely, this was one idea with which Wesley could not possibly quibble.

He flatly refused.

Why, she had demanded. For God's sake, why not?

His reply had curdled the last remaining bit of affection she still held for him. *Drop it, Aunie,* he had said in that damnably peremptory tone of voice of his, the one that expected instant obedience. *You're not having a baby. It will ruin your figure.*

He had hurt her in the past and he'd made her angry. She'd known he was a man who sought perfection in his possessions, but it had never truly occurred to her before then that that was all she was to him— just another objet d'art. She began to consider the notion the day he flatly rejected her proposal, gave her that preposterous justification, and then turned away as easily as if he had just settled a minor altercation with one of his gallery employees.

She went to her mother and tentatively broached the idea of divorce. It was the first time she had mentioned the word out loud, and she supposed she should not have been surprised to discover her mother was appalled at the mere thought.

I can't continue to live this way, Mama.

Don't be foolish, sugah. You have all the wealth and social advantages a woman could desire.

Mama, it's not enough; haven't you heard a word I've been saying? I'm nothing more to Wesley than a pretty possession. I'm not allowed to work; I'm not allowed to bear a child. Unless he wants to show me off, he acts as though I don't even exist. Surely you can see that it's simply not enough.

I can see that you're an ungrateful child.

Her marriage limped along for several more months, but the idea of divorce, once planted in her brain, would not give Aunie a moment's peace. Finally, the day came when the voice whispering in her mind was louder than any rationale she could summon to counter it.

She made an appointment with a prominent attorney, Jordan St. John. When Wesley came home from work that evening, she told him she had filed the papers.

Of all the reactions he could have made, she did not expect the one she got. He laughed.

I'm serious, Wesley.

Don't be ridiculous. Go put on your red Scaasi—we have dinner reservations at eight. She could still see his manicured fingertips impatiently tapping the crystal of his Rolex watch and the irritation in his eyes when he looked back up at her. *And for God's sake, do something with your makeup. You can't be seen in public looking like that.*

When she finally convinced him that she was, indeed, serious, she was terrified he was going to have a stroke. He was enraged; there was no other word for it. He threatened her with all manner of legal harassment; he told her he would see to it that she was left penniless and socially ostracized if she insisted on going through with her insane proposal.

By that time, she'd reached the point where she truly didn't care. She just wanted to feel that she had some worth in this world that didn't begin and end in her looks. She also knew deep in her heart that she would never feel worthwhile or even entirely *real* as long as she was married to Wesley.

She told him to do what he had to do.

To her amazement he made a complete turn-around and agreed to an amicable settlement. Suddenly as gracious as he'd been in their courting days, he insisted that she keep the house and the Mercedes. He moved into his club and instructed his own lawyer to settle a generous sum in her name. She was baffled by his abrupt change of heart, but she didn't question it. She was simply grateful that the fighting was at an end. When their divorce was ultimately finalized, she felt as though she had gained a whole new lease on life.

It was not a feeling destined to be long-lived.

James flipped on the light that was mounted to his drafting table, dropped onto the padded seat of his secretarial chair, and picked up a pencil. Ten minutes later, he tossed the pencil aside and drummed his fingers against the slanted edge of his table in an irritated rhythm, no closer to inspiration than he had been when he'd first sat down. Damn. He was restless and edgy and concentration was simply beyond him.

He popped the cap off a cold Dos Equis and

prowled the apartment but there wasn't a thing there capable of holding his interest. The book he'd been enjoying last night was suddenly boring and dry; there was nothing worth viewing on television, and what in hell ever happened to the days when FM radio meant listening while smooth-voiced DJ's played an entire uninterrupted side of an album? He couldn't even find anything good to eat in this place.

James killed off his beer and grabbed his scuffed leather jacket. He had to get out of here for a while; he was going nuts.

He stopped at the grocery store and bought some provisions, bypassing the chocolate-chip-mint ice cream regretfully. He wasn't in the mood to go home yet; and unfortunately by the time he was, the ice cream would most likely be reduced to a soggy puddle in the back of his Jeep. Storing the groceries, he headed for a nearby tavern that served excellent barbecued-beef sandwiches.

A sandwich, a beer, and the smoky, noisy atmosphere of the tavern began to unravel his uncharacteristic tension. He put a quarter on the pool table to reserve himself a place in the lineup waiting to challenge the current champ and ordered another beer. Leaning an elbow on the bar, he sipped his beer slowly as he watched the tavern patrons.

The little blonde by the jukebox reminded him vaguely of his new tenant, the Southern belle. God, she had *hummed* while she was sanding the wall this afternoon. She couldn't carry a tune worth a damn, but still, who would have expected that kind of cheeriness from someone eating plaster dust? Especially someone like her. Otis was right: he'd only made the offer in the first place from a contrary desire to embarrass her. Her eagerness in accepting and her cheerful industriousness had knocked him on his butt. *You were right, Mistah Rydah, sandin' keeps you nice and warm.*

Offhand, he could think of about a dozen ways of keeping her warm that would be a helluva lot more enjoyable.

James sucked in an involuntary breath and aspirated beer into his lungs. He coughed harshly. Where in hell had that thought come from? He didn't go for the petite, vulnerable type; he liked them tall and experienced, girls with big tits who knew the score and were no smarter than they had to be. He enjoyed good-natured women who didn't expect more from him than a night's pleasure.

Hell, he was horny; that was all. All that edgy restlessness that had driven him out of his apartment was simply a result of having gone too long without any good, raunchy, uncomplicated sex. That was the *only* reason those mind images featuring the Magnolia Midget in glorious technicolor had popped with momentary vividness into his brain. Jeez.

He took another sip of beer and rolled the cool bottle across his flushed forehead.

"Hello, James."

James lowered the bottle and found himself staring smack dab into a truly spectacular set of mammaries showcased in a thin tank top and framed by a loose, open jacket. His face creased in half-a-dozen places as he grinned. Well, all right. This was more like it. He raised his eyes. "Shelley! Haven't seen you for a while. Sit down. Let me buy you a drink."

She smiled in pleasure and slid onto the vacant stool next to him. "Thanks, I'd like that. Make it white wine."

James motioned for the bartender.

He felt himself returning to normal as the evening progressed. He flirted, laughed, and teased. He pushed aside the stray thought that Shelley's skin wasn't as smooth and clear as he remembered almost in the same instant that it formed in his mind. He enjoyed the way she pressed her lush breasts against his arm when they talked and how she encouraged him when he went up against the pool-table champ. Unfortunately, the encouragement didn't do him a world of good. The guy was exceptional, and one game was all that James got. He was just grateful he'd only had two balls left on the felt by the time his opponent finally sank the eight ball . . . at least he hadn't been totally skunked. Shelley's brand of commiseration took the sting right out of his defeat in any case.

It was growing late when he leaned over and nuzzled her ear. "Wanna take me home?" he breathed. "You can show me all those new colors you were telling me about." Shelley was a manicurist who specialized in acrylic nails.

"Oh, James, I can't. Me and my roommate painted my room, and I have to sleep out on the couch tonight." She leaned close, cuddling his bicep between her full breasts again. "Let's go to your place."

For just an instant, James was tempted to break his number one cardinal rule: Never bring the ladies home. Shelley was, after all, exactly what the doctor ordered.

Then the moment passed. "Uh, that won't work. I've got one of my brothers staying with me." Once women spent the night, he'd discovered the hard way, they had a habit of forever after dropping by unannounced and making themselves at home. Then he always ended up hurting their feelings when he told them he didn't want someone to cook his dinner or straighten up his living room. Or worse, they noticed his work on the drafting table, discovered who he was, and then the trouble really began.

According to Lola, he was a real pig, but that was just the way it was. He didn't need the complications.

James visited with Shelley for another hour, but when he finally left, he left alone.

This had just not been his day.

CHAPTER 3

Lola pulled the basal thermometer from her mouth and made a notation on the chart next to the bed. She reclined back on her pillow, feeling depressed. It looked like tomorrow was going to be the day, and Otis would be gone. His rotation at the station began this afternoon. Damn! She tossed aside the covers and slowly climbed from the bed.

She was brewing herself a cup of herbal tea when Otis sidled up behind her. He wrapped his strong arms around her waist and nuzzled her neck. "Mornin' baby."

"Mornin'," she responded glumly and when Otis's mouth returned to the side of her neck, she hunched her shoulder irritably. He slowly straightened.

"I can see you're in a wonderful mood. Thermometer give you some bad news this mornin'?"

"It looks like tomorrow."

"So recreational sex today is out of the question,

I guess.'' His voice turned bitter. ''Gotta save up all those sperm for when they'll really count!''

''I don't suppose you could come home for a while tomorrow.''

''No, dammit, I can't.'' He grabbed her by the shoulders. ''How long are we going to keep putting ourselves through this, Lola? Remember when we used to make love just because we felt like it, not because some friggin' chart said it was time?''

''I want a baby, mon!''

''So do I, girl. But I don't want to sacrifice our entire life to the project in the meantime. There must be hundreds of black babies out there just beggin' for a good home. I want you to give some serious consideration to adoption.''

''I want your baby,'' she maintained stubbornly.

Otis stiffened and dropped his hands. They'd been over this before . . . too damned many times. It was starting to drive a wedge between them. Lately, he'd been getting the feeling she wouldn't really welcome his lovemaking unless there was the possibility it would impregnate her. The thought hurt more than he could ever let her know. Angrily, he turned away. ''I'm going to work,'' he said stiffly. Grabbing his jacket from the closet, he headed for the door.

''Otis.''

He stopped in the open doorway but didn't turn back to her. Lola came up behind him and wrapped her arms around his waist, resting her cheek against the warm muscles of his back. ''Don't go. You don't have to be there for hours.''

He remained stiff in her embrace. ''I'm sick of this, Lola. We had something so rare and good, and I can feel it slippin' away. I want to be wanted just for myself again, not because it's time for me to play the stud.

And I swear, if my brother offers his services one more time, I'm gonna flatten him."

"I know." Her hands slid down his hard thighs, then slowly rose again. Long, brown fingers brushed seductively back and forth across the fly of his slacks. "I'm sorry for my lousy attitude, mon. I love you."

He remained where he was standing but slowly reached out and closed the door.

"Let me start over again," she whispered. "Say 'mornin' baby.'"

"Mornin' baby."

"Mornin' yourself, soldier boy. Wanna fool around wid an island girl . . . just for the heck of it?"

"Yeah." He turned in her arms. "Oh, baby, yeah."

"Happy Halloween, Lola," Aunie said cheerfully when the door opened to her knock. "Otis home?"

"No. He's on his rotation at the firehouse."

"Oh, rats. The lamp in my bedroom quit working and I was hoping he could help me fix it."

"*Help* you?"

"Okay, fix it." Aunie's unrepentant grin slowly faded when it was not returned.

"James is home," Lola said flatly. "Get him to fix it for you. He's better wid the electrical stuff anyway."

Aunie frowned. "Lola, have I done something to offend you?" Ever since the day they'd met, Lola had felt like a very good friend. Friends had never been overabundant in Aunie's life. Today, however, she was receiving the distinct impression she was not welcome, and her self-esteem dropped a notch lower than usual. She backed up a step.

"No." Lola reached out and gripped Aunie's wrist. "I'm sorry. I'm just depressed today, and I'm takin' it out on everyone around me." Her dark eyes filled with quick tears. "I made Otis angry wid me earlier and now I'm hurtin' your feelin's."

"My feelings will survive. You want to talk about it or should I go away?"

Lola pulled her through the door. "I want some company."

"The doctors, they can't find anything wrong wid either of us," she confided awhile later. Her chin rested on her updrawn knees as she gazed unhappily at Aunie. "We've been married for seven years and tryin' for a child for nearly four, but I just cannot seem to get pregnant. For a long time it didn't matter so much, but lately it's practically all I can think about. It's become such a sensitive issue, Otis's sister Leeanne dreaded to tell me she was pregnant, and wid good reason. I was hoppy for her, but also I was so jealous I could have screamed. Now, it's startin' to drive me and Otis apart; and, Aunie, if I let that hoppen, if I drive him away because I can't stop obsessin' 'bout having a baby, I don't know what I'll do. I love that mon so much."

"Have you ever considered adoption?"

"That's what Otis wants to do, but I don't know . . . I want to give him his own child."

"I wanted a baby when I was married," Aunie said slowly. She had never admitted this to anyone except her mother and lawyer, and it was difficult to admit to now; but perhaps, if she could make Lola see how lucky she was to have Otis . . . "My husband refused even to consider the possibility. The reason he gave me was that it would ruin my figure." When Lola stared at her incredulously, Aunie met her eyes and continued, "Kind of gives you an idea of my importance in his life, huh? I envy you Otis so much, Lola.

It's obvious he's crazy about you, and he doesn't strike me as a man who would love a child any less just because that child wasn't created from his own seed.''

She left Lola's apartment a short time later and returned to her own. It wasn't until she entered the bedroom and flipped the switch on the bedside lamp that she recalled her original reason for going downstairs. Damn. If she wanted the thing fixed anytime soon, she was going to have to ask James Ryder to help her.

She'd really rather not.

On the other hand, she'd also rather not wait for the four days or a week or whatever it was that comprised one of Otis's rotations at the fire station. That was a long time to be without her lamp, and she had not yet reached the point where she could once again sleep in the dark. She sometimes wondered if the night would ever come when she would be able to.

Feeling like an idiot for the way her heart was beginning to pound over what was basically a minor request, she walked down the hall and tapped lightly on James's door. Relieved when there was no answer, she tapped once again just so she could tell herself she wasn't really a craven coward. Then she turned away.

"What'd y'do, call me from a phone booth on Broadway?" Aunie jumped to hear his voice through the closed door and reluctantly turned back. "I told you to come in a half hour!" The door was yanked opened. "Oh. Sorry," James said, startled. "I thought you were my brother."

She didn't reply; she couldn't. She was too busy staring at the sight that greeted her.

Her eyes were at chest level when the door opened and they widened with surprise, then refused to move any higher. He must have hastily donned his clothes when she knocked on the door. He was wearing a shirt and a worn pair of jeans, but neither garment was fastened. The shirt hung open, framing a broad, lightly furred chest and hard stomach The zipper of his jeans was unzipped and once Aunie's eyes had bemusedly tracked the sparse stripe of blond hair down his muscular abdomen to the loose, open waistband that rode low on his hipbones, she couldn't seem to drag them away. She could practically feel the strain she was imposing on her eyeballs trying to get a peek into the shadows beyond that gaping fly.

As in the black-and-white photographs on her bedroom walls, the sensuality was more in what was hidden than in what was revealed. Only this was no photograph. This was three-dimensional, warm, alive, and smelling of damp, healthy male.

It was more exciting altogether.

She licked her lips. God. She'd never seen anything quite so sexy in her entire life as this tantalizing, close-up glimpse of James Ryder's half-clad body.

Which just went to show how barren her own sex life was, she supposed. Gawd, girl, get a grip, she admonished herself and slowly dragged her eyes upwards. "Uh, I've got a lamp that quit work . . ." Her voice trailed away and she felt her jaw literally sag when her eyes finally reached his face. There was a bloody hatchet sticking out of his forehead.

It wasn't real, of course. It took her a moment, however, to remember that today was Halloween and to realize that the hatchet was obviously a prop. But a clever prop . . . Lordy, it was clever. Her lips were just curling up in appreciation, when he wagged one eyebrow at her, making the hatchet shift.

"Don't s'pose you've got any aspirin on ya?" he

asked in a hopeful voice. "I've got a killer of a headache."

Startled laughter exploded out of her. Then she laughed again, harder, and it was all downhill from there, for once started she couldn't seem to stop. Finally, tears running down her cheeks, she slid loosely down the hallway wall and flopped over on her side, still gasping with laughter as she clutched her stomach. Every time she thought she was finally getting a handle on what was turning into a nearly hysterical case of the giggles, she'd catch his eye and he'd raise an eyebrow at her and it would set her off once again. Finally, deeming it necessary to do something other than just lie there curled up on the floor making a fool of herself, she began to crawl away. Out of sight, out of mind . . . or so she sincerely hoped.

James grinned as he watched her drag herself down the hallway on her hands and knees, still laughing that wholehearted, surprisingly deep laugh. Talk about a great reaction . . . who would have thought to get that kind of response out of the prim little Confederate belle? Without removing his watchful gaze, he tucked his shirttails into his pants and zipped up.

Aunie's mirth mercifully began to subside halfway down the hall and she started to push herself to her feet. Unfortunately, she glanced back over her shoulder and caught James grinning at her and the whole ridiculous business started all over again. She collapsed back onto all fours.

He swooped down on her and hooked one brawny arm around her waist, scooping her off the floor. She laughed harder and went totally limp. Letting her dangle like a broken doll from his forearm and hip, he packed her to her front door. "Where's your key?"

"It's o . . . o . . . it's *ooo* . . ."

"Open," he supplied helpfully. "Gotcha." He opened the door, maneuvered her carefully through the doorway, and then packed her into the living room, where he dropped her in a giggling heap on her couch. She immediately rolled off. "Ooh, Gawd, I'm gonna wet my pants." Emitting silly snuffling noises, a result of trying to swallow her laughter, she trotted with knock-kneed awkwardness into the bathroom, slamming the door behind her.

Grinning and shaking his head, he stared at the closed door for a moment and then turned away. He looked around her living room with curious eyes, finding it warm and friendly and surprisingly informal. Somewhere, he'd formed the impression she'd decorate with thousand-dollar vases and furniture designed more for style than function. But although the teal linen couch with its touches of rose appeared obviously costly, it also looked invitingly comfortable. And her accessories, to his further surprise, were more along the line of street-fair-craftsmen funky than designer original. Hell, there was even a mug of his design holding some pencils and pens next to her stack of books on the dining room table. Tilting his head to read the spines, he raised his eyebrows over the titles of some of her texts. He wouldn't have figured her for a heavy math load, either. She struck him as more of the liberal-arts type. He shrugged, thinking that sometimes it just didn't pay to jump to conclusions.

There were three lamps in the living room and dining area, and he checked each one, finding them in perfect working order. Until she emerged from the bathroom there wasn't much more that he could do, so he dropped down on the couch to wait, propping his feet up on the coffee table.

He glanced at the door again. He hadn't expected to like her, and he still wasn't sure that he did. But you had to appreciate someone who laughed like that.

In the bathroom, Aunie lectured herself sternly about the perils of hysteria as she used the facilities, but it was difficult to give it the serious attention it deserved when she was still snickering. She splashed frigid water over her face until she got herself under control, then raised her dripping face to stare at her reflection in the mirror. She supposed she should be embarrassed about acting like such an idiot in front of him, of all people, but the truth was it had felt good. She hadn't laughed like that in . . . she couldn't remember how long. It had been years, though. She ran a brush through her hair, slapped on a dash of lip gloss, and left the bathroom to rejoin James in the living room.

When he tilted his head against the back of the couch to look up at her, she had to bite her lip to keep from sniggering; but the worst of her uncontrollable laughter seemed to have passed, thank God.

"So, tell me," he said coolly, recalling that it was best to keep this woman at arm's length. "Can I assume by your reaction that y' think my Halloween effort is moderately amusing?"

"It's never smart to assume anything," she replied crisply, stung at his sudden change of attitude. *Now* she felt foolish and she experienced a flash of resentment that he'd apparently gone out of his way to dampen the first good laugh she'd had in much, much too long. "I was merely being polite."

He laughed incredulously. "Polite? Honey, *this* is polite." He demonstrated a sickly simper. "Crawling down the hallway laughin' your head off is amused."

"Have it your way, James. I'll concede I was a *little* bit amused." Why was he being so nasty? She had actually felt comfortable with him for about five minutes there.

"Well, well, well. You finally said my name."

"Ah beg your pardon?"

"You said *James*. You've never called me anything but Mistah Rydah before now. . . . We must be makin' strides. Why, before you know it, we'll probably be all the way up to casual acquaintances."

She gave him a slow once-over. "Well, I don't know. I do have my standards, you know." She didn't mean it to come out quite as snooty-sounding as it did, but she excused herself with the knowledge that she was merely responding to his inexplicable attitude. "Would you mind getting your feet off my coffee table?"

He dropped his feet to the floor and stood up. Jesus, but she could make him feel like a clod. "Show me the lamp that needs fixing."

"It's in the bedroom." He followed her down the hall but stopped dead just inside the doorway.

"Great bed," he remarked, and this time his tone wasn't sarcastic. The bed was large and covered by a beautiful burgundy satin-and-ecru lace coverlet, but the head- and footboards were its crowning glory. The headboard was tall, made of solid rattan, and the footboard was only slightly shorter. Both curved gently and had rounded edges of intricate weave and subtle shadings.

"Isn't it gorgeous?" Aunie ran an affectionate hand over the headboard. "It was my divorce present to myself. This is the problem lamp," she said, indicating the small Tiffany creation on her nightstand. "It worked fine last night, but this morning it was dead."

He sat on the side of the bed, picked up the deli-

cately crafted lamp, and inspected it. "Hit the overhead, will you? I can't see." She did as he requested.
"Problem continued when you changed the bulb, I
take it?"

"What?"

He raised his head and stared at her. "Aunie, you
did change the light bulb, didn't you?"

If the floor could have opened at that moment and
swallowed her up, she would have welcomed it. Tears
of mortification filled her eyes. Would she never have
the brains to do the most basic tasks?

James's knowing grin disappeared at the sight of
the tears swimming in her lower lids, making her
brown eyes—large before—appear enormous. Christ,
she didn't know the simplest things, but still . . . "Don't
cry!" he commanded roughly. "Everyone fu . . . er,
messes up occasionally. We all make mistakes; you're
old enough to know that." He hotly resented the
strange rush of protectiveness he experienced.

"Not brainless ones like this," she retorted unhappily. "Anybody with the least bit of intelligence would
have thought to check the bulb first. But not me,
boy; it never even *occurred* to me. I'm totally *useless.*"

"Bull. You sand a mean wall, and nobody who can
hum while she's sanding plaster is totally useless."

Aunie brightened. "Yeah?"

"Yeah. You bet."

She smiled at him. "I take back every rotten thing
I ever thought about you, James Ryder. You're a nice
man."

"Yeah, I'm a prince. I'm only amazed you could've
thought anything rotten about me in the first place."
All right, Ryder, his mind whispered, you've done
your good deed for the day. Time to get the hell out
of here. He looked away and for the first time since

entering the room, noticed the photographs on the walls. His jaw dropped. "Holy shit."

There were eight of them, framed black-and-white photographs of men in various stages of undress. Men with dark hair and men with light hair, two black men and an Oriental, each showcasing a different portion of their anatomy: chests, stomachs, backs, buns, shoulders or legs. James inspected them, then turned to Aunie, raising an eyebrow. "Beefcake?" Somehow, he wouldn't have pegged her as the type to have all that male pulchritude gracing her bedroom walls.

"My fantasy boys." She laughed at the expression on his face. "Okay, I admit it: I'm going through a delayed adolescence. Mama raised me to be a perfect little lady, and posters of movie or rock stars on my bedroom walls were *not* quite the thing. I went from high school to a year of finishing school to marriage to an older man to divorce. Now I'm catchin' up on all the stuff I never got to do as a teenager. I'm wearin' jeans instead of designer dresses, runnin' shoes instead of heels, going to college instead of A-list functions, and collecting pictures of pretty, almost-naked men. When I work up the nerve, I'm even gonna have a red-hot affair . . . providin' I can find someone promisin' to have it with." She bit her lip in sudden self-consciousness, hardly believing she was telling him this stuff. This was the man who didn't even want her living here.

Mentally, she shrugged. Well, if he didn't like what he was hearing he knew where the door was. She had made a vow to herself that she would never again arrange her life to suit someone else's idea of propriety. She glanced at him speculatively from beneath her lashes and decided that with his street-wise looks and given those eyes of his and the way he'd opened the door to her only half-dressed, he probably wasn't the type to be shocked by anything she had to say anyway. "I bet you've had some red-hot affairs, huh?"

Christ. He looked at her standing there looking too fragile to handle a really hot kiss, let alone a session of down and dirty rough sex. She was the type you'd have to be real slow and careful with . . . the type he had always assiduously avoided. "No," James said shortly. "No affairs. I'm not big on commitment." He stressed that, just in case she had any thoughts of practicing on him. To his irritation, he could feel himself growing half hard at the thought. Knee-jerk reaction, he decided and said bluntly, "I've had some great sex in the one-night-stand department, though." There. That oughta turn her off.

She merely raised one dark eyebrow and gave him half a smile. "Lucky you," she said with total sincerity. "I haven't had great sex, period. I've never advanced beyond mediocre." Her eyes closed and she smiled dreamily. "I want *passion*." Her eyes shot open and met his as her face suffused with a sudden influx of blood. "I can't believe I'm telling you this."

"That makes two of us," James muttered.

"It's just that . . . well, you look like you'd know about these sorta things."

"Listen, don't go getting any . . ." James hesitated, not quite sure how to put this without sounding overbearingly conceited. Then he plunged ahead. Better to sound vain than have a future misunderstanding. The fact was they *did* have to live in the same building and the less friction between them the better. "Don't go getting any ideas about including me in your plans, okay? You're not my type, and I don't mess with novices."

"Who asked you to?" Aunie asked with an affronted

dignity that made James feel about two feet tall. So what if she'd thought for maybe three seconds that he'd make a splendid teacher? She knew he was out of her league.

"Perhaps I shouldn't have said what I said," she told him in a stiff little voice, "but I wasn't fishing for an offer to be sexually coached, so you can relax. Nor am I harboring any secret designs on your body, and believe me, I'm not looking to trap any man. In fact, the only thing you and I most likely have in common, Mister Ryder, is a deep-seated desire to avoid commitment."

Something in her expression made James remember the vicious abuse that had been done to her face, and for the first time, he really wondered about it. What kind of a man could apply his fists to that face? But then she gave him a polite, social smile and he let it slip away, sure he didn't want to know anyway.

"Forget what I said about wanting an affair, okay?" she requested in a cool little voice. "It was a stupid thing to blurt out to a man I barely know." She laughed suddenly, a deep, rich sound. "Do you have any idea how difficult it is to have a serious conversation with a person who has an ax sticking out of his head?"

He grinned at her cockily and tipped an eyebrow again, making the hatchet move.

Someone pounded on the door and Aunie jumped. "You expecting someone?" James asked.

"No." Her eyes were huge as she returned his look. "Except for Otis and Lola, I don't really know anyone in this town; I haven't lived here long enough to meet very many people."

James noted her sudden tension. He also noticed when she casually palmed a small, sharp pair of scissors off the nightstand and slipped them into her back pocket. Frowning, he stuck close to her as he followed her out into the living room.

She opened her front door cautiously. There was a large man standing on her threshold, scratching his head as he looked down at her. He looked vaguely menacing, with his unkempt hair in need of a cut, his huge barrel chest and stomach. He was wearing a pair of threadbare jeans that sagged in the seat, an old, stretched-out, no-color T-shirt with a faded Harley Davidson logo on the chest, and a ratty denim vest. There was a tattoo of a rose-entwined dagger on his forearm. He looked vaguely familiar, but she was certain they'd never met. Perhaps it was only that he reminded her of pictures she had seen of members of the Hell's Angels motorcycle gang. She looked up at him uncertainly. "May I help you?"

"Jimmy here?" He had a surprisingly melodious voice. "Otis's old lady said he might be."

"My brother," James informed her without enthusiasm when she glanced at him over her shoulder.

Of course, that was where she'd seen the man before—going into James's apartment. She opened the door fully, smiling up at him. "Come in."

"Thanks." He lumbered through the doorway. "I'm Bob. Hey, Jimmy." He stared at the hatchet in his brother's forehead. "Gawd Almighty, boy, ain't you ever gonna grow up?"

"No," James replied shortly. Hell of a question, he thought sourly, from a guy who—unless he missed his guess—was here either to borrow money or have his younger brother help untangle him from the latest mess he'd gotten himself into. "Aunie, this is my brother Bob. Bobby, Aunie Franklin."

"How nice to meet a member of James's family,"

Aunie said with the graciousness that had been instilled in her from birth. "How do you do?" She offered her hand.

It was swallowed up in his large, meaty grasp. "I've had better days, little lady. But it's nice meetin' a pretty little thing like you."

"We'll get out of your hair, Aunie," James interrupted. "C'mon, Bobby; let's go down to my apartment."

"Thanks for the help with my lamp," Aunie said, and then blushed when she remembered how unnecessary his help would have been if she had used an ounce of common sense and changed the bulb when it burned out.

Bob grinned at the high color in her cheeks, misinterpreting its meaning. Aunie saw him elbow James as they started down the hall. "You stickin' it to the little girl with the big eyes, Jimmy? Not your usual type, is she? I mean, the face is a genetic masterpiece, no doubt about it; but she's got no tits."

"Shut the fu . . . just shut up, Bob," James snapped. "Aunie's an acquaintance . . . hell, barely even that. I'm *not* sleeping with her."

Aunie shut the door and gazed down at her breasts with a rueful smile. She had a bosom. It just wasn't a particularly *memorable* bosom.

James turned to his brother the minute the door closed behind them. "So, what do y'need this time?"

"A beer would be nice."

James uttered some truly creative obscenities beneath his breath before he remembered he was trying not to do that anymore. He went to the refrigerator and pulled out two bottles of Dos Equis, handing one to his brother.

Bob popped off the cap and took a healthy swig.

He wiped his lips with the back of his hand. His voice grew defensive when he met his brother's unrelenting stare. "Jeez, kid, can't a guy come visit his kid brother without being suspected of some ulterior motive?"

James just looked at him and Bob shifted uncomfortably. "Okay, okay. I need a loan—but unlike the others, I think I've got a real shot at paying this one back."

"What is it this time?"

"You should get a real bang outta this. I want to buy a half interest in a couple of limos."

James dropped onto the nearest available chair and regarded his brother with interest. This was different from most of Bob's harebrained schemes to get rich quick. At least this one was in Bob's field of expertise—he was one of the best mechanics in town. "Tell me about it."

The couch creaked in protest when Bob settled his considerable weight on it. "Y' remember T. J. Wexler? He's got a line on a pretty sweet deal for a couple of used limousines. Only twenty-eight thousand miles on one and thirty-one thou on the other. We figgered if we could scrape up the cash between us, we'd buy 'em and start a service. Satin Doll Limousines. He'd be the driver and I'd keep the cars running sweet. I can fill in as driver, too, if need be. If it pans out, we'd invest in a third car and another driver and— who knows?— maybe someday we'd have us a fleet." He peered at his brother. "Limos are a hot commodity right now, Jimmy. Hell, even teenagers are laying down their cash to rent 'em."

"How much would you need?"

"I've got it all written down here." Bob rocked up on one hip and pulled a many-times-folded sheet of paper from his back pocket. He unfolded it carefully and passed it to James. "This would cover my half of the cash outlay for the cars, plus insurance, business license, advertising, a separate phone line at the Wexlers' to handle the calls and maintenance for six months. This here's the total." He pointed to the figure near the bottom of the page.

Bob had had ideas before that had never quite panned out, but James, in spite of himself, was impressed this time. His brother hadn't merely figured the cost of the cars and let it go at that. He'd obviously put some thought into what was needed both to get the business off the ground and to keep it going. Bobby had a sweet touch with anything mechanical, and this proposition looked almost . . . viable.

"I'll sign a loan contract if y' want me to. I figgered your interest would have to be lower than a shark's."

"Stay away from the frigging loan sharks, Bobby. Haven't you learned that lesson yet?" James scowled at his brother. It was a recurring problem: Bob borrowing from the street hoods who made loans at exorbitant interest rates and then took it out of the borrower's hide if they couldn't repay. "I'll give you the money. Keep your interest." He got up and hunted through the messy desk drawer for his savings passbook and checkbook. He pulled them out and turned to look at his brother over his shoulder. "This sounds well suited to you, Bobby. I hope you can make it work."

"I'm gonna," Bob replied adamantly. "Christ, Jimmy, I'm thirty-nine years old. I figgered it was about time I made *something* work. I'm gonna be smart for once in my life and put my money into something I actually understand. I'm even keeping my job at the car workshop until we see if this puppy's gonna fly. T.J.'s keeping his day job, too. We figgered the prime rental time is early evening to early morning, but his old lady's gonna man the phone durin' the day. If we do get a daytime gig, T.J.'ll take the time offa work."

James wrote a check and carried it over to his brother. He held it out. "Hang onto this until tomorrow, okay? I've got to transfer the funds to cover it."

Bob accepted the check and folded it in half, slipping it into his back pocket. "Thanks, Jimbo." He reached out and touched a gentle fingertip to the handle of the hatchet protruding out of his younger brother's forehead. "You always were a weird little son of a bitch," he said. "I ain't never understood you, Jimmy, and that's the truth. But I love y' anyway." He smiled wryly, and for a second the family resemblance was apparent. "Folks never believe me when I tell them it's my kid brother who draws 'A Skewed View.' "

"No? Fat lot they know, huh?" James was touched that his brother had bragged about him, and for the first time in a long while he remembered the way Bob used to defend him back when he was a skinny little kid running the gauntlet of street hoods and pushers in the Terrace. "Hang on a sec," he said. "Sit down and finish your beer." James went over to his drafting board and sat down. Fingers moving swiftly, he sketched out a tiny self-portrait, complete with hatchet. Reaching for his colors, he filled it in. At the top, in his bold, distinctive printing, he wrote: To Big Brother Bob. He signed it: Love, Jimmy (AKA J. T. Ryder). "Stick that in your wallet. You can whip it out the next time someone doubts the word of a Ryder." He grinned with self-deprecatory humor. "That and a buck will buy you a beer."

"Hell, boy," Bob retorted with a grin, "offhand I can think of a couple a bars where this and a buck will probably earn me a healthy return on my investment." He slid the caricature carefully into his wallet and stood. "I guess I'd better be shovin' off. Now that I've got my half of the financing, we can put an ad in a couple of the high school newspapers. With the holidays coming up, it's a good time to launch this venture." He ran a meaty hand through his unkempt hair. "Thought I'd get me a haircut, too. Can't look too ratty if I'm pressed into service as a driver."

James walked him to the door. "Y'need any help on the artwork for the advertising?"

"Hell, yeah." Bob grinned down at him. "You willin' to do that? That'd be great."

"Tell me what you need. I'm best at 'toons; but if you're looking for elegant, I could probably limp something out."

"Let me discuss it with T.J.," Bob replied. "I'll get back to you tomorrow." His face sobered as he stared down at his younger brother. "Thanks, Jimmy. You're gonna get your money back this time. I mean it."

"Just do me a favor," James said. "If you run into any kind of financial difficulties, come to me. Don't take your troubles to the sharks."

"Gotcha."

"Give me your word, Bobby."

"I give you my word."

"All right, then." He watched his oldest brother lumber down the hall and then slowly closed the door. He thought of this newest venture of Bob's; then his thoughts wandered down the hallway to 2B.

He and little Ms. Franklin would probably never be friends and no doubt that was for the best. At least the hostility had apparently been shelved. The corner of his mouth tipped up when he thought of all those photographs on her bedroom wall. What had Bobby called her? The little girl with the big eyes? It was true in more ways than one, evidently. What a surprise.

He sat down at his drafting table and picked up a pencil, fingers moving swiftly as a cartoon took shape. This had turned out to be one hell of an interesting day.

CHAPTER 4

How could everything be going along so swimmingly one moment and fall to pieces the next? It wasn't supposed to work that way . . . not here in her new life. Yet it only took one telephone call to bring everything crashing down around Aunie's ears.

She was laughing at something Lola said when she picked up the receiver. Fifteen seconds later, the smile was wiped from her face.

"No," she whispered. Then louder, "No!" Clutching the receiver in both hands, she slid down the wall. She could hear a spate of words on the other end of the line, frantic-sounding in their rush to reassure, but they seemed to be in no particular coherent order. She blindly fumbled the receiver into its cradle. She could see the concern on Lola's face, watched as her friend's lips moved, but the words Lola spoke didn't quite penetrate the fog that shrouded her brain.

"Go home, Lola," she whispered. "I'm fine. Really. Go home."

But she wasn't fine. Maybe she never would be again. Her lawyer had just delivered news that wrapped a chill around her heart.

"Aunie, please, let me in," Lola called through the closed door. She bounced the apartment key in her palm and then knocked harder. "Aunie!"

The door down the hallway opened and James stuck his head out. "Lola?" he said irritably. "What the hell's going on?"

Lola gave the key in her hand another uncertain glance; then she turned away from Aunie's door and hurried down the hallway. "Oh, James, I don't know what to do. I'm worried 'bout Aunie." Lola saw that she had his immediate attention. The expression of impatience that he habitually wore when anyone interrupted his time at the drawing board had disappeared. "Why?" he demanded, pushing away from the doorway.

"I was visitin' wid her this mornin' before she had to get ready for school. She received a phone call while I was there that upset her somethin' fierce, and she asked me to go. So I did, mon, but I kept a eye out for her . . . to be sure she was all right, you know. She was that upset."

"Yeah? And?"

"And she hasn't left the apartment, mon. That girl's serious 'bout her grades; I don't know if you know this, but she wants to qualify for the U next year." James hadn't known, but he nodded anyway. "Well, before the phone rang, she'd just finished tellin' me she had an important test this afternoon, but she hasn't budged from that apartment and she won't open the door or answer me. This is the third time I've been up here." She showed him the key. "It's my duplicate. I've been debatin' . . ."

"Use it."

Aunie's apartment was dark when they let themselves in, illuminated only meagerly by a waning finger of light that filtered through a slat that hung awry in one of the dining room windows' miniblinds. Feeling their way cautiously until their eyes had a chance to adjust, they entered the living room, halting in the entrance. They were greeted by a blast of hot air. "Aunie?" Lola called softly. There was no response and James said brusquely, "Aunie, answer us, dammit."

Aunie raised her forehead from where it rested on her kneecaps and peered through dull eyes at the two dim figures standing just inside the living room. "Go away," she said hoarsely and hugged herself tighter. God. The last thing she wanted at this moment was company. When they didn't move, she said plaintively, "Please? Just go away." It didn't occur to her to ask how they'd gained entrance to her apartment. Wearily, she lowered her head once again.

"We can't do that," James said flatly and made his way to the nearest lamp. He turned it on, casting a pool of light.

Aunie was sitting on the floor in front of the heat register. Her knees were drawn up to her chest, arms hugging her legs, and her forehead was pressed to her kneecaps. She was swaddled in a rose-colored woolen afghan.

Concern written clearly on her face, Lola started to bend down. James neatly hipped her out of his way and squatted in front of Aunie. Ignoring the

eyebrow Lola cocked at his cavalier treatment, he
asked her gently, "What's going on?"

She didn't answer or raise her head up off her
knees. James reached out and stroked her hair. It
flowed through his fingers like satin streamers.
"Aunie? Lola said you got a phone call that upset
you."

A sharp bark of bitter laughter into her woolly
cocoon was his only reply.

Christ, wasn't she roasting in there? It must be
eighty-five degrees in the living room. James shook
his head sharply and told himself to concentrate on
what was relevant. "Tell me about it. Tell me about
the phone call."

Her head jerked up suddenly and James was unprepared for the unbridled hostility that met his gaze as
she glared at him head-on. "Oh, you want to hear
about my *problems*, Mistah Rydah? Is this the same
man who said he'd stand back and wave my husband
by when he showed up lookin' for blood?"

James's expression froze. How the hell had they
gotten back to this Mister Ryder shit? A fierce wave
of reciprocal anger swept through him, and for a
moment, he was tempted to turn her over to Lola,
get up, and get the hell out of there. Yes, dammit,
he *was* the same guy and he appreciated the reminder
because, for a second there, he had almost forgotten.
He didn't need any additional problems. He had
enough to do just trying to stay one step ahead of
his brothers' assorted troubles. She didn't want him
here? Fine. He'd just get the hell out of her way. He
didn't want to know why she was huddled in the dark
in this vastly overheated room, anyway.

His anger drained away as rapidly as it had surfaced.
Ah, hell, who was he kidding? Yes, he did.

"Tell me about the phone call, Aunie," he repeated in a carefully neutral voice and Aunie's face crumpled. Tears rose in her eyes.

"He was *acquitted*," she wailed and then her words all ran together, barely coherent. "Oh, God, James, I'm so scared. I thought he'd be put away for a long time—Jordan said he would—but he's free, and if he finds me I know he's gonna kill me this time. He's so crazy and obsessed . . ."

Elbows digging into her drawn-up knees, she buried her face in her hands and sobbed. James and Lola exchanged concerned, puzzled glances. "See what you can do," Lola whispered. "I'll make her some tea." She left the room and James looked back at Aunie.

Her afghan had slipped from her shoulders to pool around her hips in a delicately tinted puddle of wool, revealing the brown satin chemise she wore tucked into her jeans. For an instant, James was mesmerized by the gentle upper curves of her breasts, so white against the dark satin. Ever since his brother had made that crack out in the hall a couple of weeks ago, he had caught himself at odd moments wondering about the size of her breasts. Whenever he saw her she was invariably wearing a baggy sweatshirt or a thick sweater that hid her shape and made it impossible to tell what was underneath. But he could see now that her chest wasn't as flat as Bob had decreed it to be. Oh, her breasts were petite, just like the rest of her, but there were definite curves there, sweet as honey.

James shook his head impatiently, irritated with himself. What the hell was he doing? She was sitting there sobbing her eyes out after telling him that someone was going to kill her, and instead of finding out what the story was, he was satisfying a curiosity he had no business entertaining in the first place. *You're a deep guy, J.T.*

How the hell did he go about consoling a woman? He was accustomed to dealing with male problems, but he didn't think an uncomfortably offered thump of encouragement on the back and a little straight talk was going to do the trick in this instance. Think, Ryder, he urged himself. Women liked to be held, didn't they?

He reached out and encircled one fragile wrist with his fingers, prying her hand away from her face. "C'mere," he whispered and tugged at her hand. She struggled to extricate herself from his grip, but he held on. "Shh, shh, easy now," he crooned, applying leverage. "I know we don't have much in common, but just for today you and I are gonna try to be friends. Y'need a friend right now, right? I'm just gonna hold you for a minute. C'mere."

She dove into his arms.

He knelt on the floor, legs spread wide, and held her tight as she continued to sob. He could feel her heart thumping frantically, and she was damp and overheated. But her arms clung to his neck in a death grip, one hand clutching his ponytail, and her face burrowed into his chest. James stroked her silky hair from crown to nape with one hand, his other on her back pressing her to him with wide splayed fingers. He murmured words of comfort, ignoring the spreading patch of wetness on his shirt front. A distant corner of his mind registered the fact that her skin felt just as soft as it looked. He resisted the urge to shift with discomfort. Christ, it was hot in here.

He didn't attempt to discourage her crying jag, but he was mightily relieved when it eventually wound down on its own. By the time Lola reentered the room with a tray of cups and a steaming pot of tea, Aunie was lying limply against his chest, tiny shudders occasionally rippling through her. Her nose was so stuffed she had to breathe through her mouth; and wiping at her eyes with the back of her wrist, she sniffed inelegantly.

"Here," Lola said in a soft but firm voice as she pressed a wad of Kleenex into her hand. "Sit up, blow your nose, and pull yourself together, woo-mon. James and I don't understand exactly what you been talkin' 'bout. You're gonna have to explain it to us."

Aunie's arms slipped away from James's shoulders and she sank back onto her heels. She wiped her eyes, blew her nose, and fumbled blindly along the floor for her blanket, wrapping herself up in it once again. James winced as he watched her rebundle herself in wool. How the hell could she stand this heat? He was dying. But when he opened his mouth to raise the issue, Lola, as if she read his mind, squeezed his shoulder warningly. "Shock," she murmured. "I turned down the thermostat, but don't argue with her about staying all wrapped up. Let's just try to get some sugared tea down her . . . it should help."

The afghan kept slipping off Aunie's right shoulder as she sipped her tea; and watching her, waiting for an explanation, James felt something inside himself winding tighter and tighter. He raised his arm and wiped the sweat from his forehead with his sleeve. The elevated temperature in here certainly wasn't an aid in trying to get a handle on his growing tension.

Finally, the silence got to him. "Who were you talking about when you said he was acquitted?" He knew his tone of voice was too aggressive, but he couldn't seem to help himself.

She started violently, turning big, haunted eyes on him. Her eyelids were swollen and red. "Wesley," she whispered. "My ex-husband."

He had pretty much figured that out already, so why did having it confirmed disturb him so much? "So he's the person responsible for the state of your face the day you came to rent the apartment?"

She nodded. The teacup rattled against her teeth and she set it aside. Drawing deep, shaky breaths, and with her small white teeth planted firmly in her lower lip, she tugged the afghan closer, hugging herself to contain the trembling. The attempt she made to pull herself together was painfully visible.

"How long did he abuse you before you got out of your marriage Aunie?" Lola asked gently. At the same time, she none too subtly elbowed James in the ribs. The look she shot him said, Take it easy!

To their astonishment, Aunie laughed. It was edged with bitter cynicism, but the fact that she was able to find a vestige of even the blackest humor in this situation was astounding. Then her laughter died as abruptly as it had begun. "He never touched me when we were married," she stated flatly. In more ways than one, she could have added, but didn't bother to voice that particular irony aloud.

Her composure was hanging by a thread, and the identical looks of patent disbelief that Lola and James wore as they stared at her were enough to sever its fragile hold. "You think I'd *protect* Wesley?" she snarled. The afghan fell unnoticed to the floor as she surged up on her knees to confront them, her hands ruthlessly plowing through her hair to hold it off her face. "What do y'all take me for, a fool? Tell me why the hell Ah would botha to lie about somethin' like that!" Her eyes, feverish with anguished fury, were the only spots of color in an otherwise starkly white face.

James didn't know what the hell to think. As she said, why would she lie? On the other hand, she was looking a little less than rational at the moment. Lola said gently, "Battered women sometimes deny the length of the period that they've suffered abuse because they're ashamed to admit that they stayed locked in the pattern for so long."

Aunie's mouth tightened. "Oh, do they? Well, that's unfortunate, isn't it? Y'all'll just have to excuse me, howevah, if Ah find it a little bit difficult to understand a woman who stays around to become a punchin' bag." She stood up. "Look, why don't y'all go home," she said wearily. "You seem to have it all figured out; I'd hate to clutter up your tidy theories with the messy facts."

"Why don't you go put on a sweater and then we'll sit down and talk about the facts," James snapped.

She turned jerkily to face him. "What?"

"You seem to be so damn cold but you can't keep your friggin' blanket on, so go put on a warm sweater. Then come on back out here, sit us down, and set us straight. Lola will pour you some more tea."

Aunie was tempted to suggest he take his autocratic orders and his tea and shove 'em where the sun didn't shine. But she did desperately need to talk, and in all fairness she knew she must look like some sort of crazed woman to them. How could she expect them to understand automatically what she, who had been living with it for a long time, didn't understand herself? Aside from Otis, Lola was the only friend she had made in Seattle. James didn't quite qualify as a friend; yet he was here, involving himself in her problem after he had specifically stated he would not.

In truth, she didn't know what she would do if she alienated them.

Without a word, she walked out of the room.

Lola turned to James the moment she was out of earshot. "Don't you think you're pushin' it a little?" she demanded. "She's on the edge."

James was more than a little edgy himself and was more than happy to take it out on Lola. "Sympathy makes her cry," he snarled, "but if you think you can do better, just say the word. I'd be happy to disappear."

"Go then."

That stopped him in his tracks. "What?"

"You heard me." She faced him with her hands fisted on her rounded hips. "You're so full of crap, mon. It'd take a stick of dynamite to get you out of here, so don't go deliverin' no idle threats to me! And you take it easy on her, James. If you're all bent out of shape because you're gettin' caught up in her problems against your better judgment, then maybe you'd *better* disappear. The woo-mon does *not* need you snappin' and snarlin' at her heels."

"Yeah and I suppose you're gonna tell me the gentle approach has really turned the trick, huh? I saw just how far your pop psychoanalysis got you: She was ready to chuck us both out on our butts. I may be a little rough, but you'll notice it gets an aggressive response from her instead of a flood of tears."

Aunie returned wearing a thick, warm sweater, and Lola thought the timing was fortunate. Two seconds later and she would have gone for the jugular. She would have brought up the fact that it wasn't just the knowledge that he was being dragged into Aunie's problems against his better judgment that had James all hot, bothered, and restless as a caged cat. His main problem was he couldn't handle the sight of a little skin. And that observation would most likely have had the effect of making him blow in fourteen different directions. He was so damn busy denying to himself that he was the least bit attracted to her, because James Ryder was already overburdened with responsibility and James Ryder did not have the time or patience to get involved in more than a surface, sexual way with women.

"Let's sit at the dining room table," Aunie suggested quietly. She had used the time in her room to do a hasty paste-together of her shattered composure. She would freely admit the veneer was a thin one. But for the moment at least it was all in place. "James, do you want a beer? There's some Dos Equis in the fridge that I bought for Otis and he mentioned once that it was your favorite, too." What a good little hostess you are, a snide voice whispered in her ear.

"Sounds good," he said and waved her toward a seat. "Sit down. I'll get it."

Aunie waited until he had rejoined them, pulling out and twirling around a chair to straddle, before she said, "Wesley *never* hit me when we were married." She drilled them both with the intensity of her stare. "I want you to get that straight. A man might get away with striking me once . . . everyone is probably capable of losing control at some point in their lives. But he would never get away with striking me twice."

"How do you think you could prevent it, Aunie?" James asked quietly. "You're a tiny little thing; it'd be a cakewalk to overpower you. And if he had gotten away with it once, it stands to reason he'd believe he could get away with it indefinitely."

"Sooner or later he'd have to go to sleep, though,

wouldn't he, James." It was not a question. "An iron fireplace poker could be a great equalizer."

James snorted. An image of her palming a sharp pair of scissors the day Bob had knocked on her door flashed across his mind. "Okay, I get your point. And we're sorry for thinking otherwise, all right?" Lola reached across the table and squeezed her hand to underscore the apology. Aunie nodded.

"Will you tell us just what the hell did happen?" James asked, and this time his tone was temperate. "And slowly, this go-around, so we can understand."

"Wesley was furious when I told him I wanted a divorce, and he made all sorts of threats." Aunie's voice was low and she spoke to her clasped hands on the tabletop. Her hair slid against her cheeks as she shook her head in puzzlement. "But then, just like that"—she snapped her fingers—"he turned around and agreed. He insisted on giving me the house, the car that I ordinarily drove, and a large settlement." She looked up. "I was stupid enough to be grateful that it was all so amicable, so . . . civilized."

James tensed, because he knew the civilization had been stripped away somewhere along the line. He had felt her heart pound with fear against his abdomen, had felt it beating so hard the throb had registered against his palm on her back.

Aunie's entwined hands tightened their grip. "He began . . ."—she searched for an articulate way to phrase it, then shrugged in defeat—"showing up. The first time, we'd been divorced about four months. I'd begun attending classes. I really desired to learn something this time, the way I hadn't bothered to in high school. I wanted to give myself a foundation, a preparation for accepting total responsibility for myself for the first time in my life." She stopped speaking, pressing her lips tightly together. After a moment they relaxed and she unclenched her hands and took a sip of her tea. Lowering the cup, she said to the pale liquid in the bottom of it, "Anyway, one day when I got home from school, he was there waiting for me. The maid had let him in."

She pushed back from the table suddenly. "I think I'll have some wine. Lola, would you like some?"

Lola consulted her watch, saw that it was almost seven o'clock, and accepted. Then a thought struck her. "Aunie, have you had anything to eat today?"

Aunie pulled a bottle of wine from the tiny rack atop her refrigerator. "I had breakfast." Rummaging through a drawer, she located a corkscrew.

"How 'bout I make you an omelet?"

"Oh, I don't . . ."

"I want one, too," James said. "It's past my dinnertime."

"I'll make you one, too," Lola agreed. To Aunie she confided, "James, he's a cranky mon when he's hungry."

Aunie struggled to extricate the cork for several moments, then abruptly set the wine bottle down. She held out her hands and stared at the fine tremors that set them to trembling. "I guess I do need to eat something," she muttered to herself. She brought the bottle and corkscrew to James, silently handing them over. A few deft twists of his strong wrists and the cork popped out. He offered her the bottle. "You look like you've got the d.t.'s, Magnolia. Y' want a swig straight from the bottle or you gonna be a lady and let me fetch you a glass?"

"Fetch me a glass." Then, holding his eyes defiantly, she tipped up the bottle and took a healthy swig. He grinned at her and surged to his feet in one fluid motion. The wine hit her empty stomach like a warm explosion. She plucked a napkin out of the holder and primly blotted her lips. Then she guiltily wiped the neck of the bottle.

"Here." James straddled the chair once again and reached for the wine. He poured two glasses and pushed one across the table to her. There was amusement in his narrowed moss green eyes. "Mind your manners."

For the first time since she had received her lawyer's phone call, Aunie smiled. Crooking her little finger daintily, she raised her goblet and took a sip. Then she took a gulp. She could feel its effects rushing to her head. "Funny advice," she murmured, "from a man whose personal motto is probably Anarchy Now."

"Cute," James said, but he couldn't suppress a crooked smile. In the kitchen Lola laughed.

Aunie took another sip. "I think perhaps I'm gettin' the tiniest bit loaded," she confessed. "But, look"— she held out her hands—"they're growin' steadier. That's an improvement, don't you think?"

James thought the touch of color along her cheek-bones was the real improvement, that and the fact that her eyes had lost most of the haunted look that had dulled them.

"Wesley became this obsessed person," she suddenly said. "But it was such a gradual process that it took me awhile to catch on. He'd show up out of the blue or call and expect me to go to some function with him. It infuriated him to see me in jeans or without makeup. He acted as if we were still married and I was supposed to drop whatever I was doing to accommodate his plans. It was bizarre and it was annoying but not really frightening . . . at least, not at first.''

Lola brought plates from the kitchen and slid them across the table to their respective places. She handed forks and knives to Aunie. Aunie arranged the place settings and reached for the napkins. "You want orange juice?" Lola asked her.

Aunie contemplated the level of liquid in her glass and reached for the bottle, topping off her glass. "No, thanks. I'll stick with wine."

"James?"

"Yeah, I'll have some juice."

"Then one night I finally realized that he wasn't quite . . ." She hesitated over the word.

"Sane?" James suggested.

"Yeah. Not normal, at any rate. I guess I should've remembered his reason for not wantin' me to get pregnant, but once we were divorced I'd put it out of my mind. It wasn't until this one particular night that I ultimately realized that Wesley had lost all semblance of rationality. I had a late class and I had stopped off for a pizza with a few of the other students. When I got home, Wesley was there and he had another couple with him.''

Lola slid a golden brown omelet onto her plate and said, "Eat." She served herself and James and passed around a plate stacked high with buttered toast. Aunie took a bite of her egg; then she took another. Three bites later, she looked up and said, "This is fabulous. Thank you, Lola."

"You're welcome. Have some toast."

James ate his dinner, but he didn't want to talk about the food.

He wanted to know how Aunie had finally come to the conclusion that her ex-husband wasn't quite sane. And what, he wondered, was the reason she should've remembered for her husband not wanting her to get pregnant? "Wesley had pulled two other people into his delusions? . . ." he prompted.

"Yes," Aunie said around a bite of toast, "and all three of them were in my house!" She pressed her fingers against her throat and swallowed the inadequately chewed bread. "I had dismissed the maid a couple of weeks previously, and I was makin' do with a cleaning service that stopped by twice a week. The maid had been hired originally by Wesley and I couldn't seem to get it through her head that she should *not* let him in whenever he dropped by. He could be extremely charmin' when he put his mind to it . . ." Her voice trailed away.

Then she set her fork down and looked across the table at James. "That night I discovered that all along he had kept a set of keys to the house," she said with remembered indignation. "*My* house. 'Delusions' is right. He'd made himself right at home; and the minute I walked through the door, he started jumpin' all over me, sayin' there was no excuse for my tardiness because I knew the reservations were for eight and now I was goin' to make them all late and what the *hell* would the Addisons think? I didn't know what on earth he was talkin' about and said so. This poor couple sat there on the couch lookin' like they wished they were anywhere but where they were while Wesley's rantin' on and I'm gettin' angrier by the minute. I must have demanded ten times that he give me back the keys to my house, but I might have been speakin' Swahili for all the attention he paid me. He just went on and on about how I was makin' them late and then tossin' in suggestions as to what I should wear. Gawd," she whispered, rubbing her temples.

"It was such a mess. Those people, the Addisons, they got him out of my house that night and I had the locks changed first thing the next morning, but from that point on it just kept getting worse. There was simply no gettin' away from him. Wherever I went, he was there. On my lawyer's advice, I got a restrainin' order. Fat lot of good it did me in the end."

She picked up her wine and took a large sip. "It was spooky the way he would appear out of nowhere and scarier yet how he'd only hear what he wanted to hear. It's impossible to talk to a person like that. I'd tell him to leave me *alone* or I'd call the police, and he'd say, 'Go put on the amber Bill Blass; we have reservations in half an hour.'"

"Did he, er, try to resume your sexual relationship?" James had a picture in his head of this Wesley person calmly undressing her while she struggled to keep her clothes on, ignoring her protests the same way she said he ignored conversation he didn't care to hear. Rape was an ugly business, and he didn't like the image one bit.

"What?" She stared at him incredulously, then quickly raised her glass to her lips to mask her reaction. Their sex life had been such a miserable joke that the unexpected question struck Aunie as totally incongruous and she giggled involuntarily. Unfortunately, she was in the process of finishing off her wine, and the combined actions caused bubbles to foam around her mouth. "Oh," she said, pressing her fingers to her lips, "maybe I'd better have that orange juice, now. I think I've had more than enough wine."

Lola nodded and rose to pour her a glass. Aunie turned to James. "Our sexual relationship was practically nonexistent even when we were married," she admitted and then blurted, "much to my disappointment. That's one of the reasons I want to have a really hot love affair. But I don't know," she said pensively. "I've only been kissed with real passion a few times . . . and never by Wesley. I might not have what it takes to pull off an affair." She didn't bother to tell them she was too shy to instigate such a thing in any case. It was merely a fantasy she liked to dream about, not something she expected to become a reality. At least not for a very long time.

"Have James give you some pointers," Lola suggested as she handed Aunie a glass brimming with cold juice. "He's reputed to be a really good kisser."

"Yeah?" Aunie studied him with interest over her glass of orange juice and James scowled at both of them.

"Forget it," he snapped. "I've already told you I don't tutor novices. Get your practice somewhere else; I'm not in the market."

"Gawd, James," Aunie murmured, "you are so conceited." Perhaps he *was* the most masculine man she had ever met and, yes, she'd admit she would probably find it exciting to have him kiss her. It didn't necessarily follow, however, that she was going to inflate his ego by admitting it to him. Besides, this was the second time he'd put her down by refusing to do something she hadn't even requested of him in the first place! And both times, in the process, he'd managed to make her feel like an elementary-school girl begging to be included in a grown-up game.

James jerked upright. "Whataya mean, conceited?"

"Who asked you?" she demanded. "Besides, you say you're not in the market as though one kiss from you would have me trailin' you around like a devoted puppy."

James smiled with lazy confidence, scoring attractive lines from the corners of his eyes to his cheeks and deepening the three tiny creases next to his mouth. "Like Lola said, sugar, I'm good."

Aunie snorted. James did *not* like that reaction. "Anyway," he added insolently, "you're too fragile to stand up to a really hot Ryder special."

"Too fragile!" Aunie thumped her half-empty juice glass on the table. " 'You're a tiny little thing, Aunie'," she mimicked in a voice she'd deepened in an attempt to sound like his, " 'You're too fragile, Aunie. I'm such a hot kisser they name them after me.' What did you call it—the Blue Plate Special? 'If I kissed you, Aunie, you'd probably shatter in a billion pieces.' God, Ryder, you are *so* full of . . ."

Lola thought it was time to intervene, even if she had instigated this particular line of conversation. No, come to think of it, that had been James's doing. She had merely mentioned his rumored abilities as a kisser. "What made Wesley do what he did to you, Aunie?" she asked.

Aunie had her head tipped back and her eyelids lowered to a sexy half-mast. She slowly licked her upper lip, then made a truly credible Marilyn Monroe moue at James, just to show him what he was missing before she turned her attention to Lola. He glowered at her mouth.

She realized suddenly that she wasn't nearly as frightened as she'd been earlier, and her jumpiness, whether due to the wine she'd consumed or James's and Lola's company, even if James *did* aggravate the hell out of her, had disappeared entirely. She felt nearly cheerful, which was probably not the wisest emotion for the occasion. "I guess what finally drove him over the edge," she admitted, "was the information he received from the private detective he'd hired to follow me. He didn't like it."

"He had you followed?" James put aside the irritation that the unexpected introduction of her sexuality into the discussion had called forth. The muscles in his stomach knotted uneasily. "That's pretty cold, given you were no longer married to the man. What did he discover that was so disturbing it made him go off the deep end?" He wanted to know. He didn't want to know.

Christ.

"I'd begun dating a young man named Geoff Lemire. Now *there* was a hot kisser," she informed James, but her heart really wasn't in needling him anymore. Too many memories were crowding in on her, and her spurious feeling of cheerfulness was fading fast. "Actually, it was pretty tame stuff and to anyone in a rational frame of mind, I'm sure it would've been considered inconsequential. Geoff had taken me out three or four times; we'd shared a few kisses that showed promise of better things to come; but basically, that was it." She shrugged. "Kid stuff. But the detective had a photo of Geoff kissing me, and when Wesley saw it I guess it just tipped the scales." She started to tremble.

"You don't have to tell us any more, Aunie," Lola said softly. "There's no need for you to relive it."

But Aunie didn't hear. She was locked into a nightmare memory from which it was too late to retreat. Words, rendered obscene by the violence they portrayed and the confused terror they recreated, spilled from her lips.

James and Lola, listening, felt sick.

CHAPTER 5

It was the sort of day to make a person feel nothing could possibly go wrong, a day for picnics or washing the car. A beautiful late September afternoon of hot Georgia sun, it was one of those days of blindingly blue Southern skies and light winds, the debilitating summertime humidity a thing of the past. Aunie juggled purse, book bag, and two grocery bags in her arms, closing the car door with her hip. She had to hurry; she only had about forty-five minutes before Geoff was due to pick her up for their trip to the zoo, and she still had a hundred things to do.

Halting on the walk and raising a thigh to arrest the downward slide of one of the grocery bags, she looked up at the grand facade of her house. She really should put it on the market, she thought as she secured her grip on the runaway bag. It was entirely too much house for one woman and it held far too few warm memories. She would much prefer to live somewhere cozier.

She let herself in, dropped her book bag to the floor of the foyer, kicked it out of harm's way with the side of her foot, and sidled up to a small entryway table. It was a trick, but she managed to maneuver her purse off her shoulder, down her arm, and onto the table without dropping her groceries in the process. Leaving the front door open to help circulate the breeze, she stepped out of her shoes and padded on bare feet to the kitchen.

She dropped her burden onto the kitchen table, opened the back door, and slanted the blinds to cut the glare coming off the pool. Humming to herself, she unloaded the bags, contentedly arranging the deli items, condiments, bread, wine, and service for two in the small cooler she had hunted up that morning. She placed it on the table next to a comforter she'd pulled off a guest-room bed. Nothing in this house had ever been allowed to grow old or worn, so she'd simply picked a spread she had never particularly liked. The house was full of items like that, another good reason to get rid of the bulk of it. She'd really love to furnish a home to reflect her own taste and personality instead of living in a house filled with accessories that had been picked to fit some designer's scheme. She wanted a place that could truly be called her own.

But she certainly didn't have time to do anything about it at the moment, she decided, glancing at her watch. Tomorrow would have to be soon enough to begin sorting out what she didn't care to keep. And she could call a realtor, too. She took the stairs two at a time to the second floor.

Entering her bedroom, she peeled out of her

clothes and took a quick shower. She blew her hair dry, reapplied her makeup, and rattled through padded satin hangers in search of something appropriate to wear. Her wardrobe, at least, was something she had already begun to rectify. When she and Wesley had first divorced, she'd packed most of her designer originals and moved them to a closet in another room. The clothes were all very beautiful, but she was only twenty-six years old, for heaven's sake, not forty-five. She was tired of wearing only the sophisticated apparel that Wesley had deemed appropriate.

She slipped on a sapphire jersey top with a neckline that dipped low in a drapy cowl in back, tugged up a pair of floral cotton sheeting pants, adjusted the belt on the "paper bag" waistband, and picked up a sweater in case it grew cooler once the sun set. Sliding her feet into a sleek pair of sandals, she paused briefly in front of the mirror to give herself a quick once-over and then left the room. She hummed beneath her breath as she loped down the stairs.

Entering the kitchen, she stopped dead in the doorway, her voice trailing away in midhum. Wesley lounged indolently on a kitchen chair, his fingertips nonchalantly trailing back and forth along the cooler's handle as he smiled at her with deceptive tenderness.

Apprehension dried her mouth. Ever since that night when he'd used his keys to let himself and the Addisons in, she had managed to keep him out of her house. Unfortunately, she had not been equally successful in preventing the growing number of ensuing confrontations, each one of which had been more disturbing than the one preceding it. At least they had all taken place in public. It might be embarrassing to have strangers witness those humiliating encounters, but she knew it was safer.

Then apprehension faded and outrage took its place. How dare he keep intruding on her privacy this way! They were *divorced*. She shoved away from the door frame, stepped into the kitchen and demanded, "What are you doing in my house?"

She regretted the aggressiveness of her tone before the last word had left her mouth. Wesley continued to smile at her, but there was an ugly expression in his eyes. Cautiously, she tried to edge around him to the phone.

He angled his legs to block her way. "You've been cheating on me, Aunie," he said, and the very gentleness of his voice made the short hairs on the nape of her neck stand on end. His smile and his voice were so civilized, but his eyes were not civilized at all. They looked as psychotic as those in a picture she'd seen of Charles Manson. She took a cautious step backwards. Attempting to reach the phone in the kitchen had been a mistake. What she should have done, what she was going to do now, was try to reach her bedroom, with its nice sturdy lock. Then she would worry about calling the police.

"I don't know what you're talkin' about, Wesley," she said softly and took another step backwards.

"I have photographs, Aunie," he said in that same silky, terrifyingly normal voice. His smile never wavered. "Photographs of my wife kissing another man."

She didn't bother to tell him she was no longer his wife. His eyes stated clearly that he was beyond listening to reason. Instead, she tried to stall for time. "I don't understand. Whoevah would take such a photograph?"

"Why, the detective I've had following you, of course."

She should have kept edging backward, but renewed outrage stilled her limbs. Her hands hit her hips and her chin angled stubbornly skyward. "You hired a detective?"

"Of course," he replied tenderly. "How else could I keep tabs on my wife's movements?"

"And is this detective followin' me still?"

"No. I paid him off once he showed me those disgusting pictures. I knew then what needed to be done."

She took another step out of his reach, but to her horror, he suddenly stood and took a step toward her. "I haven't slept with any man but you, Wesley," she informed him in a conciliatory whisper. She hated herself not only for her tone but for her haste in assuring him, but she was not a fool. This was not the time to cling to her pride. Better the humiliation of placating him than to cling obdurately to her rights and possibly—no, *probably*—get hurt.

She was not deceived for one moment by that well-bred smile or cultured voice. He looked as if he would very much *like* to hurt her.

All of a sudden, he was much too close. His elegantly manicured hand reached out and one finger idly flipped the silver hoop that pierced her left ear. Aunie's stomach knotted ferociously, and she abruptly suffered a shamefully overwhelming desire to use the bathroom. She pressed her thighs together and tightened all the muscles necessary to prevent herself from doing right there in the kitchen doorway what her body was frantically urging her do.

"You're missing the point, Aunie," he whispered gently. "You see, you're *my* pretty little toy." His finger slipped into the hoop. "*My* possession—no one else's. You don't make a move unless I give you permission to do so." Something twisted and sick lurked in the depths of his eyes. "I gave you everything a woman could possibly want." His finger exerted pressure and her ear began to hurt where the wire pressed against fragile flesh. He shook his head sadly at her. "But you let me down anyway."

He yanked the earring with vicious strength.

Aunie screamed as she felt her ear tear, instinctively placing her hands on his chest and shoving with all her might. Wesley stumbled backward several steps before he caught his balance.

She didn't wait around to see how he fared. Pivoting on the ball of her foot, she raced for the stairway.

She could hear his pursuit of her, but she dared not look back. *Oh God, help me,* she prayed. *Oh God, oh God, he's so crazy. Please help me. Please.*

He tackled her near the top of the stairs. The wind was knocked out of her, and when he slammed her over onto her back, she hit the stairs at an awkward angle. Pain shot up and down her spine. She kicked out at him feebly, and with a distant feeling of satisfaction, she heard his grunt of pain.

"Why, you little bitch," he said in that horrifyingly friendly tone and she saw him cock back his fist. *Mistake!* her brain screamed. *Ah, God, Aunie, don't try to fight back. He'll hurt you even worse.* But even as her mind tried to warn her, her instincts made her reach weakly for his eyes. It was just not in her nature not to fight back. Not anymore.

His fist came crashing down and Aunie tried to scream as she felt her nose break, but blood filled her mouth, her throat, and she gagged weakly.

She lost track of how many times he hit her after

that. She was vaguely aware that some of the blows were openhanded. . . . They were marginally less hurtful than when he used his fist. The only thing that registered fully, however, was the pain, the terror she experienced at the possibility of choking to death on her own blood, and that damned refined voice telling her that if she wouldn't decorate his arm anymore, well then, he would simply have to see to it that she never decorated anyone else's either.

She never heard Geoff's startled exclamation when he walked unsuspecting through the open front door; neither was she aware of him pounding up the stairs, securing Wesley in a hammerlock, and wresting him off her. She was cognizant of hearing a pathetic whimpering somewhere in the distance, but oblivious that it was from her own split and swollen lips that it issued.

Geoff managed to hold Wesley, contact the police, and call an ambulance. Within moments, sirens were moaning into silence outside the door and the high-rent neighborhood was temporarily, uncustomarily awash in a pulsating swirl of blue and red lights.

Aunie barely remembered the ride to the hospital. She floated in a dim netherworld of acute pain and hallucinogenic colors that flashed behind closed eyelids.

The emergency room was a whirling confusion of glaring, white lights and loud voices all talking at once. One voice kept asking her over and over if there were anyone they could call for her. She dimly remembered giving her mother's number.

She was oblivious to the prick of a needle that pierced the soft skin of the inside bend of her elbow, but the pain began to recede and a lightheaded sensation of floating overtook her. The next thing she knew, she was awakening in a quiet private room. For a moment, she couldn't recall how she had come to be there. All she knew for sure was that she hurt.

God, how she hurt.

In fits and starts her memory returned, and with it came a paroxysm of acute anxiety. Wesley would have maimed her; she didn't doubt it for a moment. The nurse who came in to take her vital signs commented on her heightened blood pressure and rapid pulse. She urged Aunie to stay calm and then dispensed pain medication. Her lawyer and her mother arrived within moments of each other, and two doctors stopped in to discuss her prognosis, administering professionally cheerful encouragement for a complete recovery.

By the time everyone finally left and she was once again all alone, the physical pain was in abeyance. The fear that remained, however, went deeper than a transient battering of her flesh. Jordan had assured her that Wesley's brutality would guarantee him a good, long stretch behind bars. She wanted desperately to believe him.

But Jordan hadn't lived with Wesley; he didn't fully comprehend the charm her ex-husband could exude when it suited his purpose to do so. Neither had he looked into Wesley's eyes this afternoon. Aunie had, and she couldn't afford to take any chances.

Against the doctor's advice, she checked herself out of the hospital and went home to pack.

"I feel like I've been raped by the system, but I suppose I shouldn't be all that surprised to hear of his acquittal," she said in a dull, defeated voice, speaking more to her hands folded on the tabletop than to either James or Lola. "My own mama was appalled at the damage he'd done to my face, but once the doctors assured her there would be no permanent scarring, she insisted it must have been some sort of mistake." She laughed, a brief, humorless exhalation of breath, and shook her head. "She and the rest of the family had pretty much washed their hands of me once I decided to divorce Wesley, of course, but a *mistake?* I know they never believed I had a brain in my head, but even I know the difference between a methodical beating and a slight error of judgment." She closely studied the bend of her thumb, a cynical smile twisting one corner of her mouth. "I wonder if Mama sat behind Wesley at the trial to demonstrate her support."

"Feeling a little sorry for yourself, Aunie?" James asked in a voice lacking any trace of sympathy. As he had been doing all evening, he ignored the reprimand in Lola's eyes. Privately, he thought Aunie's mother sounded like a real piece of work, but he knew better than to say so. It was one thing, he had learned a long time ago, for a person to gripe about their own family members. Hell, everybody did it at one time or another. In most instances, however, it was something else entirely to have someone outside the family do the same. So he swallowed the words he was dying to say, buried the cold rage he felt for what she had endured, and hoped to shock her out of her lethargy. It was a waste of time to dwell on the wrongs that had been done to her, anyway, and James didn't believe in wasting time. He wanted to see her spitting mad. She needed to be angry enough to fight and he doubted that sympathizing was the best way to get her to do so.

Aunie was emotionally drained, however, and she

refused to rise to the bait. "Yeah," she agreed softly
to James's dismay. "I'm feelin' extremely sorry for
myself. It's been a hard day, James," she said propping
her chin in her hand and staring lethargically at him
across the table. "I'll pull myself together tomorrow,
all right? For today, though, I think I'll just indulge
in a little self-pity."

Her exhaustion was evident, and Lola pushed her
chair back from the table. "Maybe we should go,
James," she said. "As she said, it's been a hard day. Let
the woo-mon get some rest."

James didn't budge. "You go ahead, Lola," he said,
his chin still firmly planted on his muscular forearms
stacked atop the back of the chair he was straddling.
"I'll head back to my place in a sec."

Aunie rose from her chair and accompanied Lola
to the door. "Thank you," she said softly. "I don't
know what I would've done if . . . well, you've helped
immensely just by being here, is all. I don't feel quite
so alone now. And thank you, too, for dinner."

"It was your food, Aunie. I merely cooked it."

"Nevertheless," Aunie replied firmly. "If not for
your efforts, I probably wouldn't have eaten at all and
the meal really helped. I'm grateful."

Lola inclined her head. "Then you are welcome."
She leaned closer and lowered her voice. "I know it
is easier said than done, but try not to worry. If this
mad Wesley mon should ever track you to Seattle,
Otis and James will see to it that no harm come to
you." She cocked her head in James's direction.
"James, he talk a tough game, but takin' care of
people is in his blood."

James, who was brooding in his chair, didn't hear,
which was probably just as well. He still tended to get
a bit touchy when the subject of his multitudinous

responsibilities was raised. The low-toned conversation by the door didn't register, however. He was busy staring at Aunie's back and stewing over her unexpected defeatist attitude.

He didn't like it. She was a fighter not a quitter; she'd made that abundantly clear the very first day they'd met. Yeah, so, all right, maybe she had every right to feel sorry for herself tonight, but what the hell good would it do her? Angst was an emotion with which he had little patience. It never got anyone anywhere and the thought of her spending the rest of the evening paralyzed with fear because of that gold-plated psycho made his teeth grind.

He knew Aunie was terrified at the thought, but he almost wished old Wesley would show up. He wouldn't be averse to an opportunity to demonstrate exactly how it felt to be mercilessly beaten by someone larger and stronger, which he assumed he was. Hell, if he wasn't, Otis was sure to be. And while the gentleness of Otis's nature would surprise a hell of a lot of people who never bothered to look beyond outward appearances, he did possess a temper. It just took a lot to bring it out; but knowing something like this had been done to someone as small and helpless as Aunie would do the trick.

James tugged on his ponytail and frowned. Fantasies of beating Aunie's ex to a pulp were all very warming, but they didn't do a thing to address the immediate problem—which was how the hell he was going to shake her out of her depression. Then a creative idea occurred to him, and a lopsided smile tugged up one corner of his mouth.

It was a sacrifice on his part, of course, but what the hell. Someone had to do something to prevent her from brooding all night long. As Aunie closed the door behind Lola and turned back into the room, James stood. He didn't understand why a small ripple of excitement should slither up his spine, so he ignored it.

"Oh," she said as she walked back into the dining area and saw him turning his chair back into its proper position. "Are you leaving, too?"

"Yeah. I've still got an hour or two's worth of drawing that needs to be done tonight."

There was a part of Aunie that wanted only to be left alone. She craved a measure of solitude in which to curl up and hug her fear to her breast. There was another tangled emotion, however, that clamored with disappointment that he was leaving. She kept remembering the safety she had felt when he'd held her in his arms and let her cry out her fear and rage. God, except for those brief moments, it had been so long since anyone had held or hugged her. Then she admonished herself to grow up. *It was your own damn desire for independence,* she reminded herself dully, *that led to this mess with Wesley in the first place. Let James go. Then you can indulge in a nice, long bout of self-pity.* "I'll walk you to the door," she offered softly. *After all, he's already given you a large chunk of his time, and this from a man who doesn't want to know about your problems.*

They were at the door when James suddenly turned to her. He knew his height was only average, but standing this close to her he felt as oversized as Otis. For some reason, her lack of stature continually took him by surprise.

He gave himself a mental shake. So, okay. Forget her size and get on with it. Keep it gentle and friendly so no one gets hurt, and maybe it'll help put a dent in that damned lethargy enshrouding her. James's mouth tilted up on one side as he looked down at her. "Just so your day won't be a total loss," he said smoothly, "I've decided to give you some pointers in kissing after all." His smile turned to a full fledged grin at the stupefied look on her face, then to outright laughter. He reached for her.

Aunie realized her mouth was hanging open in pure surprised reaction and closed it with a snap. She dodged his hands. What on earth was he up to? He reached again, still grinning like an idiot, and she slapped his hands down. Irritation started to surface. This hadn't been the best day of her life and she truly didn't think she cared to wrap it up by being the butt of his joke. Aunie looked him over with a jaundiced eye. "Well, lucky, lucky me," she muttered sarcastically. "What brought on this sudden change of heart? Remember me? I'm the novice who's too *fragile*." She invested the word with the same disgust she might have used to say *socially diseased*.

"I guess I'll just have to exercise a little care."

Aunie bristled and said nastily, "What, no Blue Plate Special?" Was he still harboring that absurd fantasy that she couldn't withstand a *kiss*? The man persisted in being insulting.

"*Ryder* Special." He was beginning to get a little irritated. He was only doing this for her.

"Whatever." She shrugged. "In any case, thanks, but no thanks. I'm not in the mood."

James forgot he was supposed to be friendly and gentle and reverted to type. He snorted. "No, wait, let me see if I've got this straight. Looking-for-a-hot-affair Franklin is not in the mood? I-want-passion Aunie—not in the mood? Get real. You know you're dying of curiosity."

Aunie's depression was fading fast as hot anger rushed in to take its place. Color burned high in her cheekbones and her dark eyes flashed fire at him. "Gawd, but you're arrogant," she snapped. "If y' think you're such a damn good kisser, then hadn't you better employ a little caution? What if I get hooked? Did you consider that? Why, I could start hauntin' your apartment day and night, shadowin' your evra footstep, beggin' for more and more and more kisses. You might never get another moment's peace as long as you live. . . ."

James laughed and reached out to snag her arms. He forced them behind her back and jerked her up against him, his blood running hot and furious through his veins. "Don't take it so seriously, Magnolia. This is just a little therapy between friends."

"Oh, so now we're *friends?* Mercy me. And here I thought we were just casual acquaintances."

"Whatever." He spread his legs, pulling her between them, and bent his knees to bring his face on a level with hers. Securing her wrists behind her back in one long-fingered hand, he reached up with his free hand and grasped a handful of her silky hair, tilting her head back. "I don't like the idea of your spending the night all depressed and feeling sorry for yourself, so I decided I'd give you something else to think about. Maybe it'll take your mind off Wesley."

Rage exploded in Aunie's stomach. "Why, you dirty, rotten, *low-down* son of a bitch!"

"Oh, yeah, talk dirty to me," James mocked her and his face creased engagingly as he grinned. Then his head bent and his mouth slanted across hers, cutting off her tirade. His tongue, hot, supple, and insistent, thrust into her mouth. Aunie bucked in his hold, but James simply jerked her hands warningly, pressing them into the small of her back. Knowing she was outmatched physically, she tried next to expel his tongue from her mouth with a hard jab of her own, and the kiss abruptly changed nature.

The sudden damp slide of Aunie's tongue against James's made them both inhale sharply, simultaneously. Moss green eyes impaled dark brown ones and all was still for one second . . . two seconds . . .

Then awareness of the transferral of individual flavors that passed from tongue to tongue intruded into their heightened senses, and what had been an urge to tease her out of her lethargy on his part, disillusioned anger on hers, suddenly exploded into a mutual conflagration of passion.

Aunie's objection to James's kiss was driven entirely out of her mind. Her eyes slid shut and her breathing quickened as she rose up on tiptoe to strain closer. She had never felt anything quite like this in her life. His mouth was hot; his tongue was aggressive as it pumped and withdrew with a repetitive, suggestively sexual rhythm, and ah, Gawd, he was so warm and hard.

James released her captured wrists; he widened his stance, and his newly freed hand slid inside the waistband of her jeans, fingers splaying across the small of her back. Unadulterated lust drove any semblance of gentleness from his kiss. His teeth scraped her lips . . . his mouth sucked strongly . . . his tongue speared inside her again and again.

Breathing choppily, Aunie looped an arm across his broad shoulder and grasped his ponytail in one small fist. Her breasts flattened against his chest, and the fingers of her left hand slid up the length of his neck to splay across his jaw and cheek. His skin was hot and slightly rough with evening stubble.

James lifted his mouth fractionally to change the angle of the kiss and Aunie shuddered when he suddenly sucked her finger into his mouth. His eyes, heavy-lidded and not entirely focused, stared blindly into hers as he drew strongly on the small, white digit in his mouth, then his eyelids fell shut and he groaned. His thighs tightened around her hips; his fingers dug into the heated flesh just above her bottom, and he thrust his pelvis with demanding urgency against hers.

Aunie dragged her finger from his mouth and grasped the back of his neck, pulling his mouth back to hers.

"Oh God, you taste good," he said in a hoarse voice and then drove her head back with the force of his kiss.

His hands left her hair, slipped out of her jeans, and closed around her waist. He suddenly straightened his legs, surging to his full height while synchronously hoisting her in the air. He pressed her back against the door and crowded up against her, pinning her in place with his body. Aunie drew a sharp breath of surprise and clutched at him for balance. Her feet dangled off the floor and instinctively she wrapped her legs around his waist, crossing her ankles behind his back. James's hands slid down to her hips, then edged around to grasp her buttocks. He was aware of the way his big hands nearly swallowed up her little butt, but the rounded flesh under the worn denim beneath his hands was surprisingly sturdy, warm, and resilient. He positioned her to align the heavy denim seam over her mound with the hard length of his erection and then slowly pumped his hips. She sighed deep in her throat and arched her hips, widening the spread of her thighs.

His mouth twisted over the soft fullness of hers as he turned his head to come at her from another

direction. He was on the edge of control and the
force of his mouth pushed the back of her head
against the door. Christ, he wanted her; oh, Christ,
he wanted to peel those damn jeans that were
obstructing the access he desired right down to her
ankles and . . .

Christ. What the fuck are you doing?

Sanity didn't creep back softly into James's consciousness; it exploded like a grenade. He ripped his
mouth away from her soft, clinging lips and tightened
his hands convulsively around her bottom, jerking
her away from the rigid proof of his arousal to the
safer territory of his waist. His forehead dropped next
to her head with a dull thud as it hit the solid panel
of the door, and he ground it slowly back and forth
while he attempted to control his ragged breathing
and pounding heart. Oh God. How was he going to
extricate himself from this fiasco he'd created?

Aunie was wondering the same thing. She knew
the highly erotic explosiveness of this unanticipated
little session against the door had affected James every
bit as much as it had her. She also knew, however,
that right this minute he was most likely flaying himself alive for starting something with the little novice
down the hall. He was probably scared to death that
she'd start expecting all manner of attention from
him. Well, he needn't worry, for she knew perfectly
well that she wasn't really his type. She should; God
knows he had made a point of telling her often
enough.

As he lowered her slowly to the floor and stepped
back, it flashed through Aunie's mind that by kissing
her at all, he had, in his own unique fashion, been
trying to be her friend. He had made his position
crystal clear on more than one occasion; yet he'd

violated his own ironclad code and kissed her anyway. It had aggravated her almost beyond bearing when he'd bragged he'd take her mind off today's stressful events, but by God, she had to hand it to him. He had done just that.

It was only fair then, that in return, she should at least attempt to spare him any discomfort that resulted from his impulsive action. James's methods might be different from most people's, but she supposed his heart was in the right place—just look at the way he and Lola had shown up here today and taken care of her. She'd been practically catatonic before their arrival.

Oh, Gawd, she had to do something! It was a singular moment of passion that had gotten out of control, and that was all it was. Somehow, she had to let them both off the hook so they could run into each other in the hall without embarrassment.

Hoping her legs wouldn't collapse beneath her, she pushed away from the door. James was standing a few feet away, head down and hands awkwardly stuffed in the pockets of his Levi's. Dull color stained his cheekbones, and he still hadn't said a word. Aunie shook back her hair and took a deep breath, silently expelling it. Submerging the final vestige of her embarrassment and praying her voice would not emerge in a croak, she said, "So, okay, you're a *moderately* good kisser. But I thought you promised me addictive."

James's head jerked up. Aunie was regarding him from a few feet away, her hands on her hips, an eyebrow elevated, and her mouth cocked in a wry smile. Relief creased his face into its familiar, quirky lines and his teeth flashed white as he grinned back at her. Oh thank God, she hadn't taken it seriously.

He had messed up royally this time and he'd been at a dead loss how to rectify the situation. What had seemed like a platinum idea at the time had climbed so far beyond his control, so damned fast, he hadn't had a clue how to salvage it.

But she had done it. She'd dispelled the awkwardness and simultaneously let him know she didn't expect anything from him.

He nudged her with his elbow. "C'mon, admit it. It was the best you've ever had."

Oh Gawd, it was. But that would just have to be her secret. Palm down, thumb slightly elevated, she rocked her hand from side to side, signifying she'd had better.

"Well, hell," he muttered in mock irritation, "I've been insulted by better folk; I don't have to take this from you, too." Then he dropped the facade and looked down at her seriously. "You gonna be okay, Magnolia?"

"Yeah." She reached out and lightly touched his arm. "Thank you for all you did for me today." She prayed she wasn't blushing as she got a quick mental flash of what *all* had entailed.

She forced the image from her mind. "You and Lola really helped me over a rough spot tonight, and I appreciate it . . . I mean that."

James shifted with obvious discomfort and she gave him a slight push toward the door. "G'on. I know you have work to do tonight, and I've gotta tuck in the boys."

James snorted at the thought of her gallery wall of half-naked men. "You'll understand if I don't have you give 'em all a good night kiss from me." He opened the door, but just stood looking down at her for a moment. Finally, he said, "G'night, Aunie."

"Good night, James. Sweet dreams."

She shut the door behind his departing back and leaned back against it. She had a sinking feeling she shouldn't have added that last bit.

Between the news of Wesley's acquittal and James's life-altering kiss, it was going to be difficult enough falling asleep tonight. She was afraid she knew exactly whom her dreams would feature—supposing she had any—and it was the absolute last thing in the world that she needed.

Why did the most passionate kiss she had ever received in her life have to have come from him?

CHAPTER 6

James had had an excellent brain long before he ever developed brawn. He thought perhaps that was how he had come to be saddled with responsibility for his family.

It certainly wasn't because he was the oldest. Hell, except for Will, he was the youngest of the four Ryder brothers. But his wit was quick, his tongue was facile, and his methods, while unorthodox, were effective, and by the time he was sixteen years old, he'd found himself locked into a seemingly perpetual custodianship of his brothers' problems.

A prototype of behavior had already emerged: His brothers got themselves into trouble and James promptly maximized whatever tools he had at his disposal to bail them out. For a kid lacking financial means, who hailed from an area where power was not endemic, his tools were astonishingly functional. He utilized his native intelligence, his offbeat sense of humor, an ability to think on his feet, and—as he grew older—his rough language and the reputation he had gained on the street for being unpredictable and maybe just a little bit crazy. Folks never knew quite how to take it when James Ryder smiled and made those bizarre remarks that a person couldn't help laughing at; not when in the next breath he could spout the meanest obscenities they'd ever heard and appear perfectly willing to slit the throat of anyone who got between him and the accomplishment of his objectives.

Despite the impression he gave, he had always managed to avoid any outright violence in his quest to keep his brothers in one piece. It was a little like tiptoeing through an urban minefield, though; he never knew from one moment to the next if one of his bluffs was going to blow up in his face. It had exhilarated him when he was a kid, but as he'd matured it had taken its toll. Now, he was just plain tired of it.

Neither he nor his brothers had had more than a modicum of parental guidance growing up. There was only Ma, and while she had done the best she could, she'd had to work two jobs just to feed four growing boys and keep them in shelter and shoes. The old man had disappeared so long ago James hardly remembered him. His teacher, therefore, and that of his brothers, was most often the streets of the project, and a faithless slut she could sometimes be. All four of the Ryder boys, it seemed, had learned a different lesson from her.

James credited Otis's mother for instilling many of the values he'd ultimately adopted. Muriel Jackson ran her family like a marine unit, and hanging around her apartment as much as he did, he was automatically included when she drilled morality into her kids. She had ironclad opinions on what was right and what was wrong, and she was not hesitant to express them. Neither was she reluctant to tear the hide off anyone foolish enough to ignore her sterling edicts, and that included James.

He was converted early to the work ethic, thanks largely to her influence. What he ultimately wanted for his life, the streets didn't begin to offer, and Otis's ma made him realize that no one was going to simply hand him his dreams on a silver platter. That being the case, with the single-minded determination he applied to everything he did, he set out to accomplish his objectives on his own.

He had three priorities, and if they did not appear to be of earth-shattering importance to anyone else, they were fairly ambitious for a son of the Terrace. For one thing, he desired more than a high school education. That was a rarity in itself in a neighborhood that counted a high school diploma a triumph. Secondly, he saw beauty where many saw decrepitude, particularly in architecture, and he wanted one day to own a place whose former glory he could restore with his own two hands. Third, most important, and the most difficult to achieve, he wanted to be a professional cartoonist.

The first was easy. James didn't give a damn if he earned a degree; he simply wanted the education. To that end, he worked construction by day and audited classes when he could. His interests were eclectic, and he pursued them with his customary diligence.

His other goals, unfortunately, were not as easily attained. Between his own living expenses, the cost of his mother's funeral his third year out of high school, and his brothers' needs, saving money was practically impossible. And God knew, no one was breaking down his door, begging to publish his 'toons. He had expected some initial rejection, of course; he just hadn't been prepared for the damage to his sense of ability that went along with it. Rejection hurt; there were no two ways about it. It hammered the ego and battered his faith in his own talent. Was he fooling himself? Hell, probably—how many times had he vocalized his sense of the ridiculous only to elicit blank looks from half the people around him? Maybe his stuff wasn't as humorous as he'd have liked to believe.

Otis said that was pure bull, and deep inside, that's what James believed, too. But sometimes it was a struggle to continue cranking it out. He hardly had a free minute as it was. Why waste what little he had on something that wasn't paying off?

In the final analysis, however, it proved to be a matter over which he didn't have a real option. It was simply something he felt compelled to do.

The only aspect of his life over which he *did* seem to have complete control was how and when he'd allow females into it, and damned if he planned to relinquish that. He liked women, but he lacked all desire for a steady relationship with one. Hell, the last thing he needed was yet another person demanding more of his time than he was willing to give.

Females demanded so much attention and ultimately always seemed to expect marriage and children. No thanks. He had inherited his familial responsibilities by default, and he felt compelled to draw. He didn't also, however, have to commit himself to some woman who'd further constrict his limited privacy. Give him the good-time girls, preferably tall, blonde, and stacked, whom he met in bars. They were usually looking for the same things he was seeking: a little light flirtation; some good, vigorous, uncomplicated sex; and a bit of lighthearted social interaction.

When his cartoons finally began to sell it surprised him to learn that success could be a two-edged sword. He'd never expected it to have a downside.

He was indignant to read in a national magazine that he was an overnight success. "Fancy that," he'd said to Otis, with more than a little sarcasm. "Am I a friggin' miracle worker, or what?" He didn't dispute that shortly after it had appeared in his hometown evening paper, "A Skewed View" was rapidly picked up by papers nationwide and almost as quickly expanded into commercial rights. But that damned article had completely discounted the nine years he'd struggled to keep producing while the rejection slips had mounted up.

Overnight success, his ass.

Hell, he used to put himself to sleep sometimes, fantasizing about seeing just one of his cartoons published. He'd always sort of assumed it would make his life perfection itself.

He should have known better. For all his creative mental flights of fancy, he was ultimately a man whose life was firmly grounded in reality. Yes, having his cartoons finally accepted gave him a very real feeling of validation. And there was no denying that the financial aspect was rewarding. He finally had the means to purchase his dream in the form of this apartment house, and he'd enjoyed every damned minute spent restoring the place. He was able to repay Otis's faith in him, if just a little, by providing extra income for the help Otis gave him during his off hours and by offering him and Lola free rent in the guise of managing the rental aspects of the apartment

house. So far, that had meant renting to Aunie, but
as they restored the remaining eight apartments, the
Jacksons' managerial duties would expand. James
supposed it would be nice to have the place pay for
itself, but he was in no particular hurry to see it filled
up with people.

The confusion and lack of satisfaction stemmed
from his personal life, which was nowhere near perfection. As his financial worth grew, so, it seemed,
did the scope and magnitude of his brothers' problems. Now they assumed he had unlimited resources
to fund the bailing-out process for whatever current
difficulties they might find themselves in. And women
who had been perfectly content to while away a few
hours with him when he was just James Ryder, construction worker, suddenly wanted more from J. T.
Ryder, cartoonist.

That really caught him unprepared, the way so
many people suddenly began to treat him as if he
were someone new and exotic. He sure as hell didn't
understand it. He hadn't changed; only their percep-
tion of him had; so go figure. The way a lot of them
acted, though, you'd think he'd all of a sudden
become some sort of Hollywood personality living life
in the fast lane. What bull; he was the same old James
he'd always been. Give him a couple Mexican beers,
a few good friends, and an occasional evening of
recreational fornication, and he was a happy man.
They could keep the bright lights, premieres, and
intrusive yellow journalism that other people seemed
to visualize. He was basically a private man, already
jealously guarding what little privacy he could
scrounge up to call his own. Who needed more people poking into his life?

He'd ultimately dealt with the awkward onslaught

of intrusive, fawning attention by changing the bars he had frequented. He took his business to where he wasn't known and he started over. When the new women he met asked what he did for a living, he told them he worked light construction, restoring an apartment house. It was the truth, after all. Maybe not the entire truth, but fact nonetheless. And for the past three years it had effectively protected his anonymity, which in turn had provided him the bit of isolation he craved. He required frequent periods of solitude, and if withholding pieces of information about himself was the only way to get it, then that was what he'd do. It had worked to his satisfaction thus far.

So life should be a chair of bowlies, as that Engelbreit lithograph in Lola's hallway said. Only it wasn't. His brothers seemed destined to keep repeating the same old mistakes right into the twenty-first century, and he had grown infinitely weary of cleaning up after them. He wanted them to grow up and take responsibility for their own lives. And if that weren't enough to keep him occupied, he had this damned business with Aunie now to contend with as well.

James was finding it much harder than he had expected to put his encounter with her out of his mind.

He didn't understand it; this shouldn't be happening. He knew the drill. Hell, he had invented it; he *ought* to have it down pat by now. He didn't get involved . . . not with anyone, not ever. He got so stressed just contemplating the idea, he practically broke out in hives. The complication that would come of an involvement with any woman, let alone Aunie Franklin, was the last thing he needed.

And yet . . .

He kept remembering that night in her apartment, the feel of her, her response . . . God, that response.

It infuriated him. He'd never had a problem putting a woman out of his mind before—why should it be any different this time? It was bad enough he was going to be dragged into Aunie's problems should old Wesley ever show up. All right, in truth he wasn't that averse to the idea of getting his hands on the ex-husband. He had a very real desire to hurt the man for what he'd done to her, and hurt him badly.

But that was as far as it went, dammit. They weren't even *friends*, he and Aunie, not really. He was not about to get involved with her sexually, and that was the beginning and end of that. Hell, that's all he'd need . . . a lover who lived in the same building as he did. He thought his privacy was limited now . . . just imagine what it would be like with someone who lived right down the hall. She would expect things from him that he simply wasn't equipped to give.

Provided, that is, that she was interested in having an affair with him in the first place, which was assuming one hell of a lot. He kept hearing her voice in his head saying, "Gawd, James, you're so conceited," and it made him feel like the vainest of fools.

All right, so maybe she'd made more of an impression on him during that episode against her entry door than he had made on her. She *had* laughed the whole thing off; and the few times he'd run into her since, there hadn't been so much as a hint in her manner to indicate she even recalled the incident.

So much for her claim to be looking for a red-hot affair.

Of course, she'd never claimed to be looking for one with him. That sure hadn't stopped him, however, from telling her more than once not to expect him to play the stud for her. That was what really made him squirm, the idea that he'd warned away a woman with her sort of classiness when she had never once indicated his attentions were even desired by her.

As if she'd have any use for a guy like him, anyway. He had seen things and been places she couldn't even begin to imagine, while she possessed an inherently untouched quality that even the punishment she'd taken at her ex-husband's hands had been unable to tarnish. She probably had some yuppie type in mind for her affair, someone real clean—a doctor or lawyer with soft, smooth hands.

So, it wasn't a problem then, was it? Neither he nor she was looking for a sexual liaison with the other, so he didn't have to worry about adding one more complication to an already overcomplicated situation. He'd been working overtime this past year to make his life less complex, not more so; but it really would be vain of him to include Aunie in his responsibilities. She'd never once asked him to be accountable for her. She had, in fact, bent over backward to demonstrate her independence—it seemed to hold some special significance for her. The best thing he could do by far was simply to forget the way he had forced that encounter between them and get on with the important things in life. No worries.

Why was it, then, that he couldn't quite shake the feeling she was about ninety-eight pounds of pure dynamite primed to explode directly into his life?

Aunie put down her lipstick brush and surveyed her image critically in the mirror. Did she look all right? Except for her complexion, which even she could see was flawless, she had never quite understood what all the fuss was about when people raved on about her looks. She had taken shameful advantage of it, but she'd never fully understood it.

It was important to her, however, that she look her best today. She twisted around, peering over her shoulder to check the drape of the cherry red, thin wool skirt in the full-length mirror. She turned back and adjusted the fringe of her scarf over the neckline of her silk blouse. She was meeting James's and Otis's families, and she was more than a little nervous.

Would they resent her presence? It was Thanksgiving, after all, a day for families. She had been dreading its arrival all month as she'd listened to different classmates discussing their plans. It was painful to hear other people's planned festivities when she knew she'd be all alone. Then last week Lola had cornered her and insisted she spend the holiday with them.

Aunie hadn't admitted it to a soul, but her self-confidence had been at an all-time low ever since Wesley's attack. She was very unsure of her welcome anywhere; and in the presence of strangers—which included most of the population of Seattle—her old shyness had a tendency to reemerge with a vengeance.

She almost blushed when she thought of the way she had spouted off to both James and Lola about having an affair. Talk about a lot of hot air. She hadn't even managed to exchange more than a few words with most of her classmates. She was friendly with those who approached her first but hesitant to initiate contact herself. So when Lola extended the invitation, she was leery of intruding on a family gathering and had tried to demur. Lola and Otis, and even James in his own way, had been wonderful to her. But this was a day for celebrating with one's loved ones, and she wouldn't feel right horning in on their plans.

Lola, however, wouldn't accept no for an answer. "You have other plans, woo-mon?" she'd demanded, hands on her shapely hips as she'd regarded Aunie through narrowed eyes.

"No, but . . ."

"Then you come. And bring some vegetables wid you. Not Brussels sprouts, though. Otis, he hate Brussels sprouts."

"But, his family . . ."

"They aren't so crazy 'bout Brussels sprouts, either."

"That's not what I meant, Lola Jackson, and you know it. Ah shouldn't be intrudin' on his time with his family."

Lola, who had wised up to Aunie's habit of unconsciously intensifying her Southern accent when she was feeling unnerved, grinned and gave her a little bump with her hip. "You kiddin', girl? Intrudin's 'bout the last thing you'll be doin'. Otis, he say: Get her down here. He's hopin' your presence will inhibit his brother Leon from offerin' stud service once again. Then Otis won't have to squash him like a bug, which would really put a damper on the festivities. 'Sides, James and his brothers will be there, too."

That information did nothing to reassure Aunie. If anything, it reinforced her idea that Thanksgiving was a time for family. "Oh, Lola, I don't know."

"Well, I do. Otis, he say for such a dainty little thing, you got attitude. Don't go makin' a liar outta my mon by turnin' all chicken-hearted on me now. Be there, two-thirty P.M. And don't forget the vegetables."

And then she'd left.

Aunie dabbed a meager application of her favorite perfume on her pulse points. She took a deep breath, gathered key, purse, two containers of vegetables, and a potted chrysanthemum, and juggling them carefully, let herself out of her apartment.

Downstairs, she hesitated outside the Jacksons' apartment. On the other side of the door she could hear the raised voices of a large group of people all conversing at once, and she drew a deep breath to calm her nerves. She'd worn her highest-heeled boots—the ones that made her feel almost tall and gave her confidence. Using the toe of one, she tapped it against the door.

It was swung open by a man who bore a startling resemblance to James. He had the same rawboned, Scandinavian sort of looks, with his blond hair, big-boned wrists, and large hands. This man's hair was short and styled, however, and he appeared younger and perhaps just a bit more polished, a bit less fit and tough-looking than James.

"Well, hel-lo, pretty lady," he drawled. "Welcome. You must be the Aunie everyone's been talking about." He stood back to let her enter, flashing her a practiced smile. "They didn't begin to do you justice, beautiful."

Aunie returned his smile, but hers was just the tiniest bit reserved. She'd recognize his type blindfolded on a moonless night. He was a womanizer like her Uncle Beau.

Inside, the air was redolent with turkey and baked goods. As James's brother herded her to the living room entrance, she was overwhelmed by the faces and the cacophony of voices.

People sat or sprawled on every available piece of furniture and upon the floor. Everyone seemed to be talking simultaneously as a football game blared from the television, and children were in perpetual motion, rolling over or skipping around obstacles.

Aunie hesitated at the entrance, balancing her flowers, purse, and the dishes containing her vegetables. She looked at all the unknown faces and smiled uncertainly.

"Will!" an authoritarian voice suddenly said. "What are you doing just standin' there when that chile's holding all that stuff? Give the young woman a hand."

All conversation ceased and every eye in the room focused on Aunie. In the sudden silence, she felt her cheeks heat until she feared they must rival the color of her skirt. Oh Gawd, she knew it. She should have stayed home.

"Hey, hey, Aunie," Otis rumbled as he dislodged the child he'd been bouncing on his stomach and surged to his feet. "Didn't see y' come in. Lola!" he bellowed. "Aunie's here."

James materialized next from another room, and Aunie suddenly felt like a sports car caught between a convoy of big rigs as he, his brother, and Otis hemmed her in. "Well, look at you, Magnolia Blossom," James said, inserting a long, rough-tipped finger into a soft, shiny brown ringlet and stretching it out. "Curly hair." He let it go, watching it bounce back into place.

Aunie would have reached up self-consciously to touch her hairdo but her hands were full. Did it look stupid? She'd thought it looked pretty good before she'd left her own apartment, but now she wasn't so sure and James had obviously said all he'd had to say on the subject. "Here," he said, reaching for her precariously balanced dishes, "let me take some of this stuff for you." He relieved her of the vegetables.

Lola appeared in the doorway, wiping her hands on a towel. "Hi, Aunie." She looked at the vegetables

in James's hands. "Well, don't just stand there lettin'
them cool down, you fool mon. Put 'em on the war-
min' tray in the kitchen."

"Yes, ma'am," he murmured before he raised an
eyebrow at Aunie and left to do Lola's bidding. Aunie
slid her purse onto the bookcase. "These are for
you," she said, handing the flowers to her friend.

Lola's face lighted with pleasure. "For me? Oh, my,
I can't remember the last time I received flowers."
She stroked several petals reverently, then looked
up with a blindingly white smile. "They're beautiful,
Aunie. Thank you." Tucking the flowers into the
bend of one elbow, she guided Aunie with her free
hand. "Come. I'll introduce you to the mob."

The blonde who had opened the door for her
turned out to be Will, James's youngest brother. The
woman with the air of command was Otis's mother,
Muriel Jackson, and in short order Aunie was also
introduced to two of Otis's sisters, their husbands and
children, Otis's brother and his wife and children,
and one unmarried brother. James's brother Bob she
had already met, and his other brother Paul had not
yet arrived. She tried to fix all the names to the correct
faces in her mind, but she was afraid she wasn't doing
a sterling job of it.

James's brother Will flirted outrageously; his
brother Bob was totally friendly; but everyone else
acted stiff around her, and Aunie feared she had
been correct in assuming they would resent her presence. In reality, except for Muriel, who was intimidated by no one, they were a bit awed by her. She
didn't comprehend the effect she had on them, with
her beautiful manners, cultured Southern voice,
expensive clothing, and exquisite appearance. All she
knew was that Otis's sisters quit joking and laughing

when she accompanied Lola to the kitchen; the children watched her with big eyes and fell silent when she returned to the living room, and the men avoided eye contact whenever possible. She felt she was ruining everyone's good time, and it made her miserable.

More than anything she desired to slink away, but she gave herself a stern lecture and stayed put. Dammit, she wasn't the useless decoration she used to be. She was learning to stand on her own two feet, and part of being an independent adult meant proving to herself that Wesley hadn't irreparably damaged her self-esteem. She could remain a shy, pampered child, stick close to Lola and Otis all day, and then escape at the earliest opportunity. Or, she could test her maturity by setting aside her discomfort and trying her best to fit in.

She sat down on the floor next to Muriel Jackson's feet and initiated a conversation. She found the woman's air of competent authority fascinating and soon became absorbed in their exchange. She didn't realize anyone else was paying attention, but those around the two women listened in and discovered that Aunie was interested in the same everyday subjects that interested them. Once they understood that they wouldn't be expected to converse about opera or the arts or be asked to fetch her a mint julep, as they had half feared, they too joined in. Then the children, seeing their parents chatting so easily with the princesslike lady in the flowing red skirt, followed suit.

Before she knew what was happening, Aunie was having a marvelous time.

James watched her from across the room but kept his distance. He had never seen her all dolled up as she was today. She looked good.

Hell, the truth was, she always looked good, but

this afternoon she looked *real* fine. That thing she'd done with her hair was . . . oh, shit, it was sexy. No two ways about it.

He was unaware of Will's presence until he nudged him on the arm. "Sweet lookin' babe," Will said, following his eyes. "*Real* sweet. She as good in the sack as she looks?"

The depth of anger that surged through James took him by surprise, but he turned neutral eyes on his brother. "I wouldn't know," he said flatly. "Aunie and I are barely acquainted." Why did people keep assuming otherwise?

"Good; then it won't make any difference to you if I take my best shot at her myself." It wasn't a question, and yet it was.

"Knock yourself out," James retorted through his teeth. His fool brother wasn't very bright if he couldn't see he didn't stand a snowball's chance in hell with a woman like Aunie.

Will shifted his weight from one foot to another for a moment. "Uh, listen, Jimmy," he finally said. "I was, uh, like wonderin' if I could borrow a few bucks. I've got a job interview Monday and I need a couple a things. Gotta look my best."

"What happened to your job at that nightclub?"

"Well, see, there was this hostess workin' there and an absolute babe she was, too. Legs that reached to heaven, tits out to here. Well, hell, Jimmy, how was I s'posed to know she was the owner's daughter? Anyway . . ."

"Never mind," James said wearily. "I think I've heard this story before." He fished his wallet out of his back pocket. "How much?"

"Well, uh, the rent's almost due and . . ."

James swore beneath his breath and replaced his

wallet. "C'mon. We'll go up to my place and I'll write you a check."

When they returned a short while later, Paul had arrived. He was standing by the bookcase, fingering Aunie's purse. His hand dropped to his side when James approached him. "Hiya, kid," he said, eyes darting uneasily, never alighting long on any one object.

"Hi yourself, Paul." James nudged the purse his brother had been fondling further back on the book-shelf. "This belongs to Aunie," he said in a low voice, watching his own thumb rub back and forth over the smooth leather. "She's a guest in this house."

Then his head whipped up and he impaled his brother with furious, moss green eyes. "You rip her off and I'll wring your junkie neck, Paul. You understand me?"

"Sure, Jimmy, sure." Paul thrust his hands in his pockets and hunched his shoulders. "I wasn't gonna open it; I was just feeling it. It's real leather, real soft."

"Yeah, right," James agreed cynically. "And if I'd walked in two minutes later, Aunie's cash would be history. Her purse too, probably, if you've managed to locate yourself a new fence."

He ignored his brother's protestations of innocence. Not too long ago James had hit the streets, contacting all the receivers of stolen goods whom he knew Paul to be currently using. By threatening them with every manner of mayhem and violence his fertile mind could conjure up if they continued to deal with his brother, he had temporarily shut off Paul's sources. Scum like that proliferated on the meaner city streets like rabbits in a hutch, however, and it was more than likely that his brother had already found someone new to replace those James had managed to scare away.

It was a never-ending battle that James felt he was steadily losing.

His brother had turned into a thief to support his cocaine habit and James didn't know what to do about it. He hated to give him too much cash, for then he felt he was enabling Paul in his addiction. Yet if he kept him in short funds, his brother stole. God, he was so tired of it all.

When Bob approached him a short while later, he braced himself for more bad news. It had rapidly been turning into that kind of day.

To his surprise, however, he was not asked for money. In fact, Bob was feeling pretty ebullient. "I can't pay you back yet, Jimmy," he said, thumping him on the back with a beefy hand. "But I wanted you to know that Satin Doll Limos is doin' pretty well. It started out a little slow, but business has been pickin' up lately and we've already got us several bookings for the Christmas season." His face split into a wide gun.

James felt the mellow mood with which he'd begun the day starting to seep back into his system, and he grinned, too. "That's the best news I've heard all day, Bobby."

"Yeah. And I wanted to tell ya that the artwork you did for the ad was good stuff. A couple customers mentioned it when they called in." He laughed, shaking his head in wonder. "I'm finally makin' something work out for myself and I gotta tell you, Jimmy, it feels good. It feels damn good."

"I'm proud of you, Bob."

"Proud of myself, Jimbo, proud of m'self. It's a real sweet feelin'."

Lola called everyone for dinner. Muriel admonished the children, who were at their own table, to settle down; and as soon as it quieted she said grace. Platters began to make the rounds.

"So, Otis," Bob said as he heaped turkey on his plate and then passed the platter. "When're you and Lola gonna have a couple little rug rats runnin' around here? You guys been married for—what?— five, six years now?"

"Seven," Otis replied quietly. "And we're workin' on it."

"Yeah, I can see where that'd be the fun part," Bob agreed amiably, not realizing that he'd blundered into a sensitive area. He accepted the bowl of mashed potatoes from Otis's sister and slapped a mound on his plate.

"I've told y' before, bro," Otis's brother said with a grin. "I'd be more than happy to lend my ser—"

"Leon," Aunie interrupted him. "Your mother tells me that you're a personal trainer at a local gym." She flashed him her most charming smile. "Tell me about it. I've been considering joinin' one ever since I came to town, but I don't have the first idea what to expect." Okay, so she had belonged to a club in Atlanta. She was still interested in what they had to offer up here. "Could someone like me become stronger without addin' all those bulky muscles?"

"Yeah, sure," Leon said enthusiastically and leaned forward to discourse on one of his favorite subjects. He forgot all about offering stud service to Lola.

Lola, in turn, shot a grateful glance Aunie's way, but the turkey she was eating seemed suddenly dry and tasteless. Damn it. Couldn't she get through just one day without worrying about her lack of fertility?

It was Thanksgiving, and the good Lord knew she had plenty of other things to be thankful for.

Beneath the table, Otis's massive hand squeezed her thigh.

She had Otis. That was the biggest blessing of her life. But when she thought of him, with that face and body of his that made him appear killer-mean, playing so gently this afternoon with his nieces and nephews, she wanted to cry. He should have his own children to dandle on his knee and roughhouse with. Little boys or little girls. It didn't matter which. He looked so formidable and rough if you didn't know him; yet he was the tenderest of men and he'd make an excellent father. He should *be* a father. Did it really matter so much if the children didn't come from her own womb?

For the first time, seated at the table surrounded by Otis's family and their friends, she gave serious consideration to the idea of adoption. She wasn't one hundred percent certain it was something she wanted to do. But she'd think about it.

Suddenly, her food had flavor once again.

The men attempted to sneak off to watch more football once dinner was complete, but Lola had other plans in mind for them. "If you think the woo-mons are gonna cook this dinner and then do all the cleanup, too, you have another think comin'," she said. "Clear the dishes."

"Ah, c'mon, Lola," Will wheedled. "That's woman's work."

"Wid thinkin' like that, Will Ryder," she retorted tartly, "it's no wonder I've never seen a female at one of these functions wid you." She handed him a stack of soiled dinner plates. "Get busy."

He looked to Otis, who shrugged and picked up

several platters. "Don't look at me, boy. I married me a strong-minded woman, just like my mama. I just do what she says."

Muriel patted Otis's cheek, then reached past him to gather up the serving bowls. "This here's the smartest of my boys," she said as she laughingly dodged the dish towel Leon whipped at her bottom.

Aunie was enthralled. Never had her own family interacted with such warmth and casualness. Thanksgivings at home had always been such formal affairs. The homes of her relatives had been more elegant, the table settings richer, and the food served and cleaned up by silent servants. But they hadn't been nearly as enjoyable.

"Jimmy looks right at home doin' woman's work," Bob called from the kitchen where he was drying plates passed to him by one of the Jackson children, who stood on a chair to rinse the dishes handed to him by his mother. He tugged James's ponytail when he passed by. "You ever gonna cut off all that hair, boy?"

"Nah, I thought I'd just grow it forever and give up wearing clothes. Save a few bucks that way."

The women hooted and made ribald comments that expressed unanimous approval at the idea of a naked James. Aunie tried very hard not to, but she could visualize that. Graphically. For in the picture that flashed through her mind, James's hair might reach the ground but it was still pulled back and clubbed at the nape of his neck with a rubber band. She shivered and industriously scrubbed down counters while she tried to conjure up less inflammatory images.

Late that night, as she lay in bed, she thought about

this holiday with the Jacksons and the Ryders. Difficult now to believe she'd actually dreaded it.

When she'd set off from Atlanta to move to an unknown city on her own, it had seemed like the hardest thing she'd ever done. But it was funny: Seattle was beginning to feel more like home than home ever had felt—that was due entirely, she acknowledged, to the warmth and acceptance of her new friends. And after today's test run of her ability to fit in, she felt she was finally ready to take the next step.

She was prepared to tackle a few acquaintances outside this apartment house.

CHAPTER 7

The private detective leaned back in his leather chair and gazed at his client across the massive expanse of his polished mahogany desk. His immediate impression was of a sophisticated man of obvious wealth. The P.I. wondered, however, if the client quite grasped just how expensive this prospective venture could become.

"You haven't given me much to go on, Mr. Cunningham," he said, and consulted the sparse notations on a yellow legal pad at his fingertips. "Your wife could be anywhere in the United States. She is probably using her maiden name, which is Franklin, and is possibly attending college. She has most likely opened an account at a bank, in which she will have deposited a sizable amount of money. The only correspondence that you are aware of her making is through her lawyer, although it is possible she may have contacted a man named Geoff Lemire." He looked up from his notes. "Have I left anything out?"

Wesley crossed his legs, fastidiously hitching his trousers until the creases were aligned just so. "No," he replied.

"As I said, it's not much." The detective tapped his gold pen against the pad. "Has she a particular friend anywhere? Someone she would go to who might help us narrow down the location?"

"No."

"Then I must warn you, sir, that it could take us a long time to locate her. The blue slip in the packet I gave you earlier specifies our rates." He watched the man pull out the slip and give it a cursory inspection. He appeared bored. "As you can see, with the amount of man-hours a case such as this could generate, the cost is likely to become most prohibitive."

Wesley didn't care how long it would take or what it was going to cost. That bitch had had him arrested and put through the public humiliation of a trial. He pulled his checkbook from the inside breast pocket of his custom-tailored suit jacket. He wrote for a moment and then detached the check, handing it across the desk. The private detective's eyebrows rose at the size of the retainer and Wesley rose to his feet.

"Find her," he said in a flat, emotionless voice and walked briskly from the office.

Aunie sat with a group of students at a long table in the campus cafeteria. She didn't contribute a great deal to the conversations swirling around her, but she nevertheless enjoyed being included in the camaraderie.

She was feeling pretty pleased with herself; she'd

followed through on her Thanksgiving Day resolution to extend her circle of acquaintances. Of particular pride was the way she'd done so without resurrecting her phony old social-butterfly persona, since it had always been a role that had felt fraudulent and forced. She'd created it originally as a tool to assist her in the fulfillment of her family's expectations, but she'd never felt comfortable with it.

She gave Lola and Otis the lion's share of credit for her new willingness to make herself accessible to others. From day one, the Jacksons had treated her with a natural, easy acceptance that had made her feel that just by being herself she was a worthwhile and valuable friend. Otis's description of her as a woman with attitude in all likelihood hadn't been anything more than a casual comment to him. But to Aunie it had been an enormous ego booster, going a long way toward giving her the courage to trust her true personality to strangers. Her reception by his family on Thanksgiving Day had given her further reinforcement.

She wasn't vivacious; she was quiet. But their acceptance helped her realize that that didn't necessarily preclude the possibility of people liking her anyway. Even James, she somewhat grudgingly admitted, had unknowingly added to her confidence, simply by aggravating her. She discovered she liked the way she acted around him. He irritated her so much sometimes, she completely forgot to be shy and became quite aggressive. She liked that; she liked it a lot. Except for her one defiance in divorcing Wesley, she'd never been particularly assertive, and learning that she was capable of standing up for her rights felt like a giant step forward in her quest for independence.

With a secret smile, she thought about the addi-

tional boost her self-assurance had received when
he'd kissed her that night in her apartment. Granted,
it was in an entirely different area, but she fiercely
hugged to her breast that isolated proof of her desirability as a woman.

"Anybody heard anything new on the caller?"

Aunie swallowed the french fry she'd been nibbling
and leaned forward to look at the speaker seated
further down the table. "What caller?"

Mary, a new friend who was seated on her right,
turned her head to look at her, her round blue eyes
even bigger than usual. "Haven't you heard about
the guy who's been calling the female students here?"

That prompted a niggling sense of familiarity, but
Aunie couldn't pinpoint its origin so she shook her
head.

Mary gave her a nudge. "Can I have a couple of your
fries?" she requested and Aunie pulled the cardboard
container along the table until it sat between them.
"Thanks." Mary helped herself.

Holding several fries suspended between container
and mouth, she said, "It's really creepy, Aunie. Some
guy keeps calling a bunch of the women students
here. No one knows how he gets their numbers, but
nearly a dozen women have filed complaints." She
leaned forward on her forearms and looked down
the table. "Joe. Pass the ketchup, will ya?" She poked
the fries into her mouth and half closed her eyes in
appreciation of their salty flavor.

"Obscene calls?" Aunie inquired.

"Not really," Mary replied with her mouth full,
then self-consciously covered her lips with her fingers.
"Sorry," she mumbled around them and swallowed.
Her face turned pink with embarrassment. "Jeez, not

only am I eating your food, I'm acting like a pig while I'm doing it."

Aunie smiled. "Help yourself," she invited. "I can't finish them all anyway." She butted Mary's shoulder with her own. "And relax, Mary. Emily Post isn't around, so who the heck cares if you have a couple fries in your mouth while you're talkin'? I won't tell if you don't tell. I'm more interested in what you were sayin'."

With her natural friendliness, curly blonde hair, and pretty voluptuousness, Mary was outgoing and well-liked. She had a natural confidence that came of knowing herself to be popular. Sometimes, however, she couldn't help comparing herself to Aunie's daintiness and obvious breeding, and the mental comparison tended to make her feel oversized and clownish. She found herself trying not to appear as slovenly in her manners and speech in Aunie's company, something she never particularly worried about with anyone else. Now, however, she grinned in appreciation of the way Aunie had rescued her from her own sense of awkwardness, filled with a warm glow of affection for her new friend. The more she got to know Aunie Franklin, the better she liked her.

She had noticed her, of course, when Aunie had first entered their trig class a week after the semester had begun. Hell, who hadn't? There was just something about her that had fascinated them all.

She was drop-dead gorgeous for one thing, and for all her diminutive size, she had the type of bearing that attracted a lot of attention. The guys in their lunch group had practically salivated over her, but she'd seemed rich, reserved, and sort of stand-offish, so everyone had pretty much given her a wide berth.

They'd sure talked about her, though. She appeared to be older than most of the students here and worlds more sophisticated. Her jeans were plain old Levi's and Lees like everyone else's, but she topped them with fabrics even the uninitiated could tell were ritzy. It was glaringly obvious she was from a very different background than the rest of them.

Speculation had run rampant about her reasons for attending a dinky little community college when she looked more the exclusive, ivy-league type. Neither Mary nor her lunch partners had entertained any real hope of ever having their curiosity satisfied, however, as Aunie had always sat alone in the cafeteria during lunch, her nose in her textbooks, and rarely had Mary seen her speak to anyone.

But she sure knew her stuff in the two classes they shared and it was obvious to everyone that she was smart. Therefore, when Mary ran into trouble understanding a particular assignment, she had picked Aunie to query about it. To her surprise, she had found her to be very friendly in a low-key sort of way.

She'd half expected to be politely rebuffed, but instead Aunie had immediately sat down with her and explained the mathematical process needed to solve the problems. When Mary'd still had a difficult time grasping the concept, Aunie had demonstrated the process in a number of different ways until she'd finally hit on one that Mary understood. Her patience had been phenomenal. She hadn't volunteered any private information during that time and she'd still sat off by herself at lunch, but she'd smiled at Mary when they'd caught each other's eye and had stopped to talk if she were spoken to first. It seemed a ludicrous notion, but Mary began to wonder if her aloofness might not actually be shyness.

Then the Monday after Thanksgiving, Aunie had

approached her and asked if she'd be interested in being her study partner. Mary had agreed enthusiastically and offered to introduce her to the group with whom she ate lunch. Prepared to have Aunie reject the suggestion, Mary had been surprised when instead she'd accepted with every appearance of pleasure.

In view of everything they'd said behind her back, the lunch group had been a little stiff in her presence at first. Her quiet warmth and graciousness had ultimately worked on them the way it had on Mary, however, and by degrees everyone had begun to relax around her. There was still a lot Mary didn't know about Aunie, but she felt that they were nonetheless slowly becoming friends.

"So, where was I?" she asked.

"Oozing potatoes between your teeth," Joe retorted and passed the ketchup.

"What a charmer you are," Aunie rebuked him in her mannerly way but took the sting out of her gentle reprimand with a smile. She prompted Mary, "I asked if the calls were obscene and you said not exactly."

"Oh, yeah." Mary curled her lip at a flushed Joe before she turned her attention to Aunie. "The caller doesn't make sexual suggestions or talk dirty, from what I've heard, but what he does is almost worse. He seems to know all sorts of personal stuff about the women he calls." She shivered. "Can you imagine anything creepier than having some total stranger know everything about you? Take Alice Zablinski, for instance. She just got engaged the other night, and practically before her boyfriend finished putting the ring on her finger, this creep was on the phone describing the weight and shape of the stone."

"It was the next day that he called," one of the girls sitting further down the table contradicted her.

"Close enough." Mary shrugged. "Aunie knew what I meant." She leaned into the petite brunette at her side and murmured, "God, what a fussy attention to detail. My version has more flair, don't you think?"

Aunie's dimples flashed in amusement. "Entirely more dramatic," she agreed.

Other students sitting at the table began to contribute stories they had heard about the man they'd nicknamed the Campus Caller. The whole affair sounded strange and disturbing, but Aunie was affected the way she might have been by one of those gory slasher movies that teenagers seemed to love. She was repulsed by the anonymous caller's actions, but basically felt removed from them. Perhaps it was because she didn't know any of the principals involved or perhaps it was simply because she had concerns of her own that seemed more pressing.

Either way, she didn't feel it had all that much to do with her.

The next several weeks in Aunie's life were a healing period. Determined to go forward rather than stagnate in fear, she put Wesley and the injustice the legal system had dealt her out of her mind, concentrating on the present. Her friendships with both Lola and Mary deepened, and her confidence grew daily.

It used to be she mentally cringed at comments on her looks. She had always feared that, should they suddenly disappear, it would be discovered there was nothing of substance behind them and she'd be exposed as a fraud. Attractively cased, she'd been afraid people would say, but basically a nonperson. One didn't have to be overly endowed in the intelligence department to realize that an accident of genes did not constitute a personal accomplishment.

Recently, however, she'd discovered she possessed something much more consequential than good bones and flawless skin: She had a brain. It was a realization that made her feel truly substantial for perhaps the very first time in her life.

It still amazed her that she should be drawn to math and computers, of all things. She hadn't even seen a computer back in high school, except for a basic keyboarding class, and she'd barely scraped by in math. On the other hand, she had never taxed herself in an attempt to comprehend either. She'd taken her family's assessment of her intelligence at face value and automatically assumed she was lacking in the necessary mental fortitude required for the precise sciences.

She'd had no choice but to take a required math class when she'd signed up for college following her divorce from Wesley, and she'd enrolled in a computer course in an attempt to drag her skills kicking and screaming into the nineties. Determined to gain a well-rounded education, she had struggled to understand them at least well enough to get a passing grade. To her amazement, by the end of the year she'd begun to believe she had an actual aptitude for mathematics and computers. To test herself, she'd loaded her schedule with an abundance of both when she'd picked her courses at the community college in Seattle. Each day that passed with an increase in her comprehension skills added to her growing self-esteem. Now she was tentatively beginning to believe she might actually possess what it took to go the distance toward a goal she never would have dreamed, a few short months ago, she was smart enough to tackle. Software engineering.

Mary's friendship was an additional ego booster. Aunie was treated by her new friend as if she were a card-packing member of Mensa.

One day, studying in Aunie's apartment, Mary suddenly threw her pencil on the table and flopped back in her chair in disgust. "I don't understand this stuff at all," she snarled, plowing her fingers through her curly hair. "God, I'll be lucky if I pull a C out of this course. Why can't I be smart like you?" She scowled across the table. "Forget your dainty bone structure and that skin; I'd give a bundle to have half your brains."

"Oh, Mary, honestly?" Aunie's dimples punched deep into her cheeks as she smiled radiantly at her friend. "I think that's probably the nicest thing anyone has ever said to me."

Mary propped her chin in her palm and chewed on her pinkie finger. "Oh, yeah, right," she said skeptically. "Like you don't know you're the brain of the CC calculus circuit."

"It's news to me," Aunie replied with perfect honesty. "Until this past year, I never suspected I had any sort of brain at all."

"You kiddin' me? I figured you for one of those whiz-kid genius types. Brains *and* beauty—what a gagger. I couldn't figure out what you were doing at this rinky-dink community college."

"I'm here because my high school grades weren't good enough to get me in anywhere else." Aunie laughed. "Gawd, but you're good for my ego."

"Glad to hear it," Mary replied glumly, picking up her pencil. "Anytime it needs a stroke, just give me a jingle. But in the meantime, I really need you to help me understand this shit.''

"C'mon, c'mon," Mary muttered, leaning on the buzzer. "I didn't slog through the rain for four stinking blocks for this." There was still no answer. "Damn!"

She hesitated, then pressed the button beneath the label that read Manager.

Static crackled. "May I help you?"

Mary leaned into the speaker. "Yes, please. My name is Mary Holloman . . . I'm a friend of Aunie's. Apparently she's not home and I was wondering if I could leave a message for her."

"She has told me of you," the exotically accented voice replied in a calm, lilting cadence. "Please to come in. You will find her on the second floor learnin' from the mons how to paint." The intercom crackled again, then fell silent. An instant later the door buzzed and Mary pushed it open. As she climbed the stairs she thought to herself—for about the hundredth time—what an enigma Aunie Franklin was.

Apparently, she'd discussed her with the woman with the accent; yet she'd never said a word to Mary in return about the exotic-sounding woman. Aunie had told her a little about her upbringing, enough to explain, anyway, why she was unceasingly flattered at Mary's unshakable opinion of her as a brain. Mary had an intuitive feeling, however, that there was more to Aunie's story than she had yet heard.

She truly hoped that someday they'd be close enough for Aunie to trust her with the entire story of her life. She was endlessly interested in her and

thought they had the potential for a deep and lasting
friendship.

"Dammit, Aunie, don't slop!" Mary heard a masculine voice say irritably just before she reached the top
of the stairs.

"You bumped the ladder!"

"I was nowhere near the damn ladder."

"Oh, sure. If that isn't just like a man to weasel
out of taking responsibility." There was a rumble of
choked laughter that was hastily turned into a deep-
timbre cough. Then Aunie's voice again, saying with
sweet insincerity, "It was all my fault, Mistah Rydah,
Ah'm sure. I am evah so sorry."

"You'll *be* sorry, if you don't stop with that mister
bullshit. I've wised up to you, Magnolia—I know
damn well you just do it to piss me off."

"Why, James, I'm appalled you should think such
a thing."

"Like hell. You're probably tickled pink that it
works."

Mary stood a few steps away from the top of the
stairs and eavesdropped with unabashed fascination.
She and Aunie shared a kindred sense of humor and
over the past few weeks they'd laughed together quite
a bit. For the most part, however, she was accustomed
to her friend's habit of being gracious but somewhat
distant to most of the people she came into contact
with. She'd never before heard her quite like this, all
feisty and argumentative. It was yet one more facet
revealed in a multifaceted personality. Mary grinned
and bounded up the remaining stairs.

She caught sight of Aunie standing on a ladder
between two men who looked like they'd be right at
home in a street brawl, and she paused, eyeing her
friend's companions warily. The black man was gigan-

tic and looked like he ate babies for breakfast. It probably had something to do with that bald, scarred head and massive physique. The other one, the blonde with the ponytail, while lankier and nowhere as tall as his dark-skinned buddy, was still solidly built; and his eyes, drilling holes at the moment into Aunie's back, were *not* civilized. His expression suggested he was the type who'd dare to do just about anything. Mary was a little surprised that Aunie had the nerve to give him any lip—hell, to sass either of them, for that matter.

Then she shrugged. First impressions weren't always the best criteria to judge a person's worth by . . . look how wrong she'd been about Aunie. Obviously, if Aunie was comfortable enough to jerk a few chains with impunity, then she must be fairly friendly with the two men. Mary grinned once again in a humorous sort of wonder. They weren't exactly the type of company she'd have expected her well-bred little friend to be keeping.

Mary set herself in motion once again. "I expected you to be crackin' the books, Franklin," she called as she strolled down the hallway. No one had noticed her arrival as they'd painted the wall, and in unison their heads swung around at the sound of her voice.

"Mary!" Aunie's voice was warm and welcoming. She set her paint pad carefully in the tray attached to her ladder and wiped her paint-splattered hands on the black smock she wore.

"It's a damn good thing you're home," Mary informed her as she walked up to the three of them. "I came to study with you for tomorrow's final and I had to park four blocks away. Four blocks! It's pouring out there and I wasn't a happy camper when you didn't answer your buzzer. Luckily, there was a lady with a pretty accent in the manager's apartment, and she told me what you were doing and let me in. My name is Mary," she said in a friendly aside to the two men. "Who are you?"

"I'm sorry," Aunie said, climbing off the ladder. "I should have introduced you. This is my friend Mary Holloman," she said to the men. "Mary, this is James Ryder and Otis Jackson. It was Otis's wife Lola to whom you spoke."

"Nice to meet you," Mary said and immediately turned back to Aunie. "What are you doing painting walls during finals week? I thought I'd find you hip-deep in textbooks."

"I needed a break from studying," Aunie replied. "So Otis and James offered me the opportunity to learn how to paint." She gestured at the wall behind them and smiled happily. "Isn't it great? I've never done this before."

Puzzled by Aunie's attitude, which seemed to suggest that a very special favor had been bestowed on her, Mary turned to study the two men. "Big of you to make her such a generous offer," she said skeptically. Both of them just grinned, and their smiles gave Mary her first glimmer of the personalities behind the tough, street-aware exteriors. She couldn't help smiling back before she returned her attention to Aunie. "Speaking of breaks, when's your last final?"

"Friday morning."

"My last one is on Thursday afternoon. Let's go out Friday night and celebrate, whataya say?"

"Just you and me?"

"Yeah. Slap on some red lipstick and curl your hair. I know a good bar where the music's hot and the men are good-lookin'."

"Ooh." Aunie regarded her friend with interested eyes. "I'll wear somethin' short and tight. And my highest heels."

"That's the ticket." Mary grasped Aunie by the arm. "Well, I'm sure you'll excuse us, fellas," she said to the two men. Otis was still smiling, but she observed that James was regarding her with eyes that had become abruptly unfriendly. She gave them both her sweetest smile. "I'm afraid your paint job will just have to get along without Aunie's help. We've got studying to do." She dragged Aunie down the hall.

"Thanks for showin' me how," Aunie called back over her shoulder as she trotted to keep up with her taller friend. She laughed at something Mary murmured to her and then a moment later her apartment door banged closed behind them.

The men resumed painting. It was silent for several moments before Otis said with thoughtful slowness, "I imagine that little gal will look mighty fine in somethin' short and tight, wearin' her highest heels." He turned guileless ebony eyes on James. "Don't you?"

James slapped his pad into the tray with unnecessary force, splashing white paint over the rim. He swore softly, staring blindly at the mess. Then he turned green eyes on his friend. They were wiped free of all expression. "Yeah," he replied emotionlessly. "I'm sure she'll look just fine."

"*Real* fine," Otis ruthlessly amended. He wasn't above twisting the screw a bit. Jimmy was usually self-aware to a fault. Lately, however, he'd been downright obtuse.

"Sure," James agreed flatly. "Real fine."

* * *

Aunie and Mary jostled for space in front of the mirror in Aunie's tiny bathroom. Being the smallest, Aunie stood in front. She pulled down her lower eyelid and carefully applied liner. Satisfied with the results, she picked up the mascara wand but paused, meeting Mary's eyes in the mirror.

"I don't know quite how to say this without sounding rude," she said, "but I was really pleased that it was only you and me going out tonight." She stroked a coat of brown-black onto her lashes. "It's not that I'm not appreciative of the way you've introduced me to everyone or that I don't like them, you understand. It's just that most of them seem so . . . *young.*"

"They are young," Mary replied around the lipstick she was carefully applying.

"And untried and innocent."

Mary laughed. "And you aren't?" She blotted her lips on a tissue and used the side of her little finger to remove a minuscule smear that had strayed outside the natural lines.

"In some ways, perhaps. But in others . . ." Aunie hesitated. Then, lowering the hand she had raised to apply her own lipstick, she met Mary's eyes in the mirror and told her about her marriage. She intuitively felt she could trust Mary with her private life, and if she couldn't . . . well, she'd find out soon enough.

She liked Mary's response. She didn't exclaim or commiserate. Instead, she listened quietly, and when Aunie was finished speaking, she reached out and squeezed her shoulder. "I've been married, too," she confided in return. "My story isn't as dramatic as yours; in fact it's pretty common. But it was still painful to me." Her voice trailed off.

"What happened?" Aunie inquired.

Mary gave her a tiny, wry smile and then reached past her to pick up her earring off the shelf. She hooked it through the hole in her ear. "You've probably heard it a million times. We got married too young and then grew in different directions. I wasn't even eighteen yet, and Billy was nineteen."

When she didn't say anything further, Aunie pulled a brush through her hair for several silent strokes, then ventured to say in a soft voice "Things just didn't work out?"

"No, things didn't work out." Mary looked pensive then made an effort to shake off the gloomy mood that had settled over them. She fluffed her curly hair. "Well, this is getting pretty grim. Hell of a way to start a celebration, don't you think?"

A horn honked out on the street and Aunie gave Mary the hip. "That's probably our cab. Let's go paint the town."

They were laughing as they tripped through the front entrance of the apartment house and they didn't see James coming up the walk until they'd barrelled into him. Aunie bounced off the worn, soft surface of his leather jacket and might have fallen if he hadn't grabbed her shoulders to steady her.

He looked down at her, noting the red lipstick. It accentuated that damned little mole over her upper lip. "That's right," he said. "It's your big night out, isn't it?" His eyes ran slowly down the rest of her. "Well, don't keep me in suspense, Magnolia. Unbutton your coat; let's see how you look."

His voice was perfectly level, but Aunie picked up an intimation of something uncivilized beneath the

surface. She peered up at him with a trace of suspicion, but she was unable to decide if it was justified.
His eyes were noncommittal; his tone was not snide,
so maybe it was only in her imagination that he'd
managed to make a straightforward request assume
the connotation of stripping down to the skin. But
just in case it wasn't . . .

Chin rising fractionally, she unfastened her coat
and spread it open. She struck a deliberately sexy
pose. "Whataya think?"

Ho-ly shhh . . . James's Adam's apple rode the column of his throat as he swallowed dryly. She hadn't
been kidding when she'd said she was going to wear
something short and tight. "You look like you're
ready for that red-hot affair, Aunie," he said through
a tight throat. His eyes rose slowly from their intense
contemplation of her body to spear into hers. "Have
fun."

Abruptly, he turned and strode away. The front
door clicked softly closed behind him.

Mary looked at Aunie quizzically as they climbed
into the taxi. "What is it with you and that guy?"

"What?" Aunie asked vaguely. All those feelings
she'd managed to suppress from that night in her
apartment had suddenly resurfaced with a vengeance.

Mary jerked her thumb at the rear window of the
cab in the direction of the receding apartment house.
"What was that all about?"

Her unapologetic curiosity was like pulling the plug
in Aunie's dammed-up emotions, and words tumbled
from her lips in a near incoherent rush. "Oh, gawd,
Mary, I've been so stupid. Like an idiot I told him
I'd like to have a red-hot affair. I don't know what
possessed me—it's just a fantasy I have; I'd never have
the nerve to actually instigate any such thing, and

why I should brag to James, of all people . . ." She shrugged. "Well, anyway, he said not to expect to have it with him, and Lola said he was a hot kisser but I poo-pooed the idea, so then he *kissed* me. Before I knew it, I was plastered up against the door with my legs wrapped around his waist and his hands gripping my rear end, being kissed to within an inch of my life; and Mary, I've never felt anything like that in my *life*, and I wanna have an affair, only I want to have it with *him*, but that's never gonna happen 'cuz he told me so, so now I'm even worse off than I was before I opened my big mouth . . ." Her words choked in her throat as she ran out of breath.

Mary's eyes were round with amazement. "Jeez," she said admiringly, "you sure do lead an interesting life."

Aunie's bark of laughter was tinged with hysteria.

"I wouldn't be too sure about not getting your affair with him either," Mary advised. "Did you see his face when you opened your coat? He looked at you like you were the reincarnation of his hottest wet dream."

"He didn't!"

"Yeah, yeah, he did. This is the second time I've seen the two of you together, and both times there's been this atmosphere around you like some big electrical storm brewing. He might say he doesn't want an affair with you, but I'd lay odds that right about now he's chafing something fierce over the thought of you having one with someone else."

"Oh, I doubt that," Aunie replied with total honesty, but acknowledged to herself that the thought was immensely cheering. "In any case, let's forget about him and just have a good time."

And they did. The bar Mary had picked was dim

and atmospheric, the drinks strong, the band good if loud, and the men flatteringly attentive. Her feet were sore from dancing, her throat hoarse from shouting to be heard over the music, and she freely admitted she was a tiny bit inebriated by the time the taxi dropped Mary at her car and then pulled up in front of Aunie's apartment house. She paid the driver and climbed out of the cab.

Humming off-tune, she executed an intricate dance step up the walk. Suddenly she tripped over an unseen object and in her quest to keep her balance dropped her purse. It fell to the walk, scattering its contents.

"Well, shit," she muttered. Squatting down, she began to retrieve the strewn contents. The lipstick had rolled down the walk; her brush was lying against the door. She began to giggle as she plucked stray change and bills off the ground and stuffed them back into her evening bag. "ID, ID, ID," she whispered to herself as the Georgia driver's license she used for identification continued to elude her. "Wherefore art thou, IDeo . . . ahah!" It had slipped off the walk and was resting near the trunk of the rhododendron. "Slippery little beggar," she murmured and reached for it. Depositing it in her bag, she rose to her feet, staggering slightly as the alcohol in her system shifted her center of gravity. "Whoops." It might be prudent, she decided tipsily, to get inside and go to bed before someone caught her making a spectacle of herself. She'd hate for either Lola or James to see her in this condition. In truth she didn't often drink, but undoubtedly after the way she'd blown bubbles in her wine the night Wesley was acquitted, she'd have a hard time convincing them it was a fact. Not, at any rate, if they could see her now. Instead, they would probably think she was the worst sort of lush.

She was inserting her key in the lock when the early-morning silence was broken by the sound of a car a few blocks away traveling much too fast for the narrow, residential streets. The sound grew, obviously heading at dangerously high speed in this direction. Then suddenly it was roaring up the block. Aunie had extracted her key from the lock and was opening the door, but her head whipped around just as the car screeched to a halt in the street directly in front of the apartment house. The passenger door opened and she caught just the briefest glimpse of two large men before a body was roughly shoved out of the car. Something rude was yelled; glass exploded against the curb, the door was pulled closed with a slam, and the car picked up speed again. It roared away as the person so summarily discarded rolled twice across the grass parking strip before flopping to a standstill.

Oh, my Gawd. Aunie stared in horror at the inert form. Her first impulse was to rouse James or Otis, but bleary logic demanded she at least check the person to determine what sort of aid was needed She forced herself to move, ashamed that her first thought was not compassion for the injured's plight but rather embarrassment for herself, knowing James was going to learn she'd drunk too much after all. She propped open the front door with her evening bag and made her way down the walk, approaching the body cautiously.

The person moaned deep in his throat as Aunie squatted down next to him, giving her the first indication he was male. It had all happened so fast, but when the car's interior light had blinked on she had glimpsed a flash of thick, straight blond hair, which she'd mistakenly thought feminine. Even curled face-down in the fetal position, however, she could see there was too much bulk, too much breadth of shoulder for this to be a woman. She reached out and grasped a leather-covered shoulder, rolling the man onto his back. The texture of the jacket beneath her hand registered familiarly the merest instant before she saw the man's face, half obscured by a wing of loose blond hair.

Oh, God. Aunie's hand flew reflexively to her breast. It was James and he'd been badly beaten.

CHAPTER 8

James knew he was in the wrong frame of mind for a return to the old neighborhood even as he headed there. He harbored a passionate dislike of the Terrace in general and its dark alleys where drug deals went down twenty-four hours a day in particular; yet here he was, heading for that very destination in the wake of a frantic call from Paul.

He cruised the streets slowly, looking for his brother. God, he'd worked so hard to get away from this place. The day he had finally saved enough money to move out, he'd sworn he'd never be back. It was a promise he'd been forced to break again and again, for his brothers didn't seem to share his abhorrence for the project. Bobby with his loan sharks and Paul with his drug buys, his dealings in stolen merchandise, had drawn James back more times than he could count. Someone had to extricate them from whatever mess they were currently embroiled in, and if he didn't do it, who would? Other than him, there was only Will, who unfortunately was more inclined to think with his dick than his brain. James shook his head at the thought of his younger brother being responsible for anyone. Hell, Will needed to be rescued nearly as often as the other two, although in his defense James had to admit that *he* at least usually managed to get into trouble in a less dangerous part of town.

James's resentment of his brothers' propensity for drawing him into their never-ending predicaments had been growing steadily over the past year. They wouldn't grow up, which effectively prevented him from outgrowing his background. And *that* had long been one of his fiercest ambitions.

But he also loved them. In the back of his mind there lurked memories of a time before the advent of the Jackson family into his life, memories of a time when Bobby and Paul in particular were all that had stood between him and the dark influence of the streets. He loved them; he hated them for what they were doing to his life and their own. No matter which direction he approached it from, however, the bottom line always came down to the fact that he had to do whatever needed to be done to keep them safe. They were his family.

Blocking out any thoughts that didn't directly apply to his reasons for being there had always been James's first rule of survival when he entered the Terrace. Lack of attention could be deadly in this part of town, but tonight he found it difficult to command the necessary concentration. Was Aunie home yet? he wondered. Maybe she'd met someone with whom she could instigate that red-hot affair. Christ, he hadn't been able to get that damned dress out of his mind, and she'd been out in public in it all night long. Guys must have been hitting on her right and left.

He'd been restlessly prowling through the rooms of his home when Paul's call had interrupted him. Even now, when he should be focusing every ounce of concentration on finding his brother, his mind was only partly attuned to locating him. His thoughts kept drifting back to his second-floor apartment where he'd been pacing for hours, haunting the windows overlooking the street. It grated on him to know he'd been waiting and watching for the arrival of the taxi that would bring her home.

His headlights, as he slowly cruised the streets, swept across dark corners and illuminated the hollow-eyed denizens of the night. Prostitutes in stiletto heels, fake furs, and overblown hair styles leaned into car windows or lounged against storefront walls; pimps decked out in garish colors and rich fabrics cruised by, driving pricy cars; junkies with nervous mannerisms cut deals with their contrastingly imperturbable suppliers. So far, however, he'd hadn't caught so much as a glimpse of his brother. He wondered just what the hell kind of mess Paul had gotten himself into this time. He'd merely said he needed help, had given him a general location where he could be found, and had hung up.

Then suddenly he was there, easing out of an alley as James pulled up to a light. He pulled open the passenger door and climbed in. "Hit it, Jimmy," he directed, looking uneasily over his shoulder. "We gotta get out of here."

James was in no mood to take orders. He draped his forearm over the steering wheel and turned to face his brother. "What the hell's goin' on?" he demanded.

"I'll tell ya as soon as we're outta here, okay? *Move.*"

James had just put the Jeep in gear when a car came roaring up on his tail, headlights off. "Oh, shit," Paul whispered as the driver's door was wrenched open and James was hauled from the seat. Another face appeared at his window. Swiftly, he punched down the lock on his side, slid over into the driver's seat, and ground the ignition to start the car that had stalled when James's foot was jerked from the clutch. "Bobby's," he yelled and roared off into the night.

That left James facing two very large, very muscular, no-neck men, and one look was all he needed to know he was way out of his league on this one. He'd faced enforcers before, but these two had the emotionless eyes of professionals. Enforcers from Hell, he decided with dark humor. He'd never dealt with pros before and there was a difference to this situation that he intuitively recognized. Twisted humor and fast talking weren't going to get him out of it; neither was tough language nor an intimation of violence. These two looked right at home with violence; they looked, in fact, as though they'd been weaned on it, and he had a sinking feeling that nothing short of a semiautomatic would be capable of slowing them down.

Which he didn't have. *And,* he was working blind, not having the first inkling what Paul had been up to. Son of a fuckin' bitch. He was dead.

He stuck his hands in his pockets and smiled at his adversaries. "Hey."

Okay, the cocky attitude was probably a mistake, he thought as the one with the stubbled skull hauled him off the ground where his partner's punch had landed him. He was jerked to his feet by his ponytail, his head craned back to a painful degree. Jesus. He wasn't exactly a lightweight himself, but these two were practically as wide as they were tall and every inch of them was solid muscle.

"Doan speak 'less yer spoken to and doan give us no shit, you long-haired freak," said the one with the intricately shaven pattern in his close-cropped black hair. "Unnerstand?"

"Yeah."

"Where'd the weasel go?"

"I don't know . . ." This time the blow doubled him over, but the knee to his jaw straightened him right back up again. He sagged in Stubble-skull's grasp and gingerly touched his tongue to a loosened front tooth. *Let them leave my hands alone*, was all he could think. *Oh God, they can do anything else. Just let them leave my hands alone.*

"I *said*, where'd the weasel go?"

"I don't know what the fuck's goin' on," James answered truthfully. "He gave me a call to pick him up and I'd just done so when you two showed up. What'd he do?"

"Tried to rip off his dealer, freak."

Oh, wonderful, he really was dead. "I don't know anything about . . ." Stubble-skull took a giant step backward and gave him a vicious knee-punch to the kidneys.

"Lookit all this pretty blond hair," the man said in his gravelly voice. "I think we got us a girly-boy, Butch."

Butch, James thought blearily. Jesus, it figured.

His head was yanked back so hard the rubber band holding his hair clubbed at the nape of his neck split. He looked up into Stubble-skull's eyes and what he saw there did not reassure him. "You a split-tail, boy?"

"No."

Fancy-cut's foot kicked him swiftly in the crotch and James sagged completely within the hold of the man behind him. Nausea rushed up his throat. "How 'bout that," Fancy-cut murmured. "Boy sure enough does have balls. Who woulda thunk it? Course, he ain't gonna feel much like dancin' with the ladies tonight."

They worked him over with systematic thoroughness after that, removed his wallet from his hip pocket, then stuffed him in their car. He kept drifting in and out of consciousness, only vaguely aware of his surroundings. He was surprised, therefore, when he peered through one slitted eye and recognized his own neighborhood. The two hoods were passing a pint of Cutty Sark back and forth and listening to a country-and-western station on the car stereo.

"This here was in the nature of a warnin', freak," Stubble-skull said as they roared up his block. "Tell the weasel he's a dead man, he ever tries to do what he did again. We even see him on our turf, he's gonna get the same as you." The car slammed to a stop, throwing James against the dash. The door was opened, and the next thing he knew, James was sailing toward the curb. He passed out cold the instant he hit the parking strip.

Soft hands were cautiously brushing his hair from his face when he came to. "James?" a softly accented voice whispered. "Jimmy? Oh, gawd." He felt the soft-skinned fingers move down to his throat and press against his pulse. "Please, please, please," he heard her whisper. "Wake up. James, can you heah me?"

He pried open one eyelid. There were two Aunies

hovering over him, their coats open to showcase that damned short dress that hugged her curves like a second skin. Slowly, the two images coalesced into one. He licked his split lip, tasting blood. "Aunie?" He felt ridiculously pleased that she hadn't gone home with some stranger after all.

"Oh, James, thank God you're awake! Wait heah, I'm goin' to get Otis. No, Otis is at work. Ah'll call an ambulance. Anyhow, I'll be right back. Don't try to move." She started to rise to her feet, but James's hand reached out and gripped a handful of her coat, staying her.

"No ambulance," he croaked. "Just help me get up to my apartment."

"Don't be foolish, James," she argued heatedly. "You need medical attention. Now let me go—"

"No." His fist tightened on her coat and she nearly toppled on top of him. "Help me up."

"Jim-meee," she moaned in protest, unconsciously using the name his brothers and Otis generally used. "At least let me get Lola to help."

"There's no sense wakin' her up. We can do this."

"Gawd, you're stubborn." She squatted down as he gingerly pushed himself to a sitting position and maneuvered her shoulder under his armpit. It was a struggle, but she finally got him to his feet where he swayed weakly, sweating freely and swearing. Standing, the top of her shoulder only came to his diaphragm, so she wrapped her right arm around his waist, looped his left arm over her shoulder and held him in place by gripping his big, rawboned wrist in her left hand. Inch by agonizing inch, they shuffled up the walk and through the door.

Aunie leaned him against the wall while she retrieved her purse from where it had been propping open the exterior door. She hung the evening bag around her neck by its golden chain and approached James. His eyes were closed and he was breathing heavily. "How're you doin'?" she whispered anxiously.

One eye opened a crack, showing the merest glimmer of moss green behind its swollen purple lid. "I love your accent."

Aunie swallowed an hysterical urge to giggle. "Do you?" she managed to reply. "My mama always said it made me sound downright common."

James made a rude noise and in his pain forgot his policy of never criticizing another's family. "Your mama sounds like a real pain in the ass," he said roughly and reached for her. "Ready to tackle the stairs?"

"I think so. The question is are *you*?"

"Yeah. Might as well get it over with. You gonna be able to navigate in those heels?"

Aunie looked down at her four-inch spikes. "Oh. Maybe I'd better remove them. I'd hate to be responsible for toppling us down the stairs." She took them off and stuffed them in her coat pockets.

With her shoes removed, the top of her shoulders only came to his abdomen but she followed the same procedure as before, arm around his waist, his arm over her shoulder, securing him by her grip on his wrist. James's strength was deserting him fast and he leaned on her more heavily with every step they climbed. They were both perspiring by the time they neared the top of the stairs. Suddenly, he started to overbalance and Aunie threw her weight at his torso to direct him into the wall rather than allowing him to tumble headlong down the flight of thinly carpeted steps. They banged up against the wall and James groaned low in his throat as every muscle in his body

protested the twin battering of being caught between
her resilient weight and the ungiving plaster surface.
"God," he said between his teeth. "And here I always
thought you were such a lightweight."

"I'm sorry," she wailed, stepping back to relieve
him of her weight but gripping his biceps and
pressing them into the wall to keep him upright. She
tried to evaluate his condition by the expression on
his face. "Are you all right?"

"Yeah. Give me a second to catch my breath."

"I swear I'll never drink again," Aunie muttered
to herself. "Never, never, never."

James tipped his chin into his neck and peered
down at her. "You been hitting the bottle again,
Magnolia?"

"Honestly, James, I'm not ordinarily much of a
drinker," she avowed. If he'd thought he could have
gotten away with it without inflicting a great deal of
pain on his abused mouth, he would have grinned
at her big owl eyes as she stared up at him with such
solemn sincerity. "You've just caught me in a couple
of weak moments."

"Nobody thinks you're a lush, sugar. That is . . .
you did use a glass this time, didn't you?"

"Oh! You are such a *pig*!" She laughed throatily
and spontaneously swung a playful punch at his chest.
Remembering his injuries just in the nick of time,
she pulled her punch before contact was made.
"Think you can make it the last few steps?"

"Yeah." He cautiously straightened and drew a for-
tifying breath. "Let's go."

They were at his door before he remembered his
lack of keys. Propped weakly against the wall, eyes
closed, he swore with creative fluency for several
moments. "Paul gets my keys, my car . . . I get his

beating. That son of a bitch; I think I'm gonna kill him myself." He rolled his head and opened one eye to peer at Aunie. "I'm sorry, Magnolia. I guess you'll have to wake up Lola after all."

Aunie bit her lip in indecision. Then, resigned, she slipped to his side once again and assumed the position. "C'mon," she said wearily and led him down the hall to her door.

She hesitated inside until he said tersely, "Bathroom." Once there she flipped down the cover on the toilet and eased him onto it. Through a haze of exhaustion, he watched her divest herself of her coat and toss it out into the hall. She helped him out of his leather jacket and tossed it carelessly after her own. Then she swept aside a clutter of cosmetics, opened the medicine chest and began removing half its contents, lining the items up on the counter like tin soldiers on parade. Filling the basin with warm water, she dipped in a clean washcloth, wrung out the excess moisture, and gingerly cleaned the dried blood from his face. "I still think we ought to get you a doctor. There's a gash over your eyebrow that looks as though it could use a few stitches."

"Just slap a Band-Aid™ on it," he said without opening his eyes. "I'll be fine."

"Oh, big, tough man," she snapped, angry that he was taking this so lightly. His face was a mess, and someone with more medical expertise than she possessed should be caring for him properly.

"I am tough, Aunie," he reassured her, "and the guys who did this were professionals. They aim for the maximum amount of pain with the minimum amount of permanent damage. Help me outta this shirt will you? The collar's getting soaked."

She set down the cotton ball she had just soaked

in hydrogen peroxide and reached for his sleeve, efficiently unbuttoning and stripping the shirt from his shoulders. Her breath hissed in sharply. "Oh, James, look at you." Her fingers skimmed lightly over the bruises on his chest and stomach. "Who did this to you?"

"I told you . . . professionals."

"Yes, I heard you, but what does that *mean?*"

He stared at her. He'd forgotten that she was innocent of the sort of experience he took for granted, and the sudden reminder made him feel lousy for exposing her to the dark realities that often comprised his life. Christ, he'd been rolling in filth for so long, he sometimes forgot that not everybody did. Aunie, however, was like no one he had ever known: so pristine and untouched. And right now she felt sorry for him because he was hurt. If she ever realized even a fraction of the things that he had seen or done, it'd make her sick. *He'd* make her sick. Tonelessly, he said, "That's not important. It wasn't meant for me, specifically. It was meant for Paul. I just got caught in the middle."

Aunie didn't understand any of this, but she held her peace and silently disinfected the cuts on his face. She pinched together the edges of the gash over his eyebrow and applied several strips of adhesive, hoping it would be adequate. On impulse, she leaned down and pressed her lips gently to the bandage.

James went very still. "What are you doing?"

"Kissing it better." Embarrassed, she busied herself cleaning up.

James had been taking care of himself and everyone around him for so long now, he didn't rightly know how to react to being mothered. He was tempted to point out several other areas that could stand kissing better, but he feared it would offend or embarrass her. So rather than say the wrong thing, he decided to say nothing at all. But that little gesture made him feel good. It made him feel real good.

"I've got some pain pills left over from . . . well, left over," Aunie said. "You want one?"

"Yeah."

"Here." She tipped the prescription bottle over his open palm. "You're probably twice my weight, so it should be safe to take two."

He washed them down with water and then she helped him to his feet. They were in her bedroom before he realized where she was leading him, but the instant he did he came to a halt. "I can't take your bed."

"Yes, you can. The couch is long enough for me, but it wouldn't be for you. Don't argue with me, James," she commanded with credible authority when he showed signs of digging in his heels. "Just get in the damn bed. I'm not in the mood for an argument." She left him upright if slightly swaying while she flipped back the covers.

He was too tired to argue. "I've got to call Bobby first."

"Give me the number and I'll call him. You get in bed before you fall on your face."

"Yes, ma'am," he said with uncharacteristic meekness, recited the number, and lowered himself to the mattress. "Tell Paul . . . watch his ass. They're lookin' for him."

Aunie eased his jeans down his long legs, trying not to wince at the additional bruises she uncovered. She pulled the sheet and blankets up around his shoulders and tucked him in. Then, turning off the light, she left the room.

James rolled painfully onto his side, sliding his hand beneath the pillow to force it into the contour he desired. His fingers touched something satiny and he grasped it, pulling it forth. It was a neatly folded, cinnamon-colored satin slip—obviously Aunie's nightwear. Feeling her pain pills beginning to take effect, he brought the slip up to his nose and inhaled. Then he gingerly raised his head, tucked it between his cheek and the pillow, and fell asleep.

Bob picked up the phone on the first ring. "Jimmy?" His voice sounded anxious.

"It's Aunie, Bob. James is here."

His pent-up breath sighed out gustily. "He okay? I've been worried ever since Paul showed up."

"No," she said in agitation. Reaction was beginning to set in. "He's not. He's been badly beaten and he wouldn't let me take him to a doctor. He said the men who beat him were professionals, as if that makes any difference, and . . ."

"If he said he'll be okay, he'll be okay, Aunie. He's tough."

"Dammit, don't you tell me that, too! You should see him, Bob. He's black and blue all over, and they just threw him out of the car like so much garbage, and it took me forever and ever to get him into the house and up the stairs, and *then* he didn't have his keys, because his brother has them . . ."

"He at your place?" Bob interrupted her in a calm voice.

"Yes. I cleaned him up and put him to bed. He wanted to call you but I wouldn't let him."

"What's your phone number?"

She recited it to him.

"What's his message?"

"He . . . he said to tell Paul to watch his rear end because they're lookin' for him."

If Bob hadn't been so worried he would have grinned at her wording. It was doubtful Jimmy had ever said *rear end* in his life.

As it was, however, he *was* worried. "Paul got away from me," he reluctantly admitted. "He was kickin' himself for leaving Jimmy with those thugs and went back to find him."

"And you let him go? What am I gonna tell James, Bobby?"

"I didn't exactly have an option," Bob informed her dryly. "Paul is an addict, Aunie, and addicts are wily folk. He told me he was goin' to the can, but when I went to check up on him I discovered he had slipped out the back door." He sighed. "How much did Jimmy tell you about what happened tonight?"

"Nothing. Not a darn thing, except that the men who beat him were professionals."

"Yeah, that's Jimmy. He's not one to share his problems—he always has to handle everything himself. Well the fact is, girl, Paul called him to be rescued after tryin' to rip off his dealer, which is about the stupidest thing an addict can do. He didn't even do a good job—he dropped his stash trying to get away. From what he told me, they apparently called in their heavy artillery to teach him an object lesson, but he got away and they were left holdin' Jimmy instead. Drug folks are not noted for their tolerance."

"But if James had nothing to do with it . . ." Aunie protested.

"We ain't talkin' about the kinda people you're gonna find in the silk-stockin' neighborhood you hail from," Bob told her flatly. "They were told an example needed to be made and they had a bird in the hand, so to speak, so they did their job.''

"Well, that stinks.''

"Yeah, that it do." He sighed. "About the only positive thing you can say about tonight's mess is that before he gave me the slip, Paul was seriously talking about seekin' help to kick his habit. He's been through rehab four times already and he's always gone back to the stuff. But it's been a long, long stretch since the last time he even tried to go straight. Last couple years, he's turned a deaf ear to anyone who suggested rehab, so this is a good sign." Or it will be if he doesn't get his head kicked in first, he qualified to himself but did not say aloud. No sense in freakin' her out.

"Y'know," he said instead, "it's mostly because of me 'n him that Jimmy didn't get to be a kid for very long. Paul knows it as well as I do, but this's the first I've seen that maybe it bothers him as much as it's been botherin' me.''

"But if he goes back there and those men are still around, they're goin' to beat him, Bobby.''

"He's two years older than Jimmy, girl; that's just a chance he's gonna have t' take. Hell, he's a thirty-six-year-old man who's still lettin' his kid brother take his punishment for him, and I think it's finally stuck in his craw. High time, too. If Jimmy wakes up, you tell him nothin'. He's got an overblown sense of responsibility, which Paul and me encouraged 'cuz it suited our purposes to have him take care of us. But this is one time we're gonna handle things on our own. Now that I know Jimmy's safe with you, I'll go lookin' for Paul. You see to it the kid gets a night's rest and I'll call tomorrow to fill him in, okay?''

"Okay.''

"Thanks for calling, Aunie, and thanks for takin' care of my brother. Good night."

"Bobby!"

"Yeah?"

"Be careful."

He laughed. "You're okay, kid. I will take care, all right? Night now."

"Night."

Aunie rifled quietly through her dresser drawers in search of a nightgown. Somehow, her favorite sleep slip had made its way out from under her pillow and was now caught beneath James's cheek. There was no way she could extricate it without waking him, for what wasn't pressed into the pillow by his face was tangled in his long fingers.

She had stealthily removed the second pillow from the bed, located a nightgown and blanket, and was tiptoeing from the room when the phone rang. Whispering a curse, she dove across the carpet to snatch up her bedside extension before it could awaken James. Kneeling alongside the bed, she brought the receiver to her ear. "Hello?"

A second later she replaced the receiver in its slot. James stirred restlessly and she rose up on her knees to check him. She brushed his hair off his face and retucked the blankets over his shoulders. Then she gathered the items she had dropped when the phone rang and rose to her feet.

"Who was that on the phone?" His husky voice, coming out of the dark, startled her and she whirled to face him, her hand clasped to her breast.

"No one," she whispered. "That is . . . I don't know. They hung up."

"Probably a drunk," he said groggily, "else a twelve-year-old with an extension in their room."

"Probably." She approached the bed. "How are you feelin'?"

Like I've been run over by a truck, he thought, but a healthy sense of machismo prevented him from admitting as much out loud. "Okay. Kinda thirsty."

"Want a glass of water?"

"Yeah. That'd be nice."

She left the room and returned moments later to find him struggling to sit up. "Let me help you," she said, hurrying to his side. Setting the water on the nightstand, she slipped an arm around his back and eased him to a sitting position. His skin was warm where her bare arm met his bare back. She arranged his pillow and slipped her arm free, twisting to retrieve the water glass. She handed it to him.

"Thanks," he murmured and drank thirstily. To divert herself from watching the smooth glide of his throat muscles, Aunie looked around for her slip, but it was nowhere in sight. She shrugged. It must have slipped beneath the covers when he was struggling to sit up.

He handed her the empty glass and grunted with pain as he lowered himself to a prone position once again. She was pulling the covers up when the phone rang again. "Oh for heaven's . . ." She snatched up the receiver. "Hello?"

Click.

"Damn!" It took an effort not to slam it back into its cradle.

"Maybe you'd better unplug it for the night," James suggested.

"Yeah, maybe I should." She squatted down to do so.

"What time is it?"

"Around three-thirty."

"Did y' get hold of Bobby?"

She was glad his back was to her so he couldn't see her start of nervousness. She'd always been an awful liar. "Yes. He said for you to get all the rest you can, and that he would handle everything at his end."

"Good." James sighed, exhaustion pulling at him. "Good night, Aunie."

"Night, James." She gathered her items and left the room.

He waited a few moments, then delved down under the blankets with his right hand. Pulling out her satin slip, he raised up his head enough to slide it back between his cheek and the pillow. Then, with a sigh, he closed his eyes.

Moments later, he was sound asleep.

Aunie debated unplugging the living room extension of her phone but decided against it. As long as it didn't disturb James's sleep she thought she could put up with a few nuisance calls if she had to. As he'd suggested, the caller was most likely a drunk or a child playing games. In any case, Bobby might try to contact her, and if he did, she wanted him to be able to get through.

Wearily, she picked up the coats she'd tossed in the hallway earlier and hung them in the closet. She made up a bed for herself on the couch, then shimmied out of her dress and draped it across the arm of the chair. Yawning with enough force to make the joints of her jaw creak, she pulled off her pantyhose and panties, donned her nightgown, and padded down the hall to the bathroom. She washed her face, brushed her hair and her teeth, then returned to the living room. Flopping down on the couch, she pulled the covers up, hesitating only a moment before she snapped off the light. With James in the apartment, she didn't think it would bother her to sleep in the dark.

Which was a rather amazing concession, considering the shape he was in. If push came to shove, *she* could probably whip him tonight.

Still, there was something reassuring about the presence of a man who could take in stride the beating he had just endured. That kind of toughness was beyond her comprehension. What sort of life must he have led . . . he and his brothers, too; for, as though they were everyday events, Bob had talked about things that up until tonight she'd half believed only existed in the movies. He'd talked about addiction, stealing, rehab; about examples being set, strong-arm men and . . . Lord, she couldn't even keep it all straight. Despite her experience with Wesley, she thought her own life must have been pretty damned sheltered in comparison. She didn't half comprehend matters the Ryders took for granted.

Her last thought before drifting off to sleep was a wry one. At least now, she thought with groggy humor, I can tell Mary that James T. Ryder slept in my bed. Maybe I'll leave out the fact that he had to be beaten black and blue to get him there.

CHAPTER 9

It was late when Aunie awakened the following morning and for a few disoriented moments she couldn't quite comprehend why she was sleeping on the couch. It was the sight of her spike-heeled evening pumps, one upright, one lying on its side, that sparked remembrance of the early morning hours of the previous night, and she pushed herself to a sitting position, yawning and raking a hand through her hair.

Was James still here?

He was, she discovered a few moments later when she peeked into her bedroom. He was lying on his back in her bed, the covers kicked loose. Except for the sheet with its English Garden pattern draped over his loins and one leg, he had managed to dislodge the rest of her bedding and it sagged off one side of the mattress. He looked large and masculine against her feminine sheets and even more beat-up than he'd appeared last night.

Aunie tiptoed into the room and quietly raided her closet and drawers. Twenty minutes later, showered, shampooed, and dressed, she let herself out of the apartment.

Lola answered the door and smiled welcomingly when she saw who her visitor was. "Good morning, woo-mon! How was your big night out wid your friend Mary?"

"It was fun until I got home," Aunie replied wryly and then filled Lola in on the early morning events with an economically worded report. "Do you think you could give me a hand? Someone should be there in case Bob calls back and to sit with James until he awakens. But once he wakes up, he's gonna need something easier to don than what he was wearin' last night. Do you think he'd mind terribly if I let myself into his apartment to gather a few things together?"

"The mon better *not* object, not after the way he commandeered your help last night and then took over your bed." She eyed her friend in concern. "You should've awakened me, Aunie. He couldn't have been easy to maneuver."

"Believe me, I wanted to . . . if for no other reason than to help me talk some sense into him. He really should've seen a doctor, Lola. But he wouldn't hear of it. Even all beat-up, he can be incredibly stubborn."

Lola laughed. "That's James, all right. And determined. If you hadn't been there to help, the mon most likely would've dragged himself up to his apartment on his own."

"He might have tried," Aunie agreed wryly. "He wouldn't have gotten any further than the front door, though. Apparently, along with his car, his brother has all his keys as well."

Moments later, Aunie let herself into James's apartment with Lola's duplicate key. She hesitated a moment in the hallway, feeling awkward about being there without his permission. He had been in her apartment several times now, but she'd never before been in his, and somewhere along the line she had gained the distinct impression he jealously guarded whatever privacy he could find behind these four walls.

She knew she couldn't stand here waffling about it all day long, however, so she finally flipped on a light and stepped into the living room. Immediately, she came to a halt, staring around her in wonder. She had the uncanniest feeling she could've been shown a dozen different apartments and instinctively would have picked this one as his. It looked just like him.

It was masculine and offbeat, like James. The furniture was black leather, chrome, and glass; the walls were white. Books, magazines, and a number of gadgets were stuffed haphazardly onto the bookshelves until they overflowed; but the rest of the room was almost painfully neat, except for two empty beer bottles and an ashtray full of burnt matchsticks on the coffee table.

Aunie tried to picture James sitting on his couch, sipping from his bottle of Mexican beer while he struck matches and tossed them into the ashtray, but it was a difficult image to conjure. It was her impression he was always on the move. The kind of boredom that heap of spent matchsticks seemed to convey was hard to envision in conjunction with the man she'd perceived him to be.

She dragged her eyes away from the coffee table and glanced around the walls. His artwork was, to say the least, eclectic. Two exceptionally fine prints shared space with a Lynda Barry "Poodle with a Mohawk" poster and a limited edition Olivia De Berardinis lithograph. There was a classic Wurlitzer jukebox with bubbling colored lights in one corner of the living room and a white formica drafting table with black trim and mounted light in the other.

Feeling as furtive as a trespasser but unable to resist, she crossed the room to peek at his work in progress. Fingers skimming over the cartoon on the drafting table without actually touching it, she lightly traced its outlines in the air.

Her mouth tilted up. What must it be like to be so creative? Somehow, this morning, that aspect of his character seemed almost incongruous for a man who'd been beaten all but senseless the night before by enforcers from a subterranean drug world. She didn't half understand him; that was a fact. But not for a moment did she doubt that James Ryder was one complex man.

Aunie gave herself a mental shake. She had no business snooping through his belongings like this. Briskly, she entered his bathroom and located his deodorant and toothbrush. In his bedroom she rapidly rifled his drawers until she found a pair of grey sweatpants, clean underwear and socks, and a forest green boat-necked cotton sweater. Not allowing herself another moment to explore as she would have loved to do, she let herself out of his apartment, carefully locking up behind her.

The smell of freshly brewed coffee greeted her when she opened her own front door. Lola stuck her head out of the kitchen doorway. "You ready for a cup?" she inquired, hoisting her own mug. "All's quiet. James is still sleepin' and so far Bobby hasn't called. I got hold of Otis at the station and he say to tell you not to worry 'bout James. He say if Jimmy say he didn't need a doctor, then he most likely didn't need a doctor." She made a face, shaking her head. She had looked in on James as soon as she'd arrived and she'd seen his condition for herself. Aunie had not been exaggerating. "Mons," she said with expressive disgust. "You ask me, they don't none of 'em have the sense they were born wid. Anyhow, Otis, he be here as soon as his shift is over this afternoon . . . in case James and his brothers need his help."

"Thanks, Lola," Aunie replied. She'd been rather proud of the way she'd handled last night's situation all on her own, but it was a relief nonetheless to share the burden. "If you'll pour me a cup of coffee, I'd appreciate it more than I can say. I'll be right back." She held up the small stack of James's belongings. "I just want to put these in the bedroom."

James's first conscious thought as he slowly surfaced from the comalike depths of a healing sleep was that his entire body ached something fierce. It reminded him of the unrelenting agony of an abscessed tooth he'd once had; only this time the pain throbbed throughout his entire system. Nowhere was he immune from it.

What the hell happened? he wondered groggily as he pried his eyelids open. And where in hell was he? He stared without comprehension at a black-and-white photograph of a shirtless man, which was the first thing his gaze encountered. He looked down at the daintily flowered sheet draped across his lap, noticing its feminine ruffle next to the bruises on his stomach and legs. He wasn't in a hospital, obviously, not with this decor.

Inspecting his surroundings more closely, he eventually recognized them. Oh, hell, this was Aunie's bedroom. He should've known the instant he'd seen the beefcake photographs gracing her walls. But it was the ornate wicker footboard that ultimately prompted his memory. So, okay, now he knew where he was. But what in God's name was he doing here?

It all came back to him then: his inability to settle down last night, the call from Paul, Stubble-skull and Fancy-cut beating the crap out of him, Aunie finding him and helping him into the apartment house, Paul having his keys . . . and even Aunie's little satin slip that he'd hidden from her and used like some damned two-year-old with a security blanket.

Jesus.

He'd told her not to expect him to get involved in her problems; from the very first, he'd warned her against that. Yet somehow, to some extent, he'd still found himself entangled in them. As if that weren't bad enough, now she appeared to be just as deeply entrenched in *his* family's messy affairs.

She hadn't asked to be involved in the aftermath of last night's beating and he knew it was irrational to blame her because she had been. Hell, all she'd done was lend him a hand.

But he was in pain and his pride still smarted furiously from the way he'd mooned around his apartment last night like some pimple-faced adolescent, keeping his eyes peeled for her return, jumping at the sound of every car driving down the block. And irrational or not, he *did* resent her involvement.

Damn her, what the hell was she doing getting all tangled up in his life?

Despite his pain, which severely undermined his habitually ironfisted self-control, he might have been able to keep his disgruntlement under wraps if he hadn't noticed the little stack of his belongings on her nightstand. But first the familiarity of the sweater caught his attention; then he recognized the rest of the stuff. He knew then that she had been in his apartment, that she'd trespassed his only remaining sanctuary, and a lifetime of hard-earned discipline flew out the window.

"Magnolia!" he roared furiously; then he swore, grimacing at the sharp stab of pain that was a result of stretching his mouth. Unreasonably, he deemed her accountable for that, too.

She was in the room practically before the echoes of his wrath had faded, searching his features with concern as she approached the bed. Lola was right behind her, but James failed to notice. His eyes were trained accusingly on Aunie.

She leaned over him, brushing his hair gently away from his face. "Are you in pain?"

"Hell, yes, I'm in pain. What'd ya think, I'd feel like running a friggin' marathon?"

She recoiled from the venom in his tone but firmly instructed herself not to react to it. People were often sharp-tempered when they were hurting.

He pushed himself painfully to a sitting position. "Just who the fuck gave you permission to go snooping through my apartment?" he demanded belligerently.

Aunie flinched guiltily and flushed a painful red. Because that was exactly what she felt she'd been doing, she didn't have one word to offer in her own defense.

Lola, however, was a different story; she felt no such

compunction. Whipping an arm the color of café au lait around Aunie's shoulders, she hugged her protectively to her side and glared at James. "I did," she said flatly. "And if you were any sort of a mon, James Ryder, you'd be thoroughly ashamed of yourself for even askin' such a thing. This little woo-mon dragged your sorry butt up a flight of stairs, patched you up, and put you in her own bed, and you *dare* chastise her wid your filthy mouth for entering your precious apartment?"

Put like that, it did sound a little less than reasonable . . . never mind ungracious. James opened his mouth to apologize, however grudgingly since he was still irrationally furious, but Lola was on a roll and she rode right over whatever he might have said. As far as she was concerned, James had had his chance and he'd blown it.

"For your information, Mr. Big Shot," she informed him coolly, "Aunie was in your apartment for seven minutes, maximum. She'd have to be mighty fast to snoop through your pitiful, raggedy belongings and still have time to locate and gather the stuff she thought you needed." Her deep brown eyes, filled with scorn, transferred from his face to that of the petite woman hugged to her side. They immediately softened. "Come," she said gently. "We go back to the living room and let this big baby sulk in peace. It's a sorry day when a woo-mon tries to do something to make a mon more comfortable and gets the nasty side of his tongue for her efforts." Wheeling them both around, she marched them smartly out the door, slamming it shut behind her.

That left James to stew all alone with a pain-riddled body, an enormous anger he didn't have the first idea how to handle, *and* a galloping case of the guilts.

He whispered a long string of obscenities, but it didn't make him feel better.

Creaking like an old man with arthritic joints, he slowly dragged himself out of Aunie's comfortable bed. He picked up the disputed gear she had accumulated and shuffled with painful slowness out of the room and down the hall to the bathroom.

He helped himself to two of Aunie's pain pills and took a hot shower. His face was too ravaged for him to consider shaving, and eyeing the apparent dullness of Aunie's razor, he decided it was probably just as well. His guilt rose up to kick him in the teeth when he saw that she had included a rubber band to club back his hair, and then again when he noted the ease of donning his sweats as compared to wrestling his way back into last night's jeans. Ah, hell. He longed to hang onto his righteous indignation, but the more he thought about the way he'd attacked her after all she'd done for him, the more of a horse's ass he felt.

Bobby was in the living room drinking coffee and chatting with the women when James emerged from the bathroom. He lowered himself carefully onto the couch, and when Aunie silently handed him a mug of coffee and started to turn away, he caught her by the wrist, staying her. It felt fragile and small in his grasp.

"I'm sorry," he said stiffly when she looked down at him without speaking. She shrugged one shoulder and turned away, forcing him to drop her hand. He glared at her back. He'd said he was sorry, hadn't he? What'd she want, roses?

"They really worked you over, didn't they, kid?"

James looked over at Bob, who was studying him closely. "Yeah," he replied. "They knew just what they were doin'."

"No concussion?"

"No."

"Pissed any blood?"

"No."

"I guess you're gonna live, then. Bet it hurts like a son of a bitch though."

James grunted his agreement.

Bob shifted his bulk uncomfortably. He sipped his coffee, scratched under his collar, then finally looked his brother in the eye. "Paul's in the hospital."

Every muscle in James's body screamed in protest at his sudden start. "What? How?"

"He felt bad about leaving you, so he went back to find ya."

"And you let him?"

"Christ, now you sound like Aunie. You *know* what he's like when he sets his mind on something, Jimmy. How do you think—"

"Aunie *knew* about this?"

Aunie walked out of the kitchen where she'd gone to avoid James. She met his accusing stare head-on. "I didn't know about him being in the hospital until Bob got here, but I knew he'd given him the slip."

"And you didn't tell me?"

"To what purpose?" she inquired coolly. She'd just about had it with his surly attitude, pain or no pain.

"To what? . . . Christ, I coulda—"

"Hey!" Bob angrily interrupted. "Don't blame her. I told 'er not to tell you. Shit, Jimmy, ain't you the guy who's been broadcasting how fed up he is with taking care of everybody's problems? What the hell do ya think you could've done, anyway? From what I heard, you couldn't even get up the walk without the help of this little lady here."

James scowled. Did everyone have to keep throwing that in his face?

Bob's tone softened. "By the time I found him, so had the goons. But I'll tell y' somethin' interesting, Jimmy. Last night was the first time I've ever seen Paul pass up a chance to score some blow. He lost his supply, y'know, getting away from the dealer he tried to rip off. Ordinarily, you know damn well that woulda had him hittin' the streets in search of a new score. But for once in his life he was more concerned with someone else's problems. He was pretty damn shaky, which is how they caught him, I imagine, but still . . ."

"Where is he now?"

"Harborview."

James pushed himself painfully to his feet. "Let's go."

Bob knew better than to argue with him. Jimmy was as muleheaded as they came once he'd set his mind on a chosen course and Bob knew from experience it was a waste of breath to try to change his mind. He lumbered to his feet.

Aunie was tempted to try to dissuade him, but she held her tongue. He should be in bed, but clearly whatever good sense he might have once possessed had been knocked out of him the night before. She ground her teeth in impotent anger, her feelings for James T. Ryder at the moment somewhat less than fond. She couldn't help wincing in sympathy, however, to see the awkward slowness in this man who was usually as quick and agile as a cat. Silently, she went to the closet to retrieve his battered leather jacket. "Try not to do anything stupid," she recommended as she held it out for him to slide his arms into.

Bob turned his startled laugh into a cough. "Uh, thanks for the coffee, Aunie."

She smiled at him with genuine warmth. "You're more than welcome." For all his unkempt looks and occasional bad grammar, she found Bob immensely likeable.

Bob turned to James and gave him a pointed look. James rolled his shoulders irritably, but reached out and cupped Aunie's throat in his large palm, tilting her face up. He rubbed the calloused pad of his thumb over her soft lower lip. "Thanks," he said shortly. Then he released her and walked away.

"Don't mention it," she muttered to the door closing behind his back.

Paul looked even worse than James felt. That wasn't too surprising, according to the doctor with whom James and Bob had spoken out in the hall.

"Your brother is severely undernourished . . . not an uncommon affliction in an addict," he said, stuffing his stethoscope into a pocket. "He didn't stand up to the beating he took as well as you did." He leaned forward to examine James's contusions. "Want me to check you over while you're here?"

"No, I'm okay."

The doctor nevertheless whipped a small penlight out of the breast pocket of his white lab coat, pulled down James's lower eyelid, and examined his pupil reactions. "No concussion," he concurred. "Any blood in your urine?"

For the first time that day, James almost smiled as he tipped his head in his brother's direction. "Like I told Dr. Bob here, no blood."

The doctor grinned at Bob. "You've gone over the list, hmm?"

"Yeah." Bob shrugged. "We grew up in the Terrace." He knew there was no need to elaborate. Not only was the project just one bluff over from Harborview Medical Center, divided only by the entrance to the I-90 corridor, but the hospital itself had the best trauma care in the city, so it got a lot of business from Terrace residents. Rapes, gunshot wounds, stabbings, beatings, all were sent there first. "Y' learn young what needs medical attention and what you can fix yourself and still live with."

"Ah." The doctor nodded in acknowledgment of Bob's blunt assessment. "Well, as to your brother Paul," he said, "the bad news is he has multiple contusions, a broken nose, a cracked rib and some bruised internal organs. But he'll live. We've got him on a high-protein drip to build up his strength and we'll give him as much food by mouth as he can handle. He's got a few loose teeth, so it'll have to be soft food for now. The good news is he's expressed a strong desire to kick his dependency, a desire fueled, apparently, by the thought of you"—he tipped his head at James—"taking a beating that was meant for him."

James wasn't overwhelmed with hope. "He's been in rehab before," he commented glumly. "It never seems to stick."

"I've got a program in mind that's a little bit different." The doctor went on to outline an experimental program that used a drug widely prescribed for epileptic seizures. "We've had some amazing results with this."

"Is this anything like the methadone program?" James inquired dubiously. He wasn't about to get excited over a drug that was every bit as addictive as the substance it replaced.

"No, that's the beauty of it," the doctor replied. "Methadone substitutes one narcotic for another. CBZ is not addictive. It's a specific antidote to cocaine craving in the brain."

Bob scratched the side of his neck. "Run that antidote business by me one more time."

The doctor explained about a process called kindling, which he likened to an electrical impulse in the brain's limbic system. "Kindling is like a cellular memory of cocaine, which is what causes the intense craving," he said. "CBZ eliminates or significantly reduces kindling. In effect, what it does is give responsibility back to the individual. By curbing the craving for the drug and getting involved in therapy groups, the recovering addict can control his cocaine use. So, you see," the doctor said, tucking his hands into his pockets and rocking on the balls of his feet, "if your brother consistently attends counseling and takes the CBZ as prescribed, he has a markedly better chance of recovery than he's ever had before."

James shook his head, trying to absorb the novelty of hearing good news for a change in relation to Paul's addiction. "It sounds pretty damn miraculous," he said and glanced at Bob to see how he was taking it. Then he stuck out his hand. "I'm having a hard time taking it in, but thanks, Doc."

"You're wel—" His beeper went off and the doctor thrust the hand he'd been reaching out to James into his pocket to turn it off. "Oops, gotta run." He turned on his heel and in only moments, it seemed, had disappeared down the corridor with a ground-eating, brisk stride, his lab coat flapping behind him.

James and Bob exchanged incredulous looks, then

simultaneously broke into smiles. They pushed open the door to their brother's room and entered. A television was turned on and tuned to a Saturday afternoon sports program but Paul was dozing. He awoke a few moments later when James clicked off the wall-mounted set. "Hey," he said thickly, and worked his tongue unsuccessfully against his dry lips. He gestured weakly toward the roll-away tray that held a pitcher, plastic cup and straw, and a box of Kleenex™. "Gimme a drink, will ya?"

Bob held the cup of water for him to drink. The small effort required of Paul to sip it through the straw seemed to exhaust him, and his head dropped back on the pillow, his eyes closing.

"We talked to your doctor, Paul," James said.

Paul's eyes opened and focused briefly on his younger brother. "Jesus, you look about as good as I feel," he mumbled. "I'm sorry, Jimmy." His eyes drifted closed, then opened once again. "Doc tell ya 'bout the CBZ?"

"Yeah. Sounds pretty great, doesn't it?"

"Sounds too fuckin' good to be real, but the doc swears he ain't jerkin' me off." Paul could feel his nose threaten to drip and instinctively started to raise the back of his hand to it. He was brought up short by the IV. Bob whipped a Kleenex™ out of the box and handed it to him. "Thanks, Bobby," Paul said as he accepted it. He blotted the moisture from his nostrils. "Will one of you call Willinger for me Monday mornin' and let him know I'll probably be out the rest of the week?"

"Sure." It had always been a source of amazement to James that Paul had managed to hold the same warehouseman's job for the past seventeen years, despite his longstanding addiction. James wasn't quite sure how he'd done it, if he stayed straight at work or if he was simply wily enough not to get caught tooting in the men's room. But the fact remained that up until about the middle of last year, he'd juggled his payroll check to cover both rent for the cheap room where he boarded and his escalating habit. Then it had begun to slip beyond his control and he'd resorted to stealing. Only incredible luck had kept him out of jail.

But all that actually had a chance of changing now.

James felt almost euphoric by the time he and Bob left their brother to rest. Some of the stiffness had worked out of his abused muscles and he was moving with more ease. Plus, Paul's prognosis was more promising than he'd ever dared hope. Altogether, the day was turning out a helluva lot rosier than it had looked this morning. All that was left was to ask Otis to go with Bob to fetch his Jeep from the Terrace, since he didn't quite feel up to the constant shifting of gears that would be necessary to drive it home himself. Then he could take it easy for the rest of the day. Well, just as soon as he talked to Aunie, he could.

He had come to the reluctant conclusion that he owed her a larger apology for his behavior this morning—not to mention thanks for her help last night—than he'd begrudgingly given her so far. Okay, so he still wasn't thrilled to have her entangled so thoroughly in his life. The fact remained that she had gone out of her way to help him. When he thought of her tipsy ninety-odd pounds supporting his one-eighty frame, he reflected with wry humor that it was a wonder they hadn't both landed in a heap at the bottom of the stairs. He had to admit that she'd given it her all. And as much as he hated to, he also had to admit that while she was about it she'd been generous, concerned, efficient, and gentle. . . .

And funny. God, he loved humor; it was the cornerstone of his life. How was it that she could always seem to make him laugh?

Dammit to hell, she was working her way under his skin and he didn't know what to do about it. He hated the fact that she'd been in his apartment this morning. Really hated it. He'd found it difficult enough to drive her from his mind before . . . just witness his asinine behavior last night when she was out with her friend. Now that he knew she'd been inside his home, maybe even handled his possessions, it was going to be ten times worse. He didn't care that she'd only been thinking of his comfort. His apartment was his fortress, dammit, and she should have stayed the hell away from it.

Still . . .

She had lent him—and his brothers—a helping hand, and she hadn't asked a lot of dumb questions while she was doing it. He'd repaid her help with obscenities and surly, adolescent behavior.

So . . . he'd apologize.

But then he was staying the hell away from her.

Again.

"Where is everyone?" Otis hung his jacket in the closet. He walked over to where his wife was seated, bent down, and gave her a kiss. "I figured the place would be jumpin'." He grinned and gave her another kiss. "Instead, it's like a ghost town."

Lola set aside her needlepoint, turned down the reggae she'd been listening to on the CD, and filled him in on the morning's events. She hesitated for the space of a few heartbeats at the end of her recital, then took a deep breath. "Can we talk, mon?"

"Sure, babe. Let me grab a cold one first. You want some pop?"

"Please."

She waited while he popped the top off a bottle of beer and poured her a glass of cola. When he was settled next to her on the couch, she rattled the ice cubes in her drink for a moment, straightened the bright cotton of her skirt with uncharacteristic fussiness, then finally looked up at him. "The way James treated Aunie this morning made me angry, Otis."

"Babe . . ."

"He acted like a spoiled brat wid her. The woo-mon knocked herself out to help him both last night and this mornin' . . . and her reward was to have him snarl at her for enterin' his precious apartment. He sounded as if she'd spent hours in there, goin' over the place wid a fine tooth comb. I tell ya, Otis, I felt like grabbing him by the collar and . . . what's the word?"—she searched her mind, then suddenly snapped her fingers—"*impartin'* a few home truths for the mon to chew on."

Otis groaned. "I'm sure that would've gone over real big, Lola, especially on top of last night's beating." Very gently, he continued, "Baby, it'd be obvious to a blind man that Jimmy wants that little gal. But he's gonna have to come to terms with it on his own. Your smackin' him upside the head with the knowledge is *not* gonna help the situation."

"I know."

The beer bottle paused midway to Otis's mouth. "You do?"

"Yes, mon, I do. The way he acted angered me, but in here," she thumped her fist against her breast—

"I understood he's runnin' scared from feelin's he doesn't want to be feelin'." She glanced away. "That's not the problem."

She had placed her feet in his lap while she was talking and automatically, Otis picked one up in his large hand and began to massage it. "So what is?" he asked as his thumb kneaded her high arch. He searched her face in fascination. One of the things that kept their marriage lively was Lola's unpredictability. After seven years, he still never knew exactly what to expect from her.

"The problem, mon, is that his attitude this mornin' reminded me . . . of me. Of the way I been actin' over this baby business." She paused and took a deep breath. "I think I'm ready to talk to the peoples about adoptin' a baby, Otis."

His hand stilled on her foot. Slowly, a blindingly white smile spread across his face. "You *think* you're ready? Or you're sure?"

"I'm sure."

He jerked upright from his indolent slouch, slammed his beer bottle down on the coffee table, and reached for her. "Oh, God, baby," he muttered hoarsely into her fragrant hair, "that's great." Her arms were wrapped tightly around his neck and he could feel the thump of her heart against his abdomen. "That is really great." He pulled back and dipped his chin to see into her eyes. "When?"

"Monday," she said. 'We'll call Monday and find out what we need to do."

"Good." He kissed her. Pulling back, he threw back his head and laughed uninhibitedly, then kissed her again. "I love you, Lola Jackson."

"I love you, too, mon." She grinned at his delight and wondered what had made her think this was such a difficult decision. She'd half decided in favor of adoption on Thanksgiving Day but then had skittishly shied away from committing herself fully. Suddenly, this morning, as she had watched James unconsciously sabotaging any hope of getting what he really wanted, it had come to her in a blinding rush that she'd been doing the same thing in a different arena. And it had also come to her that she was finally going to do something about it. She felt good about this. She felt very good. She gave Otis her little three-cornered smile. "We're gonna be parents, mon. What do you think about that?"

"I think, baby," he said as he gave her a hug that threatened to crack a few vertebrae, "that we're gonna be the best damn parents in greater Seattle."

"In King County," Lola averred.

"Hell, in the state of Washington."

"Why be so modest, mon? We're gonna be the best damn parents in the universe."

"Yeah. Damn straight." He settled back in the corner of the couch, holding her in his arms. She started to reach out for their drinks, but he stayed her hand. "Leave 'em, baby. I've got a better way to occupy your hands."

She raised a dark eyebrow at him. "Ooh."

His head was lowering when the doorbell rang, effectively halting its descent. "Shit," he muttered. They sat up and Otis hooked his beer bottle by the neck as he rose to answer the door. "Remember where we were," he instructed Lola over his shoulder. Then he reached for the doorknob.

"Hiya, Otis," James said as he and Bob walked in. He eyed Otis's beer. "Got another one of those? No, on second thought, I guess I'd better not. I haven't eaten anything all day."

"I'll take one," Bob interjected.

"Help yourself," Otis said. He inspected James's face. "They worked you over pretty good, bud."

"Yeah," James replied with surprising cheer.

"Tell 'em what the doctor said," Bob called from the kitchen, his head buried in the Jacksons' refrigerator. James did.

"That's very encouraging, James," Lola said, watching him closely. "It's wonderful news. Is that why you look happier?"

"Yeah. That and the fact that I'm not quite as stiff as I was this morning." He turned to Otis. "I've got a favor to ask of you. I'm sorry to impose the minute you get home, but I wondered if you'd go with Bobby to pick up the Jeep." He glanced down at himself ruefully. "My reflexes aren't all they should be and I'm afraid that clutch would kill me before I drove a mile."

"No problem."

"Thanks, Otis. I owe you." He edged toward the door. "Well, I think I'll go upstairs and make myself a milkshake. Then, uh, I've got to talk to Aunie." He smiled sheepishly at Lola. "I know I won't get an argument from you when I say I owe her both an apology and thanks for her help."

"No argument, mon. But Aunie's not home."

"Oh." He battled his disappointment. He'd really wanted to get this over with. Then one well-muscled shoulder inched toward his ear. "I'll catch her later then, I guess."

"James, it'll have to be a lot later. She's gone, mon."

James went very still. Slowly, he turned his head and pinned Lola in place with the intensity of his stare. "Whataya mean, gone?" Christ, she hadn't moved out, had she? He knew he'd been a little rough, but, shit, that was no reason to just pack up and leave.

"Her friend Mary called shortly after you left for the hospital this mornin' and invited her to spend the holidays wid her family. They live somewhere over on the canal." Lola watched James carefully. "Aunie accepted."

"She's not gonna be here for Christmas?"

"No."

It was just as well, he told himself . . . just as well. Hell, it actually made things simpler.

He didn't know why his gut, all twisted up in knots, didn't seem to agree.

CHAPTER 10

Aunie could hear her phone ringing through the door as she fit her key into the latch. Mary had just dropped her off after their holiday with her family and as Aunie was burdened with purse, suitcase, and a large sack of groceries, she didn't rush to unlock the door. Not many people knew her unlisted number, and of those who did, Mary was on her way home; she was planning to go down and visit Lola as soon as she unpacked; James wasn't likely to call her, and neither was his brother Bob. The college office had her number but they were closed for the holidays, and she'd only received a handful of other calls which had invariably turned out to be either wrong numbers or an occasional charitable organization that had somehow gotten hold of her unlisted number.

By the time she had unlocked the door, closed it behind her, and unloaded her purse and suitcase on the nearest chair, the phone was no longer ringing.

She shrugged indifferently. It could have been her attorney, she supposed, but if that were the case, he'd call back. She carried her groceries into the kitchen.

She'd had a wonderful time at Mary's parents' house, but she was glad to be home. Fed up with James and his inexplicable attitude the morning following his attack, she had jumped at the opportunity to get away. But it hadn't been long before she'd begun to wonder how he and his brother were faring in the aftermath of their ordeal. She had also missed the Jacksons.

As soon as she had put the groceries away and unpacked her suitcase, she gathered the Christmas presents she had bought for Lola and Otis and let herself out of her apartment. Minutes later, she was knocking on the Jacksons' door.

"Hoppy New Year, woo-mon!" Lola exclaimed upon opening the door. She reached out and gathered Aunie to her breast in an enthusiastic hug. Aunie hugged her tightly in return. After a lifetime spent with an undemonstrative family, she was still getting used to being embraced this way. Unaccustomed to it as she'd been, at first she'd felt stiff and uncomfortable with Lola's tactile ways. But it was a habit to which she was discovering she could rapidly acclimate, as it always left her feeling appreciated and flushed with warmth.

She spent the next couple of hours visiting with her friend. They exchanged Christmas presents and news of how their time apart had been spent.

"James is back to normal," Lola informed her almost immediately. "Paul's recuperation has been slower, but he has been released from the hospital. He's in a new program to kick his drug dependency, and so far, he's doin' very well." She explained the way it worked, then waved a hand impatiently. "But that is not the big news." Momentarily she looked shamefaced. "Of course, it is big news; it's very important. It's just not *my* big news."

"Tell me *your* big news," Aunie demanded. She could sense Lola's suppressed excitement.

"Otis and me, we signed up wid the adoption peoples," Lola blurted. She laughed exuberantly. "Aunie, we're goin' to get a baby!"

"Oh, Lola, that *is* wonderful news! When? How?" Lola's laughter was infectious and Aunie joined in, reaching out to squeeze her friend's hand. "Start from the beginning and tell me everything. I want details, lots and lots of details."

Lola grinned into the cup of tea she held in both hands. Looking up, she rolled the cup between her palms while she related all the pertinent information. Her smile never diminished.

Aunie learned it would take approximately six months for the Jacksons to get a child. First they would have to complete a series of interviews, home studies, and physicals, as well as have their financial and family histories reviewed.

Lola asked Aunie if she'd be willing to write one of the three personal references the Jacksons were required to obtain from nonfamily members. Gaining Aunie's assent, she launched into a description of the scrapbook she was trying to put together. Of all the information the caseworker had furnished them with, Lola was most intrigued by the family album they were asked to provide.

"It's to show to the birth mother," she explained. "And we can also write her a letter explaining why we would like to adopt her baby, specifyin' what our values are and what kind of parents we think we'd be. The birth mother is given three albums to choose from, and if she wants, she is given the opportunity of meetin' us. I'm real excited 'bout it, Aunie. The only problem I can see is gettin' pictures that don't make Otis look like a killer."

"Just make sure he smiles in them," Aunie suggested. "He has those beautiful, whiter-than-white teeth and his smile changes his entire appearance."

"Yes," Lola agreed. "And I wanna get at least one picture of him playin' wid a niece or nephew. He's so big and looks so mean, but he's always so gentle wid the childrens, and it shows."

"Remember Thanksgiving, when all the kids were hanging on him when he walked across the room?" Aunie smiled in reminiscence. "God, Lola, remember how he laughed? That would make a great picture."

"Ooh, woo-mon, I like that idea very much. I want to get some shots of Otis's entire clan anyway, to show the birth mother that her baby would be comin' to a family ready-made wid a grandma and aunts and uncles and cousins. Maybe I can get them all together this weekend and use up a couple rolls of film."

They discussed the possibilities for an additional forty-five minutes before Aunie finally rose to go. She was reluctant to leave the warmth and excitement of Lola's company but feared overstaying her welcome. Lola was probably anxious to contact the various members of Otis's family to arrange for the weekend photography session, and with everyone's busy schedules, that was bound to be a time-consuming endeavor. She was too polite to make her calls while Aunie was still there or to ask her to leave, so Aunie took matters into her own hands by thanking her for her Christmas present once again and asking her to give Otis his when he returned from the lumber store, where he and James had gone to pick out baseboards for the upstairs hallway. She reiterated her congratulations on the Jacksons' decision to adopt and took her leave.

She knew the prospect of a little solitude should be appealing after the more than a week she'd just spent being constantly surrounded by people at Mary's family home. But once back in her apartment, Aunie found herself at a bit of a loss for something to do. Looking around at the dust that had accumulated during her absence, she decided somewhat despondently that cleaning was probably as good a way as any to occupy her time.

Admiring one last time the new addition for her gallery wall of boys, which had been Lola's Christmas gift to her, she set it aside and built a fire in the fireplace. She changed into a Penn State sweatshirt and a pair of leggings, twisted a bandana into a band to tie her hair up off her face, and got out her dust rag and vacuum. Turning up the stereo, she took her time, removing all her books and decorations from the bookshelves and tables, dusting each surface and item separately instead of employing her usual slapdash method of a swipe here and a swipe there.

By the time she got around to chasing dust bunnies across the hardwood floor with a dust mop, she had admitted to herself that part of her restlessness stemmed from a latent disappointment that she hadn't seen James. She had half hoped he and Otis would return while she was still at the Jacksons'. She'd really wanted to see for herself that he had fully recovered.

Face it Franklin, a little voice whispered in her ear as she opened one of the dining area windows and vigorously shook the dust mop out of it, *you just wanted to see him, period.*

Convinced it would be dangerous to do otherwise, she had tried assiduously to put her one amorous encounter with James completely out of her mind. Except for sometimes late at night or during an occasional unguarded moment, she had been fairly successful at it, too.

But during the holidays, she and Mary had taken several walks on the beach. And during the course of one of them, the subject of sex had been introduced into their conversation. Aunie had found herself describing the dismal failure of her love life with Wesley.

"I always thought I'd be a natural at sex—you know?—the way some people are at certain sports," she'd confided. "I'd had opportunities before Wesley, but I always chickened out. It just didn't seem right, somehow, to lose my virginity to someone I only knew superficially. Then, with Wesley, I thought: This is it. Look out world, 'cause you're about to meet the last of the red-hot lovers. Instead, it turned out I was totally inept."

"From what you've told me, it sounds more like a case of Wesley's being a lousy lover."

"Do you think so?" Aunie had asked hopefully.

"Yeah. I do. You know what you oughtta do, Aunie? You oughtta take a stab at seducing James. I bet he's a regular hotshot in bed."

"I bet he is, too," Aunie had replied glumly. "The only problem is, I'm not his type. In fact," she'd said, eyeing her friend with a hint of sourness, "you're more his type than I am. I hear he likes them tall, blonde, and busty. Just my luck I'm short, brunette, and practically bustless."

"That may be, toots, but I noticed he didn't spare me a second glance the night we went out. *You* he looked at like he wanted to eat you up with a spoon."

Ever since that conversation, the memory of that night in her apartment had kept coming back to haunt her with increasing frequency.

He'd made her feel things, that night, that she'd only dreamed of feeling before. For the first time in her life, she had felt totally desirable as a woman, sexy and seductive. After Wesley's lack of passion, the way James had effortlessly dominated her every sexual response had left her shaken and weak-kneed . . . and although it probably wasn't very liberated of her to admit, she'd loved it. She'd loved her own helpless response and his hunger. She'd loved the uncompromised passion, unleashed and utterly demanding. It had undermined her control as few things in her life had ever been able to do. Imagine . . . up against a door. She couldn't help wondering, had the act been followed through to its natural conclusion, would he actually have made love to her in that position?

Knowing James . . . probably.

She'd only had sex in a bed, with the lights off and her body properly bathed, perfumed, and gowned. She had a gut feeling, however, that none of those little niceties were prerequisites in James Ryder's personal book of carnal knowledge.

And this is the man you'd like to seduce? her properly raised alter ego demanded with fastidious horror.

She didn't even have to think about it. *Yes.*

Yes, yes, yes.

The only problem was . . . she had grave doubts about ever actually summoning the nerve to attempt it. Not without encouragement at any rate, and despite Mary's heartening words, she didn't believe that was something she was likely to receive.

Aunie sighed. Tucking her new photograph under her arm, she grabbed her dust rag and rolled the vacuum cleaner into her bedroom. She might as well clean up in here and then decide on the perfect spot to hang her newest hunk. Looking at her prospects realistically, she had to accept the fact that it was quite likely her boys were as close as she was likely to get in the foreseeable future to an unclad man.

And if that wasn't a depressing thought, she didn't know what was.

Considering the licentious nature of her thoughts, it wasn't too surprising that when the doorbell rang and she opened it to find James lounging against her door frame, her heart kicked hard against her chest wall and then commenced a furious drumming. She was completely flustered. One dusty hand flying self-consciously to her tied-back hair, she wet her lips with a nervous tongue. Oh, great. Here she'd been fantasizing the big seduction, and he had to show up when she looked like Chambermaid Cathy.

Life was so unfair.

"Hiya, Magnolia," he said, pushing away from the door frame and sauntering uninvited into her apartment. She had to step back hastily to keep from being bowled over. "How was your Christmas?"

"Fine," she croaked. Oh Gawd, she had to get a grip. Her mouth was dry, her cheeks felt flushed, and she had an awful sensation of imminent exposure, as if a neon sign were about to blink on over her head, broadcasting her thoughts. "And yours?"

"Not bad," he replied. He stuffed his hands in

his pockets and shifted uncomfortably. "Listen, the reason I stopped by . . ." His words trailed away when she abruptly shifted to block the entrance to the short hall that led to the bedroom and bathroom. Why the hell was she looking so guilty? A thought struck him and his eyebrows drew together. "What's goin' on, Aunie? Y' hidin' a man in the bedroom?"

That struck Aunie as almost funny, considering. "Don't be ridiculous," she retorted with an unnaturally high-pitched laugh. "I've been cleanin' and . . . and hangin' my newest hunk."

"Yeah?" he said doubtfully. The little pulse in the base of her white throat was fluttering like a trapped bird, and her elegant cheekbones were flushed scarlet. "And what else? Fantasizing about him while you gave your vibrator a test flight?"

"Mistah Rydah!" The outrage was unmistakable.

"I guess not, huh?"

"Most certainly not!" Her cheeks felt as if they were on fire. As if she would ever admit to such a thing even if she *had* been doing it! Did the man's gall know no bounds? "What, exactly," she inquired through her teeth, "do you want?"

"Huh? Oh!" *Nicely done, Ryder,* James thought wryly. *You came to apologize and instead you've already managed to piss her off.* He still thought she looked more like a woman who'd been caught with some guy's hands down her pants than someone doing a little light housecleaning. The thought, however, had the ability to make him inexplicably irritable, so he shoved it aside. He scratched beneath his lower lip. "Listen, Magnolia, I didn't come here to give you a bad time."

The look she shot him said you could have fooled her, but James plowed on doggedly. "I never really thanked you properly for everything you did for me last week." He rolled his shoulders uneasily. Reaching out, he tweaked the perky little tails poking straight up from the knot of the colorful headband that held back her shiny hair. He thought they were cute— they looked kind of like little rabbit ears. "And I owe you a major apology for the way I acted the next morning. It was uncalled for, and I'm sorry."

"You were hurtin'," Aunie excused him and James marveled at her generosity. She was mighty quick to forgive, he noted, as she stepped closer and inspected his face, her ire of a moment ago apparently forgotten. "You seem to be fully recovered," she finally decided. "How's your brother? Lola tells me he's in a very promisin' rehabilitation program."

"It's nothing short of miraculous, Aunie," James informed her enthusiastically. "I never thought I'd see the day when Paul had a real chance of kickin' his habit, but so far he's doing incredibly well."

"I'm glad," she said softly. Then, as if remembering something, she exclaimed, "Oh! Wait here. I'll be right back." She whirled on the ball of one foot and trotted from the room. An instant later she was back, extending a small, exquisitely wrapped present. "This is for you."

Oh shit. James stared at it, feeling rotten. "I wish you hadn't," he muttered. "I didn't get you anything." He didn't tell her about the cherry red sweater that had drawn him over to a table in Nordstrom's three separate times before he'd finally walked away for good, leaving it unpurchased.

Aunie smiled. "Don't worry about it, James; I didn't expect anything from you. Believe me, this is not extravagant. Open it."

He did so, reluctantly. But when he opened the

little white box. his eyes snapped up to lock with hers and he laughed. "Coated rubber bands?"

"I noticed you use actual rubber rubber bands for your ponytail," she said with a smile, pleased with his reaction. "Any woman could tell you they're the absolute worst for your hair. They break it off."

"No kidding. That must be one of those little beauty secrets only females ever seem to know." He reached up and slid off the rubber band holding his hair clubbed back, wincing as it snagged a few hairs.

"They also pull," Aunie observed.

"Yeah, they do do that." James grinned and plucked one of the coated rubber bands from the box. He swore mildly as a hank of hair escaped his grasp and he looked down to meet her eyes. "Got a comb?"

Mama's edict on never sharing one's personal grooming items flickered through Aunie's mind, but she shrugged it aside and reached for her purse, digging through it until she located her brush. She extended it to James. "This okay?"

"Yeah, thanks." He dragged it roughly through his hair, tossed it back to Aunie, then whipped the new rubber band around his hair twice. He grinned at the snug fit. "This is great. Thanks, Magnolia." He leaned down to give her a brief, friendly peck on the lips, then straightened up smartly before he forgot himself and did something incredibly stupid.

He'd better get the hell out of here.

"Well, hey," he said. "I hate to unwrap and run, but I've got some stuff that's gotta get accomplished tonight. Thanks again for your help last week and for these." He hefted the little box as he edged toward the door. "I'll, uh, see you around, huh?"

"Yes, see you around," Aunie said softly. She was

confused and disappointed by both the brevity and
the brotherliness of his kiss and by his abrupt departure. She stared at his back as he strode down the
hallway and then closed the door with a soft click.
Leaning back against it, she pushed out her lower lip
and blew in frustration, making her bangs flutter.

God, he was an enigma. One minute he made her
mad enough to spit—then the next he made her
laugh. And always, it seemed, he could make her feel
so incredibly carnal.

She sighed and pushed away from the door. No
two ways about it. What James Ryder truly did best
was make her crazy.

CHAPTER 11

The new year started out uneventfully, which in Aunie's opinion was exactly as it should be. Uneventful, to her way of thinking, equated with safe.

She kept herself busy. Classes resumed shortly after the new year and the little time not expended in class or studying was usually spent socializing with either Lola or Mary . . . or occasionally both.

She acquired a fascination for the various steps in the adoption proceedings Lola and Otis were required to go through in order to qualify them eligible as adoptive parents. Lola kept her apprised of all the latest developments, dispensing frequent updates made colorful by her personal observations and feelings. After agonizing for hours over her recommendation to the adoption agency, Aunie eventually completed a draft that satisfied her and she sent it off.

She hardly ever saw James. She didn't know if it was a deliberate evasion on his part, but she acknowledged that for her own peace of mind she was doing her utmost to avoid him. She had once again shelved her one paltry erotic memory and her unrealistic fantasies. She was supposed to be striving for adulthood, which meant it was time to get on with it and quit dreaming of never-never land.

She called Otis's brother Leon and joined the gym where he was a trainer. Four afternoons a week, she taxied to the health club and undertook a vigorous workout. Leon proved to be a relentless taskmaster, always pushing her a little bit further than she thought it was possible to go. At first, as her body screamed its protest, she was convinced he was a closet sadist trying his best to cripple her. Eventually, however, as her muscles acclimated to the vigorous sets and repetitions, she began grudgingly to appreciate his efforts. After about a month, she turned into an outright fan. In addition to strengthening her body, the workouts helped clear her mind. Studying seemed to come easier on the days she visited the gym. Enthused about the benefits, she tried to convince Mary to join also, but the only response she elicited was a sarcastic, "Yeah, right."

During the last weekend in January, she accepted her first date with a man named Tim Dwyer, whom she had met at the gym. He was a nice man and he showed her a very good time, but unfortunately they lacked chemistry. When he kissed her good night outside her door, it was merely pleasant. She wasn't even vaguely tempted to invite him in . . . and somewhat to her own surprise that was all right. She didn't feel desperate to commence her much-talked-about affair. The important thing was that she'd taken the first step; she was making a well-rounded life for herself in Seattle.

The tension she'd learned to live with for so long was finally beginning to ebb, and she even felt cautiously optimistic about her chances of avoiding future contact with Wesley. She went days, sometimes weeks now, without giving him a single thought. Neither did she often think of Mama or Daddy or any of her other relatives. Her life was growing in directions which they'd never understand, let alone approve of, but she was very happy with the changes she had wrought. She had found something in Seattle that she'd never had in Georgia: a feeling of purpose and belonging, a sense of competency. She was growing up fast—if belatedly—and she was proud of the strides she had made. It was nice to feel she no longer had to look over her shoulder, nicer yet to be filled with confidence that life was finally getting back on course.

Then the telephone calls began.

At first, they were easy to ignore. The phone would ring, but the caller would hang up without bothering to identify himself. It was an intrusion and irritation, but they came with such sporadic irregularity that Aunie assumed it was merely a mannerless person reaching the wrong number but too rushed or rude to say so before disconnecting. By the middle of March, however, the calls had started to become a habitual nuisance.

It never occurred to her to be frightened by them; they were simply an annoyance. Then the occasional call turned into a daily bombardment, but it happened with such gradualness that by the time she felt there was cause for concern, she couldn't even begin to guess whether they were being placed by the same person.

The method, at any rate, was the same one. The phone would ring; she'd pick it up and say hello; they'd disconnect. If it were the work of the same person who had sporadically called in the past, it had grown to the point where unlike those occasional intrusions, which had had a gap of several days between them, the caller would now immediately redial—only to once again hang up the instant she answered the phone. It made her seethe with impotent frustration.

After putting up with it for more than a week, she called the tele-abuse line only to be informed she needed a police case number before they would take a report. Not quite ready for such a drastic step, she went shopping for an answering machine instead.

She hadn't mentioned the calls to anyone, hoping the anonymous caller would grow weary of his game and give up. It was rapidly becoming apparent, however, that that had been wishful thinking on her part. Such being the case, upon returning home with her newly purchased machine, she stopped off at the Jacksons' apartment to have a talk with Otis and Lola.

Mary sat on the edge of her bed with the phone receiver cradled between her shoulder and ear. Hunched over one updrawn knee, her heel on the the mattress and her foot flexed, she applied a second coat of Iced Rosewood nail polish to her toenails as she waited for Aunie to answer her phone.

The line on the other end was suddenly connected and Mary sat a little straighter. She reached up and steadied the receiver with two fingers, prepared to launch into a long conversation the moment Aunie said hello. But it wasn't Aunie's expected voice that came down the line.

"You have reached 323-0194," a deep and menacing masculine voice snapped. There was a beat of silence, then the demanding voice barked, "WHY?" *Beep.*

Mary couldn't have said why she slammed down the phone; it was simply an instinctive reaction. Her heel slid off the bed; toes that were spread apart by cotton stuffing still flexed toward her leg. Slowly she replaced the brush applicator in the bottle and twisted the cap tightly.

"323-0194," she whispered to herself. That was Aunie's number. But her friend hadn't mentioned getting an answering machine and who the hell had recorded that message? The man had sounded huge, impatient . . . and not someone with whom a sane person would care to tangle.

Otis, most likely. But why?

Mary used her blow-dryer to speed the drying process on her nails. Then, yanking the stuffing from between her toes, she tossed it in the general direction of the wastebasket and pulled on socks, jeans and boots. She grabbed her jacket and purse and slammed out the front door.

"I vote for filing a police report," Mary said decisively the instant Aunie had finished explaining about the calls. "I'm surprised you haven't done so already." She looked to Otis and Lola for support and found Lola nodding in agreement. The Jacksons had still been at Aunie's when she'd arrived, visiting after having helped set up her new answering machine. "Have either of you heard about the man who's been making calls to some of the women students on our campus?"

Otis slowly straightened. "That's your campus?" he asked. "I've read about it in the papers, but the exact location was never mentioned. It's always been referred to as a local college." He turned questioning eyes on Aunie.

"It never even occurred to me," she admitted. "But now that you mention it," she added with slow consideration, "I really doubt that it *is* the same person."

"Based on what, exactly?" Mary demanded. "Aunie, you can't make that kinda judgment without a few facts to support it!" She paced irritably in front of the fireplace.

"Think about it, Mary," Aunie retorted tightly. "From everything you've told me about this college guy, he *talks* to the women he calls. He knows details about their lives." She ran tension-stiffened fingers through her hair. She'd already caught hell from Lola this afternoon. Mary's added belligerence and the new possibility she had raised had the effect of winding her nerves tighter and tighter. "*My* caller doesn't say a word. He hangs up as soon as I pick up the phone."

"Well, yeah, that is different," Mary agreed reluctantly. "But still . . . I don't like it."

"I don't like it either, woo-mon," Lola injected, reiterating an opinion she had already emphatically stated before Mary's arrival.

Aunie's emotions snapped like an overwound spring. "Do you think I do?" she demanded angrily. She confronted her friends combatively, hands fisted on her hips. "I'm not exactly ovahjoyed, myself, to be harassed on a daily basis by some idiot with a touch-tone. But I'd like to exercise a few preliminary options before Ah go runnin' to the police—is that all right with the two of you?" Chest heaving, she glared at them. "*Do* Ah have your permission?"

Otis patted her on the shoulder. "Easy girl, easy," he murmured. "They're on your side. They're just concerned about your safety, Aunie. We all are."

Aunie expelled a harsh breath and slowly regained control. "I know," she said softly. "And I'm bein' a bitch." She looked at her two friends. "I'm sorry, y'all." She rubbed her temples where an incipient headache was threatening. "This's got me all shook up. It's just . . . I thought I was finally leavin' the shit behind me, y'know?" She laughed without amusement. "Where *do* I get these absurd notions?"

"You don't think it could be Wesley, do you?" Mary asked hesitantly.

"Oh Gawd." Aunie collapsed onto an overstuffed chair. She propped her elbows on her knees and buried her head in her hands. After sitting thus for a few silent moments, she sighed unhappily and plowed all ten fingers through her hair as she slowly straightened. She was suddenly overwhelmed with fatigue and her head lolled against the chair's headrest as her hands dropped limply to her lap. "I don't know, Mary," she eventually replied. "I didn't think of him, either." She blew a disgusted breath. "Pretty stupid, huh? I guess I just sorta automatically assumed it was some clown randomly punchin' up my number."

"And now?" Otis asked.

Aunie gave the idea several moments' silent consideration. Finally, she admitted, "I just don't know. My past experiences with Wesley lead me to believe he wouldn't call and then hang up without sayin' anything. Always before, he's been extremely vocal."

"If it's not a random caller," Otis said slowly, "who

would you choose to be more likely, Wesley or the campus guy?"

"I'm a math major, Otis," Aunie replied with a grim smile, "so I know a little somethin' about probabilities. The odds against one person receivin' telephone calls, at an unlisted number, from two separate, unrelated psychotics, must be about a million to one. Attendin' the college from which one of the crazies is currently operating would naturally alter the probabilities a great deal, but still . . . I guess if those are my only choices and knowin' how obsessed Wesley is, then I'd have to say it was him." The mere thought was enough to make all the natural color drain from her face and an involuntary shudder wrack her small frame.

Otis patted her hand. "Listen, Aunie, chances are you were correct in your first supposition. It probably is someone who randomly punched up your numbers. That sorta thing happens more frequently than we think, I imagine. Why don't you stick with your original decision to give the answering machine a few days, and then if the calls persist, you can file a police report."

"Otis," Lola protested.

"Shut up, babe," he requested in a genial tone. "A couple of days aren't gonna make that big a difference. We're going to keep an eye on her, so there's no need for you to go aggravating the situation. As it is, we've probably seen to it that she's not gonna be sleeping any too well tonight."

"I could stay with you, Aunie," Mary offered.

"Would you?" Aunie jumped at the offer. It was a measure of how far she'd progressed since her move to Seattle, she imagined, that Wesley hadn't automatically popped to mind at the very first phone call. In truth, she hadn't even thought to be frightened by the calls until her friends had raised all these horrific possibilities. But now that they had ... "It's silly, probably, but suddenly I'm a wreck. I really would appreciate the company."

"No problem. I'll just run home to pack a few things and grab my books. I can be back in an hour."

"Could I ride along with you?" Aunie had a sudden desire to get out of her apartment. "I didn't get anything out for dinner, but if you don't mind stoppin' at a restaurant along the way, I'll buy you a meal."

"Sounds like a deal to me."

Lola and Otis rose to go. Lola came up to Aunie and stood staring down at her solemnly. "Are you angry wid me, woo-mon?"

"Of course not." Aunie rose up on tiptoe to give her a hug. "I love you to pieces for caring so much. Only ... I need to try this my way for a day or two, okay?"

"All right," Lola agreed. "You keep us informed, though, huh?"

"I will." Aunie turned to Otis. "Thank you," she said. "Thanks for hookin' up my machine and for the message and ... well, everything." *Thanks for considering my point of view when no one else would.*

He reached out and touched the tip of her nose with a large, dark finger. "It was nothing ... but you're welcome anyway. Try not to worry too much. I'm sure everything will be fine."

But everything wasn't. Aunie very badly wanted to believe that her anonymous caller was some stranger who had haphazardly picked her number, and for a while it appeared that might be the case. The answering machine cut down dramatically on the nuisance calls and she started to relax. Then, six days after her machine was installed, she received a call from her lawyer in Atlanta and she knew she could no longer afford to leave her situation to chance.

As usual, she had allowed the machine to vet the call. But it wasn't a disconnect this time. Jordan's voice spoke through the recorder.

"Aunie?" it said uncertainly after the beep. Recognizing the voice, she rose from her studies at the dining room table. "Uh . . . have I reached the correct number? This is Jordan Saint . . ."

Aunie picked up the receiver. "Hi, Jordan, it's me."

"Aunie! That's some recording. Where on earth did you get it?"

"My downstairs neighbor recorded it for me."

"Very effective," he said. "Is your downstairs neighbor quite large by any chance?"

"Extremely."

"African-American?"

"Yes."

"As mean as he sounds?"

"No," she replied. "He's a pussycat, actually; although if you didn't know him, you most likely wouldn't think so."

Jordan laughed. He hesitated a moment, then said, "I'm not quite sure how to tell you the reason I'm calling, dear. I don't want to frighten you unnecessarily, because it's probably nothing, but my office was broken into a couple weeks ago."

Aunie tensed all over. "Oh Gawd," she whispered. "Wesley?"

"It's very unlikely, Aunie," Jordan replied. "But your phone number was in my personal Rolodex, so I felt you had the right to know. It didn't include the area code, though, and without that there's no way to know in what state it originates. The only record of your address, of course, is in your file, which was under lock and key."

"I've been receivin' nuisance calls, Jordan."

He swore. "Does it sound like Wesley?"

"I don't know; the caller never speaks. He hangs up as soon as I answer. That's why Otis recorded the message on my machine."

"Wesley has never been the type to keep silent, dear. It's quite likely those calls are entirely unrelated."

"That's what I thought . . . what I hoped," she replied. "But now . . ." Now she had a very bad feeling. Things had been going just too well to last—she should have known better.

They conversed for a while longer before Jordan finally rang off. Long after the call was terminated, Aunie remained on the couch with her legs drawn up, her arms wrapped tightly around her shins, and her forehead cushioned by her kneecaps. Shadows grew long across the hardwood floor as afternoon turned into early evening, but she never noticed. God in heaven, she kept thinking over and over again. God in heaven.

Was the madness to begin all over again?

Lola and Mary went with her to file a police report. She was, by then, convinced her caller was Wesley. Once the officer taking her report learned which college she was attending, however, he was equally certain they were dealing with the man harassing her fellow students.

"In either case," he finally said with strained patience the third time she attempted to argue with

him about it, "the procedure works the same. Call
this number and the tele-abuse line will tell you how
to proceed."

"I have a restrainin' order against my ex-husband,"
Aunie informed the officer. "But it didn't prevent
him from beatin' me black and blue once before.
Can you at least promise you'll respond quickly to a
call for help from me if it does turn out to be him?"

"Yes, ma'am. That I can do." He scribbled a notation on her report. Resigned to the fact that it was
probably the best she could hope for, Aunie rose.
She offered her hand. "Thank you, officer. I appreciate your time."

He shook her hand, tipping his head politely.
"Ma'am."

"Well, that was pretty much a waste of time," she
commented glumly once she, Lola, and Mary hit the
street.

"At least you have a case number," Mary said with
uncertain optimism.

"Yes, I have that." She squinted against the bright
March sunshine, took a deep breath, and slowly
expelled it. "So. I suppose my next step is to contact
the telephone company."

Lola dug in her purse for a pair of dark glasses.
"Let's go get somethin' hot to drink, woo-mon," she
suggested. "And something chocolate. We'll find us
a place that overlooks the mountains, have us a latte
or tea, eat somethin' fattenin', and relax."

"Sounds like a plan to me," Aunie said, perking
up. "Mary?"

"You guys navigate and I'll drive."

They ended up at a small restaurant in Post Alley
across the street from the Pike Place Market. Over

tea and decadently rich desserts, Lola asked, "You ever consider askin' James for advice?"

"No!" Aunie stated emphatically. Her prickly, hard-earned independence demanded she handle it herself. Then she amended truthfully, "Well . . . yeah, I did *consider* it. Briefly."

"The mon can be wickedly inventive when it come to handlin' this sorta thing, Aunie."

"I know . . . or at least I've guessed as much," Aunie admitted. "It's those damn eyes of his . . ." She straightened defensively. "But he's made it pretty darn clear what he thinks about me and my problems, Lola. And besides, I'm supposed to be learnin' to stand on my own two feet." She shook her head. "No. I don't think I'll be sayin' anything to James Ryder about all this. I'll deal with it on my own."

She girded herself for Lola's argument, but to her surprise Lola merely shrugged and changed the subject.

When Aunie got home, she called the tele-abuse line at the phone company. Upon reciting her police case number, she was told a trace would be put on her line and she was instructed to keep a precise record of the date and exact time of each suspicious call. She was further instructed to phone in her list of said calls each Friday. Once she'd hung up, she sat drumming her fingertips on the arm of the couch.

She had a nasty feeling that too little was being done. She felt like a sitting duck and she detested the sensation. If her caller were Wesley—and she had an awful feeling it was—and if he were able to proceed in a natural progression that would advance him from step A: having traced her unlisted number, to step B: tracking down her actual address . . . Oh God.

She was as good as dead.

The total defeatism of that thought put the starch back in her spine, and she pushed out of her chair, pacing militantly back and forth in front of the fireplace. She had progressed a long way from the girl she'd once been. She'd discovered strengths in herself and a depth of intelligence she never would have guessed she possessed a little over a year ago.

Bully for you. It doesn't mean diddly if you can't figure out a way to utilize your swell new accomplishments.

She had gained a certain degree of competence, dammit, earned through hard work and trial and error. She was *not* a useless decoration, willing to sit still like a good little victim, just waiting to be attacked. Not again, not ever. She was damned if she was going to let Wesley's sick obsession destroy everything for which she'd worked so diligently.

That being the case, how did she go about preparing herself so she *wouldn't* be a sitting duck?

You're a smart woman. Think!

She chewed the skin around her thumbnail as she paced. Damn! If she were supposed to be so darn smart, then why was her brain working with such appalling sluggishness? The only thought that came readily to mind was that any confrontation with Wesley would have to be brought to her and as such would be out of his natural territory. She'd take any advantage she could secure, of course; but as a strategy it was a little on the passive side.

Frankly, as a strategy, it was downright pitiful.

When her doorbell rang, she was grateful for the interruption and jumped up enthusiastically to answer it. This searching for a workable solution was a lot like having a name on the tip of her tongue that she couldn't quite recall. The harder she tried, the bigger the blank she drew. Perhaps if she shelved it for the moment, the solution would come to her.

She opened the door, expecting to see Lola.

Instead, it was James who lounged against her door frame. He was wearing a leather carpenter's belt, riding low on his hips and bristling with tools. A drill was loosely clasped in one large hand. As she stared up at him in surprise, he slowly pushed away from the doorjamb.

"Hi there, Magnolia Blossom," he said with a lopsided smile as he strolled uninvited into her apartment. "Lola tells me you've been receiving a rash of nuisance calls." He closed the door behind him, leaned back against it, crossed his arms over his chest, and looked down at her. The light in his moss green eyes made him appear even more of a rabble-rouser than usual.

"So?" she inquired blankly.

"So," he stated, wagging the drill beneath her nose. "I'm here to take you in hand."

Aunie pushed the drill aside with a dainty fingertip. "Ah *beg* your pardon?"

He grinned at her imperious tone. "You heard me. Lola said the cops think it's the same person who's been harassing some other students from your college, but you believe it's Cunningham."

"Lola said a lot, apparently," Aunie muttered. No wonder she hadn't bothered to argue with her earlier in the afternoon about involving James. She probably hadn't wanted to give Aunie the opportunity to flat-out forbid her to drag him into this. Aunie leveled her dark brown eyes on James's. "Thank you very much for your concern," she said coolly, "but I can handle this on my own."

"Uh huh," he said agreeably and unlooped the cord to the drill. He extended the end to her. "Here, plug this in for me."

She ignored it and stood her ground to block his way, hands on her hips. "James, are you listenin' to me? I said I appreciate your willingness to help, especially considering everything you've said to the contrary in the past, but . . ."

"I want to do it my own self," he concluded for her, making her sound like a recalcitrant four-year-old. He picked her up by the waist and moved her out of his way. Kneeling down, he plugged the drill into the wall socket, then straightened and fed out the cord to the front door. Hefting the drill in his right hand, he glanced at her over his shoulder. "Come here."

"Now listen heah, Mistah Ry—"

"Come here!" There was such authority in his voice that she found herself automatically taking several forward steps before she caught herself and stopped. By then, however, the damage had been done, for that involuntary response to his peremptory command had brought her within James's range. He reached out a long arm and snagged her wrist in one rawboned fist, yanking her forward. "Now," he said, grasping her shoulders and whirling her around to face the closed door, "stand still. I'm gonna measure for a peephole."

"Oh." That wasn't a bad idea. She probably would have thought of it herself . . . tomorrow.

He shook his head in amazement as he bent down, leaning over her shoulder to make a pencil mark on the door. "Christ," he muttered under his breath. "It's a damn good thing I purchased the swiveling kind or all you'd see from this height would be a bunch of navels.''

Aunie had been hearing comments about her lack of stature all her life and rarely had she allowed them to affect her one way or the other. There was, however, such a thing as timing, and James's was somewhat less than fortunate. She was already feeling railroaded by the way he'd barged right in and taken over. The last thing she needed at the moment was to hear a sarcastic remark about her height.

She whirled to face him, giving him an angry shove to the diaphragm that took him off guard and backed him up a pace or two. "Ah didn't ask you here,'' she spat out, "and I have no intention of putting up with you or your stupid comments.'' She whipped open the front door, then grasped his forearm with both hands, fully intent on throwing him out of her apartment. "You can just get out of my home right now.''

His bare arm was warm beneath her gripping hands, hard with muscle, soft where the veins stood out, and rough with hair. It didn't budge so much as an inch when she yanked on it. Aunie could have screamed in pure frustration.

James looked down at her. He reached out his free hand and rubbed a calloused thumb over the arch of her cheekbone. "I'm sorry for that crack,'' he apologized. "It was rude and uncalled-for.'' Aunie felt somewhat mollified until he ruined it by adding, "Now back off, will ya? I've got work to do.''

Reining in her anger, she sighed in defeat, accepting that he wouldn't leave until he'd accomplished what he'd set out to do. She released his arm.

James fished a flat case out of one of the pockets in his carpenter's belt, selected a bit, and squatted down to fit it in the drill. Moments later, the scream of metal ripping through wood filled the apartment, along with a faint scent of sawdust. Aunie watched him work for a minute, then walked away, settling herself at the dining room table to study.

She heard the front door open and close awhile later and thought he had left. A moment later, however, she heard the door reopen, a soft rumble of wheels, and then the high-powered whine of a shop vac. She decided he must be cleaning up.

James stuck his head in the room. "All done," he said. "Want to come check it out?"

Aunie ignored him.

"Guess not." He stepped into the room. "I suppose my chances of being offered a beer are pretty slim, huh?"

She ignored that, too.

"You gonna sulk all night?"

Her head snapped up. "I am not sulking!"

"Of course you aren't," he agreed, resting a hip against the table and bending down to finger her lower lip. "This is always pouting out to here."

She slapped his hand away, shoved back her chair with a screech and stood. Going to the kitchen, she retrieved a Dos Equis from the refrigerator, popped the cap, and returned to the dining area, slapping the bottle down on the table next to him. "Here" she said. "It's to go."

He pulled out a chair, whirled it around, and straddled it. Taking a long draw on his beer, he held the bottle loosely between both hands and looked at her. "Why are you so mad?"

"Because you're just like every damn man I've ever met," she spat. "They all think I'm either too stupid or too helpless to do anything for myself."

A muscle in his jaw jumped. After hearing about

some of the men in her life, he wasn't exactly thrilled to be lumped together with them. "I don't think you're stupid at all," he said evenly, "and if you'd climb down off your high horse and let me help, I could teach you ways to minimize your helplessness." When she didn't immediately snap his head off, he asked, "What have you come up with so far? How do you plan to handle the situation?"

Oh God, he *would* have to ask. "Wesley's goin' to have to bring the confrontation to me," she said softly.

"Presuming it's him."

"It is. At least . . . the probability that it's him is a lot greater than that of it bein' the Campus Caller or some other stranger. Well, actually," she amended truthfully, "I did opt for the stranger theory until I found out that my lawyer's office had been broken into. But not now." When he didn't argue, she continued, "Anyhow, it won't be in Wesley's natural territory this time. It'll be in mine, and I'm gonna work on learnin' it well." She waited for him to scoff at her feeble plan.

"Damn straight," he agreed to her surprise. "And I can help. I was born and bred here." When she didn't snap up his generous offer but sat there staring at him with those big, brown, noncommittal eyes, he said in a surly tone, "You say you aren't stupid, right? If you're so damn smart, then act like it. Just stow your effin' independence for a while and accept all the help you can get. The trick is to survive."

She pursed her lips. "I'll think about it."

Christ, she was stubborn. James surged to his feet, grabbed Aunie's elegant little chin in one hand, and tilted her face up. "You do that," he instructed crisply. "You think about it long and hard."

He released her and stalked out of the room. Aunie could hear him gathering his tools together and then, a moment later, the click of the front door shutting softly behind him.

Once she was sure he was gone, she immediately got up to inspect her new peephole.

CHAPTER 12

She had the opportunity to try it out first thing the following morning. The doorbell rang as she was tossing texts and notebooks into her book bag. Stopping only long enough to slip on a pair of shoes, she crossed to the door and peered through the peephole. She was greeted by the sight of a male chest and she quickly adjusted the swivel upward. James's face was slightly distorted but still readily recognizable.

She opened the door. "Now what do you want?" she demanded ungraciously. "I'm on my way out."

"Yeah, I figured as much," he replied equably. "I wanted to catch you before you left. I need your key."

"Why?"

"I'm gonna run some wires in here for an alarm."

She immediately forgot her resentment over the way he was assuming command of her life. "Really? How will it work?"

"You got time for an explanation?" he inquired dryly.

"Oh!" She looked down at her watch. "No. Rats, I don't." She handed him her key. "How am I supposed to get back in?"

"This is not a speedy procedure, Magnolia," he responded dryly. "It's gonna take me awhile. Buzz up here when you get home and I'll release the front door lock for you. If I'm gone, buzz Lola and get her spare key. I would have gotten it myself, but she and Otis aren't home right now. Besides, I knew you'd have a tizzy if I let myself in without asking."

"I think you've got that backwards, James. *I'm* not the one who got all bent out of shape the last time someone entered an apartment without permission." Without waiting for a response, she grabbed her cashmere jacket, picked up her book bag, and sailed out the door.

James watched her depart, then shook his head and closed the door behind her with a low, sardonic laugh. Trust her to remind him of that.

The moment Lola had informed him about this newest travail in Aunie's life—the phone calls and Aunie's belief that her ex-husband was responsible for them—he'd been resigned to taking a hand in its resolution. He might have fought against his involvement in her problems from the first day they'd met, but somewhere in the back of his mind he'd always known that, one way or another, he was going to be roped into them.

She needed taking care of, and knowing that, he was incapable of leaving her twisting in the wind. It wasn't, as she had suggested yesterday, because he considered her too brainless to fend for herself. She was about as bright as they came. What she wasn't, however, was notably streetwise; and if she weighed in at an ounce over a hundred pounds, he would eat his shorts. He'd seen how well she'd fared the last time she had come up against Wesley in a physical confrontation. He was determined to do everything in his power to improve her odds should the man ever turn up seeking a second round.

Whether little ol' Magnolia Blossom liked it or not.

Hell, he was resigned to doing what needed to be done, and once having accepted the necessity of taking her in hand, he found it slightly irritating that she wasn't equally as accepting. Wasn't he backing down on every single vow he'd ever made—loudly and publicly—to remain uninvolved? Yes, he was, dammit, and the least she could do in return was not fight him every damned step of the way. It was her ass he was attempting to save here.

James spread out his plans on her dining room table. He'd been up until nearly three A.M. the night before working on them, but he counted the little bit of lost sleep worthwhile, for he was pretty pleased with the final result. Old Wesley was in for a surprise if he arrived here expecting to find Aunie all alone and helpless.

His main dilemma had been whether to put sirens in each hallway that were loud enough to turn Wesley on his ear once the switch was flipped or to go for the silent alarm method. He'd talked it over with Otis and ultimately they had opted for a signal that would sound in both their apartments without alerting Wesley. They had agreed that the man was unstable enough already. No telling how he'd respond to an obvious alarm, and they sure as hell didn't want to risk precipitating an action in which Aunie would be the ultimate loser.

The corner of his drawing began to curl inward and James picked up Aunie's little laptop computer and used the edge of it to anchor it. After studying the plan, he let himself out of her apartment and went to gather the tools be would need from his basement workshop. Once he had everything assembled, he made a pot of coffee and set to work.

Otis arrived at noon. "Here," he said, tossing a long white bag at James, "I brought you a sub." He crossed over to the table where the drawings were laid out. Planting his large fists on the tabletop, he leaned over to study them.

James joined him, dropping into a chair and pulling his sandwich out of the bag. The smell of vinegar wafted up as he unrolled the inner wrappings.

"This looks like a slick little arrangement, Jimmy," Otis commented, glancing up at him. Then he turned his attention back to the set of plans. "I don't see a place for the switches, though. Do you have 'em marked?"

James leaned over and tapped a spot on the blue-print with one long finger. "Here, on the underside of the lip of her nightstand," he said. "I haven't marked the living room switch yet, because I'm still undecided. If he should somehow manage to get in here undetected, next to the door's not gonna do her any good. He's not apt to let her go in that direction. Kitchen's a maybe. She's got a nice set of knives in there that she could use to hold him off, but I don't know ... once in there, she's also trapped—and given her weight and size, I'm afraid most weapons could be turned against her. I like the middle of the living room best ... it gives her more options and more room to maneuver. But how do we run the wires along the hardwood floors? They're either noticeable or they're a hazard."

"How about drilling a hole and snaking it through?"

James shook his head. "Works going down. That's what I'm doing in the bedroom. But coming up is another matter ... we need a hole at least large enough to accommodate my hand. I haven't checked yet to see if we can pry up a board. The subflooring's not a problem. We can always knock a hole in that." He balled up the waxed paper that had held his sandwich and pushed back from the table. "Thanks for the lunch. Let's get to work."

When James buzzed Aunie in later that afternoon, she raced up the stairs two at a time, anxious to see what progress he had made on the alarm system. She was smiling with anticipation as she barrelled through the front door, but she came to a dismayed halt just inside the entrance to the living room. "Oh, m'gawd! What have you done to my walls?"

"It was necessary, " James informed her tersely. Raising his voice, he called, "Okay, Otis! Snake 'er through." He shined a flashlight into the hole he'd knocked in the wall, then spared a glance at Aunie's stricken face. "I'll fix it, Aunie. It'll look good as new when I'm done; I promise."

Dazed, Aunie sank down on the couch cushions. She hadn't really considered how a person would go about installing an alarm. Staring at the black T-shirt stretched tautly across James's shoulders and back as he hunched muttering to himself over the hole in her wall, she realized she had naïvely assumed it was merely a matter of hooking one up. Not one of her brighter assumptions, obviously. The thing had to have a source of electricity and electricity meant wires, and James had *told* her he was going to run some wires, but . . . well, she simply hadn't given the matter enough thought.

Lola breezed in moments later. She took one look at Aunie's face and whipped across the room in a swirl of cotton skirts. Sitting down next to her on the couch, she reached over to pat her hand. "The mon didn't warn you about the mess, woo-mon?"

"No. I guess I should have realized . . ."

"You're not an electrician, girl, no reason you should. Come." She stood and pulled Aunie up with her. "You come wid me. Load your purse wid money . . . we go do some shoppin'. Make you forget the mons turnin' this place into a madhouse."

"Oh, Lola, that sounds like an excellent idea." Aunie picked up the book bag she'd dropped in her surprise and carried it to the dining room. She retrieved her purse from the bedroom—where she found Otis down on all fours next to the bed, feeding wire down a small hole in the carpet—then she returned to Lola. "I'm ready."

The phone rang and everyone stilled.

Aunie picked it up, only to hear the party at the other end disconnect. Glancing at her watch, she noted the time on the pad placed next to the phone for that purpose. She looked up to find James regarding her tensely over his shoulder.

"That him?"

"Yes. At least . . . yes." She supposed it remained to be seen if it were Wesley, but it was definitely her caller.

"Shit," he whispered and turned back to his work.

Aunie and Lola spent the rest of the afternoon

shopping. They spent more than an hour in the infant department at one store, exclaiming over tiny little shoes and stretchies, narrowing down future choices for decorating a nursery.

Aunie insisted on cooking a special dinner for everyone as a partial payment for all the hard work they were doing on her behalf, and on the way home they stopped at a grocery store for the ingredients. She went to work in the kitchen as soon as they returned.

Dinner was finished, the alarm installed, and the walls replastered by eight o'clock. James watched Aunie gaze around her in dismay as they gave Lola and Otis enough time to reach James's and the Jacksons' apartments before testing the new system. "The plaster has to set," he informed her gently. "I'll touch up the paint tomorrow afternoon."

She turned to him, reaching out to touch his arm. "Thank you, James," she said softly. "For everything. You must think I'm spoiled rotten, but I really do appreciate—"

The phone rang.

When she answered it, it was Lola. "Flip the switch, woo-mon."

Aunie glanced at James and he nodded. She flipped the switch that he had installed on the underside of the end table next to her couch.

Over the phone, she could hear a faint beeping and she laughed, turning to James. "It works!" Spontaneously, she threw her free arm around his narrow waist and hugged him tightly. "You are so clever!" Releasing him, she spoke excitedly into the phone.

Later that evening, Aunie thought a great deal about her relationship with the three people who had just left. It was her belief, generated by hard experience, that adversity, more than any other factor, most accurately measured the depth of a friendship. When times were tough, one established rather quickly who one's real friends were. That had been emphatically driven home when she had divorced Wesley and discovered herself to be quite without any, her many acquaintances nowhere to be found. For the first time, she'd been made to realize that, in spite of having been surrounded by people all her life, she'd never had a genuine friendship with anyone.

So when she'd started taking courses at the college in Atlanta, she'd been determined to change all that. She had forged a few tentative new relationships despite the hindrance of her shyness. She liked to believe they would have eventually progressed had Wesley's actions not forced her to flee. She already knew, however, that she hadn't been accepted as readily or as immediately by anyone back home as she had been by Lola and Otis Jackson. From the very first day when she had arrived bearing the fresh marks of Wesley's beating, they had made her feel welcome. Without question or reservation . . . never once had she felt that their acceptance was conditional on the way she looked or the amount of money she possessed.

And then there was James, who, despite his many protests to the contrary, had nevertheless been there to offer his help every single time she was in need of it. She loved all three of them.

She was *in* love with *him*.

As she sat curled up in the corner of her couch, staring at the raw patches of plaster that changed the appearance of her living room from upscale yuppie to tenement tacky, she didn't know whether to laugh

hysterically or to cry. God. She'd never dreamed she'd
fall in love with a man whose hair was longer than
her own. She'd never thought she'd fall in love with
a man who swore at her, ordered her around, and
assumed command of her life when it suited him,
without the least regard to her own wishes or protests.

And she certainly never dreamed she would fall in
love with a man who repeatedly told her she wasn't
his type and refused the use of her body before she'd
even thought to offer it.

But she had. Lord have mercy . . . she had.

She'd realized it this afternoon as she'd watched
him working so competently on the installation of
her alarm, but she had a feeling it had been brewing
inside her, unacknowledged, for quite some time
now. She should have considered the possibility the
very first time she had wondered what it would be
like to make love with him.

For, if the truth were known, she had a sneaking
suspicion she was one of those depressing women
who had to be *in* love in order to make love. It would
explain why, in all those years when the subject of
sex had filled her mind with erotic fantasies, she had
always shied away from any actual opportunities to
experience it for herself. It wasn't until she'd fallen
in love with Wesley that she'd truly felt prepared to
seek carnal knowledge . . . and then she'd been raring
to go.

For all the good it had done her.

But that was really beside the point. The question
was: What was she going to do now?

How did she go about reconciling her need for
independence with James's propensity for barging in
and taking over? She might love him to pieces, but
never again would she relinquish her own plans and

dreams in order to fall docilely into line with some masculine vision of what was supposed to be.

But to be utterly fair, there *was* one fact she had to acknowledge. Both of the ideas that James had brought up thus far were indisputably viable. They were inventive, designed for her protection . . . and, dammit, she hadn't thought of them on her own. Having admitted as much, she supposed it wouldn't hurt to take it one step further. In all likelihood, he'd probably known what he was talking about as well when he'd spoken of showing her ways to mitigate her helplessness. So, perhaps . . .

Oh, what the hell. She'd let him take over—for the time being at any rate—*and* as long as he didn't attempt to force her into doing something she didn't want to do. At worst, she might learn something. At best . . .

Well, at best, she would at least get to see more of him.

Aunie was involved in an animated debate with two of her fellow students as she exited her last class of the day. They paused in the corridor outside the classroom, and she hefted the strap of her bulky book bag to a more comfortable fit on her shoulder as she leaned forward attentively to listen to the argument being presented by one of her companions.

"Aunie." The voice was a deep rumble and her head whipped around in surprise. Otis lounged against a nearby wall, a huge, dark, monolithic presence who drew sidelong stares even as those watching were careful to skirt around him. The overhead light picked out the ridge of scar tissue on his hard, ebony skull, and the small golden hoop with its tiny bead of onyx that Aunie had given him for Christmas gleamed in his ear. Even covered by a lightweight sweater and jeans, his physique was formidable. Aunie excused herself from her wide-eyed classmates and crossed the hall to him.

"Hi, Otis," she said with a smile. "What are you doing here?"

"I've come to escort you home," he said in a deep, soft voice that nevertheless carried, and Aunie almost laughed at the preponderance of dropped jaws around her. She spotted Mary in the distance. Her friend's cocked eyebrow seemed to ask, What's up? and she headed in their direction. But before she could successfully navigate her way to them against the flow of student traffic, Otis had wrapped one meaty hand around Aunie's elbow and steered her toward the exit. She looked over her shoulder and grimaced, shrugging in response to Mary's bewilderment as she allowed Otis to guide her out the door.

"Just one more of James's little plans, I take it?" she commented mildly as he opened the passenger door of his illegally parked candy-apple red Thunderbird for her. She made no move to get in.

Otis eyed her warily, but before he could respond Mary raced up. She skidded to a halt before him, out of breath. "What's going on?"

"Where are you parked?" was his only reply.

"Over by the reservoir."

"Get in," he said and flipped the seat forward for her to climb in the back. "I'll drive you over." His expression and tone clearly said *Don't push me,* and both women climbed into the car.

"Now," he said as he pulled into a parking spot that had just been vacated behind the reservoir, "here's the deal." He turned to Aunie. "We only have your supposition that your caller is Wesley. Could be you're right. But it's not beyond the realm of possibility that you're wrong." He waited, wondering if she'd argue with him.

Aunie shrugged. "True."

"If it should turn out that your caller is not your ex-husband, but rather the same person who's been harassing the other students at this college," Otis continued, "and if, as seems likely, he is a student here himself, then Jimmy feels a show of strength is called for."

"And that's you."

"And that's me. Today. If your caller is a student here, he's gonna see for himself that you are not unprotected."

Mary slapped the back of the front seat. "I love it!"

Aunie didn't share her enthusiasm, but she had to admit that it made sense. That was the damnable thing about James's plans. She always felt an instinctive desire to protest his interference, but she never did, because his ideas always made sense.

And she always wished she'd thought of them first.

James stuck his head out into the hallway when Aunie returned from her workout at the gym. "Where y' been?" he inquired, and she knew she would have bristled at his presumption if his tone hadn't been so friendly.

She found he was a hard man to resist when he was feeling friendly.

"Workin' out with Leon."

He stepped out into the hall. "That's right. Otis mentioned something about that."

Aunie shrugged uncomfortably. "Yeah, well . . . I don't know if it'll do me much good if it ever comes down to hand-to-hand combat with Wesley, but . . ."

"Hey, it builds endurance," he interrupted her. "It can only help."

"That's what I thought. If nothin' else, I can always outrun him."

He came closer and reached for her hand. He studied it for a moment, then let it go, transferring his gaze from her fingers to her eyes. "Grow your nails."

"I beg your pardon?"

"Your fingernails. Let 'em grow. Long nails are an excellent weapon."

"Oh." She studied them herself. "Okay."

"What time you gettin' home tomorrow?"

She looked at him askance but politely replied, "About the same time as now, I imagine. After school I usually study for a while and then I go to the gym for a workout." She tilted her head to one side inquiringly. "Why do you ask?"

"I'm gonna teach you some of the basics for fightin' dirty." He grinned at her expression. She was looking at him as if he had suggested she dance topless on a gin-joint tabletop. "Wear something comfortable."

"You've had some really good ideas, James," she replied with a certain inbred haughtiness, "but this is not one of them. *This* is certifiable."

"Yeah?" In a flash, he had her pinned to the wall, her hands pulled high above her head and rendered immobile by one large fist, her lower body trapped by the strength of his legs. "So whaddaya gonna do?" he breathed into her hair. Closing his eyes, he inhaled her scent.

"Spit in your eye?" she suggested between her

teeth. She hated it when he was right. Hated it, hated it, hated it.

She felt warm and soft and smelled even better, pressed between his body and the wall, and James's body responded enthusiastically. His erection was painful and immediate. Dammit! What was it about this one little woman? He didn't understand this at all.

Oh, not the hard-on; that came as no major surprise. But these feelings all churning around inside of him ... Something had to be done about those. They were so damn intense. The only other thing he'd ever felt this strongly about was his 'toons.

And that didn't make a goddamn lick of sense.

He stepped back and released her. "Wear something comfortable," he reiterated with studied casualness. Then he turned and walked away.

Aunie walked out of her last class on Friday expecting to see Otis once again. But it was Bob who leaned against the far wall.

"Hiya, kid," he said, pushing himself erect. He offered his tattooed arm. "Your chariot awaits."

"Oh, no," she protested weakly moments later when he stopped in front of a huge, black Harley Davidson. She had never ridden on a motorcycle in her life.

"You'll be safe as houses," he assured her, patting the bike seat with pride. "She's a full-dress hog, and I brought a helmet just for you." Rummaging through the saddlebag, he extended it to her. Out of the other one, he pulled a wadded-up leather jacket. "Here. Jimmy thought y' might need this, too." He took her book bag and arranged it in the storage space, then watched as she donned her borrowed safety apparel.

Grinning at the picture she made in Jimmy's jacket, which was large enough to wrap around her twice and had sleeves that dangled well below her fingertips, he flipped up the tinted visor to her helmet. "You're okay, kid," he said, peering in at her wide brown eyes. "Climb aboard and hang on." He flipped the visor closed again and boarded his motorcycle.

Aunie gamely climbed on behind him and put her arms around his waist. She saw several of her fellow students eyeing Bob and her with amazement as he roared away from the curb. Mary had gleefully informed her yesterday that the new word around school was that Aunie Franklin kept dangerous company.

James would be tickled to hear it, she was sure. Wait until her schoolmates got a load of *him*. They hadn't even seen him yet, and he was probably the most dangerous of them all. She was beginning to think that facile mind of his was downright scary.

James watched from his apartment window as she climbed off his brother's bike a short while later. Seeing her in his jacket, he got another of those weird churnings in his gut. As he watched, she reached up with invisible, leather-covered fingers to remove the helmet and hand it to Bob. She shook her head as she spoke to him, and her expensively cut, shiny brown hair flew gently around her face until it gradually all swayed smoothly into place, once again hugging her nape and jaw. Whispering an obscenity, James turned away from the window.

Down in the yard, Aunie voiced the question that had just occurred to her. "Shouldn't you be at work, Bob?"

"I'm headin' back now," he replied. "I took an hour off."

"Just to get me? Oh, Bobby, you shouldn't have."

"You took care of my brother when he needed it."
Bob shrugged. "Jimmy said he wants everyone at your
school to know you've got friends who'll take care of
you. I owed you, kid, and I wanted to do it. It's no
big deal."

"It is a big deal," she insisted and rose up on her
tiptoes to give him a quick peck on the cheek. She
followed it up by gently dabbing at the small smear
of lipstick she'd left behind, erasing it with her thumb.
"Thank you."

"No problem." He handed her the book bag and
grinned once again at her small figure in its big jacket.
"I can trust you to return Jimmy's coat to him, right?"

"Right."

"Okay, then. See ya around, kid." He turned and
lumbered over to his bike. Mounting up, he gave her
a small salute and roared away.

James acted rather testy when she returned his
leather jacket, so Aunie didn't linger. She let herself
into her own apartment and called the telephone
company to report her list of dates and times from
the previous week's calls. She was instructed to start
a new list.

The week that followed was much like the last. Each
day when she left her final class of the day, she was
met outside her classroom by one of the men. Otis
met her twice, Bob once, and James twice. They
brought her home; she studied; she worked out with
Leon . . . and she had lessons in how to fight dirty.

Out of all James's multitudinous plans, those lessons
were her least favorite. They were too . . . difficult.

In every respect.

Yes, she was learning to function under pressure,
to redirect emotions, to concentrate her awareness.
But it was difficult to be with him, know herself to

be in love with him, and have him treat her like his
not-so-bright little sister.

And that was usually the highlight of the lessons,
when he was encouraging her.

When he tested her with a practical application of
the knowledge he'd been hammering into her, he
raised difficult to an entirely new dimension.

She knew her emotions were overloading. The dis-
parate sensations he raised in her made her feel
schizophrenic. When he was her instructor he
touched her, he pinned her down; he gave her
directions in his usual blunt way, in his usual blunt
language. She absorbed and she learned, but underneath it all Aunie itched with a need for a different
kind of recognition. He made her crazy with his intimate touches that held no trace of intimacy, his sexual
references that had no real reference to her. Unknowingly, he taunted her with the weight of his body on
hers, the feel of his skin as she grappled to break his
hold, his scent, his voice . . . Gawd. And because he
wanted her to learn, he was never satisfied to show
her a move once and let it go at that. Oh no. He had
her repeat the movements over and over again until
she thought she'd scream with pure, unbridled frustration.

But when he staged practice attacks to test how well
she had absorbed what he'd taught her, sex was the
furthest thing from her mind. That was not the vaca-
tion it might have been, however, because at those
times, he just plain frightened her. He stalked her,
regarded her with someone else's eyes, talked to her
in a voice devoid of his usual intonations, and she felt
genuinely threatened. Knowingly, he took personal
knowledge that she had given him and goaded her
with her own fear.

No, the lessons were not a picnic, not in any respect. If she wasn't tormented in one manner, she was tormented in another.

On Friday, she snapped.

"Once more," James said as he pushed off her prone body and climbed to his feet. He extended a hand to her, and wearily, Aunie reached for it to be briskly hauled erect for the umpteenth time that day. "Now, pay attention, dammit," he growled and she gathered herself. "Concentrate on what needs to be done. Wesley's just busted through the door and his only desire is to hurt you. You're scared; it's okay to be scared. But . . . what did I tell you about emotions?"

"Control them; don't let them control you. Don't lose your temper. Don't panic," she droned automatically. She knew what he said made sense. She should . . . God knew he'd drummed it into her often enough. He'd told her repeatedly not to allow herself to be taunted into losing her temper and not to give in to panic. *You can't fight effectively, Aunie, if rage or terror is ruling your brain.*

Her mind was stuffed full of such advice. *Take that adrenaline surge and turn it to your own advantage . . . it can give you strength. Watch every move he makes, Magnolia. Read the damn body language to learn which way he's gonna move.* He'd told her all kinds of stuff, demonstrated even more, but she was tired . . . dead tired and sick of the whole business.

One more time. She'd do this one more time this evening, and then she was through. She hadn't had a night to relax and do absolutely nothing in much too long.

"Okay, sit at the table," he instructed. "You're studying." She tensed. Instruction was over. It was practical application time. She sat as instructed and he walked out into the hall. Suddenly, he reappeared from out of nowhere, the way she'd told him Wesley used to do. "Hello, Aunie," he said in a monotone, staring at her with emotionless eyes. "I told you I'd be back for you."

Aunie's awareness of everything around her was suddenly heightened, and she stood. Keeping her eye on him, she edged for the panic button on the end table. *Use a moderate tone of voice, Magnolia. Don't spook him into action.* "Wesley," she said calmly. "What are you doing here?" She reached the table and paused with her back to it, blocking it from his view. Casually, she curled her fingers around the edge, one of which reached out and touched the switch. If this actually had been Wesley, the alarm would now be on and he wouldn't know it. James's voice in her head said, *Unless it's unavoidable, don't broadcast what you're doing.*

"You've been cheating on me, Aunie," James said in a flat voice as he moved nearer, and Aunie nearly shivered. She hated this part . . . when James used words that Wesley had used the last time he'd hurt her. She picked up the phone behind her back and felt along it for the M1, M2, or M3 buttons, all three of which had been programmed to dial 911. Pretending to push one, she dropped the receiver on the couch cushion. James had told her that police responded quickest to calls that were on an open line yet gave no information or were cut off in the process of giving information. 911's computer automatically scrolled up the phone number and corresponding address for the incoming calls.

He was moving in on her and Aunie experienced the spurt of adrenaline that never failed to surprise her. She knew that this was James; yet her body forever insisted on recalling Wesley's attack during these sessions.

Never removing her eyes from him, she edged around, angling for the door. That was her primary objective, if at all possible. *If the opportunity presents itself, Aunie, don't dick around. Get the hell outta there.* But James suddenly moved, blocking her way. She correctly judged his intent on his next three moves by watching his body language and she successfully dodged him.

Then he was on her.

Aunie reached for his eyes, and this time her nails were only centimeters away before he got a grip on her wrist. With her other hand, she jabbed for his Adam's apple. James's hand whipped out to stop her. She slammed her knee up between his legs.

She came the closest she'd ever come to reaching her objective. But ultimately she failed, and in the end, he had her down in her usual position, spreadeagled on the floor, her wrists pinned to the hardwood on either side of her head, his body weighing her down. Dammit!

He released her hands and placed his own on the floor to push himself off her. Suddenly enraged, she gripped his hair, twisted her head to the side, and yanked with all her might, trying her damnedest to smash his face into the floor. James grunted as he felt several hair roots give. Instinctively, he grabbed her wrists and slammed them back to the floor.

"Good girl," he panted. "That last was a great little piece of improvisation. You came close this time, Magnolia." He released her wrists once again and started to push off. "Okay, let's give it another try."

She made no move to rise. "No."

That single, flatly stated negative halted him in his tracks. He dropped back over her, propping himself up on his forearms. "Whataya mean, no?"

"Just what I said. *No.* Ah've had enough."

James didn't consider how hard he'd been pushing her. He overlooked the signs of strain on her face. He had demons of his own riding him; her defiance enraged him, and he reacted with instinctive aggressiveness. "You've had enough?" he demanded furiously. Unreasonably aggravated, he jammed a hard muscled thigh between her legs and curled his hand into the thin material at the loose neckline of her Betty Boop T-shirt. He twisted his fingers and hauled on the material, making her back arch. "Is that what you're gonna tell Wesley when he shows up?" he snarled, his face thrust close. "Ah've had enough? Dammit, Magnolia, he could have this little shirt ripped off of you in two seconds flat and rape you where you lie. Now, what're ya gonna do to stop him?"

That did it! He'd done this before—in fact, he did it all the time. He was forever introducing the possibility of rape into the conversation whenever she dared balk, but she was way past allowing such tactics today. "Wesley would never rape me," she snarled right back. "How many times do I have to tell you that before it'll sink into your thick skull? *You* want to rip my shirt off, James? Then rip it! But don't go attributin' that particular motive to Wesley. He never much cared for my little ol' lily whaht body." She lay on her back, knees bent around the thigh pressed up hard between her legs, breasts heaving against the backs of his fingers.

James was twisted into a thousand knots. He'd just spent the past couple of weeks hammering at her not to allow her emotions to go unchecked, and here his own were totally beyond discipline. For weeks, for months, he had denied, denied, denied.

Something different was pushing him now.

"Yeah, well maybe I'm not old Wesley," he said with soft menace. "Maybe I'm the phone guy from the college, and doll baby, *he'd* rape you in the blink of an eye."

It suddenly hit Aunie that he was aroused. She could feel him against her inner leg, hard and hot, and it infuriated her. Because she knew him and his insufferable self-control. He'd go stick it in a knothole before he'd avail himself of her. "I don't think we're talkin' about Wesley *or* the Campus Caller," she said venomously. "I think we're talkin' about *you.*" The irony of it hit her and she laughed bitterly. "Gawd, James, that's funny."

He stared at her with uncomprehending fury, denial written all over his face, and she sighed. "Oh, James, you just don't get it, do you?" she asked. "You just don't get it at all. I guess I'll have to spell it out for you. Because, if we're talkin' about you here . . . if you're the one who wants to make love to me, Jimmy . . . then, sugah, go ahead; I'm more than willin'. It sure as heck wouldn't be rape!"

CHAPTER 13

"Christ!" James recoiled from her as if he'd been scalded. He released her shirt, withdrew his thigh, and shoved to his feet. "Listen, Aunie," he croaked, thrusting his hands through his hair. "Don't talk like that. I've told you before, you're not . . ."

"If you say I'm not your type one more time, I swear I shall scream," she bit out between clenched teeth. She rose to her knees, staring up at him defiantly. "I'm sick of you tramplin' all over my ego with that excuse. If I'm not your type, why are you sportin' that?" She indicated the erection straining behind the fly of his worn jeans. He opened his mouth as if to reply, but she rode right over whatever he would have said. "And why is it you can't seem to be in my company for more than five minutes without introducin' sex into the conversation? Y' do, y' know . . . every darn time we're together. So, what's the story, Jimmy? Either you're nothin' but a big ol' lily-livered coward or . . ." She tilted her head as if she were considering. James was standing only feet away, his big hands now at his side, clenching and unclenching into fists. "Or," she continued slowly as she climbed to her feet, "you're one of those men who's all talk and no action. Is that it? Ooh. I bet it is. James Ryder," she imprudently mocked him, "thinks he's a stud, but he's only a pony."

James forgot all the reasons why he couldn't touch her. All he could think of was that he didn't have to take this. Not on top of the past couple of weeks he'd had. Shit, he'd put himself on the line for her, exposing his dark side in order to teach her a little street savvy. He hadn't wanted to do it. Up until now, she hadn't seemed to fully realize just how different the worlds from which they came were, and he hadn't wanted to be the one to clue her in. He'd known damned well that once she'd seen what he was capable of, it would be driven home to her like a stake through a vampire's heart.

And, dammit, it had been. He knew she hated these sessions; he'd seen her fear of him every time he'd had to test her on how well she was learning, and it had twisted him up in knots. To cap it off, he'd thought he'd go nuts, rolling around on the floor with her, keeping his hands to himself, and now she was calling him a *pony*? Well, no more Mr. Nice Guy. If it was a stud she wanted, then it was a stud she'd fucking well get. He almost laughed aloud at the thought. Appropriate choice of words, those.

He was towering over her in two giant steps. "What did you call me?" His hands wrapped around her hips and he picked her up and stood her on the couch so their eyes were on a more even level.

If he thought she was going to back down, he was

crazy. Aunie's chin jutted towards the ceiling. "A lily-livered—"

"No, after that." His eyes ran over her from head to foot, taking in everything, missing nothing: her bright eyes, her flushed cheeks, the long, white neck, that T-shirt that had taunted him all afternoon with its cropped neckline that slid all over her shoulders, those skin-tight little grey leggings. "Say it to my face."

"I said it to your face the first time, you big blond baboon. You think you're a stud, but you're only a . . . umm . . ."

James's long fingers had tangled in her hair and his mouth cut off her words. He wanted to force her to eat her words, literally, but then he tasted her mouth under his, felt her bare arms wrap around his neck, felt her body plaster itself up against his, and his brain short-circuited, all coherent thought erased.

His mouth was avaricious on hers, lips tugging greedily, tongue pumping insolently, licking up her flavor, showing her who was boss, demonstrating what she could expect if she messed with James T. Ryder. She moaned and opened her lips wider, raking the newly grown nails of one hand across his scalp until her hand reached the coated rubber band that clubbed his hair back. She wrapped her small fist around it.

He bit her bottom lip, tugging on it, worrying it, then opened his heavy-lidded eyes in time to see her tongue snake out to lick along the edge of her upper teeth. He groaned and went after it, sucking it into his mouth. Releasing it a few moments later, he gripped a silky handful of hair and tugged, forcing her head back, exposing the long white arch of her throat. He sank his mouth into the soft skin just below her earlobe, then slowly dragged it down the length of her throat, pausing to lick, to suck, to rake it with his teeth. Small patches of red began to bloom against the milk white expanse. Aunie shuddered and rolled her head to the side to give him better access.

He took full advantage.

One of Aunie's knees slowly rubbed up the outside of James's thigh and hip, eventually hooking around the back of his waist. James laughed low in his throat and slid his hands down her back until they were cupping her buttocks. He hauled her up and she wrapped both legs around his waist. "Oh, God, you like this position, don'tcha Magnolia?" He bounced her up and caught her bottom in his hands again, squeezing lightly. His mouth returned to her throat.

"Umm," she agreed and rubbed her hands down his spine, grasping handfuls of his shirt and inching it up his back. James bent his knee into the couch cushion and lowered her to a prone position, falling across her, her ankles still locked around his hips. His shirt was bunched under his armpits, and she reached over his shoulders to grab the bottom edge and tug it over his head. It stretched from bicep to bicep in front of him as he planted his hands on the couch next to Aunie's head and stiff-armed his upper torso away from her. She wrestled it down his arms, sliding it off over each of his large hands as he picked up first one and then the other. She tossed it aside.

James dropped down upon her, driving her into the cushions, sliding his arms beneath her back to arch her into his mouth. He slid down her body and nosed her T-shirt away from her stomach. Kissing the skin there, he found it to be white and firm and of an incredibly soft texture. He nosed the material higher, then looked up at her, his eyes more green than usual, the grey burned out by the force of his emotions. "Take it off," he demanded.

It never occurred to Aunie to argue. She reached down and crossed her hands over her abdomen, grasping the hem and pulling it up over her head. When she shook her hair free and looked down again, James had gone very still. He was staring at her little lace bra and swallowing hard.

"Jesus," he whispered hoarsely and eased one arm out from under her back. He pushed up on the other elbow and the fingers still lodged beneath her back splayed across her spine. The hand that he lifted to touch her shook with a fine tremor.

His long, hard fingers lightly traced the outline of her bra, then slid inward to chart the pattern of pink lace that covered her breasts. He hesitated a second over her nipples, which poked like little pink pencil erasers against the material constraining them. Then he brushed his fingers against them, back and forth, back and forth, inflaming them further with the abrasive rub of the lace. They distended yet more and he caught one between his thumb and finger and pulled at it, squeezing it gently. Aunie sighed deep in her throat. James groaned deep in his.

His heart pounding furiously, he fumbled with the front catch between her breasts. He was usually adept at removing a woman's bra, but wouldn't you know that with her the damn thing would behave as though she'd bonded it together with superglue. Abruptly, it gave, and he peeled aside the little lace cups. His Adam's apple rode slowly up and down the column of his throat as he stared at the alabaster perfection of the curves he'd exposed. He brushed the straps off her shoulders and Aunie shrugged off the wispy garment. "Jesus," he said again, and for once in his life it wasn't a curse. Reverently, his calloused fingers grazed the delicate curvature of her breasts.

Aunie watched him. For some reason, the sight of her breasts had halted the frantic pace at which they had been devouring one another. After everything she'd ever heard about James's propensity for women with big breasts, she had half expected him to be disappointed in the size of hers, but he seemed to be fascinated by them instead. His eyes hadn't left them since the moment she'd removed her top. His fingers roved over their dainty curvature with a delicacy that made her wonder if he thought they'd fall off in his hands if he handled them roughly.

"Jesus, these are sweet," he whispered to himself, gathering them cautiously in his rough-skinned palms. Little jolts of electricity skittered to Aunie's loins. She watched the wry smile that tugged up one corner of his mouth and creased his cheek. "Almost a handful," he whispered.

"Yes," Aunie agreed dryly. "And if you push them together or sit me up, you'll even see a little cleavage." She didn't know whether to be offended or amused that he'd apparently forgotten the breasts he found so interesting were attached to her.

James's startled eyes flew to hers and then he grinned at her sheepishly, licking his lower lip. "That a fact? Let's see." He shoved to his feet, pulling her upright. Taking a seat on the middle cushion, he tugged her onto his lap, guiding her leg over his hips to kneel astride him. She braced her hands on the hard rounded muscles of his bare shoulders while she found a solid purchase for her knees on either side of his hips, then lowered her bottom to sit in his lap. She adjusted her position and felt the sensitive cleft at the juncture of her thighs bump against his erection. She sucked in an involuntary breath and, hands sliding down to grip his biceps, rocked back and forth helplessly. Her head fell back and her eyes drifted shut as she ran the tip of her tongue around suddenly dry lips.

"Oh God, Aunie!" James dug his fingers into the supple skin of her back and jerked her against him, arching his hips to maintain contact. For the first time their bodies pressed together skin against skin, and he thrust rhythmically with his hips while his wide-splayed fingers on her back moved her upper body in slow circles, flattening her breasts against the solid wall of his chest, feeling her softness glide and rub against his hair-roughened hardness.

His fingers gripped harder and the muscles of his biceps stood out tautly as he pressed upward, forcing her to rise up on her knees. She moaned a protest over the loss of the delicious hardness upon which she had rocked, but James was relentless. He moved her until her breasts were on a level with his face. Watching for her reaction, he slowly extended his tongue to delicately lap a straining pink nipple.

Aunie jerked. "James?" She thrust her shoulders back, pushing the breast be was attending closer, needing more . . . needing less gentleness. "Jimmy?"

Her responsiveness, her unapologetic desperation, made James feel powerful, more so than he'd ever felt in his life, and he laughed deep in his throat. "What do you want, Magnolia?" he demanded in a low, raspy voice. "Tell me what you want."

She gripped the back of his head and tried to force it nearer. With her other hand she cupped the underside of the breast he teased and pushed it up, bringing it in closer proximity to his lips. "Suck me," she whispered. "Please, Jimmy, touch me harder. Please."

"Jesus." She was staring down at him, her pupils dilated and her eyelids heavy, begging him—oh, shit, *begging* him—to do what he'd been dying to do anyway but had been half fearful she was too fragile to withstand. His hard hand replaced hers on her breast, gripping it until the distended pink nipple stood out in stark relief; then his lips clamped down on it and pulled strongly. She moaned and clutched his hips with her knees, thrusting her pelvis forward in an age-old rhythm, seeking a relief that wasn't forthcoming.

James tipped over onto his side, laying her down on the cushions. Raking his teeth over her nipple, he hooked his thumb into the waistband of her stretchy grey leggings and thrust them down to her knees. His hand slid back up her thigh and wedged between her legs, shaping itself to the feminine mound that arched greedily into his touch. Her little lace panties were damp beneath his fingers, and James groaned.

"Ah God, you're so wet." He delved beneath the lace, using his fingertips to separate slick petals of feminine flesh, sliding them up and down, rubbing a plump, slippery lip between his thumb and fingers. Then the rough pad of his thumb was reaching higher in search of her clitoris. He felt it, small, sleek, and hard, peeking out of its hood, and he rubbed light circles around it, pressed it with his thumb, flicked it with his thumbnail. Her little moans, the sweet way she opened and closed her thighs around his hand, drove him on.

Aunie clutched his ponytail in one hand. The other fumbled desperately at his fly, small, delicate fingers rubbing at the distended hardness behind it one moment, wrestling with the zipper the next. "Oh gawd," she whispered. "I want you inside me. I'm goin' to . . . James, I want you *inside* me!"

The hand between her legs grew more insistent. "Next time," he promised, watching her. "This time's just for you. Let it go, Aunie. I want to see you come."

"Oh no," she protested weakly, but she could feel it building. "Oh no, James . . . oh please . . . *oh God!*" And she thrust into the fingers working their magic, clamping her thighs around his hand as all that interior sensation exploded with volcanic power. Her hips jerked helplessly and the hand in his hair pulled mindlessly until James's neck was arched beneath the force of her grip. Her stomach muscles rippled once, twice . . . then she went limp, burying her face against his chest.

Triumph, like potent brandy, exploded in James's brain. He'd known a few power junkies in his life and had never quite understood what it was that drove them. For perhaps the first time in his life he appreciated the rush that absolute power could produce. Watching his big, rawboned hand slide out of her little pink panties, he admitted he'd *enjoyed* being able to control her that way. He wrapped his arms around her and held her tightly, inhaling the scent of her hair as he rubbed his jaw against the crown of her head, tugging her up higher to bury his lips in the contour of her neck. He was stiff as a pike and throbbing painfully, but he ignored it, knowing his turn would come. Right now, he just wanted to savor this feeling of mastery that making her climax had given him, to feel her soft skin for a minute, hot and damp against his stomach and chest, to revel in her tiny shudders and clinging arms. Oh, Jesus . . . he wanted to relive again the sweet music of that soft, escalating whine as she had exploded beneath his fingers.

A rush, indeed.

Aunie kept her face hidden, grateful for the strength of his arms holding her so tightly, the feel of his body wrapped around hers, the big hands soothing her. She yawned. She'd never known it was possible to feel this relaxed, this physically satisfied. She felt so good, but at the same time she wanted to squirm with embarrassment. No man had ever done anything like that for her, and it had felt so incredible. But for him to *watch* her while she was . . . Oh gawd, it was a little bit mortifyin' and wasn't she sort of selfish not to have done something for him in return?

She wished she had more experience. She wanted desperately to make him feel as good as he'd made her feel.

She pressed her mouth against the light pattern of hair that fanned across his pectorals, then turned her head and rubbed her cheek against him like a kitten. Loosening her grip on his ponytail, she slid her hands to his neck and pulled herself higher, kissing his throat, his Adam's apple, the damp skin beneath the angle of his jaw. She shivered at the damp, slick rub of her breasts against his smooth abdomen as she stretched higher to reach new areas, shivered again at the rougher feel of his chest hair. Her nipples, newly softened, shriveled into hard little nubs. She wouldn't have thought it was possible so soon, but she was getting excited all over again.

James made a noise deep in his throat and tangled his fingers in her hair, tilting her head back. He bent his head to touch his tongue to the little mole on her upper lip, and she lifted her mouth to him with an eagerness that twisted his gut. He teased her with broken kisses, mounting forays at her mouth that he pulled at the last minute, loving her helpless reaction: the parted, swollen lips, the reach of her tongue, the heavy-lidded eyes. God, she was so gorgeous, and for the moment at least, she was all his. Damned if he wasn't going to wring every last drop of enjoyment out of their encounter today.

For he couldn't help but feel that tomorrow this dainty little apparition was going to wake up and be horrified that she'd let herself be sullied by the big, rough hands of an ex-tenement rat.

Aunie's hands were running down his hard stomach to the waistband of his jeans and James abruptly stood. She blinked up at him in confusion and he pulled her to her feet, stooping in the same movement to get a shoulder under her stomach. He surged upright, hoisting her in a fireman's lift.

"Mistah Rydah!" she protested.

He smacked her on the butt. "Don't call me that!"

Aunie stilled, reacting to his tone, and James cursed under his breath. What could he say? *I'm sorry if I sound surly, but I think I'm going to hear that in the morning and I don't want to hear it tonight.* He stroked an apologetic hand over the pink lace he'd abused. "The couch is too short," he explained in a gentle voice. "I need room to move." He strode with her dangling over his shoulder to her bedroom. Kicking the door closed behind him, he crossed the room and flipped her onto the bed.

Aunie pushed up on her elbow, shoving her hair out of her eyes. James was kneeling on the floor, removing her shoes and socks. The tangle of leggings around her ankles was eased over her feet and dropped to the floor. Standing, he kicked off his own footwear and reached for his zipper.

She scrambled onto her knees to help him. Their hands kept bumping and tangling together until finally Aunie grabbed his by his big, knobby wrists, planted a kiss in each palm, and clamped them to her breasts. He stared mesmerized at the sight and feel of her white breasts in his weathered hands and she reached for his zipper once again.

All Aunie's spurious expertise disappeared when she finally pushed his shorts down his hips and his erection sprang free. She swallowed hard. Gawd. It was big.

Wesley had never had anything like this.

Well, of course, he'd had *something* like this, but it hadn't been nearly so long or so thick. She had occasionally fantasized about having a lover of impressive dimensions. It was one thing to imagine such things, she discovered, warily eyeing his erection. It was something else to be faced with the reality of *this*. It had been a long, long time since she had participated in any sexual activity. She wasn't sure if she'd be able to accommodate the thing.

But she was madly in love with him and she knew she would die trying.

She brushed his shorts all the way down his legs, and he kicked them off. Tentatively, she wrapped her hand around him. He was warm and rigid and he pulsed in her hand when she squeezed. A drop of fluid appeared and she used a gentle fingertip to spread it around the big, blunt head. The hands on her breasts went still.

Aunie tore her eyes away from the magnificence of his sex and looked up to find him watching her. She blushed furiously. "Jimmy?" she said in a soft, hoarse voice. "I'm afraid I'm not very experienced."

James's heart crashed against his ribcage. He eased

her over onto her back and propped himself up over her. "It doesn't matter."

"I don't want to disappoint you."

His eyes tracked slowly down her body, then slowly back up again, absorbing its perfection. "You couldn't, Magnolia." He liked the fact that she was dressed only in a minuscule pair of pink panties and a blush. The more he thought of her inexperience, the hotter he got.

Which was crazy. He'd never had a yen for beginners.

Her hands shaped his shoulders, slid down to his biceps. Knowing he was showing off like a teenager but unable to resist, he flexed them. "Gawd," she whispered in awe. He bent his elbows and brushed his chest against her breasts. "Oh!" Her fingers digging into the solid muscles she'd been admiring, she arched her back, scraping her nipples in the sparse blond fan of hair on his chest.

Pushing himself up to kneel astride her, he cupped his hands around both breasts and kneaded. He was gentle at first, but he noticed that the more firmly he handled them, the crazier she became. When he squeezed them between his fingers and thumb until his hand had swallowed up all except the distended pink nipples, her hips began a slow bump and grind. When he hunched over to gently grind first one and then the other nipple between his teeth, she whimpered and contracted her hips deep into the mattress, then thrust her pelvis up as far as his imprisoning thighs would allow. Her fingernails dug grooves into his hard leg muscles just above his knees.

He edged back further. Hooking his fingers into the waistband of her panties, he slowly peeled them off. Before she could even raise her hips to facilitate their removal, James had slipped off the bed to kneel at its side and pulled her legs over the side after him. He tossed the scrap of pink lace aside and draped her legs over his shoulders. Turning his head, he pressed an openmouthed kiss into her thigh.

Aunie raised up on her elbows. "James?" she whispered. God, she looked so decadent with her legs sprawled open, the bend of her knees caught on his round shoulder muscles. She blushed. Only her gynecologist had ever seen her that close up.

"God, this is pretty," he murmured hoarsely, staring at the luxuriant little black pelt, the flashes of pink. He felt her legs trying to close around his neck, saw her hand creep down to cover herself. "No, don't hide it," he whispered, rolling his big shoulders to unlock her grip. "It's so pretty, Aunie; don't hide it from me." And he bent his head to probe around and between her concealing fingers with his tongue.

"Oh, my gawd, Jimmy!" As if scalded, she whipped her hand away. That suited James just fine, since it left him a clear field. Lazily plying his fingers and tongue, he proved to her that when it came to this particular game, he was a professional player.

Her hips were straining high in search of satisfaction, thigh muscles standing out tautly, when James finally rocked back on his heels and reached for his wallet. He fumbled on a condom, then rose and planted a knee on the mattress. "Put your ankles on my shoulders, Magnolia," he commanded, and once she'd complied, he pressed a thumb against his erection, pushing it down to align with her body. His hips pressed forward and he sank into her a short way.

"Oh, God, Aunie." Feet planted on the floor, knees braced on the bed, he propped his hands on the mattress next to her shoulders, arms stiff and head thrown back. "You're so tight." He pressed a little

further. He'd never had a virgin—had never desired
one. He had the craziest feeling, however, that it must
be a lot like this. Gritting his teeth, he eased back
and then pushed a little harder, gaining another inch.
He tilted his head down to look at her. "Are you all
right?"

She had to struggle to accommodate him, but it
wasn't nearly as uncomfortable as she'd half feared
it would be. In truth, it felt good and she wanted all
of him. "Yes," she whispered and bent her knees a
little, planting the soles of her feet on his collarbone.
She angled her hips, pushing against the fullness
inside her. "More," she pleaded.

He swore under his breath and pressed forward.
Suddenly, the tight muscles gripping him gave a little
and he sank into her fully. He groaned. Eyes closed,
he pulled back and then thrust forward slowly. Pulled
back . . . thrust forward. His eyes slitted open and he
looked down to where they were joined. He sucked
in a deep breath and pumped his hips, watching
blond hair mesh with, then separate from, black.
Then his eyes trailed up her body. He had her bent
almost double, her knees pressed back against her
chest. "Oh, baby," he said repentantly, "you don't
look very comfortable." He lifted one hand off the
bed and slid her leg over his arm, replanting his
hand once her leg was hooked around his waist. He
repeated the gesture on the other side. "That
better?"

"Um," she agreed dreamily and he felt her inner
muscles grab him when she locked her ankles behind
his back. "Magnolia's favorite position," he murmured and commenced a slow, steady rocking.

Her fingernails dug into his forearms and she raised
her hips to meet each thrust. "Oh gawd, Jimmy," she

panted, licking her upper lip. "Oh gawd. It feels so ... um ... feels so ..." She raised her locked ankles higher up his back and pressed her head into the bedspread, arching her back. Her breath caught in ragged little moans in the back of her throat.

James thrust harder, withdrew a little further, pumped a little deeper. "Feels so?" he prompted.

"Goo-o-od," she moaned, dragging the word out endlessly. "So good."

"Oh Christ," he muttered and began to slam into her. He was close, God, he was so close. But he needed to hang on ... had to get her over first. He bent his elbows, bringing his upper body lower, and tucked his chin into his neck, his tongue extending to lap a pink nipple. He knew that would probably get her off. She seemed to have the world's most sensitive little tits.

A frantic little whine rolled out of her throat and, as before, she thrust her breasts up for closer, rougher attention. He was happy to oblige her, drawing strongly on her nipple while his toes dug into the carpet and the muscles in his buttocks contracted, pounding into her with all his might. "*James?*" Her voice climbed beyond its normal soft contralto. "Oh gawd, *James!* I'm gonna ... Uh! ... Oh, pleeeze, I'm gonna ..." And like flipping the switch on a detonator, she felt his large shaft touch something deep inside of her and she exploded into a million fragments, whimpering and raking her nails down his back as her hips slammed up to impale her on that delicious source of pleasure. Inner muscles contracted crazily and she cried out as rapturous sensations, such as she had never known could exist, grabbed her senses and shook them from their moorings.

James lost control. The sight of her lost in her

orgasm, the feel of her—hot, damp skin, raking nails, the slick, gripping sheath milking him for all it was worth—pushed him violently over the edge. He slammed into her one last time and stiffened all over, buttocks clenched to keep him deep, arms locked, head flung back, teeth gritted. A low, animal growl climbed from deep in his diaphragm, rumbled in his chest, rattled in his throat. His teeth unlocked and he roared her name to the ceiling. His entire body jerked convulsively.

The pulses beating in their eardrums gradually slowed and James's head dropped forward. Suddenly he surged against her, sending them both sliding more fully onto the bed. He collapsed atop her, driving the air from her lungs in a loud whoosh.

Head hanging, he pushed up on his forearms just enough to let her breathe. "Sorry," he muttered. He wondered if now was when she'd realize just what she had done . . . and with whom.

Aunie knew exactly with whom and what she had done, and she reveled in it. "James?" she whispered as she dug her fingers into the muscles of his back and massaged. He arched against her hands like an overgrown house cat.

"Yeah?"

"That's never happened for me before."

That brought his head up in a hurry. He brushed her hair away from her flushed cheeks and forehead with gentle fingertips and studied her face. God, she was so pretty. "You've never come?" he asked incredulously.

She didn't even blush at his blunt language. "Not with Wesley. Not ever." She wasn't about to offer the fact that she'd helped herself to a few orgasms. One simply didn't speak of such things. Well, Jimmy probably wouldn't hesitate to do so, but most people didn't. Anyway, it wasn't the same thing at all. Her ankles unlocked from his hips and she rubbed the sole of one foot up and down his calf.

"And there hasn't been anyone except Wesley?" He didn't know why the idea should make his heart pound, but it did.

She shook her head. "There wasn't even that much of Wesley." She hesitated, then confessed, "I'm sorta like those cars that the salesmen all swear were only driven on Sundays by little old ladies."

James laughed. She could always do that to him ... say or do something that caught him off guard and tickled his funny bone. It was more insidious than even the best of sex. "Yeah," he agreed dryly, "except they're usually lying through their teeth. In your case it's the truth. Low mileage, high performance."

The smile that broke out across her face made James's breath catch in his throat. She looked so pleased that he'd been pleased.

She yawned and rubbed her cheek against the damp skin just under his collarbone. James tunneled his fingers through her hair. "Tired?"

"Um-hmm. I know it's fairly early, but,"—she yawned again, raising polite fingertips to cover her mouth—"I'm beat." Her eyes drifted closed, then reopened to regard him drowsily. "I'm sorry," she murmured contritely. "You're probably hungry, huh? I think we both missed our dinners."

"Don't worry about it." He eased out of her and rolled onto his back. His arms reached out to pull her to him, one large hand cupping the back of her head to position her cheek gently against his chest. She sighed and snuggled in, looping an arm over his shoulder, her hand groping for his ponytail. She draped a leg across his thighs.

Two minutes later, she was asleep.

James held her for about an hour before the rumblings of his stomach forced him out of bed. He pulled on his jeans and let himself out of her apartment. In his own, he made two fried-egg sandwiches and washed them down with a tumbler of orange juice. He sat down at his drafting board and was pleased with both the quality and quantity of his work when he pushed back an hour and forty-five minutes later. Going into the bathroom, he flossed and brushed his teeth, removed his rubber band to rebrush his hair, and then clubbed it back again. He shaved carefully.

Then, grabbing a huge handful of condoms, he locked up and let himself back into Aunie's apartment. In the back of his mind was the thought that this might be his only night with her.

The notion shouldn't have had the power to disturb him. With other women, that was all he'd ever wanted.

He tiptoed into the bedroom and stood looking down at her sleeping form. Okay, it did disturb him. He didn't know what the hell made her so different. Usually he was satisfied with one, maybe two sessions of raunchy sex, and then he was anxious to be on his way. Somehow, tonight, that didn't seem nearly enough.

Who, however, could possibly guess what her attitude might be come morning? So, on the chance that tonight was all he'd ever get, he damn well planned to make it count.

CHAPTER 14

He woke her several times that night. Touching her, kissing her, he pulled Aunie from the depths of a sound sleep time after time. And she discovered that, as unbelievably exciting as it had been when he'd made love to her with that edge-of-control urgency he'd displayed earlier in the evening, it was almost negligible compared to when James was feeling slow and deliberate. She had to grit her teeth to prevent herself from blurting out her feelings for him as his hard body rocked over hers with excruciating laziness. Even when he rolled to his back and let her rise and fall upon him as she wished, he held her to a languorous pace that somehow triggered nerves she'd never even dreamed she'd possessed. Through pure concentration—fueled by a terror of scaring him off—she managed not to tell him that she loved him. It was completely beyond her, however, to prevent as well the low, continuous moan that escaped her clenched teeth, her compressed lips.

James awoke first the following morning. Stretching until his shoulder muscles popped, he rolled over to reach for her but stopped at the sight that greeted him. He felt the same sickening drop in his gut that he'd experienced the night Fancy-cut kicked him in the balls. The little bit of her that was visible—her face, her throat, a diagonal slice of one delicate shoulder and breast—gave every appearance of having been thoroughly debauched. He finessed the blanket away and stared down at her, swallowing hard.

He'd never known anyone with skin so pale, had never seen a woman who didn't display at least the faintest of tan lines. But from her hair line to the tips of her toes, Aunie's skin was untouched by the sun, as white and smooth as a gardenia blossom.

Usually.

This morning she looked like she'd been worked over by a brillo pad. Her skin was marred by angry, splotchy red scrapes from his heavy morning beard . . . a result, no doubt, of the last time he'd roused her, around seven A.M. The finely delineated lines of her mouth had been blurred by the roughness of his passion, lips swollen now and red, and whisker burns abraded the area around it.

But worse by far were the hickeys.

Hickeys, for Christ's sake. He'd outgrown thinking they were proof of his prowess when he was about seventeen, eighteen years old. Yet there they were, standing out as dramatically as drops of blood in the snow—on her throat, on her breasts, across her stomach and one thigh. He didn't even know when he'd produced them—the first time, second time, third . . . shit, how many times had there been? He

remembered the feel of her skin, incredibly soft
against his mouth, remembered thinking she was
downright edible, but he sure as hell didn't recall
setting out to mark her like that.

Curses, low and imaginative, whispered out of his
throat, and his beard rasped like sandpaper in the
morning stillness as he scrubbed his hands over his
face. So all right, he tried to tell himself bracingly.
You pretty much figured she'd come to her senses
this morning anyhow, right?

Yeah, right, an inner voice replied viciously, *but I
wasn't lookin' to friggin' well guarantee it.* Oh, Christ, if
she'd had any doubts before, one look in a mirror
and she'd be convinced he was nothing more than
a slum-born animal, incapable of the finer graces she
no doubt expected from a man. He dug his elbows
into his updrawn knees and clasped his hands behind
his head, squeezing his temples between his forearms.

He was still sitting that way, methodically searching
his normally facile mind for a brainstorm, when all
hell broke loose.

The fists thundering on Aunie's front door brought
James's head up with a snap. Aunie shifted in her
sleep, then abruptly came awake when the pounding
continued. She sat up, the covers tumbling to her
lap, and blinked at him in confusion. "James?" she
whispered, watching him wrestle his jeans over his
naked rear, tucking and cautiously zipping. "What's
goin' on? Who's makin' all that noise?"

"I don't know. Here." He tossed her a floral silk
kimono that he'd found draped over her little acces-
sory chair. "Put this on. I'll answer the door."

James disdained stooping down to put his eye to the

viewer. Instead, he yanked open the door in irritation. Whoever the hell was making all that racket had better have a pretty damned good excuse.

His brother Will was the last person he expected to see.

"Oh, good. You're here," Will said and shouldered past James into the short hallway. "Lola said you might be." He rocked nervously on the balls of his feet, the hands in his pockets anxiously jiggling change. "I need your help, Jimmy."

So what else is new? James thought with a twinge of bitterness, but he didn't bother to verbalize it. "C'mon in." He jerked his head in the direction of the living room. He let his brother precede him, then nearly barrelled into his back when Will abruptly stopped. Looking past him, he saw Aunie standing uncertainly in the entry to the bed-and-bath hallway.

She had donned her little cinnamon satin slip as well as the silk kimono, but nothing could disguise what he'd been doing to her the night before. Some of the violently hued marks had been covered by material but by no means had all of them been, and her hair was still rumpled, her mouth still swollen. The jumpiness in Will's body stilled as he turned to his brother and for the first time noticed his bare chest and unclubbed hair. For some reason, the sight of their dishabille seemed to lessen his own tension. "I need your help," he repeated with less edginess than before.

"I'll make some coffee," Aunie offered quietly and disappeared into the kitchen. James added a whole new twist of guilt to the mass already knotting his gut when he noted the stiffness with which she walked. Jesus. He'd always prided himself on being a fairly considerate lover. But he sure as hell hadn't used an ounce of common sense last night.

He turned to Will with a notable lack of sympathy. "What's the problem?"

"Lana's knocked up and . . ."

"Who?"

"Lana. You know, you met her at . . . oh, I guess that was Bobby. Well, anyhow, she's this woman I've been seeing and now she's knocked up."

"You didn't bother to use anything?" James demanded incredulously.

Will's retort was sullen. "I thought she was taking care of it."

"Good God." James shook his head in disgust. "Of all the stupid, idiotic . . . pregnancy aside, Will, you ever heard of safe sex? STD's? AIDS?" He shook his head again, impatiently. "Never mind. What is it, exactly, that you want me to do about it?" He absolutely drew the line at turning this place into a home for unwed mothers, so if that was what his brother had in mind, he could forget it.

"I need ya to lend me a couple hundred bucks. She can get an appointment at the clinic, but we're short—"

"Let me get this straight," James interrupted him sharply, heavy blond eyebrows drawing together ominously over the bridge of his nose. "You want me to finance an *abortion* for your girlfriend because you were too damn lazy to use a glove while you were glad-handing her?"

Will reacted poorly to the incredulous contempt in his brother's voice. "When the hell did *you* get so righteous, Jimmy?" he demanded hotly. "It's pretty damn clear you've been sticking it to *her*"—he jerked his head in Aunie's direction just as she emerged from the kitchen—"the whole night long, so don't try to tell me if she turned up pregnant, you wouldn't hustle her to the nearest clinic, same as me. Or maybe," he said with reckless insolence, his eyes once again taking in the marks on Aunie's skin, "your idea of birth control is keeping her on her knees sucking your—"

The next thing Will knew, his brother was slamming him up against the wall, a rough hand in his hair jerking his neck taut, a muscular forearm jammed against his Adam's apple, choking off his air supply. James's eyes glittered dangerously as he pushed his face aggressively close to Will's. "You *ever*," he said between clenched teeth, "talk about her again like she's one of the little sluts you associate with, and I'll tear your fuckin' tongue out by the roots. You got that, William?" Chest heaving, James stared at his brother through a haze of red. She was the purest thing that had ever passed through his life. He would friggin' well be *damned* if anyone would talk about her as if she were a round-heeled little whore.

Will nodded weakly, eyes wide and nostrils flared. Jesus. He'd seen that look in Jimmy's eyes before, but always it had been directed at someone else . . . usually while in defense of one of his brothers, never at one of them. His eyes sliced to Aunie, who was standing stock-still, regarding them both with horror. He'd made a big mistake thinking she was just another bimbo who'd fallen easily into his brother's bed. Jimmy had never been one for kiss and tell, but everyone knew his past conquests hadn't been all that dissimilar from Will's. Not only was this one a hundred times classier than his usual type, but . . . well, Jimmy didn't blow like he'd just done unless something mattered deeply to him . . . not ever. Will wondered if Aunie knew her importance in his life. Hell, he wondered if his brother knew.

He wondered if he were going to pass out for lack of oxygen before he could figure it out. He could feel himself growing lightheaded.

"James, please," Aunie said in a low, urgent voice. "He's your brother, and you're hurting him!"

He glanced at her, saw the horror in her eyes, and the red mist began to dissipate. He slowly eased his arm back, released his grip in Will's hair. Breathing heavily, he stepped fully away from his brother, shoving his hands through his own hair while he stared unblinkingly at Aunie. Then he turned on his heel and strode from the apartment, slamming the door behind him.

Slumped weakly against the wall, Will took several cautious breaths. He looked at Aunie, at her confusion and horrified dismay, and was genuinely embarrassed that she'd heard what he'd said to James. The Ryder brothers didn't ordinarily run across women of her ilk, and his only excuse for the crude comments he'd made at her expense was frustration with Jimmy's attitude ... which he supposed wasn't really much of an excuse at all.

"I'm sorry," he said, pushing away from the wall. "What I said about you and Jimmy was uncalled for, and ... well, I'm sorry."

She suddenly seemed to recall just what it was he had said and blushed scarlet, tugging the lapels of her kimono closer. Will felt even lower. Jeez, there was just something about her that could make a guy feel like the crudest of lowlifes. He didn't know how Jimmy could stand it. But then, maybe his brother didn't respond to that untouched quality in quite the same way that he did. "Look, I'll get out of your hair," he said. "It was stupid of me to come here in the first place. Jimmy's always had this moral streak . . . I think he got it from Otis's ma. I guess I should have remembered that before I told him what I needed the money for."

"Is that your only regret?" Aunie inquired in amazement. "That you didn't lie to James about the reason you wanted the money?"

Her well-bred wonderment made Will squirm with something he didn't particularly care to feel . . . conscience. "Hey, accidents happen," he said defensively.

"It occurs to me," she commented neutrally, "that they happen a lot more frequently to those who do nothing to prevent them."

"Maybe, but the fact remains, lady, that Lana's already knocked up, neither of us wants the kid, and one way or another we're gettin' her an abortion!"

"So be it," Aunie said, delicately shrugging one shoulder. "What you ultimately choose to do is your business and you have a perfect right to that choice. But rather than dragging other people into a controversy over abortion as a means of birth control, why don't you finance your decision the old-fashioned way . . . and earn it yourself."

"Spoken like someone who's never had to work a day in her life!" Will snapped. "When you pay your dues, sister, then you can talk to me about earning it myself!"

That flicked her on the raw, touching a nerve in her most persistently held insecurity. But a newly discovered pride brought her chin up. "Just who do you think is balancin' my budget and payin' my bills?" she asked coolly, looking him squarely in the eye. "Who do you suppose is workin' her tail off to get an education to prepare herself for the real world?

You don't know the first thing about me, Will Ryder, or the dues I've paid, so don't presume to tell me I've never worked a day in my life. At least I don't expect my brother to fork over money that he's accumulated through his own hard work just to make things smooth and easy for me!"

For a moment, Will looked as though he might explode, and Aunie took a leery step backwards. But then he puffed up his cheeks and expelled a long breath. "Okay, maybe you have a point," he conceded with a modicum of good grace. He even managed half a smile. "I'll consider what you say, all right?"

"All right."

His conscience pinching, Will was totally sincere as he spoke the words. He was almost thirty . . . maybe it *was* time he quit depending on Jimmy to bail him out every time he was in trouble. Maybe he should start figuring a way to take care of business for himself. He'd give it some real thought.

By the time he'd reached the main entrance door of the building, however, he was already wondering if Paul had any spare change, now that he was no longer putting all his money up his nose.

Aunie closed the door behind Will's departing back and slowly slid down it until her knees were wobbling in front of her face. Of the many times she had fantasized the seduction of James Ryder, never had she visualized a morning after quite like this one. It had turned out to be a regular circus, and now she didn't have a clue where she stood. Would James be back?

He had flat-out told her ages ago that he wasn't

big on commitment. That was something she had better keep in mind. And yet . . .

She couldn't erase from her mind the way he'd *looked* at her just before he'd stomped out of the apartment. He'd looked at her as if he needed her understanding, her approbation . . . needed her. And, as much as the viciousness of his attack on Will had unsettled her, the fact remained he'd come unglued in defense of her. Almost as if . . . well, almost as if she were important to him.

Aunie pushed up from the floor and went into the bathroom to start a bath. In her bedroom, she picked James's T-shirt off the floor and buried her nose in it, inhaling his scent. She found his shorts, shoes, and socks on the floor under the satin-and-lace spread when she pulled it up to make the bed. Gathering together the soiled items of his apparel, as well as a few discarded items of her own, she tossed them into her clothes hamper. Then she returned to the bathroom, shut off the steaming water, and removed her clothes. As she turned to drape her kimono and slip over a hook on the back of the door, she caught a glimpse of her reflection in its full length mirror and stilled.

"Oh . . . my . . . gaaawd." She stepped closer and used her forearm to wipe the steam from the mirror's surface. Lord have mercy. No wonder Will had felt free to voice those crude insinuations. She'd thought they'd simply come off the top of his head before she caught sight of herself in the mirror.

Talk about your morning afters. Caption her Tart on the Town. She'd always marked easily, so she didn't give much consideration to the splotches of red that decorated much of her body. But look at her mouth—

look at those whisker burns! They made her look so corrupt, so . . . slutty.

Slowly, slowly, her reflection's lips curled up in a wicked smile, the dark eyes took on a knowing cast.

Because, honestly, hadn't she had the most wonderful time of her life getting in this condition?

She whipped her kimono back on and went to the kitchen to mash up a couple ice cubes. Returning to the bathroom with them in a plastic baggie, she wrapped them in a washcloth, slid into the steaming bubbles with a sigh, and held the ice pack to her mouth. Ah gawd, that felt good. Her head tilted back against the rounded edge of the tub and her eyes closed.

Would James be back?

Or was she going to have to take matters into her own hands and go looking for him?

James was *not* accustomed to needing anyone, and he felt torn apart trying to deal with all the new emotions that kept surfacing. From his sixteenth year onward, his life had been spent catering to the needs of others, and aside from a growing desire for more privacy and fewer problems, he'd never questioned the rightness of his particular circumstance—it simply *was*.

When he slammed out of Aunie's apartment that Saturday morning, however, nothing appeared simple. Temper high, heart pounding, stomach churning, he paused indecisively in the hall for about six heartbeats; then he loped down two flights of stairs to his basement workshop. He crossed straight to the heavy-equipment rack, where he picked out a sledgehammer of considerable size. He was too damn

wired to work on his 'toons. Might as well do something more in keeping with his mood.

It wasn't until he bent a toe on the leg of his work-
bench that his attention was drawn to his lack of
clothing ... never mind proper work clothes. He
slapped his jeans pockets, relieved to find his apartment key still intact. Well, thank God for small favors,
at least. He sure as hell was in no mood to come
under Lola's eagle eye had he lost the damn thing
in Aunie's bedroom. He could swear, sometimes, that
Lola was part witch. One look at him and she'd probably know exactly what was eating him.

And she'd offer a truckload of unwanted advice on
what to do about it.

Hauling his sledgehammer with him, he went up
to his place. He stood under the pounding spray of
the shower for a long time, trying his damnedest to
assemble a little rational thought. It proved to be a
losing battle. He felt almost as if he had the flu: queasy
stomach, aching head, and his mind was racing too
rapidly to pin down any one thought long enough
to deal with it. Climbing out, he dried off, dressed,
and roughly towel-dried his hair. He took a brush to
it, showing it no mercy, and rubber-banded it back.
Hoping that the distress knotting his stomach was
merely hunger, he padded into the kitchen, but nothing in his refrigerator appealed to him. He slammed
the door shut. The hell with it. He'd eat later.

Digging through his files for the plans he'd drawn
for the third floor, he collapsed cross-legged onto
the floor and pored over them. He'd always planned
to convert the four apartments up there into one
large place for himself. It was a future project, but
he decided he might as well start now by knocking
out a wall or two. He could use a little catharsis.

He swung his sledgehammer at an interior wall in one of the upstairs apartments until his shoulders and arms burned in protest, but he failed to find a true measure of release for his bottled-up emotions. Usually self-aware and honest to a fault, he had built up a blind spot when it came to Aunie Franklin. A defense mechanism he refused even to acknowledge had guided his responses to her practically from the beginning ... for somewhere deep inside of him lurked an instinctive awareness that she had the power to hurt him in ways he'd never been hurt before. So he stood within a cloud of plaster dust, angrily destroying the wall, and lied to himself, just as he'd been lying for months. He told himself that it was just because the sex last night had been so surprisingly good that he was feeling a little lost and edgy today. It had nothing to do with need. Nothing.

He ignored the fact that it wasn't images of last night's sex that were twisting his guts into a relentlessly agonized mass. Visual images flashed across his mind, all right, but they were images of her delicate skin marred by his careless handling, images of the expression on her elegantly structured face when he'd gone berserk with his brother. Oh God, that look. He kept seeing it. She'd stared at him as if wondering whether he had some latent penchant for destruction that she'd missed up until that moment, and he couldn't shake that expression free of his mental viewing screens no matter how hard he tried.

Not for the world would he admit to a feeling of social inferiority when it came to her. Hell, he'd never felt inferior in his life, not to man, woman, or child, and he sure as hell didn't now.

He was just having one of those days.

* * *

"Woo-mon! I'm so pleasured to see you ... I thought you'd never get home!"

Aunie, who was barely through the oval-glassed front door, looked up to see Lola leaning out her open doorway. "Hi," she said and smiled. Her tall, exotic friend was practically bristling with suppressed excitement. "What's up? You look like you've just won the lottery."

"Better." Lola stood back, holding the door. "Please to come in." As politely as she'd expressed it, it clearly wasn't a request Lola expected to be ignored. Aunie went in.

"Sit, sit." Lola waved her to a chair. "Would you like some tea? Coffee? A Coke?"

"What I'd *like*," Aunie retorted, grabbing Lola's hand and dragging her onto the couch beside her, "is to know what's going on. You look as if you're about to explode." Her eyes suddenly widened. "Oh gawd, Lola, is it about a baby?"

Lola laughed and hugged herself. "Yes! Our social worker at the agency called!"

Aunie snapped upright. "And ... *and?*"

"And she say there is a young woo-mon there who pick our family album!"

"Oh, Lola!" Aunie grasped her friend's hands. "That's marvelous news! Tell me everything."

"She is young, only fifteen years old. She is due to deliver on June fifth."

"That's only a smidgin over two months to wait."

"If she is on time. With a first baby, it's just as likely she'll be late. But, oh, I am so thrilled. I can bear the wait if I know that at the end of it we'll be gettin' our babe. I will fill the moments until then fixin' a room for it." Her laughter was deep and rich.

It was also contagious, and Aunie laughed with her. "Oh, Lola, congratulations. Otis must be terribly excited, too."

Some of the laughter left Lola's dark eyes. "He doesn't know yet, woo-mon."

"He doesn't! Why?"

Lola bounced up from the couch, then sat down again. "The social worker, she call me 'bout three hours ago. I call Otis immediately, but he's ridin' with the paramedics today. You were gone. James, he's makin' a racket up on the third floor like he has much on his mind, and from the sound of things, I think it best not to disturb him. I thought Otis should be here when I phoned his family to give them the news. I have been going coconuts with all this excitement and no one to tell. I'm so glad you finally came home." She nibbled the skin around her fingernail. "I wish Otis would call me back."

"I'm sure he will, the moment he gets back to the station. When does his rotation end?"

"Not until tomorrow afternoon. Look," she leaned over to pick a heavy cookbook off the floor and flipped through the pages. "I thought I'd make this for dinner tomorrow night to celebrate," she said, pointing to a colored photograph of beef Wellington.

"What a wonderful idea. I'll bring down my crystal candleholders. They'd look pretty on the table." Suddenly the couch vibrated and Aunie sat upright in apprehension. "What's that?" She'd heard conversations among her fellow schoolmates about earthquakes and it flashed through her mind that this might be one. But if it were, the tremor quickly passed.

Lola squeezed her hand. "It's okay," she said. "It's

only James. He must have knocked a main support beam.''

"I thought it was an earthquake," Aunie admitted. She glanced at the ceiling. "What is he doin' up there?''

"Workin' out a load of aggression, I'd say," Lola commented. She leaned forward and gently twitched aside Aunie's flipped-up collar, studying the small, blood-red mark that had been mostly concealed beneath it. "You wouldn't hoppen to know anything 'bout James's aggressions now would you, woo-mon?"

Aunie opened her mouth to tell Lola everything but discovered somewhat to her amazement that she could not. Funny, she'd planned to do exactly that earlier. Unsure if Otis were at home, however, and knowing she'd be uncomfortable discussing something so personal in front of James's best friend, she had taken a cab over to Mary's instead.

Mary hadn't been home. Perhaps she should have paid more attention to the relief that had mixed with her disappointment as she'd turned away from her door, but until now it hadn't fully registered. All she'd known at the time was that she was too restless to return to her apartment. She had wandered the shops downtown for several hours and then killed additional time by walking home instead of calling a taxi. And during that entire time, she'd carried on mental conversations with Lola, in which she received encouragement and solid advice.

Now she discovered that what had passed between James and her last night was too personal, too important to her to discuss . . . even with Lola, who knew him well. This was one problem she simply had to unravel for herself. She bit her lip and heard herself say, "I'm not precisely certain what James is feelin' at this moment; but if you're askin' if it has anything to do with me, then I'd have to say yes, I think it does. I can't talk about it, Lola.''

Lola studied her quietly. Finally, she said, "Just tell me this. Did James give you that mark or is he up there tearin' apart the third floor because someone else did and he saw it?''

"Don't be silly. This is Jimmy's handiwork.''

"Don't be silly, she say. I've been watchin' the mon twitch like a finger on a hair-trigger for some time now, so I don't think it's silly. I don't want to see him hurt, woo-mon, so don't you go breakin' his heart.''

Aunie laughed wearily. "Oh, Lola," she sighed, "you've got it all backward. I love that man so much it's drivin' me crazy. I couldn't even *begin* to tell you what the heck it is that he's feelin' for me.''

She stood at the base of the stairway to the third floor for several long moments, trying to summon the nerve to climb the stairs and confront James once and for all about their relationship. In the end, however, she chickened out. She kept hoping he would come to her apartment. When seven o'clock came and went, when all had been still on the third floor for over an hour and still he didn't arrive on her doorstep, she didn't know what to do. This morning it had seemed so simple, so clear-cut, to say that if he didn't come to her she would go to him.

Now nothing seemed simple.

Yet . . .

Was this what she wanted? This uncertainty, this stark insecurity? When his eyes seemed to give her one message and his words gave her another, did she stake her happiness on trying to *guess* what he wanted?

Or did she take the bull by the horns like a big girl and ask him what his intentions were?

Out in the hallway, James turned away from her door for the third time while he, too, argued with himself. He was unwilling to admit that he harbored any sort of need . . . and yet, he couldn't seem to stay away from her. He lifted his hand to knock on the door, then let it drop to his side, its mission incomplete. What if she didn't want to see him?

The thought brought his chin up. If she didn't want to see him then that was just tough. She still needed his help, so she'd simply have to get used to having him around. He rang the doorbell.

The door was whipped open, and they stood face to face, hearts pounding. For several seconds they simply stared at each other warily.

Then Aunie launched herself at his chest. She wrapped her arms around his neck and pulled herself up his body, with the help of his hands on her bottom, until her legs were twined around his waist. "Oh gawd, Jimmy," she mumbled into the warm contour of his neck. "I was so scared you weren't comin' back."

CHAPTER 15

James's arms tightened around her convulsively. He stepped into the apartment with Aunie still clinging to his torso like a treed cat and bumped the door shut behind him with his hip. He leaned back against it. "You aren't mad at me then?" he asked in a hoarse voice, rubbing his jaw against her silky hair. God, she smelled so good, felt so good.

She shook her head against his throat. "Why would I be mad?"

Christ, if she didn't already know, he sure as hell didn't want to tell her. But she had already raised her head, loosened her grip on his neck, and was leaning back from the hips to look into his face, so he admitted, "For leaving hickeys all over you like some no-class teenager? I thought you'd be furious."

"Over those?" She laughed in astonishment, dimples flashing. "Sugah, I've had bruises the color of pansies and the size of your fist from merely brushin' up against a hard object. I mark easily. A few little ol' red splotches are not gonna throw me into a tizzy."

The knots in his stomach, which had begun to unravel the minute she'd thrown herself into his arms, finally dissolved entirely. He pushed away from the door and maneuvered her around until she was riding his back piggyback style. He jogged into the living room.

"Want to go for a walk around the neighborhood? I can show you some of the lesser known hidey-holes you may have missed."

"Mm." She nibbled on his earlobe. "It's dark out there. I wanna make love."

"Stop that!" He dropped her like a hot spud on the living room couch and stepped back, hands stuffed in his pockets. "Don't tease me, Magnolia. You know we can't do that."

"I do?" Aunie pushed up on her elbows and knuckled her hair out of her left eye. "We can't? Why not?"

"Why not! I went overboard last night and this morning you were walkin' around here like a cowgirl after a week-long roundup."

Aunie grinned at him and pulled up her sweater, showing him a pale blue satin-and-lace bra. "Yeah," she murmured, "but I was still walking, wasn't I?"

"C'mon," he growled, eyes glued to the pale curves of her breasts. "Don't do this to me. I'm trying to be responsible here."

"Well, don't be. Let me be responsible for myself."

"I don't want to hurt you!"

"You won't. I took a long, hot bath this morning and I feel fine James, honest I do." She reached for the button on her waistband. "Wanna see my matchin' panties?"

James grabbed her wrists and slammed them to the

cushions on either side of her head. Kneeling at the side of the couch, he glowered at her. "Yes, damn you, I do. Now, knock it off, will ya? I don't have a whole lot of control around you, Aunie, and I don't think I can stand another day like the one I just spent, feeling guilty and sick every time I thought of how carefully you had to walk because of me."

"Let go of my wrists, Yank." He did and she sat up, scooting into the corner of the couch. Pointedly, she pulled her sweater back down, picked up a throw pillow, and hugged it to her chest. "I think we'd better get a few things straight," she said in a quiet voice filled with conviction. "First of all, nobody . . . not you, not some gynecologist with ten years worth of education . . . *nobody* knows my body better than I do. I'm tired of having you judge my endurance by my size, not to mention being less than thrilled when you make decisions that directly affect me without bothering to consult me first. I'm a grown woman, James, not a little girl."

"I don't think you're . . ."

"Don't you? You've made a quite a few insulting assumptions about me since we've met. Too fragile to *kiss*, remember that one?"

"Oh." He grinned sheepishly. "Yeah."

"And you could have saved yourself the repercussions of your guilty conscience today if you'd bothered to stick around long enough this morning for a little basic communication. You didn't make love to me in a vacuum, you know! I was right there, participating my little heart out, and I think I find it offensive that you believe I'm so vain a few little love bites are going to throw me into a tailspin." She eyed him sourly. "Or maybe that's your own ego talking. Are you only gonna love me as long as I'm perfect?" Damn it, anyhow. Was she destined to keep picking men who were less interested in the total package than they were in the gift-wrapping?

Who the hell said anything about love? James wondered warily. He opened his mouth to set her straight, to warn her against building fantasies out of thin air, and instead heard himself saying indignantly, "Dammit, Magnolia, it had nothing to do with physical perfection or the lack of it. It was more a matter of . . . class distinctions." Somehow, that came out sounding stupid. Damn. It sure as hell hadn't felt stupid at the time. It had felt painful and confusing.

"What?" Aunie tossed her pillow aside and faced him squarely, seriously provoked. "Are you telling me, Mistah James T. Rydah, that I'm not good enough for you?" But, no, that simply didn't make sense. Not given the way he kept trying to protect her, whether she needed protection or not.

Glints of moss green glared out at her from between narrowed blond lashes. "Don't toy with me, Aunie."

She suddenly remembered the sting of his hand on her rear end and the tone of his voice last night when she'd called him mister. "You think *you're* not good enough for *me?*"

"Don't be ridiculous." But his voice was stiff.

"I'm not being ridiculous. Explain what you mean by class distinctions."

"We come from different worlds, Magnolia. Haven't you figured that out yet?" He was annoyed at having to point it out to her. "While you were going to country club dances in pretty little party dresses, I was wallowing in the dirt, rubbing shoulders with hookers and drug dealers."

"So, what's your point, Jimmy? If you're saying that people can't or don't change, then you're full of it

up to your handsome green eyeballs. *I've* changed
. . . and darn happy it makes me, too. I'm not the
same person I used to be; I'm *better* because I'm useful
now. And you . . . My God, look at what you've done
with your life! You sure as heck aren't associating with
that sort of person now. You're a famous cartoonist,
for heaven's sake; you own this beautiful building;
you possess all sorts of skills that I can't even begin
to comprehend. The only thing the matter with you,
James Ryder, is that damn overblown sense of responsibility of yours!"

"A sense of responsibility is a *liability*?"

"It is when you use it to make decisions concerning
my body without botherin' to consult me first!"

"Oh, shit, Aunie, are we back to that again?"

"Yes, we're back to that. How come only *you* get
to decide when we make love? I want equal say-so! I
didn't move halfway across the country just to hook
up with another man who thinks I'm too damn dumb
to know what's good for me."

James hauled her to her feet and bent down to
stand eyeball to eyeball with her. "Don't you ever
compare me to that asshole!"

The honest outrage in his voice drained Aunie of
her anger. She raised a hand and stroked his smooth
cheek with conciliatory gentleness. "No," she agreed.
"You are *nothin'* like Wesley. You're such a fine man,
James." She cupped his jaw in her palm and raised
her lips to bestow a sweet kiss on his mouth. Drawing
back, she wiped a smudge of lipstick off his bottom
lip with her thumb, looked at him with luminous
brown eyes, and said sweetly, "But don't you go
expecting that my saying so entitles you to run my
life."

James laughed. "No, ma'am, I wouldn't dream of it."

Aunie snorted, skeptical of his easy capitulation. Then with a shrug, she reached down, grasped the hem of her sweater and the polo shirt beneath it, and whipped them over her head. Her hands went to the waistband of her jeans, but she hesitated, looking up at him. One delicate dark eyebrow shot up. "So, how about it?" she inquired. "You wanna see my matchin' panties now, or what?"

James wrapped his hands around her waist, lifting her; and as usual anytime her legs were in the vicinity of his torso, they spread apart to wind around his hips. Holding onto his shoulders with both hands, she arched back from the waist and practically purred when his mouth pressed kisses from her throat to her shoulders, to her collarbone, down to the little tab that held her bra closed between her breasts. "Yeah," he finally whispered hoarsely, rubbing his face in the shallow valley of her cleavage, his big hands gripping her round little bottom to bring more of her into range. "Let's see 'em."

It wasn't until the following Thursday that Aunie realized it had been awhile since she'd received any disturbing phone calls. She checked the time and date sheet that she used to mark down each call and saw that the last one had been logged at 12:37 A.M. on Saturday morning of the previous week.

She didn't know what to make of it and was uncertain how to proceed. James, when she showed him the time sheet and explained the current lack of calls, did not share her indecision.

"We just keep on doing exactly what we've been doing," he said peremptorily.

Her newfound, hard-won independence bristled at his tone. Chin elevated, she snapped, "There you go, trying to manage my life for me again! I'll have you know, James T. Ry—"

The next thing she knew, she was flat on her back with James on his knees straddling her hips, pinning her wrists to the floor. He leaned over her until their faces were only inches apart. "This isn't up for debate, Magnolia," he informed her with cool finality.

Cheeks blazing with temper, dark eyes liquid and impossibly large, Aunie glared up at him. "Get off me, you lowdown, no-good, mannerless Yankee." It was demanded in a tone loaded with well-bred disdain.

He grinned at her. He couldn't help it; now that he knew she didn't scorn his background, he loved it when she went all Southern belle on him. "Huh-uh. Now quit squirmin' around and listen up." He rested more of his weight on her thighs when she ignored his command. "If your caller was from the college, it stands to reason that he was discouraged by the fact that you're well-protected. Therefore, the escort remains." He could tell by the way she quit bucking that she was beginning to think instead of react. He eased his weight a bit. "Now, if it's old Wesley, the calls could have stopped for a number of reasons."

"Such as?"

He really hated to say this, but it needed to be said. "Such as he's in transit. And if he's headed here, the self-defense lessons are more than necessary, Magnolia; they're mandatory."

She went perfectly still and the blood drained from her face. Her reaction made James wish he hadn't raised the possibility, which in turn made him feel defensive. Why did she have to be so damned stubborn? He hadn't wanted to confront her with the potentiality, but she always had to push, push, push. Just once, he wished she'd simply accept something he said without arguing about it.

Still . . .

"That's worst-case scenario . . . and it's only one possibility," he said gruffly, reaching out to stroke the velvet-smooth skin of her cheek. His finger brushed back and forth over the tiny mole above her upper lip. "If it is Cunningham, he has to be intelligent enough to realize that your lawyer informed you of the break-in at his office. It could be he also recognizes the likelihood of your calls being traced and he's just lying low for a while."

"I hate this, Jimmy," Aunie said wearily.

"I know, baby." James eased his weight off her and rolled to the side. She remained in the same position, only her head turning to maintain eye contact.

"Maybe," she whispered in a voice that didn't hold much hope, "it really was a chance caller who finally got bored."

"Maybe it was," James agreed without conviction. Propping his head up on one hand, he reached out his free hand to brush her dark, shiny hair away from her face. "But, Magnolia, honey, we sure as shit aren't risking your safety on that assumption."

Wesley pulled his Jaguar up to the curb and parked behind the realtor's car. For a moment, he sat behind the wheel just staring impassively at the For Sale sign posted to one side of the walkway that led to the Atlanta house he had once shared with Aunie. Rage built inside him. Drawing a deep breath to help him conceal it, he climbed out of the car and joined the real estate agent.

She preceded him up the walk, flashing him a smile over her shoulder. "As you can see, Mr. West," she said with professional enthusiasm, addressing him by the fictitious name he'd given her, "this is one of Atlanta's premier neighborhoods. You won't find a more desirable address."

That's why I bought the damned house in the first place, you stupid bitch.

Wesley tuned out most of her sales pitch as they inspected the house. Fury was escalating inside him as they moved from room to room. "I thought the premises had been vacated," he snapped in the cool, impatient tone he habitually reserved for employees and other inferiors.

"It has been," she replied in confusion. Then understanding dawned. "Oh! The furnishings. Now, this is a real bonus! All of it"—she waved her hand— "can be purchased for a song. Isn't it simply lovely? It was designed by one of *the* most exclusive design- ers." She mentioned a name and gave him a coy smile. "Perhaps you've heard of her?"

Heard of her? He'd *discovered* her. And the acquisi- tion of every *furnishing,* as the realtor's term was, had been personally supervised by *him.* This house had always been a showplace.

He had filled it with treasures and now Aunie had it all up for sale. At bargain basement prices, as if the acquisitions that were his life's work were no more consequential than flea market castoffs. It was a slap in the face.

Just one more for which, very soon now, she was going to pay.

* * *

Several times during the past few nights she had told him she loved him.

James couldn't be positive, of course, that it hadn't been said merely to gain a little sexual relief. That certainly wasn't outside the realm of possibility; after all, each time she'd whispered it had been in the heat of the moment. He brooded about it as he paced his apartment.

James had always thought he knew a great deal about women. When it came to one like Aunie, however, he admitted he didn't know jack, and his prior experiences weren't much help in this particular situation. Except for his mother, who had never been home much, he'd never lived with a woman in his life. Hell, he thought with automatic defensiveness, he wasn't actually living with a woman now.

Yeah. Right.

Okay, he was practically living with her.

For perhaps the first time in his life, he had no idea what he was going to do next. He'd thought that once he got in her pants ... Okay, the truth was he hadn't thought beyond that, hadn't even allowed himself to think of that much. But if he *had* given the matter some thought, he would have expected to be quickly bored.

That's the way it had always worked in the past.

He sure as hell hadn't expected this constant neediness, and it grated on him. About the only thing he managed to keep inviolate these days was his apartment, using it when she was out or at school, always meeting her in her place, never in his. Big deal. He kept her out; but the minute he knew she was home, he was down the hall, panting to be with her. Christ. Why couldn't he stay away?

He felt so different with her. Territorial, possessive, protective, all sorts of emotions he never in a million years would have associated with himself. Even sex was different.

Now, there was a masterpiece of understatement—sex was especially different. Always before, he'd picked big girls who liked it rowdy and a little rough. He showed them a good time and then he was out the door. From the first time he'd contemplated what it would be like with Aunie, however, he'd assumed he'd need to exercise more than a little customary care with her. To his surprise, she'd proved to like it rowdy and a little rough, too. Sometimes. But then the other night, when he'd tweaked a nipple a little too enthusiastically, he'd learned that what excited her one day could hurt her the next.

He'd whipped his hand back guiltily at her little gasp of pain, but she had reached for it with both hands and pressed it over her entire breast. "It's okay," she'd whispered. "They're a little tender tonight, is all. Just hold it like this."

For the first time in a long time, he'd remembered her fragility. He knew it drove her crazy when he referred to it, especially if he were foolish enough to intimate it might prevent her from accomplishing a given goal. She seemed to think she was ten feet tall. And most of the time, her sturdiness had surprised him. But the truth was, there were times when she *was* fragile.

He hadn't been able to handle the thought of hurting her and so he'd made love to her very carefully that night and very, very slowly. His reward was discovering that slow made her wild.

God, it had been so sweet: her hands sliding restlessly, digging into his back, pulling his ponytail, gripping his buttocks while she thrust her pelvis sharply upward. Her breath coming in shuddery little exhalations; her heavy-lidded dark eyes losing focus as they stared at him. And then the whispers, starting slow and sweet, escalating in urgency. "Jimmy? Oh God, James? Oh *Jimmy*, please . . . Uhhh? . . . Oh Gawd, I love you, Jimmy, I love you, Jimmy, I love . . . Oh *Gawd*!"

He'd felt like the top of his head was blowing off and he'd come in violent, scalding jets. And ever since then, he'd found himself making love to her slowly— God, so slowly. Holding back until his eyes began to cross and his balls turned blue.

Holding back because he knew if he did, then ultimately he'd hear her say, "I love you, Jimmy." Despising his desperate need to hear it.

Did she mean it? Or was it just some knee-jerk reaction, words she felt were necessary to express before she got off?

He always bottled up his instinctive response. He kissed her with savage concentration; he swallowed hard; he roared his satisfaction to the walls, but he bit back the words that dammed up in his throat every friggin' time.

God, I love you, Magnolia.

Why was it so impossible to admit? It just was. He could not, would not, say the words aloud. He simply couldn't. Not as long as he still saw a terror of him in her eyes every time he made her practice her self-defense.

It was getting to the point where he hated those damned sessions as much as she did. She was turning into a right fine little fighter, but he found her fear of him acutely painful.

It had to be that way, though. She wouldn't flat-out fight, not fight the way she might one day need to do, unless he could convincingly duplicate Cunningham's probable actions. There was no point in teaching her to defend herself if all those lessons went up in smoke in the face of an unexpected panic. So he generated a fear, then taught her to function through it.

But he hated it. And he knew instinctively that if he didn't keep those words locked tight in his chest, he would no longer be capable of pulling it off.

He didn't know how to deal with the confusion of all these raw emotions clawing away inside of him, but the animal instinct that had always served him so well urged him to protect himself. On a deep, rarely acknowledged level, he simply didn't trust it to last. Guys like him did not end up with women like Aunie Franklin. Sooner or later, he was sure, she was going to take a good long look at their differences; and when she did, she would probably be packed and gone so fast, he wouldn't see her for dust. So he prevented her from making any memories in his apartment, and he held a part of himself aloof— protection against future pain.

As for the here and now . . . about all he could do was bite his tongue and swallow back words that were better left unsaid.

"So, you haven't had a call in . . . how long?"

"Three weeks." Aunie had her eyes closed and her face raised to the sun. She and Mary were spending their lunch hour on the grass plaza in front of Performance Hall at school. This was the third day that the weather had reached the midseventies. There was a light breeze and students lounged in various stages of undress all over the plaza, working on their tans. Mary was already a pretty golden color. Aunie merely enjoyed the warmth, since every exposed inch of her skin was slathered with SPF 40 sun block. Without it, she'd burn, blister, and peel. In her next life, she was coming back as a six-footer with an olive complexion.

"That's good," Mary commented. There was a moment of silence, then she asked, "So, why don't you look relaxed?"

Aunie's eyes snapped open and she turned her head to stare at her friend. "Because James won't let me. God, Mary, I could really use a break from all this, but he just keeps pushin', pushin', pushin'. What's Bobby's phone number? If you've gotta fight, what's the most vulnerable area on a man's body?" She snapped her fingers. "Quick. Otis's phone number!" She rubbed the little wrinkle that had popped up between her delicate, dark eyebrows. "It seems like he's either making love to me or tryin' his damnedest to drive me beyond endurance with his little quizzes and tests. Do you know that we've never even been on a real date? He's all but livin' with me and he's never once taken me out."

"Are you unhappy with him, Aunie?"

"Unhappy? No. I just don't feel very . . . secure. He warned me a long time ago that he wasn't big on commitment and I thought I was okay with that. But I don't think I am, really. I want more, Mary. I love him so much, and I want the security of knowing he loves me, too. Sometimes, I truly believe he does. But then he gets all cool and reserved on me. He withdraws into himself and I just can't reach him. I hate worryin' that today's the day he's gonna decide he's bored with me.''

"I really don't see that happening. You ask me, he's runnin' scared.''

Aunie looked at her in amazed disbelief. "This is a joke, right?'' When Mary didn't offer the punch line, she demanded, "Runnin' scared from what? I don't think there's anything in this world that James Ryder is afraid of.''

"I think he's scared silly of you. Of you leaving him. Of you getting hurt. Jeez, Aunie, he guards you like a starving dog with a tasty bone.''

"Believe me, the last thing he has to fear is my leaving him, and he knows it. Every time he makes love to me I ramble on and on about how much I love him. I try not to, 'cuz I'm afraid it'll scare him off, but I can't seem to help myself.''

"Sex talk.'' Mary shrugged. "He won't take that seriously. Everybody does it.''

"He doesn't.''

"That just means that he's the type who, when he finally does get around to saying the words, will really mean them. Trust those feelings that tell you he really loves you. Better yet, why don't you try a little communication? I can almost guarantee that it wouldn't hurt for the two of you to climb out of bed long enough to talk to each other.''

"I know, I know. I say I wanna be a grown-up, then I whine like a seventh grader with her first real crush. But I'm a slow starter. I've never felt anything remotely like this before and I'm terrified of losing it. Every time I open my mouth to broach the subject I chicken out, because what if he says, 'No I don't love you, and I don't want your love either—all I wanna do is fuck?' I honest to God don't know what

I'd do.'' She shook off the mantle of depression this conversation had produced. "Let's talk about somethin' else. It's too nice a day for worrying about things you can't change."

"Okay," Mary replied agreeably. She planted her chin in her palm and smiled. "So, tell me. Aside from the obvious, Ms. Franklin, what *is* the most vulnerable area of a man's body?"

Aunie laughed and ticked them off on her fingers. "The obvious, of course: testicles. Then there's throat, eyes, nose, and kneecaps."

Aunie was surprised to find Paul as well as James waiting for her when she left her last class. She waved to Mary, who was making her way toward them against the flow of hall traffic, and then turned to James's brother. "Hello, Paul. It's nice to see you."

Paul gave her a shy smile. "Hi ya. Hope y' don't mind my tagging along with Jimmy."

"Of course not. Did y'all do somethin' together this afternoon?"

"Yeah. I'm moving into a new place on Queen Anne and Jimmy took me shopping for a new couch." He gave her a self-deprecating smile. "I don't trust my taste; it's been said it's all in my mouth."

"It's not an exaggeration, either," James contributed. "You should've seen the plaid Herculon monstrosity he was leanin' toward."

"I suppose you steered him toward black leather, instead?"

"Nah," Paul answered. "We ended up with something real nice." He launched into a description of it for her.

Mary, who had approached a moment earlier, took

advantage of Aunie's preoccupation with Paul and leaned toward James. "Listen," she murmured, "Aunie really wants to go out on a date."

All the good humor fled James's face and his eyes turned cold and flat. His hand whipped out and gripped Mary's wrist. "With whom?" he demanded.

Mary stared at him with openmouthed amazement. "With you, you idiot," she snapped and pried his fingers off her arm. She rubbed feeling back into her skin. "She said you've never taken her out."

Dull color climbed high into James's angular cheekbones. He noticed her still rubbing her wrist and glanced quickly at Aunie. Thank God, she hadn't noticed him manhandling her friend. "I'm sorry," he muttered. "Are you okay?"

"Yeah, I'm dandy." Mary studied him for a moment. "You don't like me very much, do you?"

"You're okay." Mary arched an eyebrow at him and he admitted, "All right, maybe I'm still a little pissed about the way you took Aunie out to pick up men."

Her jaw dropped. "My God," she said incredulously, "that was nearly five months ago! You sure as hell hold a grudge for someone who didn't even have a relationship with her at the time." She watched color tint his face. "For your information, James, I didn't take her out to pick up men, I took her out to celebrate finals and have a few laughs. If we'd seriously gone hunting for bear, buddy, then trust me, she wouldn't have ended up babysitting you that night."

James plowed his fingers through his hair until his fingertips bumped the rubber band holding back his hair. He stared at Mary as he gripped his ponytail. Finally, a large shoulder inched toward his ear. "I suppose," he admitted.

"You suppose what?" Aunie inquired, turning back to them.

"He supposes he can put up with me for dinner tonight, when what he really planned was to have you all to himself," Mary supplied smoothly when James, his expression uncharacteristically blank, just stared at Aunie.

"Good, you can feed me, too," Paul said with a small smile. "I'm afraid to drop by unannounced. Bobby said he did, and you gave him the bum's rush."

James flushed. He *had* rather unceremoniously hustled Bobby out of Aunie's apartment the other night the instant she'd returned from a session at the gym. She'd been all flushed and dewy from her workout, and he'd had a sudden need to get to her before the sweat had a chance to dry.

"If you don't mind potluck, you're both welcome," Aunie said warmly. "But, Paul, you and James are goin' to have to entertain yourselves for a while. Mary and I have to study."

"No problem."

James thought about both their guests later that evening after they had left. He supposed Mary wasn't really all that bad. She had a fairly decent sense of humor and she loved Aunie. She could be worse.

Paul's company he had really enjoyed. It had been so many years since he'd been around his brother when he wasn't high or looking to get high that he'd all but forgotten about his sense of humor. When they were kids, Paul's sense of the ridiculous had always been closely in tune with James's.

Unfortunately, of the four Ryder boys, Paul had had the most difficulty finding an identity for himself. In those days, he'd been shy and insecure with anyone who wasn't immediate family, and James imagined that had contributed a good deal to his years of addiction. In the beginning, cocaine had given him a false sense of courage. It had made him feel indomitable, and then it had systematically begun to destroy him.

But today, James could see the quiet pride of self that Paul was developing. He'd talked to him at length about the program and his encounter groups, about the feeling of self-respect he gained every day he survived without giving in to the need for a snort. He'd had a pocket full of money today, and he'd been like a kid in a candy store as they'd shopped for furniture for his new apartment, proud as a boy with a shiny new bike as he'd shown James his new place. It wasn't huge or deluxe, and Paul had known it, but he'd also known it was respectable and nice . . . a far cry from the dump he'd lived in for so many years.

It was amazing. His brothers were finally beginning to do what he'd longed for them to do . . . they were beginning to grow up and take responsibility for their own lives. Paul was getting on track; Bobby had actually made two payments now on the loan James had given him, and Will . . . Well, Will was still a horse's ass, but maybe there was eventual hope for him, too. He hadn't seen him since the day he'd come looking for money for his girlfriend's abortion and had damned near gotten his teeth knocked down his throat instead.

All of which meant James was getting his own life back, just as he'd loudly claimed to desire more than anything else. It was kind of funny then that he felt just the tiniest bit lost. He still had Aunie's problems to straighten out, of course, but that was quite a bit different. For one thing, she neither wanted nor expected him to take charge. She did everything in her power, in fact, to see that he *didn't* assume control. Her friggin' independence could be a real thorn in the side for a man who was accustomed to taking command at the first whiff of trouble.

The front door opened. Well, speak of the devil. James watched her over his beer bottle as she backed through the door and then bumped it closed behind her with her hip. She maneuvred the unwieldy laundry basket through the archway and crossed over to the couch, turning the basket on its side and spilling clean clothes all over James and the couch.

"Half of this stuff's yours," she informed him. "So you can help fold it."

James raised one eyebrow. "I just love a domineering woman."

"Yeah?" She picked out one of the bandannas she used as sweatbands at the gym and whipped it into a rope. Jumping onto his lap, straddling him with her legs, she quickly secured his wrists in the homemade bondage. She removed the bottle of beer from his hand, twisted around to set it on the coffee table, sat back, and grinned at him. "Hah! I've got you in my power now, Yankee dog, so you had better show me a little respect."

" 'Zat right? Now that you've got me, what, exactly, are you gonna do with me?"

She gave him an evil grin. "Turn you into my sex slave."

"You're dressed all wrong for this, Magnolia. Where's the black leather?"

"Well ... I've got a pair of spike-heeled black leather boots. Will that do?"

The seriousness with which she considered the matter made him laugh. "You got a whip, too? Leather bra with the nipples cut out? A spiked dog collar, perhaps?"

"I don't need all that stuff. I've got a garter belt, my boots, and . . . imagination!" Then she regarded him sourly. "How come you know so much about this, anyway?"

"Occasionally, my taste in movies is very lowbrow."

"*Dirty* movies?" Her eyes were huge as she leaned back and regarded him with fascination. "Really? Ooh, you dirty old man. Do you wear a raincoat and go to one of those sleazy theaters on First Avenue?"

James laughed. "Sorry to disappoint you, baby, but I rent 'em from a neighborhood video store and watch 'em on the VCR."

"Well, the next time you get one, I wanna watch it, too, okay? I've never seen one."

He shrugged. "Yeah, sure." He'd have to pick out something fairly tame or she'd be shocked right down to her little pink toenails.

"When? Tomorrow?"

The three creases in his cheek deepened as he grinned at her. Whoever would have guessed that his well-bred little darlin' would have a secret hankering to see a blue movie? "One of these days," he promised Then he remembered what Mary had said. "Aunie?"

She was grinning to herself over the prospect of seeing one of those movies, but his serious tone brought her head up. "Yeah?"

"Will you go out with me Saturday night?"

"Out where?"

"Out to dinner, dancing . . . I don't know. Wherever you want. On a date."

The smile that lighted her face was like the dawn breaking. "Really?"

"Yeah. We've never dated."

"I know."

"So, will you?"

"Oh, Jimmy," she said and raised his bound wrists over her head until his arms were around her. She wound her own arms around his neck and pressed her face into the side of his throat "I would really, really like that."

CHAPTER 16

Wesley sat in his beautifully appointed, sterilely clean living room, staring deep into his snifter of fine brandy and brooding. That goddam bitch. She'd ruined his entire life.

He'd given her everything. She'd been nothing but a poor, shirttail relation when he'd first met her. From a good family, certainly, and beautiful beyond belief . . . but still a virtual social *nothing*. He'd showered her with riches, given her standing, bestowed his prestige upon her. And for what?

So she could turn around and try to destroy his good name with her lies and her sluttish behavior.

He'd had to do everything for her; the tramp never had possessed an ounce of discernment. It wasn't as if he'd asked her to do anything that would tax her mind; all he'd ever expected her to be was a worthy adornment. Hadn't he supplied her with the benefit of his excellent taste by choosing her wardrobe?

Hadn't he counseled her on who was important and who was not? And what had he asked in return? Merely that she be a credit to him.

His eyes burned with a fever that was becoming increasingly familiar to those in his social and business circles. She'd turned him into a laughingstock. First by attending that third-rate college instead of keeping herself available to decorate his lavish functions as a proper wife should, then by openly running around with another man. Wesley hadn't missed the speculative glances that were cast his way, and he knew exactly where to cast the blame. She was his *wife*, yet instead of being a credit to him, her behavior had ultimately resulted in a public display in court.

Well, she wasn't going to get away with it. No one made a fool of Wesley Cunningham. Not without serious retribution.

Hers was just around the corner.

The perfect summerlike weather had broken, but even though it was grey and overcast, it was still unusually warm. Aunie and Mary shared a lunch on the shady grass plaza outside the Performance Hall.

"So, anyway," Mary was saying, "he says to me, 'Hi, I'm Lance Cameron LaRue'—do you *believe* that name? . . ."

Aunie was only half listening. Her hand kept creeping to the back of her neck and finally she craned her head around. The short hairs on her nape were standing straight up. Was someone staring at her? She scanned the faces nearby, then those further afield, but she didn't make eye contact with anyone who seemed inordinately interested in her. She turned back to Mary.

"I feel like I'm being watched," she murmured, breaking into Mary's conversation, and her friend's head snapped up. "Wait a second and then take a look around. See if you can spot anyone, will you?" She paused a beat and then gave Mary a crooked smile. "Lance LaRue?"

Mary laughed. "Yeah. Sounds like the hero of a Western novel, doesn't it? He had a personality to match. The guy seemed to assume I'd fall into his arms." Casually, she glanced beyond Aunie's shoulder, scanning the plaza. She took her time, eyes moving slowly from face to face. Finally, she returned her attention to Aunie. "I don't see anyone."

Aunie's pent-up breath was expelled in a sigh. "I'm probably imagining things."

"Still," Mary said.

"Yeah," she agreed. "Still." She thought a moment. "Lola is picking me up today," she finally said. "We're supposed to go shopping for nursery goodies. I think I'd better give her a call and tell her to implement plan REI."

"Oh, wait, don't tell me," Mary murmured. "Something dreamed up by the crusading cartoonist, right?"

"You got it."

One corner of Mary's lips quirked up in a wry smile. "This I gotta hear."

Aunie and Mary met after their last class. They walked together as far as the southwest corner of the reservoir where Mary turned left to retrieve her car. Aunie turned right, crossed the street, walked to the middle of the block, and entered Recreational Equipment Inc. through its main doors.

REI was to Seattle sportsmen and outdoor enthusiasts what Cartier's was to a serious jewel fancier. Aunie had been fascinated by the place ever since the first

time James had walked her through it while he laid
out operation REI.

She couldn't pinpoint why the store interested her,
exactly. It wasn't as if she'd ever been camping or
had participated in any sports except tennis and, back
in her school days, a little field hockey. Until her
divorce, she hadn't owned a shoe that didn't boast
at least a three-inch heel, and she was accustomed to
navigating the pavements of cosmopolitan cultural
centers, not hiking through the hills or shooting the
rapids.

Perhaps that was the very reason she found this
Mecca for the great outdoorsman so interesting.

It catered to just about every interest group, from
backpackers to kayakers. It was housed in a big, ram-
bling building, with ramps to here, stairs leading
there. Down in the basement was a bargain outlet
incongruously labeled The Attic, and the salespeople
in each department seemed to her extremely knowl-
edgeble. They sold sports equipment, clothing, dried
foods, and accessories for just about every nature-
related hobby known to man.

Aunie meandered through the various depart-
ments. Upstairs, she hung over a case filled with Swiss
Army knives; she admired the naturist artwork hung
in the stairwells; she listened to a customer and a
salesman discussing rappelling. Then, at 3:12 P.M.,
she wandered down the ramp to the men's clothing
section.

Fingering a rack of bright Gortex jackets, she kept
an eye on the ramp, watching for a tail. One minute
passed, then two, and no one appeared except one
young man in a plaid flannel shirt who only walked
halfway down before he suddenly snapped his fingers
as if he'd just remembered something, pivoted on his

heel, and retraced his steps. Aunie slipped through another department past a lone cash register, and exited onto Pike Street at exactly 3:15. Lola pulled up to the curb and Aunie climbed in the car. It immediately shot out into the traffic before she even had her door closed. She twisted around to watch the door she'd exited.

"Did you see anyone followin' you, woo-mon?"

Aunie turned back to a normal seated position as soon as they turned a corner. "No," she murmured. She glanced at Lola. "All those damn self-defense lessons and Jimmy's little quizzes must be affecting my mind. I probably imagined the whole thing."

A second later, unseen by either woman, a young man in a plaid flannel shirt rushed out of the Pike Street exit of REI and looked up and down the block. He walked to the corner and scouted that block also. Then he swore, pulled a small black notebook out of his breast pocket, and irritably scribbled a swift notation.

Trust James to have his own ideas about dating etiquette, Aunie thought in amusement as she peeked through the peephole at his knock. She opened the door. "Why didn't you use your key?" she asked as she looked him over admiringly.

"This is a date," he informed her, doing some inspecting of his own. "You don't go barging into your date's home, you ring for her." Or so he imagined. Actually, his courting practices had always leaned more toward casual pickups than prearranged engagements. If Magnolia wanted a real date, however, then he was determined to do it right. He brought his hand out from behind his back. "Here," he said coming as close to diffident as a man of his temperament ever got as he handed over a cellophane florist's box, "This is for you."

"A corsage," she said weakly. She would not laugh . . . she would not. She hated corsages, but she would bite her tongue in two before she said so. He was treating this evening out as though they were high school kids going to their senior prom, and she found his sweetness so touching that tears rose in her eyes. She lowered her head and took her time extricating the corsage from its container, refusing to look up until she had herself under control. "It's very pretty," she finally whispered. "Thank you."

He took it from her and picked up her hand. "Look, it goes on your wrist," he said, sliding it into place and admiring it against the paleness of her skin. "I thought the other kind was sort of dumb, since it was bound to get all squished when we dance."

Aunie brought the corsage up to her nose and inhaled its heady fragrance, then held out her hand to admire its adornment. Okay, she'd admit it: This one was different. It looked pretty against her wrist, and she loved it. Unlike many of the large, fussy corsages she'd worn in the past, he'd picked one that was dainty and restrained, just two tiny white gardenias nestled in a few of their deep green leaves. It looked old-fashioned and gracious. She raised her eyes to his and smiled, her dimples slowly denting her cheeks. "Thank you, James." Standing on tiptoe to give him a kiss, she then stood back and trailed her fingertips over his smooth-shaven cheeks and jawline. "You look great."

He did, too. No conservative suit for James Ryder; his formal attire was as individualistic as he was. She'd never seen him in anything but casual wear, but tonight he was wearing a pink shirt tucked into pleated slacks. A superfluous but snazzy pair of narrow, powder blue suspenders clung to his broad shoulders, bonded to chest and flat stomach. His tie was funky: blue to match his suspenders, with an old-fashioned sugar cone at its southernmost tip supporting four scoops of pastel-hued ice cream. He wore a raw silk jacket with the same casualness that he wore his habitual T-shirts, and in the lapel was a boutonniere, a dainty pink rosebud.

Standing close to him, Aunie brushed her hands over his broad shoulders, adjusted the knot in his tie, and smoothed its tail down his hard chest and abdomen. "I've never seen you in a tie," she murmured. "I've never seen you dressed up at all." She fluttered her lashes. "Ah sweah, suh, you look good enough to eat."

"Why, thank you, Miz Scarlett," he replied, inserting a rough-tipped finger into a shining curl of hair and gently pulling on it. "So do you. I'm glad you wore that dress."

It was the same one she'd worn the night she and Mary had celebrated finals. She had debated wearing something instead that he'd never before seen, but of the several outfits she'd tried on and discarded, this one had simply kept calling out to be worn. She'd curled her hair, carefully applied more makeup than usual, including glossy red lipstick, and donned her sheerest hose and tallest pair of heels.

"Give me one little kiss to tide me over and then we'll hit the road," James said. "Our dinner reservations are for eight."

Laughing at a remark James made as he held open the apartment house's front door for her, Aunie slipped beneath his arm. She grabbed his hand to pull him down the stairs with her, then stopped dead at the sight of a long white limousine double-parked in the street. Bobby, in uniform and cap, climbed out of the driver's seat, walked around the hood, and held open the back door. She turned to James, dark eyes sparkling with delight. "For us?"

"None other." He guided her into the plush interior and grinned at his brother when he gave them a respectfully solemn salute before he closed the door. "Can't have a dress this hot ridin' around in an old Jeep." He handed her a fluted goblet of champagne and leaned over to press an impulsive kiss into the exposed portion of one white shoulder. "God, you're beautiful."

For once those words were music to her ears. She wanted to be beautiful in James's eyes. She hoped he saw other, worthier attributes as well when he looked at her, but for tonight . . . she could live with beautiful.

He took her to the Space Needle. It was a mild May evening and the rotating view was spectacular. After dinner, they walked around the Center. James insisted on a game of put-put golf, and after tripping around the tiny course in her inappropriate heels, Aunie retaliated with bumper cars. Ultimately, they ended up in a dimly lighted bar in Pioneer Square, swaying to the smoky rhythms of a blues band.

It was around midnight when he heard her murmuring into his tie. He tightened his hold and lowered his head. "What?"

They swayed in place for a couple silent heartbeats. Then Aunie rubbed her cheek against his chest. "I love you, Jimmy."

Ah God. James took a deep breath and squeezed his eyes shut, heart pounding into overdrive. He had tried—God knows he'd tried—but he just couldn't fight this anymore. His hands slid upward until they were framing her face and he bent down to kiss her, there on the dance floor. "God, I love you, Magnolia," he said hoarsely.

Aunie stopped dancing and her forehead dropped against his chest. Her arms exerted more and more pressure around his neck. Finally, he heard her mumble into his shirt, "I was beginnin' to think I'd never hear you say that."

"Yeah, well." James's laugh was more an exhalation of breath than an actual verbalization of humor. He struggled with second thoughts, knowing he probably shouldn't have said anything. Nothing had really changed, after all. Hell, all the reasons he'd had for keeping his feelings to himself were still valid.

"Don't make the mistake of thinking they're magic words, Aunie," he felt compelled to warn her. "Just admitting it out loud isn't gonna make anything easier. It won't make your problems go away."

"Speak for yourself, James. Hearin' it makes things a whole lot easier for me. Tell me again."

There was so much pressure in his chest. "I love you." The words were forced out through a constricted throat.

She seemed to pick up on his tension. Dark eyes searched moss green ones. "Are you sure, James?"

Was he sure? The pressure started to ease. He might have reservations about his timing, but he wasn't the least bit uncertain of his feelings. "Oh, yeah," he replied. "I'm positive." His smile was crooked. "How about you? Are you sure?"

"Oh, yes." She pressed tiny, smacking kisses along his neck. "I'm very, very, very sure."

"God." His arms closed so tightly around her she squeaked in involuntary protest. "Sorry, baby," he murmured as he loosened his hold. His hands slid up her slender arms until they connected with her wrists behind his neck and he pulled her hands loose. Slipping them down to his chest, he pressed them against his shirtfront, one long finger nudging the browning petals in her corsage as he looked down at her. "Let's get out of here, Aunie."

He instructed Bobby to find a scenic route home and then settled back in the plush seat with Aunie tucked up against his side. He couldn't seem to get a handle on his emotions. He'd sworn to himself that he wouldn't tell her how he felt until some of her problems were resolved. Dammit, he hadn't been blowing smoke when he'd said expressing his emotions wasn't a magic cure-all. Simply saying the words wasn't going to alleviate this mess she was in; it was, in fact, more likely to complicate matters when he insisted on continuing the self-defense sessions.

On the other hand, just once, he was going to revel in the freedom of making love to her without choking back the words.

For the remainder of the weekend, Aunie walked on air. She had convinced herself it was a feeling destined to last.

Sunday provided some excitement of its own. She and James, along with Mary and Otis's sister Leeanne, helped the Jacksons put the finishing touches on their nursery. The men assembled a changing table. Mary and Leeanne washed the window and hung the balloon shade. Aunie and Lola stenciled little white rabbits as a border where walls met ceiling.

When the phone rang, the women had finished cleaning up and were attaching the frothy skirt to the bassinet. James was holding three separate parts of the changing table together while Otis tried to thread the screw through the aligned holes. When it rang a second time, Lola said, "Otis!" in exasperation. At the same time he looked up in frustration and called, "Lola, will you get the damn phone? I'm up to my armpits in the parts for this table."

Lola trotted off to answer it, and Leeanne moved to stand over her flustered brother. "If you think putting that thing together is tough, just wait," she advised him with a knowing grin. "Every bike, trike, big wheel that you buy the kid is going to say, some assembly required. They tell you it's so simple a four-year-old could put it together, but they always neglect to send along the four-year-old to give you a hand."

"Otis!" Everyone stilled at the urgency in Lola's voice, heads turning toward the door. Otis surged to his feet and Leeanne gripped his arm. "Oh, God, is it Mama?" she whispered, moving with her brother toward the doorway. "Has something happened to Mama?"

They could hear Lola murmuring into the phone, and then the sound of it being replaced in the hook. She poked her head around the wall. "Muriel is fine, Leeanne. I'm sorry if I gave you a scare," she apologized. She turned to Otis and a beatific smile spread across her face. "We're parents, mon."

"What!"

"We're parents! To a baby girl, a little premature but healthy. Five pounds, four ounces, nineteen inches long. She was born at 2:19 P.M." She laughed and executed a little dance step. "Otis, we're parents!"

"A daughter? We've got us a daughter?" Otis stared at his wife in stunned silence for a moment, then suddenly whooped. He picked up Lola and whirled her around. "When can we see her?"

"Right now." And within minutes, they had floated out of their apartment on a cloud of parental bliss and excited congratulations.

Three days later the proud new parents brought Greta-Leigh Jackson home. It was a day of extreme emotions for Aunie, for reality had intruded by then, splintering her too-brief euphoric state beyond repair.

Dammit, she hadn't even had a tiny grace period. At school on Monday, the distressing reality of her situation had once again reared its ugly head.

Okay, so she shouldn't have been taken by surprise, shouldn't have allowed her expectations to climb to unrealistic heights. James had been warning of this very thing when he'd admonished her not to expect all her problems suddenly to vanish just because she'd heard a few words from him that she had so longed to hear.

That didn't make it overwhelmingly easier to accept when she once again felt the weight of someone's eyes watching her. The crash back to earth was merely that much harder in the wake of the too-few hours that she'd flown so high. Her immediate gut reaction was anger and—as much as she hated to admit to it—self-pity. Dammit, why her? What had she ever done to deserve all this negative attention? Other women got to fall in love and act young, be carefree; why were things always so difficult for her? It was so unfair.

Well, all right, so nobody had ever actually promised her life would be fair. In a perfect world it would be; but face it, she'd known for a long time now that this world was far from perfect.

Having conceded that much, she forced herself to

take it one step further and to relinquish the dubious comfort of feeling sorry for herself. Instead, she applied some rational thought to the matter. And the first thing she thought to do was go to a pay phone.

She dug a fistful of change out of her purse and placed a long distance call. The instant she was put through to Wesley, she replaced the receiver back on its hook and slumped back against the warm brick wall, her heart beating heavily.

Very well, then. She pressed a fist to her breast and took several deep breaths. *Get a grip and review the facts.* Fact one: It wasn't Wesley who was watching her. That didn't eliminate the possibility that it might be one of his private investigators, of course; but it was comforting to know that at this moment, at least, Wesley himself was nowhere in the vicinity.

Fact two: She never felt under observation when she was in class. She didn't know if she should consider that significant, but she rather thought she should. Of course she also rather thought that in order to cause the fine hairs on her nape to stand on end the way they did, a person would necessarily have to stare rather long and hard at her. And realistically, that would be somewhat difficult to achieve with a minimum of discretion in a classroom. So where did that leave her? With fact three, she supposed: It was only during lunch breaks on the plaza that she'd felt she was being watched.

By the time Otis picked her up that Monday afternoon, brimming with excitement and Polaroid snaps of his newborn daughter, Aunie had reconciled herself to the truth of her situation. As much as she might wish otherwise, her life wasn't going to progress with fairy-tale smoothness, so she might as well learn to live with it. The knowledge had upset her; she'd held her pity party, and then she had applied herself to searching for an answer and had moved on.

It was the fight she had with James after school on Wednesday, just before Otis and Lola were due home with their new baby, that did the most damage to her wildly vacillating emotions.

Someone meant her harm, and she couldn't deny it was frightening. But the truth was, it didn't possess half the power to upset her as did the resulting tension it produced between her and James. They were living with an ever-present stress, a constant pressure that caused them to snap and snarl with cruel thoughtlessness at the first wrong word or misinterpreted look. Jimmy could fight really dirty when the mood struck him. If she were to be honest, she supposed she'd have to admit that she could, too. But it hurt when she was the recipient of his anger. It hurt a lot.

Wednesday's fight seemed to her to blow up out of nowhere. And the culprit on which it hinged, apparently, was her ability to shelve unpleasant realities for short intervals. If he could have given her just two damn seconds to explain . . .

Her adeptness at setting aside problems was a measure of how truly screwed up her life had been for a long time now. She wasn't stupid; she didn't believe trouble would simply go away if she ignored it.

But a person could only live on the edge of her emotions for so long without precipitating a crisis. To avoid emotional meltdown, she had learned long ago to temporarily set aside the problem and concentrate on the minutiae of day-to-day living. It was an unhappy fact of life that once she was strong enough to face it again, the nastiness would be right there where she had left it; but the trick was to give herself a moment in which to collect a bit of stamina. It was

a delay-and-address system she had employed for the
past few years to defuse and compartmentalize the
chaos of her life.

She *hadn't* deliberately been withholding information from James when she'd failed to mention her
suspicions that she was once again being watched.
She had forgotten, dammit. She had simply forgotten.
She'd worked past her own feelings on the subject,
had taken some preliminary steps to identify or eliminate possibilities, and then she'd set the problem
aside for a while to be considered later. She'd meant
to tell him about it, but once she was at home, other
matters had arisen to drive it from her mind.

God, the way he'd acted when she had remembered
to tell him, you would've thought she was a one-
woman commando squad charging blindly into
booby-trapped enemy territory. And *that* was when
he wasn't accusing her of being just plain blind. To
personal danger. To reality. To the most meager
ration of intelligence, to hear him tell it.

All of which was downright mild compared to his
reaction when he learned that not only had she kept
this information to herself for two whole days, but
she'd also called Wesley to verify his whereabouts.

She had given up attempting an explanation by
that point. Perhaps she should have persisted, if only
to cool him down a little, but she hadn't. Frankly,
she had been too busy reacting, quite poorly she'd
admit, to his tone, his words, his attitude. How dare
he yell at her, swear at her, talk to her as if she were
a brain-damaged infant who lacked the intelligence
to be left on her own for an unguarded instant? She
didn't have to take such treatment from anyone.

She couldn't say with any authority afterward what
the exact words had been that had triggered it, but

somehow, their furious verbal exchange had segued into equally furious lovemaking up against the refrigerator door. God, what a mess! She didn't know about James, but when her gripping legs had gone lax and he had slid her to her feet, when he had stepped back, arranged his clothes, and slammed out of the apartment, she knew that she for one didn't feel any better. Only marginally satisfied physically, and emotionally she was a wreck.

The clamor of James's furious exit rang in her ears. Her back slid down the fridge door until she was in a gangly heap on the floor, head hanging, short skirt bunched around her waist, panties dangling from one ankle. What had she said? Gawd, what on earth had she said to set him off that way? That wasn't lovemaking, that was . . . it was . . . She didn't know what it was, but it hadn't been lovemaking. She bawled her eyes out.

When Lola called a short while later and invited her down to meet the newest member of the Jackson household, she tried to disguise the damage to her puffy eyes and swollen mouth with a hastily applied ice pack. Apparently her remedy was less than successful. Lola took one look at her and silently handed her the baby to hold.

"Ooh, Gawd," Aunie whispered and cuddled the infant to her breast, absorbing comfort from her warmth and sweet baby aroma. She collapsed onto the couch and looked down at the child in her arms. "She's beautiful, y'all. Absolutely beautiful."

Greta-Leigh's complexion fell somewhere between Lola's shade of cafe au lait and Otis's ebony. She had a full head of hair already a good inch long, and it stood out statically around her tiny head like a dark dandelion in full bloom. "Oh, look at her little lips. They're so sweet." Greta-Leigh's mouth was pursed, causing the middle of her top lip to point over the bottom lip like a tiny bird's.

Aunie's finger brushed a soft, dusky cheek and she looked up at Lola and Otis. "You must be so proud." To her eternal mortification, her voice cracked on the last word and tears rolled down her cheeks.

Otis and Lola made sounds of concern and she felt like an absolute fool. "I'm sorry," she whispered and wiped at her cheeks with her free hand. She gave them a wobbly smile. "Please, ignore it. I must be premenstrual or somethin'."

But that wasn't it at all. She had just remembered that for the first time ever, James hadn't used one of his ever-present condoms this afternoon. Great. Wouldn't it be just her luck to get pregnant the first time they failed to use birth control?

She wouldn't mind so much, except her life was such a mess right now that the last thing she had any right to do was drag a child into it. Not to mention she'd always dreamed of conceiving a child in love, not anger. And, Lord, wouldn't Jimmy just be thrilled to pieces? She was pretty sure he was already regretting the fact he'd gotten tangled up with *her*. If he learned he might be a daddy on top of it he'd probably open up a vein.

"I've gotta go get some formula," Otis said. He squatted down to kiss Greta-Leigh on the crown of her head. As he stood, he rubbed an affectionate hand over Aunie's hair. Kissing Lola, he let himself out of the apartment.

Lola sat down beside Aunie on the couch. "You

want me to take her?" she asked, tipping her head at the baby with a soft smile.

"Oh, no, please. May I hold her just a little while longer?"

"Sure." Lola watched in silence for a few moments. Finally, she said, "So, what's goin' on wid you, woo-mon? And don't tell me PMS. You been fightin' wid James?"

Aunie nodded.

"Want to talk 'bout it?"

Prickles at the back of her nose warned Aunie of an imminent renewal of tears. "Can't."

Lola stroked Aunie's hair away from her face. "Just tell me this: You gonna be all right?"

"Yeah, I'll be fine." She hoped.

"Okay, good. I s'pose then that you'd like me to change the subject?"

"Please." Her eyes on Lola, Aunie rubbed the side of her face against Greta-Leigh's head. "I'll tell you about it later, when I've got a little more control, okay?"

"Fine wid me. You interested in seein' my sweet baby girl's fingers and toes?"

"Yeah," Aunie said. "I'd like that. I'd like that a lot."

The light was blinking on her answering machine when she let herself into the apartment a short while later. There was a message requesting she call Detective Garet Bell at the Seattle police department. Oh, God, what now? With hands that were not quite steady, she punched out the number he'd left.

"This is Bell," a clipped voice answered.

"Detective Bell, my name is Aunie Franklin," she

identified herself in a barely audible voice. She cleared her throat. "Uh, you left a message for me to call you?" She clutched the receiver in slippery palms.

"Franklin, Franklin. Oh, yeah, here it is. Miss Franklin, I called to let you know we've apprehended the person responsible for the rash of harrassment calls that you and several other students from your college have been receiving. According to the time and date sheets you submitted to the telephone company a few weeks ago, the number of origin on several of your calls tallies with that of the woman whose list finally nailed him."

"Oh, my God," Aunie whispered in shock. "Who was it?"

The answer was anticlimatic as she didn't recognize the name. Perhaps Mary would. Almost to herself she murmured, "I don't understand this. I've heard about the calls he'd made to other students. Why were my calls so different?"

"Interesting you should ask that," Detective Bell replied. "Ordinarily the answer would probably remain one of life's little mysteries, but this guy turned out to be one of those chatty little individuals who likes to brag about his deeds. Your name was mentioned specifically." Aunie's stomach turned over.

"He gained access to his victims' telephone numbers through a part-time job he held with Ma Bell," the detective explained. "And, miss, he took it quite to heart when your unlisted number was virtually the only information he could get on you.

"Physically, he's fairly nondescript," the detective continued, "average build, average coloring, nothing outstanding about him. He found it simple enough to blend into just about any crowd, where he'd glean

details of his victims' lives through overheard gossip
and conversations. Apparently, though, you don't talk
about yourself at school. He was rather put out that
although there is some gossip about you, no one
seemed to possess any concrete facts. There was no
personal knowledge available, none of the little
details that he used to unnerve his victims. Rather
than leave you alone entirely, he settled for calling
and hanging up; but apparently the message on your
machine took a great deal of fun out of even that. I
approve of that message, by the way. He also mentioned something about bodyguards?''

Aunie gave him a thumbnail sketch of James's
escort service, including a brief description of the
physical characteristics of her sentries, and the
detective laughed. They talked for a short while
longer and then disconnected. The instant Aunie
replaced the receiver, she was out the door and down
the hall, pounding on James's door.

He opened it and she launched herself at his chest.

His arms tightened around her convulsively.
"Aunie?" Holding her, he stepped out into the hall
and closed the door behind him. To say he was surprised to see her was an understatement.

Somehow, though, he intuitively knew her being
here now was something separate from the fight
they'd had earlier. Trying to see her face, he asked,
"What? What is it, baby? Are you all right?" At least
her instincts still had her running to him with whatever it was, instead of taking it to Otis or Lola.

"It wasn't Wesley, James," she said into his chest.
"It was some boy I don't even know."

"What wasn't Wesley, baby?" Then it clicked. "The
phone calls? They caught the caller?" When she nodded, he picked her up and carried her down the hall

to her apartment. Once inside, he set her on her feet and held her at arm's length so he could see her face. "Tell me."

She looked around with some confusion. Hadn't they been in front of his apartment? Why were they in hers when his had been closer?

"*Tell* me, Aunie."

She shook her head to clear it and then told him. "Detective Bell said it took longer to track him than it usually would because he used public phones almost exclusively. They would get a number on the trace, but they didn't have the manpower to stake out all the various phone booths he used. Then, two or three weeks ago, he began placing the calls from his home. They picked him up today."

"Christ." James tugged on his ponytail. "This is kind of hard to take in. After assuming all this time it was Cunningham."

"Tell me about it."

"But this is good," he said, rapidly assimilating and shifting facts in his fertile brain. A slow smile slashed lines from the corners of his eyes, deepened the three shallow grooves next to his mouth. "It's excellent, in fact. Y' know what this means, Magnolia?"

She wasn't thinking as speedily as he, but the facts were slowly sinking in nevertheless. "It's all over, isn't it, James?"

"Yes." He looked down at her and noticed signs that she'd been crying. His smile slowly faded. "Yes," he repeated. "It's really all over."

CHAPTER 17

It was doubtful much work was accomplished on campus the following day. It was abuzz with news of the arrest as bands of students formed and broke up ... constantly shifting and rearranging themselves into new groups as they milled about dissecting every snippet of information available. Voices rose and fell as everyone vied to relate their individual reactions to the news. A party atmosphere pervaded the halls, classrooms, and grounds.

As Aunie had suspected she might, Mary had a working knowledge of the young man arrested. She described him to Aunie, but no matter how descriptive or how many instances she could cite when he'd been on the periphery of their lunch group, Aunie was unable to pin a face to the name.

Oddly enough, for a short while as they milled out on the herringbone brick plaza fronting the building, Aunie thought she felt someone watching her. The fine hairs on her nape stood up, just as they'd been doing for the past week. Her head whipped around and she automatically scanned the crowd . . . but saw no one who seemed to be paying her undue attention.

Then she felt slightly ridiculous. Talk about an inflated sense of her own importance. In view of yesterday's arrest, it hardly seemed likely that anyone was watching her now; and in truth the sensation had only lasted for a brief instant. For all she knew, some guy had thought she was cute . . . for about fifteen seconds. She smiled slightly at the ego-puncturing thought. Nevertheless, she made a mental note to mention the impression to James—provided she saw him—and then she put it out of her mind.

She was slightly embarrassed to admit it, even to herself, but she was every bit as greedy for information about the caller as any other student present today. She liked to believe she was above the sort of gossip and conjecture that tended to run rampant around the campus, but she found herself willfully absorbing every particle of intelligence that made the rounds, be it real or speculation. If it pertained to the young man who'd managed to turn so many lives upside down, she listened.

It was still a struggle to assimilate the knowledge that it was a stranger and not Wesley who'd been calling her.

It was drizzling by the time her last class let out and Mary offered her a ride home. Aunie declined, wanting to savor the freedom of her first unattended walk in several weeks. She took her time, window-shopping along Broadway, stopping to purchase a few toiletries she'd been meaning to replace for some time. By the time she fit her key into the outdoor lock of the apartment building, she was nearly soaked to the skin, but she didn't care. It appeared that finally her life was being returned to her. And rain or no rain, she had enjoyed herself immensely.

The young man trailed more than a block behind her on the opposite side of the street. He found keeping her in sight along Broadway as easy as pie. When she turned off into the residential district and he lost the convenient camouflage of sidewalks congested with students and shoppers, it was a little trickier, but not much. She hadn't spared so much as a single glance behind her, and not for the first time that day he blessed the poor chump who'd gotten himself arrested yesterday. No doubt he was a degenerate little jerk-off, but his timing couldn't be faulted.

And timing was all, the young man thought. It was no skin off his teeth to admit he'd been starting to feel the pinch of desperation. He'd lucked onto Franklin's registration for college several weeks back and thought he'd had it made. As it happened, however, that was the last piece of luck he'd had. The address on the registration turned out to be a post office box she never visited. She hadn't applied for a Washington state driver's license; she hadn't registered a car. No one knew anything about her except that blond bitch, Holloman, and when he'd approached her, she'd refused to give him the time of day. He was not her type obviously. Either that or she didn't appreciate a good old-fashioned pickup. Some women were like that.

The primary problem, of course, was that Franklin was surrounded by men whom he for one didn't care to encounter up close. Without their vigilance, he could have followed her home the first day, but their

presence made trailing her a sticky proposition. He
hadn't missed how cautious and observant they were
when they escorted her to and from the vehicles
they'd parked illegally right in front of the college.
And they clearly knew the town well. He didn't believe
they'd ever spotted a tail, but they drove as if they
assumed one and they'd lost him every time. Who
the hell were these people?

Then, just to make matters about as dismal as they
could possibly get, tomorrow, from everything he'd
been able to determine, Franklin was taking her last
final. After that, of course, she'd be gone for the
summer. So God bless the deviate. Two days later and
he would have been shit out of luck.

Protected beneath the leafy branches of a tree one
block south, he leaned against the rough-barked
trunk, picked his teeth with a matchbook cover, and
grinned in satisfaction when she turned up a short
walkway and let herself into an old, well-maintained
apartment building. Bingo. Yes sir, this beat hell out
of waiting for the DMV to cough up the addresses
on the Harley, Thunderbird, and Jeep registrations
he'd requested. Especially since he hadn't a clue if
they'd lead him anywhere. He had sweated bullets
this past week worrying that the three beefeaters who
owned those vehicles were simply the babe's hired
talent. Now he didn't have to give a rat's ass.

He leaned against the tree and smoked a cigarette.
Anyone peeking out from behind a curtain would
assume he was sheltering from the rain for five minutes. Then, whistling, he flicked the butt away and
strolled up the street. Pulling a notebook from the
breast pocket of his flannel shirt as he passed the
apartment house, he breezed on by without a pause,
scribbling down the address as he went.

His bonus for being the one to locate Mrs. Wesley Cunningham was in the bag.

The Jacksons' door opened as Aunie was closing the entrance door behind her and Otis stuck his head out into the hallway. "I'm glad you're home," he said. "You got any plans for this afternoon?"

"Just goin' to the gym," she replied. "But it's not something I have to do; I can easily put it off." She studied him. "You look kind of frazzled, Otis. What's the matter . . . baby keep you up all night?"

"I've gotta leave for work and Lola's got the flu or something. She's feeling lousy . . . can't seem to hold anything down this afternoon." He gave her a beleaguered look, his big shoulders twitching. "Aunie, could you do us an enormous favor and watch Greta-Leigh for a few hours? My sister can take her at six; and if Lola's still feeling under the weather later tonight, I can probably get the next couple days off. I know it's an imposition—"

"Don't be silly," she interrupted him. "I'd love to take care of her."

"Thanks, Aunie. I appreciate this more than I can say. Jimmy's nowhere around, and I was coming to the end of my rope trying to figure out what to do." He gave his wristwatch a hurried glance and then rubbed his long fingers over his hard skull. "Come on in. I'll get her bottles and diapers together."

Between the two of them, they located and packed all the baby's essentials and brought her diaper bag and the infant up to Aunie's apartment. Aunie ran in to change out of her wet clothes while Otis said goodbye to his daughter.

"Daddy's gotta go to work now, honeybunch," he murmured, chin tucked into his neck as he gazed lovingly at the baby sprawled on his massive shoulder. Big, dark eyes stared up at him and the plastic clown-smile of her pacifier bobbed as she worked the nipple. "You be a good girl for Auntie Aunie and I'll see you in a couple of days." He looked up at Aunie as she walked into the room, towel-drying her hair. "Or sooner, if Lola doesn't feel better. You got my work number?"

Aunie grinned at him and recited it. "James made me memorize *everyone's* number. Don't you worry about a thing now. We'll be just fine—won't we, sugar?—and I'll take real good care of her." She tossed the towel aside and held up her hands for the infant.

Otis reluctantly peeled Greta-Leigh off his shoulder, pressed a kiss on her forehead, and handed her to Aunie. His white teeth flashed in a smile. "Thanks again, Aunie. I owe you one."

"Oh, yeah, this is a real hardship," she replied and gave him a cocky smile. "I just hate having to play with this little ol' sweetie pie all afternoon. Go on now; get to work." She walked him to the door, smiling tolerantly as he told her the time of Greta-Leigh's nap and last bottle, and gave her more information than she needed concerning the various supplies they had toted up to her apartment.

"I thought he'd never leave, didn't you, sugar?" Aunie asked the baby when the door had closed behind Otis's back. She nuzzled the incredibly soft skin in Greta-Leigh's neck. "It's just you and me now, kid."

* * *

Wesley concluded his conversation with the detective, recradled the receiver, and went into action. He buzzed his secretary and gave her crisp instructions; he called his maid and ordered her to pack.

When he was finished giving the commands that would smooth the way for his trip, he leaned back in his chair and smiled in satisfaction.

The little slut's time had come.

Aunie played with the baby for a while and then put her on a blanket on the floor and stretched out on her stomach next to her, ankles crossed in the air, to study for finals.

Half an hour later, she decided it was a good thing she already knew this stuff, because her heart just wasn't into cramming. Now that the euphoria of her walk home was wearing off, she couldn't stop reliving the same memory she'd been reliving every unguarded moment since yesterday afternoon: her fight with James, and the angry, unprotected lovemaking that had followed it.

Last night had been pretty miserable. Her emotions had fluctuated wildly and she hadn't attained even a fraction of the stability she usually received from being with James. He'd talked too much about all the wrong things, and she hadn't talked very much at all.

Why hadn't he once mentioned their fight? She'd instinctively run to him in spite of it the moment she'd found out about the caller, but it had never been far from her mind. Hadn't it occurred to him yet that they hadn't used any birth control? Didn't he care? She'd badly needed his comfort; yet all the while she'd been receiving it, she'd also been harboring a lot of unaddressed anger. When it came right down to it, she still was.

Okay, perhaps it was childish of her not to have broached the subject herself; there was too much at stake here not to clear the air. But last night she'd kept waiting for him to say something, and when he hadn't, she'd turned stubborn. Damned if *she* was going to be the first one to bring it up when he'd been the one to instigate the whole affair. Disgracefully, childishly, she still felt that way.

And would somebody please tell her just what the deal was with his apartment? Her name might not be Einstein, but she wasn't a total lackwit. It was slowly dawning on her that apparently she was not welcome in it.

Teeth clenched, stomach knotted, she knew she had to redirect her thoughts. The last thing she needed was additional anger; she was already nursing more than she could handle. With renewed determination, she applied herself to her books; and when James arrived a short while later, she put extra effort into behaving normally. She would not give him an excuse to accuse her of sulking.

He closed the door quietly behind him and walked into the living room. Shooting Aunie a quick, wary glance, he then gazed down at Greta-Leigh.

She lay on her back on a baby blanket on the floor next to Aunie, surrounded by toys but staring unblinkingly at a lighted lightbulb over her head. From her position on the floor, she had a straight view up the shade of the lamp on the end table.

"Hey little darlin'." He crouched down next to them and waved a tentative finger in front of the baby's face to get her attention. He glanced over at Aunie. "Won't that wreck her eyes?"

"Apparently not," Aunie replied, "although I can't shake the feeling it's goin' to blind the child." She stuck a finger in her book to mark her place and looked up at him. "And this is after I was forewarned. Lola told me about Greta-Leigh's little kilowatt habit yesterday. I guess babies this age are naturally attracted to bright lights. The pediatrician at the hospital told Lola it wouldn't harm her."

"Huh. Spooky."

Greta-Leigh noticed the big finger waving in front of her face and reached for it. James nudged it into her soft little palm and then grunted in surprise when she clamped down on it with unexpected strength. Experimentally, he pulled his hand in toward his body and the baby came with it, still clinging.

"Support her head, James," Aunie cautioned, smiling at Greta-Leigh, who was faithfully adhering to his finger even though her head lagged behind the rest of her body. "Her neck's not very strong yet and she lets go as abruptly as she grabs on, don't you, sugar? Put your other hand under her like this."

James complied. "You can sure tell she's Otis's kid. She's got a championship grip. Uh-oh." He wrinkled his nose. "Oh, God, Magnolia, I think she's fillin' up her pants." He gingerly pried the tiny fist from his knuckle, scooped the baby up in his big hands, and extended her to Aunie. "Here."

Aunie experienced a spurt of good humor. "Here, yourself," she replied, reaching for the diaper bag and shoving it over to him. "You are a big, strong man. I'm sure you can change one little ol' diaper."

"Isn't it time for her to go home, yet?" James held

her as far away from his body as his long arms would stretch.

"We've got her until six. Lola's sick." Aunie smirked at the expression on his face. "Everything you need is right here," she said, giving the diaper bag another nudge. "Wipes, cornstarch powder, clean diapers ... even clean rubber pants if she's overflowed the ones she has on."

"Now there's an appealing thought. Why don't I just take her out back and hose her down?"

"James."

"Okay, okay. But I'm warnin' you, Magnolia, I've got a weak stomach. If I get sick, it's gonna be up to you to clean up after both of us."

"Rinse out the diaper in the toilet when you're finished and put it in the plastic bag behind the bathroom door."

"Christ. You mean she's done this more than once?"

Aunie raised an eyebrow, and James walked off muttering to himself, still holding the baby as far from his nose as he could get her.

He was gone a long time. Curiosity finally getting the better of her, Aunie tiptoed down the short hallway.

"I don't know diddly about kids, kid," James was saying as she approached the bathroom door. He had filled the sink with warm, soapy water, rolled the baby's T-shirt up under her armpits and was swishing her legs and bottom back and forth in the basin. "Y' need three hands for this job." As Aunie watched, he draped the baby, facedown, over his left forearm, clutching her chubby thigh in his hand, and used his right hand to scoop water up over her bottom. "Your bag's got everything else in it; you know if it comes with a washcloth?" He shook excess water from his fingertips, caught the bag's shoulder strap with his foot, and pulled it nearer. He rummaged through it one-handedly. "Sure enough. I figured I could count on your mama to pack everything we'd need."

He was somewhat clumsy and his high, bony forehead was beaded with sweat by the time he reached for a towel, but he cleaned the baby thoroughly. He clamped Greta-Leigh on his thigh with one hand while he knelt and used his other to fold a clean towel in two and spread it out on the bathroom floor. Laying her down, he turned back for the bag and started when he saw Aunie propped against the doorjamb, watching him.

"Hey," he said in greeting. "Why didn't you tell me the kid was loaded when I picked her up? There was shit like you wouldn't believe from stem to stern." He pulled out a clean diaper and flopped it onto the towel. "Y' ask me, it's none too soon to begin toilet training." Locating a clean pair of rubber pants and the container of powder, he turned back to his task.

Aunie didn't reply, but she smiled as she watched him. This was the James she knew. When he slipped protective fingers between the diaper and Greta-Leigh's stomach and then promptly stuck himself with the diaper pin he was using to secure the whole operation, she laughed.

James glanced up at her. "You really enjoy watchin' me make an ass of myself, don't you?" He managed to secure both pins and picked up the rubber pants.

"Yeah," she agreed with easy honesty. "You may be a crackerjack carpenter and cartoonist, but you're sure a klutz with the kids."

James held Greta-Leigh up for Aunie's inspection and said, "I did a *righteous* job. Come on, admit it."

Aunie swept the baby into her arms. "Yeah, yeah, yeah." She stuck her nose into the baby's neck. "But it took him hours and hours to change one little ol' diaper, didn't it, sweetie pie?" Waltzing them out of the room, she called back, "Don't forget to rinse out the diaper and put it in the bag behind the door." For some reason, she felt much better, her anger diffused. They still had to talk, but at least she felt hopeful that everything would be all right.

The feeling didn't last through the next five minutes.

James found them back in their original positions on the floor when he was finished. He dropped the diaper bag on the hardwood next to the blanket and hunkered down. Great-Leigh began to whimper. "What's the matter, sweet thing?" James stroked a long finger over her silky cheek.

Whimpers turned to wails, wails to a roar.

"Uh oh." Aunie hopped up. "We know she's dry, so she must be hungry. I'll throw a bottle in the microwave."

"Don't leave me alone with her!"

Aunie was already in the kitchen, but she poked her head around the door. "See if you can find her bink."

"Her *what*?"

"You know, her little pacifier." Aunie withdrew into the kitchen once again. "It's on the blanket somewhere. Look among her toys."

James located it, blew a piece of fuzz loose, and popped it into the baby's mouth. Immediately, Greta-Leigh began working it, sucking vigorously enough to make the plastic bob. It dried her tears, but James found the artificial clownlike smile kind of eerie. "I can't believe Otis lets her use this thing," he said. "No kid of mine would ever get one."

In the kitchen, Aunie laughed. "Never say never, James," she replied. "It's an invitation for the famous-last-words fairy to kick your teeth in." She waited for one of his off-the-wall comebacks, but James had abruptly fallen silent.

When Aunie reappeared with the bottle, she immediately knew the first lighthearted exchange they'd shared in twenty-four hours was over. James had once again retreated behind a barrier. He didn't appear angry but he had withdrawn. Rage immediately surged up her throat in response, threatening to choke her. Damn him. *Damn* him. For about two minutes, she'd been able to forget yesterday's mess. What had set him off this time?

He watched her feed the baby for a while, but it wasn't long before he excused himself, ostensibly to complete a cartoon that he'd been working on. He bent down to give Aunie a kiss but she turned her face aside, so he ruffled the baby's dark hair instead. Then he left, quietly closing the door behind him.

No kid of mine. The words mocked him all the way down the hall. Inside his apartment, he closed the door with extra care, gripped the door frame until his knuckles stood white, and then deliberately, viciously cracked his forehead against the unyielding wood panels in an attempt to obliterate the chanting, sneering little voice in his brain. *No kid of mine.*

Ow, shit, that hurt. Nursing his aching head, he stumbled to the couch and sank down onto the cool leather. God. No wonder she wouldn't speak to him last night. He'd never known her to be so reserved, but in his oblivion he'd thought he understood. He hadn't been able to cough up the apology she'd deserved for the lousy things he'd said during their fight. Always articulate, he hadn't been able to express himself on the one topic that needed to be verbalized. He'd hated it that she hadn't seemed to find it necessary to make conversation at all, but now ... Oh, Jesus, she must think he was such a bastard.

All the while he'd been rushing to fill in the silences with a surplus of words, he hadn't uttered one relevant remark, hadn't asked one appropriate question. Like: Was it a safe time for her or was it a fertile period? Was there a chance he could have gotten her pregnant? What did she want to do if he had?

He had an ugly suspicion regarding the latter. She still had two years of university left and he'd lost count of the number of times she'd told him how much she looked forward to holding a job and earning her keep in the real world. The last thing she was likely to want was to be saddled with his kid.

Son of a bitch. He couldn't believe he'd been so careless. From his very first sexual encounter, safety had been his middle name; but now, with the one person who really mattered, responsibility had flown out the window. So where did they go from here?

He knew what he wanted, but he wouldn't hold his breath. She hadn't even let him kiss her. His abrupt bark of laughter was long on bitterness, short on humor. Hell, what did he actually know about lasting relationships, anyway, or about any relationship, come to that? It wasn't as if he'd ever had one before Aunie. What he'd had was a parade of one-nighters.

If he didn't get off his butt and talk to her pretty damned quick, that was all he was likely to ever have. But first he had to marshall his arguments. If he flew off the handle with this one, he could kiss everything he wanted goodbye, which was pretty damned ironic when you thought about it. His entire life, he'd been able to submerge his emotions behind a fast wit and a faster tongue and talk his way out of nearly any situation. With Aunie, however, his trademark verbal adeptness just fell to pieces. Instead, he went brain-dead and his emotions roared to the surface, dominating his every action. From the very beginning, it seemed, she'd turned him upside down without breaking a sweat, causing him in the process to react first and apply rational thought second. Just when it was most important to keep a cool head, he invariably lost his temper.

Well, he couldn't afford to do that this time. So he was going to get some rest and give this considerable thought. And then he was going to take his much-vaunted ability to fight his way out of a tight corner and put it to good use.

Tomorrow, little Miss Magnolia Blossom had better look to her laurels. Because he was playing this one to win.

The plane that landed at Sea-Tac airport in the middle of the night was more than half an hour late and the limousine that Wesley's secretary had ordered for his arrival was not waiting. He shot his cuffs in irritation and impatiently consulted his Rolex watch once a minute for an additional fifteen minutes before he condescended to collect his own baggage and take a taxi.

Just one more inconvenience for which that faithless bitch wife of his would answer.

Staring disdainfully through rain-soaked windows at what he considered uniformly bleak scenery, he reflected on all he had done for her. He had raised her from a poor relation to a woman of consequence, had given her everything a woman could possibly want. In return the ungrateful little slut had ruined his life, destroyed his reputation. His business had suffered in the past nine months, many of his friends had dropped from sight, and the agency he had hired to find her had taken their own sweet time, soaking him for a fortune in the process. That was no coincidence, he was sure.

Gazing out at the sparse traffic on the interstate, however, Wesley, a perpetually dissatisfied man, allowed himself one brief, pinched smile of satisfaction. For he had found her now, just as he'd always known he would. The moment he'd awaited was rapidly approaching. In less than twenty-four hours, he would be in a position to exact his revenge. Oh, yes, she was going to pay for every slight he'd suffered, for each and every humiliation. She was going to pay dearly.

Tires hissing over wet pavement, the taxi pulled to a stop in front of Aunie's apartment house. All the lights except the one blazing over the front door were darkened—not surprising, given the hour. Wesley sat and stared at the building with obsessive concentration, caught up in a web of dark thoughts. The driver, watching him in the rearview mirror, shifted uncomfortably. His passenger's expression was one that was becoming increasingly familiar in Atlanta circles, causing friends and business acquaintances alike to give him a wide berth. To the driver it was unfamiliar, but no less disturbing. The guy looked like a psycho.

"So, what's it gonna be, bub?"

"Wait here." Wesley opened the rear door and climbed out, ignoring the driver's protest. He walked up the path to the front door and studied the names next to the buzzer. Only three, and one of them was Franklin.

Good.

He climbed back into the taxi and settled himself. Looking at the driver down the length of his nose, he said peremptorily, "Take me to the Four Seasons Olympic."

CHAPTER 18

Independently, Aunie and James had reached the same conclusion. This impasse in their relationship could not be allowed to continue. Both had spent two difficult nights apart, and both had decided they needed to talk before everything worthwhile they'd built together was reduced to ashes. Each privately swore that the necessary conversation would be handled in a nonconfrontational manner, with logic and calm foremost, emotions strictly controlled and relegated to a back burner.

Their intentions were the best. They just didn't realize how difficult that particular promise would be to keep.

Aunie was feeling optimistic by the conclusion of her final exam. She wouldn't know for sure until she saw her grade, but she felt it had gone well and hoped it was an omen for the rest of the day. Due to the continuing inclement weather, she had accepted a lift from Mary, both to and from school, but she'd declined her friend's invitation for a celebratory lunch. Promising to make it up to her at a later date, she waved Mary off and ran, head down, up the path, letting herself in the front door. She was anxious to talk to James and settle the future of their relationship once and for all.

She'd decided on the way home that she was most likely blowing the matter of his apartment entirely out of proportion. He'd never actually said she was unwelcome. Well, he had, as a matter of fact, the one and only time she'd entered it, but that was before they'd become involved. She had to believe that the dark suspicion, which had bloomed full-blown yesterday afternoon, was nothing more than an instance of her paranoia at work following what had truly been an immensely eventful and stressful week. It didn't say much for her state of mind, perhaps, but it certainly beat the alternative, which was that James was deliberately excluding her from a large portion of his life. That was a supposition she found untenable and she refused to make herself crazy thinking about it before she had a chance to talk to him.

By the time Aunie had put away her supplies and stored her book bag on a shelf in her bedroom closet, the steady drizzle had stopped and the thick, lowering clouds had commenced to thin, allowing intermittent rays of weak spring sunshine to break through. Choosing to view the improved weather as another promising omen, she brushed her hair and her teeth and applied a dash of lipstick.

Drawing a deep breath, she decided she was as ready as she'd ever be.

She didn't bother to lock her door behind her when she exited her apartment. It was nice, now that the young man responsible for the harassment was safely behind bars, not to feel the need for extra caution. She walked down the hall, hesitated a moment outside James's apartment, and then resolutely knocked on his door.

"Hang on a sec," he said through the door, and when he opened it Aunie was reminded of Halloween day. Once again he was wearing a white shirt that was unbuttoned and hanging open and jeans that were not zipped. His hair was damp. "Hi," he said in surprise. He buttoned up his shirt and stuffed the tails into his waistband, zipping and buttoning the fly. "I thought you'd still be at school. You finish your final already?"

Some of her optimism drained away when he didn't move out of the doorway or invite her in, but she determinedly gave him the benefit of the doubt. "Yes, and I think I did all right." She looked up into his face. "We've got to talk, Jimmy."

He stepped out into the hall and closed the door behind him. It was strictly a reflex action on his part, not something he'd consciously planned to obstruct her. "Yeah," he agreed. "I know. It's been a hellish couple of days." He placed his hand on her arm and out of habit began to guide her along the hall. "Let's go down to your place."

She went cold all over. "No," she replied through constricted vocal cords, pulling her arm free. "Let's not." All her old insecurities rose up to haunt her. Had she once again fooled herself into thinking there was something more to a relationship simply because she so desperately wanted there to be? Her eyes filled with tears. "I thought you loved me."

He stared at her, dumbfounded. "I do love you!"

Suddenly, she was furious. "You love having sex

with me!" she spat at him. "Sex! That's all it is. But
when it comes down to allowin' me into your life . . .
boy, is that a different matter!"

"I don't have sex with you, Magnolia; I make love
to you."

"Indeed?" she said with flat disbelief as the episode
in her kitchen flashed through her mind. "What's
the difference?"

James paled. "Jesus," he whispered, staring down
at her flushed and furious, upturned face. He
pinched the bridge of his nose between his thumb
and forefinger. "You don't really believe that, do
you Aunie? That there's no difference between some
slam-bam, back-alley fuck and the way you and I make
love?"

"Why shouldn't I?" she demanded. "How do I
differ from your other girlfriends, Jimmy? Name me
one way, aside from the obvious of course . . . that
they all have big boobs and no intellect, while I have
a big intellect and no boobs."

"Dammit, Aunie, there's no comparison between
you and the women I used to see! They were . . .
friends. Hell, not even that, some of them. I *love* you!"

"Then why am I just as excluded from your life as
they were, Jimmy? Why haven't you *once* invited me
into your apartment, showed me your work? And how
come, if you make *love* to me the way you claim to
do, the other day in my kitchen felt more like makin'
war?" She was mortified and furious with herself when
she began to cry in earnest. "Why did I feel like Ah
was bein' punished, Gawd, Ah hate it that I can't
even remembah what was said that started the whole
thing!"

"You called me a prick."

"I didn't!" The word had arisen in her mind on

a number of occasions, particularly where Wesley was concerned, but she'd never said it aloud in her life.

"Yes you did, baby. And hearing it come from your mouth . . . I don't know, I lost what little control I was exercising up to that point. " He thrust his hand through his hair. "Dammit, Aunie!" *I was scared to death and it transmuted into anger,* he wanted to say. But Terrace machismo inoculated in the boy prevented the man from admitting it. He tried an oblique explanation instead. "Not only had you just nonchalantly informed me that someone was still watching you, you'd also put yourself at risk when you contacted Cunningham. So I guess when you called me a prick on top of it, I lost it. I decided to show you just how big a prick I could be." He moved close and touched the tears streaming down her cheeks with a rough-tipped finger. "But I'm sorry, Aunie. I am. And I swear to God it didn't occur to me until yesterday when we were talking about Greta-Leigh's pacifier, but . . . Could I have gotten you pregnant?"

She wiped her palms across her cheeks and sniffed. Knuckling her nose like a little girl, she hunched one shoulder. "I don't know. Maybe. I've gone over it and over it, and the closest I can determine is that it was right on the boundary between the days that are safe and the days that aren't. I won't know for sure for a week or so."

"Have you thought about what you wanna do, if it turns out you are?"

"Have I—? Of course, I've thought about it! That's been practically all I've *been able* to think about."

"And I suppose you've come to some sort of decision?" he queried her neutrally. He felt he'd screwed up so many things in their relationship. He regretted his aggressiveness on Wednesday: the deliberately wounding words and the way he'd taken her in anger up against the fridge. He was sorry about his failure to use a condom, which had left her unprotected; sorrier still—given that look of betrayal on her face—about not sharing the most important aspects of his life with her: his home, his work. When he'd first made the decision to keep them separate, it had seemed a smart way to protect himself in case she walked out on him. Now it merely seemed childish. He was trying to make it up to her by showing her he'd abide by whatever decision she made and not attempt to muscle her into doing what he desired.

Aunie's emotions, however, were running high, her self-esteem was at an all-time low, and she misread his intentions entirely. She equated his carefully impartial tone with indifference, thought this was his way of humoring her. She jerked back from him furiously. "Don't you patronize me, James!"

Every defense he'd built over the course of two decades threatened to slam irrevocably into place, and his temper, which up until that moment he had managed to contain, flared at the way she'd repudiated his sincerely offered overture. "Patronize! Jesus, lady, I'm bending over backward here to be a New Age sensitive guy by letting you set all the rules! This is *my* kid we're talking about if you're pregnant, but it appears to me that I'm just spinnin' my wheels because you're determined to be pissed no matter what I say. I'm damned if I do and damned if I don't. Just what the hell do you want from me, Aunie?"

Aunie plunged both hands into her hair and raked it off her forehead with such vigor her eyelids stretched. "I don't know! Maybe I'd like, just once, for you to define the terms of our relationship! Every time there's been a move to be made, I've had to make it and I'm tired of pushin' myself in where I'm not even sure I'm wanted. I want to know if you are willin' to take any risks in this, this . . . Gawd, I don't even know what to call it! Love affair? Shack-up, what?''

"Risks?" James roared. "You want risks? Fine, I've got one for you that'll make your hair curl!" He grabbed her by the wrist and hauled her along behind him, pulling her through his apartment door and slamming it shut behind them.

He dragged her over to his drafting table and pressed on her shoulders until she sank down onto the secretarial chair in front of it. "Here! Look at my stuff. Explore my apartment. Do what you want . . . just don't leave. I'll be right back." He rummaged through the desk while she stared blankly at his work in progress. Locating his wallet, he checked his cash supply, picked up his checkbook, and stuffed both in his pocket. He collected shoes and a pair of socks from his bedroom; but not trusting her not to bolt, he brought them into the living room where he could keep his eye on her while he donned them. He hurriedly brushed back his hair and whipped a rubber band around it. Then he gathered his keys and came to collect her. "Let's go." He hustled her out of his apartment again. "And tonight you're sleeping here. I'm sick of having my performance judged by that roomful of steroid-fed beefcake."

Aunie stumbled the combined length of their arms behind him, hustled along by his grip on her wrist. She had to practically trot to keep up with his ground-eating stride. Dazed by the implications of being told she would be sleeping in his apartment that night, she only spared enough mental energy to wonder where he was taking her.

James was just reaching for the doorknob on the building's front entrance when the Jacksons' door opened. Lola looked out. "Oh," she said dully, "You're goin' out."

The static aura of supercharged emotions that surrounded James and Aunie subsided somewhat as they looked down the hallway at Lola. Their expressions became concerned, for her characteristic energy was absent as she slumped against the door frame and her creamy brown skin was overlaid by an unhealthy tinge of grey. Aunie twisted her wrist out of James's grasp and crossed over to her friend.

"Sick again?" she asked her sympathetically. Lola nodded, then suddenly slapped her hand over her mouth and ran for the bathroom. They could hear the sounds of her being ill behind the hastily closed door and met each other's eyes uneasily. "I don't understand this," Aunie said. "How can one person go up and down the way she's doin'? She was so sick yesterday. But when I stopped by before Mary picked me up for our final this morning, she was feeling great. Now she's sick again. I'm goin' to call her doctor."

"Good idea," James agreed. He squatted down to peer at Greta-Leigh through the mesh in her playpen. "Hello, sweet thing," he murmured. "Your mama's not feeling too perky right now, but it's nothing for you to worry about. Ol' Uncle Jimmy and Aunt Magnolia are gonna see to it she gets fixed up."

Greta-Leigh stared up at the overhead light.

Lola emerged from the bathroom just as Aunie was hanging up the phone. She collapsed on the couch in exhaustion and watched as Aunie began gathering baby items and stuffing them into the diaper bag. "What are you doin'?"

"Packin' up. Dr. Woo had a cancellation and can

fit you in, but you have to be there in twenty minutes. James will drive you, won't you, Jimmy?" He nodded. "I'll take Greta-Leigh up to my place."

"Oh, but," Lola protested, "she hasn't had her bottle yet and it's almost time for her—"

"No buts," James interrupted and handed Lola her purse. "Aunie can handle it. C'mon, now. We've gotta get going." He helped her to her feet. Aunie trailed them to the front door where James suddenly turned back and wrapped his hand around the base of her skull. He pulled her onto her tiptoes and gave her a rough kiss. Raising his head, he stared down at her intently. "Don't think I'm gonna be sidetracked by this," he said. "You want me to take a risk in our relationship and I'm plannin' on taking one. This is a postponement, Aunie, nothing more."

"Where were you takin' me?" Five minutes ago it hadn't seemed important. Now she was consumed with curiosity.

His face creased with his smile. "Ah, now," he whispered, sliding his thumb down the side of her throat. "That'd be tellin', wouldn't it?"

"Jimmy!"

"Okay, okay. The King County Administration Office."

She stared at him blankly. "Whatever for?"

He slipped his fingers out from behind her neck and stepped out in the hall. "To apply for a marriage license," he said and closed the door in her face. By the time Aunie collected her wits sufficiently to yank it open again, he and Lola were gone.

Slumped low on the seat of a rental car on the next block, Wesley folded down a corner of his newspaper and watched as a muscular, long-haired blonde and a tall black woman left the apartment house. The man escorted the woman to a Jeep parked near the corner, helped her in, stood and stared a moment up at the apartment they had vacated, and then walked around to the driver's side and climbed in. They drove away.

Wesley's nostrils flared and his mouth curved up in a sneer. Now, if that wasn't just typical! The little bitch had found the least acceptable accommodations possible. According to the nameplates he'd read last night, there were only three apartments rented in that building and they were inhabited by niggers and hippies, for Christ's sake. Trust the slut to pick such a place; she never had possessed an ounce of social discernment. Every damned time they'd gone out, he'd needed to brief her on who was important and who wasn't.

It was fortunate for her she was a beauty, for she'd sure as hell never had a brain in her head. Well, the free ride was over. By the time he was done with her she wasn't even going to have her looks to rely on.

He'd give those lowlife tenants fifteen minutes to ascertain they weren't just running a short errand, and then he was going in. Wesley smiled to himself.

He'd waited a long time for this.

"Come on, sweetie pie, we're goin' up to Auntie Aunie's apartment." She picked up Greta-Leigh, snagged the strap to the diaper bag, and let them out of the Jacksons' apartment. She hadn't thought to ask for a key to lock up, but it shouldn't matter. The outside door was secured.

Greta-Leigh started to fuss the moment they crossed

over the threshold of Aunie's apartment. Aunie kicked the door closed behind her and walked directly to the kitchen, where she put a bottle in the microwave to warm. She changed the baby and then collected the bottle and a clean diaper to use as a burp cloth. Testing the formula's temperature on her inner wrist, she sat down, arranged the infant in the crook of her left arm, and popped the nipple into her mouth. Greta-Leigh began to suck on it enthusiastically. Aunie watched her drink but her thoughts kept returning to James's last words.

Marriage license? He had been on the verge of dragging her downtown to apply for a marriage license? God above! He hadn't been kidding when he'd said he'd take a risk that would make her hair curl. Aunie removed the bottle from Greta-Leigh's mouth, sat her up, and gently rubbed her back until she burped up an air bubble. She returned the bottle to the baby's mouth.

And she smiled. Not the most romantic proposal, was it? More of a declaration of intent, but that was Jimmy. And it wasn't as if she actually gave a rip how he worded it. The important thing was that he apparently wanted the same thing she wanted. He wanted to marry her. Oh God, she was in heaven!

The distant sound of breaking glass jerked her out of her daydream. Had that come from the basement? Oh, surely not; it must have been out in the street or perhaps from the neighbor's yard.

Greta-Leigh, who had dozed off, started violently at Aunie's own startled movement. Her eyes flew open and her little hands flew up in reflex panic. Aunie made soothing noises and the baby took some comforting pulls on the nipple in her mouth. Then her eyes drifted closed again and a moment later her milky mouth went slack. Aunie set the bottle on the end table and stood, carrying the infant into her bedroom, where she gently laid her on the bed and propped pillows around her. She tiptoed from the room and closed the door.

She was in the kitchen heating water for a cup of tea when her front door opened. Surprised James was back so soon and suddenly shy, she smoothed her hair nervously. Licking her lips, she took a deep breath and stuck her head around the corner.

Wesley was disdainfully inspecting her apartment. He picked up the telephone on the end table by the couch, looked at it a moment, and then ripped it out of the jack.

She jerked back into the kitchen, gripping the countertop with white-knuckled fingers and breathing hard. He had been looking in a different direction and hadn't seen her. But it would take about three minutes to search the apartment and . . .

Greta-Leigh! Oh, God, she had to think. She'd have to show herself before he searched the bedroom. She couldn't let any harm come to the baby, and Wesley was just insane enough to do her serious harm if it suited his purposes.

Aunie's mouth was devoid of all moisture and sweat pooled clammily in her armpits and between her breasts; it trickled coldly down her spine. Her heartbeat pounded deafeningly in her ears. But James's self-defense lessons hadn't been the nerve-wracking waste of time she'd thought them to be after all; thanks to them, she wasn't in a complete state of panic. She picked up a sharp paring knife and slid it into the back pocket of her jeans. Sparing a longing glance at the pan of boiling water, she momentarily considered throwing it in Wesley's face. But if she

missed or if she hit her mark but failed to disable
him, he would be enraged beyond her ability to control. And if he should discover the baby . . .

No. Delaying tactics were her best bet. And for that,
she would need every drop of guile she possessed.

She turned the heat down beneath the pan of water
and stepped into the doorway dividing kitchen from
dining area. Praying she could pull this off, she made
her voice as calm and welcoming as possible as she
said, "Why, hello, Wesley. How nice to see you." She
gestured into the kitchen. "I was just making myself
a cup of tea. Would you like one?"

To her own ears, she sounded as phony as a three-
dollar bill. But Wesley, who had expected fear and
rage, was obviously thrown off stride by the warmth
of her greeting. The psychotic coolness that she had
dreaded to see in his eyes was momentarily clouded
by confusion. All he said, however, was, "No. Come
out here."

She edged into the living room, frantically trying
to judge a proper distance to keep between them,
one which would protect her physical safety, yet at
the same time prevent setting him off by appearing
to be too obviously avoiding him. Casually, she made
her way to the end table with the alarm button and
flipped it on. Not that there was anyone to hear, but
on the off chance she could stay in one piece long
enough for James to get home . . . With regret she
eyed the unobstructed path to the front door. There
was a good chance that if she made a run for it Wesley
would give chase—and there was every possibility she
could lose him once she was outside. But if he didn't
follow her, God, if he didn't . . .

She simply could not risk Greta-Leigh that way.
And when it came right down to it, she couldn't

leave the baby unattended. She had promised to take care of her.

At the same time she was calculating possibilities, she prattled mindlessly. Calling on the years of experience she'd spent forcing vivacity where none had been felt, she smiled, chattered, flashed her dimples, and radiated Southern charm.

She racked her brain for words that would appeal to Wesley's special brand of snobbery. With bubbleheaded viciousness, she denigrated her apartment and its furnishings, spouted bigotry that lambasted James and her cherished friends, talked of designer fashions until she feared he would demand to see her wardrobe—which would be nothing short of disastrous. Regularly interspersing the sundry slander, she bemoaned the dearth of social nightlife in Seattle for all the world as if it were the only subject her little brain could retain for more than five minutes running. She lied with a fluency that astonished her, and for nearly fifteen minutes, she kept him at bay.

Wesley lounged on the couch, smiling slightly as he listened to her.

She never afterward could pin down where she had gone wrong. Perhaps she'd simply been whistling in the dark from start to finish. Wesley was so twisted it wasn't beyond the realm of possibility that he'd merely been stringing her along for his own perverted amusement, simply to see how far she would go.

Eventually, he interrupted her monologue. "You know, don't you," he inquired with a charming smile, "that you have to be punished."

Aunie's conversation dried up. Wesley patted the cushion next to him. "Come here."

She edged away. "No. I don't think so."

"Remember the last time you defied me?" he said gently. "I didn't let you get away with it then and I won't allow it now."

"Times change, Wesley." Emotions gone numb, she turned her back to him and headed for an area where she'd have room to maneuver.

He caught up with her, of course; she didn't for a moment expect otherwise. Mind clicking furiously through remembered instructions, demonstrations, and those hated practical applications of theory James had forced on her, her only thought was to give a good accounting of herself before she went down. She was going to hang on long enough for help to arrive for Greta-Leigh, and she *was* going to deal some pain of her own. Of that, she was determined.

Damn his eyes for arriving just when she was beginning to believe she could attain a little happiness of her own.

He grabbed her from behind, roughly grasping her arms. She'd thought she was beyond fear or anger, beyond feelings of any sort, but adrenaline surged through her veins. In her ear, James's voice whispered with blunt gruffness.

Your natural instinct is to pull away, it said. *Dammit, are you listening to me? If he grabs you from behind don't try to lunge forward out of his hold, Magnolia. Step back into it.*

She did as she'd been taught. Stepping back she snapped her arms wide and broke his hold. Whirling, she chopped at his Adam's apple with stiffened fingers. His legs collapsed beneath him, and while he clutched his throat and gasped for breath, she danced away, looking around her for anything that could be used as a weapon. God, if only the baby were close enough to grab, they could be out of here.

She was going for the nearest lamp when he tackled her. She tried to kick her feet free, but he clung, tripping her up, and they crashed to the floor. Aunie had the farthest to fall and she was momentarily stunned as she slammed onto her back on the planked hardwood, the wind knocked out of her. Wesley scrambled up to kneel astride her and slapped her hard across the face. At the apex of his swing, he immediately reversed his arm and backhanded her with vicious strength, snapping her head to the side.

As she struggled to catch a breath, her chin slowly swiveled back to face him and she stared up at him through watering eyes. Her only satisfaction was in the knowledge that at least he was no longer smiling with that insufferable smugness. Arrogance was ingrained in him up to his well-groomed eyebrows, however. He hadn't even bothered to secure her hands.

She reached down to where he knelt over her, grabbed at his crotch, and squeezed with all her might. Wesley roared with outraged pain, rained blows about her head until her grasp loosened, and then he toppled to his side. He kicked her in the hip as he fell over.

One of the blows had most likely broken her nose and the blood flowing over her mouth and gurgling in her throat almost succeeded in throwing her into a blind panic. It revived terrifying memories of that other night when pain and choking humiliation were dark companions, resurrected a degrading sensation of helpless submissiveness. Aunie's reasoning abilities began to cloud and she whimpered. She might have been lost entirely if from the corner of her eye she hadn't seen Wesley, still curled in a ball with his hands protectively cupping his genitals, smile with satisfaction at the sound of her distress.

No, dammit! She swiped ineffectually at her mouth, spit out all the blood she could clear from her throat, and pushed to her knees. She dragged herself to the end table and fumbled for the lamp. He wasn't going to win that easily. *Damned* if he was. Her hands closed around the ceramic base and she jerked, ripping the plug from the socket. Sobbing for breath, she sat back on her heels for a second, hugging the lamp to her breast.

Pain radiated along her nerve endings and she was slower than Wesley to regain her feet. His hand twisted in her hair just as she was straightening and he swung her around. When he suddenly let go, she stumbled dizzily, crashing against the fireplace. The lamp slid from her grasp, breaking harmlessly upon the floor.

Wading through the mess, Wesley grasped her by her shirtfront. He waved a broken shard of lamp in her face and then lowered it from view. She couldn't see what he was doing, but she gasped as she felt her blouse slice apart.

"Beg me not to hurt you," he demanded. A lust for power burned in his eyes as he caressed her from throat to breast with the broken ceramic.

Aunie tried to make herself smaller. "Please," she whispered. "Don't . . ." She cried out at the sharp sting of the two shallow cuts he slashed on her upper chest. There was a sensation of wetness as tiny beads of blood welled up within the lacerations.

"Whoops," he murmured. "Guess you weren't quick enough." He smiled at her and raised the brittle fragment so she could see it once again. He made several passes with it in front of her face. Aunie's eyes followed its hypnotic, weaving progress back and forth.

"You're not so pretty now, are you?" he crooned. "Not so fucking high and mighty." He casually nicked her face with the jagged ceramic tip once, twice, and she clawed his wrists frantically.

The pain of her digging nails made him tighten his hold on the improvised weapon and it cut into his palm. Snarling, he dropped it. "You goddamn bitch!" He stepped back and kneed her in the stomach, slapping at her head, neck, and shoulders with both hands. Aunie doubled over, retching.

Her ears were ringing, and at first she didn't comprehend what made Wesley go so still. Then she heard it, too. Their battle had awakened Greta-Leigh.

"What the—?" Wesley twisted his hand in Aunie's hair once again and jerked her to him. Herding her along in front of him, his grasp arching her neck to an awkward angle, he marched them down the tiny hall to her bedroom. He kicked open the door and shoved her roughly. Aunie stumbled into the room.

She stared numbly as he walked over to the bed. He ripped the phone on the nightstand out of the wall. "Well, well, well," he said pleasantly, staring down at the wailing infant. "Aunie's had herself a pickaninny. Why is it I'm not surprised?"

"She's not mine," Aunie replied weakly. Oh, God, she prayed. Please, *please* watch over her. He's so crazy and she's only a little baby; don't let him hurt her. Summoning strength, she said in a more energetic voice. "I'm watching her for the woman downstairs. She's been ill, and she had to go to the doctor."

Wesley looked unconvinced. He picked up a pillow and gazed down at the infant consideringly. Aunie felt panic claw at her throat. "Look at her, Wesley!"

she cried in desperation. "She's not even a week old. Do Ah look as though I just gave birth? Have you noticed any baby things in this apartment?"

She didn't fully breathe again until he let the pillow drop to the bed. "Shut her up," he snapped.

Aunie picked up Greta-Leigh and cradled her in her arms. She sat on the side of the bed and talked soothingly to the child. When the frantic cries began to subside, Aunie searched for and found her pacifier. She slipped it into the baby's mouth.

"Let's go," Wesley said peremptorily. Aunie started to set Greta-Leigh back in her nest on her bed, but he stopped her, saying, "No. Bring the brat along."

His hand clamped painfully on the back of Aunie's neck and he shoved her along ahead of him. In the dining room, he scraped out a chair and pushed her onto the seat. Turning sideways so he could keep an eye on her, he yanked up the wooden miniblinds. Aunie blinked against the sudden strong glare.

Wesley looked out into the quiet neighborhood for a moment. Then he opened a window and whirled back to Aunie. Before she could divine his intentions, he had grabbed the baby from her arms and was dangling her out the window, only his hands on her waist supporting her. Aunie screamed.

Wesley glared at her over his shoulder. "You've got a choice, you faithless slut," he said between his teeth. "You can continue to defy me . . . in which case, I'll fucking kill this little black bastard."

Aunie's eyes never left Greta-Leigh, who was beginning to scream in rage. Sickness filled her throat as she watched the pacifier tumble from the baby's mouth and drop from sight. "Don't hurt her, Wesley."

"Beg, you bitch."

"Please!"

"You through fighting?"

"Yes." Her head bowed, the weight of it suddenly unbearable, abruptly much too heavy for her slender neck to support. "You can do whatever you want to me; I'll do anything you say. Just don't hurt the baby."

"All right. That's more like it." He brought his hands back inside the window and passed Greta-Leigh carelessly to his ex-wife. "Put her on the couch. And don't even think of tryin' to get cute with me, bitch."

Aunie cuddled the baby to her breast. For the first time since Wesley's entrance, tears filled her eyes and spilled over. "I'm so sorry, sweetie pie," she whispered into the baby's hair. "So sorry." It sickened her to see this innocent child smeared with her blood. Carefully, she laid her on the couch and propped a pillow next to her to prevent her from falling off.

"Now, get back here."

Aunie wiped her mouth once again, and then wiped the blood from her hands against the seat of her jeans. With a start of surprise, she felt the wooden handle of the paring knife in her back pocket. She had forgotten about it. Wesley grabbed her and dragged her over to the window before she could formulate a plan that would incorporate it. He studied her misshappen face in the strong light.

"You look like shit," he said. He rummaged through her purse with one hand and pulled out a lipstick. Holding her by a handful of hair, he slashed the red gloss over her mouth and one cheek. Tossing it aside, he shoved her into the kitchen.

"Make me that tea," he snapped. He stood in the doorway and surveyed the room. "Make one move for those knives," he warned her, "and I'll snap the brat's neck before you clear the blade from the holder. Push 'em back." She complied. "Further."

She shoved the wooden holder to the far corner of the counter. "Good. Now, get your butt back over here and make me a cup of tea."

Aunie turned the burner back up under the pan of simmering water. She opened an overhead cupboard and pulled down a small box of Earl Grey tea bags. Selecting one, she set it down and opened another cupboard for a china cup and saucer. Her field of vision was rapidly narrowing as her eyes swelled shut. "Do you want lemon?"

"No."

"Cookies?" She was stalling for time.

"Why not?" He surveyed her with arrogant satisfaction. "We'll have a fucking tea party. For one. You, of course, are not invited, except to serve." When her carefully schooled face failed to register any reaction, he looked away angrily. His mind searched furiously for a new way to torment her. "This place is a dump."

Aunie grabbed the handle of the pan and tossed the scalding water in his face. Wesley screamed, clawing at his eyes. He sank to his knees, but even blinded, he managed to obstruct her exit from the narrow kitchen. One of his arms hooked around her calf, preventing her escape, and he tugged hard, throwing her off balance. She toppled over, landing half on top of him.

One of his hands fumbled along her body until it attached to her throat. Muttering promises of a long, tortuous death, he squeezed. Whimpering, Aunie fumbled the paring knife from her back pocket and slashed blindly at his arm. She shuddered as she felt the warmth of his blood join her own, but at least his grip loosened. She stumbled to her feet and ran for her life. Snatching Greta-Leigh from the couch, she raced out the door.

His obscene, screamed threats reverberated in her ears as she slammed it shut behind her.

CHAPTER 19

"Pregnant!" Lola muttered for the fifteenth time as she stared moodily out the car window. James grinned, and noticing, she scowled at him. "You think that's amusin'? I tried for *four years* to have a baby. Four years, mon! So I give up, we adopt Greta-Leigh, and what happens? In less than eight months I'm gonna have two childrens under a year old. Wait 'til Otis hears about this—the mon's gonna have a heart attack!"

James brought the Jeep to a stop at a red light and reached for the tiny jeweler's box on the dashboard. He snapped it open and stared with satisfaction at the slender gold wedding band nestled within. He ran his thumb over its narrow row of five diamonds. He had purchased it while waiting for Lola to emerge from her appointment. *There* was a risk Aunie couldn't ignore.

He forced his attention back to Lola. "It never

occurred to you it was morning sickness making you toss your cookies the past coupla days, I take it.''

"No, you fool mon, it didn't! I was sick in the middle of the afternoon. Mornin's I felt great.'' Lola turned her head to glare at him, obviously in no mood for humor. "The light's turned green, James,'' she informed him and put her hand out peremptorily. "Here. Let me see that.''

"Mercy, mercy me!'' she said in admiration a moment later. "And me widout my shades!''

"Y' don't think it's too gaudy, do you?'' he queried her anxiously. Restrained taste was not, after all, something they taught in the Terrace.

"No, mon, I think it's beautiful. As dainty and elegant as Aunie herself. She's goin' to love it, James.''

He hoped she was right.

They lucked into a parking space only a few houses down from the apartment building. James came around the hood of the Jeep and assisted Lola from the car. "Looks like Bobby's here,'' he commented, nodding toward the Harley parked on the pathway. He was smiling at her continued grumbling as he ushered her into the building, knowing that once she felt better she would probably be thrilled with the doctor's report. But the strident beeping of the alarm that greeted their ears the moment she opened her front door wiped every trace of amusement from his face.

"Oh, Jesus,'' he whispered. He pushed Lola toward the phone. "Call 911!''

He took the stairs two at a time, bellowing Aunie's name as he hit the second floor hallway.

"Jimmy?'' Bob stumbled out of the apartment, his color pasty. "Jesus, I'm glad you're here. It looks like there was a massacre in there . . .''

James shoved past him into the apartment. He halted abruptly in the entrance to the living room, reeling back against his brother's solid bulk as he came up behind him.

The room was torn apart, the lighter pieces of furniture overturned, lamps and small knicknacks scattered and broken. One of the dining area windows stood wide open, and on several surfaces throughout the apartment were drying smears and coagulating pools of blood. Its strong metallic scent mingled with an aroma of something scorched. "Where is she?" When Bob didn't immediately answer, he turned on him, gripping his shirtfront. "Where the fuck is she!"

"I don't know, Jimmy. I just got here a few minutes ago, myself." Bob grasped his brother's shoulders. "There's somethin' you'd better see." He guided him further into the room.

The man's body was sprawled out on the dining area floor, one leg stretched into the kitchen doorway. A track of blood indicated he'd dragged himself from that room. The scorched smell was stronger there, and James stepped over the prostrate form. He turned off a burner that glowed red and then turned back to squat next to the man. Nudging him over onto his back, he reached for a pulse.

Bobby hunkered down across from him. "Is he dead?"

"I can't feel a heartbeat."

"Jesus, look at his face," Bob said, staring at the red and blistered skin. "Do you have any idea who it is?"

"Cunningham, I think," James said, glancing up at his brother. "Aunie's ex. Bobby, have you checked the bedroom?"

"Yeah. No one's there."

"Oh shit, man, where *is* she?"

"Jimmy . . ." Bob hesitated, looking over at the opened window. "I, uh, haven't looked out there."

Lola arrived just then. She stopped in the doorway, took one look at the destruction to Aunie's apartment, smelled the blood, saw the body the two men squatted next to, and fled to the bathroom where she was sick. James stood. He had to force himself to walk over to the window. Bracing himself, he looked out, and his knees sagged in relief when there was nothing to see. Head hanging, he had to clutch the windowsill to keep himself upright as he gulped air deep into his lungs.

Gradually, he pulled himself together. If ever there were a moment when it was crucial to remain level-headed and utilize his intelligence, it was now. He met Lola outside the bathroom and ushered her from the apartment, Bob trailing behind them.

"Where are they, James?" Lola begged to know. "Where's Aunie and my baby?"

"I don't know, Lola. But we'll find them." He drew another deep breath and shoveled his hand through his hair. "Did you call 911?"

She blinked. "Yes. But they wanted to know if anyone was hurt before they'd dispatch a unit. I tried to explain 'bout Aunie's ex-husband and the restrainin' order and the alarm ringin', but I don't know. They said they'd send someone."

Inside her apartment, James gently pushed Lola toward the phone again. "Call Otis."

"Oh, God, what am I gonna tell him? *Where are they*?!"

It was then that they heard the baby crying. It was muffled and faint, but it came from within the apartment. James was galvanized into action before the other two even had a chance to react. He tracked the sound into the nursery.

At first glance it appeared empty, but the cry was more audible and he crossed over to the closet. Lola and Bob burst into the room just as he was opening the door.

Aunie scrambled crablike into the furthest corner, twisting to present her back, the baby against her shoulder protectively sheltered between her and the wall. She reached back with one arm, brandishing the knife toward the opening with weak awkwardness. "Back off!" she warned shrilly. "Ah sweah Ah'll kill you, Wesley, before Ah let you get your filthy hands on her again."

Greta-Leigh's wails crescendoed.

"Magnolia?" James said softly. He got down on his hands and knees on the closet floor and inched toward her. "It's okay, baby," he crooned. "It's okay. Wesley's not gonna hurt you again. I promise you, honey, nobody's ever gonna hurt you again." Bile climbed up his throat as he got his first good look at her.

"Jimmy?" Aunie peered in the direction of his voice. She tried to make out his face to verify that her mind wasn't playing tricks on her, but both eyes were swollen shut.

"Yeah, baby, it's me." He reached out and gently grasped her wrist. She shuddered at the touch and huddled further into the corner, but she allowed him to unpeel her fingers from around the hilt of the knife. He removed it from her hand. "Lola's here, Aunie. Will you let her have Greta-Leigh?"

"Let me hear her voice," Aunie replied suspiciously. She still wasn't positive she hadn't wished all this up.

"Woo-mon?" Lola knelt in the closet's doorway. "Are you and my baby okay?"

Aunie began to cry. "Ah'm sorry, Lola," she sobbed. "Ah'm so sorry. Wesley held her out the window and Ah got blood all ovah her. God, please, forgive me; Ah'd give anythin' not to have involved her."

James scooped her up in his arms and backed out of the closet. He sat down on the floor with his back against the wall, Aunie cradled on his lap, the baby still clutched possessively to her chest.

"God Almighty," Bob said faintly.

"Call 911 again, Bobby," James directed him, raising his voice slightly to be heard over the infant's roars of outrage. "Tell them we need immediate medical attention as well as the cops."

Aunie had quit crying. Her broken nose made it difficult to breathe and she laid her head wearily against James's chest, panting through her open mouth. "Greta's wet," she whispered.

Tears flowed down Lola's face. "I'll take her now, Aunie," she murmured. "Okay? Hand her to me, please. I'll clean her up and change her into dry clothes." She reached out for her child.

"Yes, good." Aunie pressed her parted, swollen lips against the baby's head and then relinquished her to her mother. "Keep her safe."

Lola blanched when she saw the blood covering her child, but the moment she peeled off her little stretch suit and used a baby wipe to clean her hands and face, she realized that none of the blood covering her was her own. Greta-Leigh's only real problem was a soaked diaper. Gnawing her lip, she looked across the room at her battered friend.

"I'm cold, Jimmy. Really cold."

James looked down at Aunie and was scared out of his mind. He had no idea how much blood she had lost, but it was obvious she was in shock and fading fast. "Lola! Get me a blanket. Oh, Christ, where's that ambulance?" Even as he spoke the words, he could hear the faint wail of sirens in the distance. He wrapped the two of them in the quilt Lola handed him. "Hang on, baby. Just hang on a little longer." He rubbed his cheek against the crown of her head. "God, I'm sorry, Magnolia. I'm so sorry I wasn't here for you. I failed you when you needed me most."

"No," she whispered. "Didn't." She panted weakly, then gathered her strength. "Saved . . . life. Those . . . lessons . . . I . . . hated." Her fingers curled weakly in his shirt. "Remembered, Jimmy. Did . . . n't . . . panic."

Bob ushered in the paramedics. They muscled James aside and began to work over Aunie. As soon as they had her stabilized, they put her on a collapsible gurney to transport her to the hospital.

It was as the medics were extending the legs of the stretcher that James noticed the dark, wet bloom of blood staining the crotch of her jeans. He watched them hang the IV on the attached stand and cover her with a blanket, and he felt as if a giant fist had slugged him in the stomach.

If she had been pregnant before, she was no longer.

"Dead?" Aunie turned her head in the direction of the detective's voice. "*I* killed him?" Her head was fuzzy from the narcotics they had given her for the pain, and she thought it was that which was causing her confusion. "I-I-I . . . *no*. He was yellin' obscenities and threats when I left. I slashed at his arm to stop him from choking me, but he was still screamin' at me when I grabbed Greta-Leigh and ran out the door." She groped along the side of the hospital bed with her right hand. "Jimmy?"

James leaned forward in his chair and clasped her hand in both of his. "Cunningham's dead, Magnolia. He was dead when Bobby and I got there."

"You nicked a main artery, miss," the detective said. "He must have bled out after you left." He looked away from her. Christ. He really didn't have the heart for this. The guy's death was too merciful.

"Am I goin' to jail?"

The detective turned back his head to observe her. The black woman whose child had been involved had showed him a snapshot of Miss Franklin before he'd left her apartment. It was hard to tell, looking at her now, but she had been beautiful. "No," he replied. "There will be no charges filed. In addition to your statement, we have knowledge of the restraining order and a report from the ER doctor here on staff. It is my belief that you acted in self-defense and in defense of the child's life. I just need you to verify a copy of your statement once we have it typed up. When the swelling goes down on your eyes, we'll need you to come down to the station, read it over, and sign it." He stood, as did the quiet young man in the corner who had recorded Aunie's statement. The detective reached out a hand to touch her arm. She gasped and jerked it away skittishly. "Get some rest," he said.

The policemen left, the door swishing closed behind them.

Aunie started to cry. She was relieved Wesley was dead—oh, God, she was *glad*—yet she felt horrible that he'd died at her hand. She had never willfully even *hurt* anyone before, let alone been responsible for a death. And yet . . .

Her emotions were so jumbled she couldn't have said with any coherency how she felt.

"Shh," James soothed her, leaning over and brushing her hair away from her face. "Don't cry, baby, don't cry. It's all over now."

Her face turned blindly in his direction. "Jimmy? Could you hold me?"

He climbed onto the high bed with her and gingerly gathered her in his arms. She sighed. It was silent for several moments, then she whispered, "Did they tell you that I'm not pregnant?"

"I already knew. I saw the blood on your pants when the paramedics were taking you out." He lifted up his head, chin tucked in to look down at her. "Were you?"

"I don't know. They said it was much too soon to tell. But I can't shake the feelin' I was, Jimmy."

"Aunie?" He hesitated a second, then said, "How did you feel about it? We both got defensive and angry yesterday, and neither of us really said what we thought. I need to know."

"Oh, James, I felt so mixed up. The thought of being pregnant right then scared me silly. I didn't think you'd want a baby, and I still have two years of school left." Her fingers curled in his shirt. "Yet, part of me really wanted to be. I've got more than enough money to care for a child and I think I'd be a pretty good mother. And besides"—she yawned hugely—"it was yours."

"It scared me, too," James said. "But I would have wanted it, Magnolia. That's kind of funny, huh? After all my howling about too many responsibilities? But I like the idea of us being a family and I'm really willing to work hard at it . . ." His voice trailed away as he realized she had abruptly fallen asleep. He smiled ruefully.

"We'll talk about this later," he whispered and kissed the crown of her head. Easing her out of his arms, he climbed off the bed and sat down in the chair next to it. His head tilted against the back of the chair. Gazing up at the ceiling he murmured, "We've got all the time in the world to talk now."

EPILOGUE

Aunie stood in the doorway to her apartment, fighting to overcome her apprehension. A small voice in her brain told her to quit being ridiculous and go on in, that there was nothing to be afraid of, but it was difficult to hear over the thunderous knocking of her heart. It had been more than a month now since that day with Wesley, and she had yet to set foot in her former home.

When she'd been released from the hospital, James had already moved most of her personal items to his apartment. He'd carried her straight to his bedroom to recuperate, and she'd been too weak then to worry about how she would feel when the time came to reenter her home. It had taken awhile for her strength to rejuvenate; but once she'd begun to mend, it had returned quickly. That was when she'd discovered that physical health was apparently restored more rapidly than mental well-being—at least in her case.

She'd never dreamed there would be a problem the day she had strode down the hall to retrieve her good nail file from the bathroom. James had overlooked it when he'd packed her belongings.

She had approached her apartment with confidence, only to stop dead in the doorway. Nothing had prepared her for the blind terror that commenced her heart to pounding, her hands to trembling. Nothing had prepared her for Wesley's horrible, echoing voice that rebounded threateningly within her mind or for the memories that played before her eyes in a red-tinted fog. She had backed away and softly closed the door. Ashamed but unable to do it herself, she'd enlisted Lola's help to retrieve her nail file. In the several attempts she had made to face her demons since that episode, nothing had changed. She hadn't been able to force herself past the front door.

But tomorrow she was getting married. She didn't want her wedding present to James to be a legacy of neurotic fear. He had given her so much when he'd equipped her with the skills to come through her experience alive, when he'd taught her how to refuse the role of perfect victim. She needed to give him something in return . . . she needed to restore something to herself. Her ordeal at Wesley's hands was yesterday's news, dammit. It was over; she had survived. She was determined to start her life as Aunie Franklin Ryder with a fresh slate.

Nails digging into her palms, she stepped into the apartment.

She half expected to see dried blood and chaos, to smell the stale ghosts of her terror, but it looked much as it had before that day. Her heartbeat began to quiet. Wandering from room to room, she slowly discovered that the memories most dominant had nothing to do with Wesley at all.

She was sitting on the bed contemplating the cream of those memories when she heard the front door open. For just a moment she tensed. It was a source of pride that she had already regained her equilibrium. before she heard James's voice call out.

"Magnolia? You in here, baby?"

"In the bedroom."

He appeared in the doorway and Aunie launched herself off the bed and into his arms. Her legs gripping his waist, her arms about his neck, she leaned back and grinned up at him. "Hi."

"Hi yourself, sugarbritches." His own grin creased his face in a dozen places. "Lola said to tell you that the beef Wellington will be done at six-thirty and not to be late." He smiled ruefully. "Now that her morning-slash-afternoon sickness is a thing of the past, she's back to being her old bossy self."

"You know she's going to make us go through a weddin' rehearsal after dinner, don't you?"

"Yeah, Otis warned me. I knew we shoulda eloped to Vegas."

Aunie's nose wrinkled. "Too tacky."

"But simple. What's to rehearse, anyway? It's just gonna be you 'n me and a few of our friends in Otis's apartment. I'll say I do, if you will." He sat down on the edge of the bed and buckled his knees from side to side just for the fun of having her grab at his shoulders and tighten her legs around his hips. Aunie laughed and jerked his ponytail.

"It's just basic stuff, Jimmy. Be good. She's gone to so much trouble to make this special for us."

"Yeah, I know." He flopped onto his back and

gazed up at her perched astride his lap. "I was kind of surprised to find you here, Magnolia."

She rolled to lie by his side, her cheek on his chest. She was quiet for several moments before she finally said, "I couldn't bear the thought of havin' unresolved fears when you put that beautiful ring on my finger."

"You're not afraid now?"

"No. The hardest part was steppin' over the threshold. Once I came in and walked around a little bit, I found that I'd been grantin' Wesley more power than he deserved by running scared this past month. There're no ghosts here anymore."

His fingers tangled in her hair and pressed her head more fully against his chest. "Ah, God, that's good to hear." He rubbed his free hand up and down her arm. "We're getting married tomorrow, Magnolia. Jeez, can you believe that?" He grinned up at the ceiling. "Just a few short hours until I can introduce you as the little woman."

"You do and I'll take a frying pan to your head." She propped her chin on his chest and looked up at him. "Jimmy, does this frighten you at all?"

"Little bit." He tilted his head to look at her. "I'm not always easy to get along with, Aunie. Hell, you know that better than anyone. And I get these spells when I just want to be alone. But I'm gonna work at this, baby. I'm gonna work at it real hard."

"So am I. I want you to know that I don't require round-the-clock entertainment. My ego won't be bruised if you want some privacy. Just as long as you spell it out for me ahead of time and don't go slammin' off or scream at me for interruptin' you."

"I don't always know how to conduct a relationship, Magnolia."

"I don't think anyone does, all the time." She smiled up at him. "Just pretend you're a recovering alcoholic. Take it one day at a time."

James laughed. "Ah, God, I love you, girl. You're the best thing that's ever touched my life." He reached down to unbutton her blouse. Rolling her to her back, he leaned down and pressed soft kisses to the two thin scars on her chest. He raised his head to stare into her eyes. "You ask me, I think we're gonna have us one helluva long and happy marriage."

"So do I, Jimmy T." She wrestled his T-shirt up over his head and tossed it aside. "So do I."

SUSAN ANDERSEN lives in the Pacific Northwest with her husband and a cat named Styx, and is the proud mama of a grown son. The inhabitants of her little piece of the world are weird and wonderful, and she credits the attempt to stay one step ahead of them with keeping her young.

Susan enjoys hearing from her readers. You can e-mail her at susan.susanandersen.com; drop by her website at www.susanandersen.com; or write her care of P.O. Box 47375, Seattle, WA 98146. Those desiring a reply to snail mail please enclose a #10 self-addressed, stamped envelope, and she will respond as quickly as possible.

Romantic Suspense from

Lisa Jackson

__Treasure
0-8217-6345-8 $5.99US/$7.99CAN

__Twice Kissed
0-8217-6308-6 $5.99US/$7.50CAN

__Whispers
0-8217-6377-6 $5.99US/$7.99CAN

__Wishes
0-8217-6309-1 $5.99US/$7.50CAN

Stella Cameron

"A premier author of romantic suspense."

__The Best Revenge
    0-8217-5842-X $6.50US/$8.00CAN

__French Quarter
    0-8217-6251-6 $6.99US/$8.50CAN

__Key West
    0-8217-6595-7 $6.99US/$8.99CAN

__Pure Delights
    0-8217-4798-3 $5.99US/$6.99CAN

__Sheer Pleasures
    0-8217-5093-3 $5.99US/$6.99CAN

__True Bliss
    0-8217-5369-X $5.99US/$6.99CAN

Call toll free **1-888-345-BOOK** to order by phone, use this coupon to order by mail, or order online at **www.kensingtonbooks.com**.
Name_____
Address_____
City_____ State _____ Zip _____
Please send me the books I have checked above.
I am enclosing $_____
Plus postage and handling* $_____
Sales tax (in New York and Tennessee only) $_____
Total amount enclosed $_____
*Add $2.50 for the first book and $.50 for each additional book.
Send check or money order (no cash or CODs) to:
Kensington Publishing Corp., Dept. C.O., 850 Third Avenue, New York, NY 10022
Prices and numbers subject to change without notice. All orders subject to availability.
Visit our website at **www.kensingtonbooks.com**.